A SPANISH TREASURE

Brave and gentle, cruel and unyielding, Tom Cavendish could have a man flogged as easily as kiss a pretty face. He knew that there would be trouble if he let his equally proud and hot-blooded younger brother, David, sign aboard the *Desire*.

But the voyage seemed to be going smoothly—until the magnificent *Santa Anna* hove into view. For aboard her was the woman who was to become the obsession of Tom's life—and the cause behind David's mutiny—the beautiful, seductively intelligent Catherine de Montoro.

Bantam Books by Jan Westcott

**THE BORDER LORD
CAPTAIN FOR ELIZABETH**

PART

1

Chapter 1

THE ANTEROOM was small. He came across its sixteen feet swiftly; he knelt.

"Madam," he said.

She used his surname: "Cavendish."

He stood with the grace of an animal. Without a word, she seated herself, spreading out her gown so that it flowed about her stiff chair, flower-like. The brocade rustled, sending its sounds into the room like the currents of excitement that the meeting aroused.

He was still standing, restlessly. She took joy from his presence. The small room caged him; it prisoned the essence of him, and she could taste it fully: the male recklessness, the strength, the cruelties and tenderness of which he was capable. For these moments he was hers, and she knew well enough there were many women who envied her.

"Sit, Cavendish," she said. "You've ridden from Plymouth."

He answered with his usual directness. "I'd as soon stand, Madam. For the reason that I've been in the saddle for hours."

She looked at him. From his fingers dangled the scarlet sea cap she had given him. On his feet were Cordovan leather boots, probably looted from a Spanish grandee. His eyes were blue, intensely blue; his thick hair was short and tinged with gray. He was thirty-one years old, and Elizabeth was as proud of him as though she herself had given him birth.

Both doors of the room were shut. Yet when she spoke her tones were low.

"You sail soon, then?"

"Thursday," he said.

"You have only two more days!"

Today was Tuesday. It was July, the twenty-second

of the month, and the day was hot. The afternoon air that fanned into the room was warm and heavy.

"I scarce love to see you leave," she said. "And I scarce think I can stay you. Yet I might try, even now."

"Do not try."

"Do not interrupt." She said it, not sternly, but as a wise mother to a child. And she paused.

"I like the men I have about me. And I need them. I have always needed them. I want them—for myself a little, for England much. I have brought peace to England. You and your kind are using peace to bring us closer to war with Spain. It is England, and not distant lands, to whom your allegiance should be offered!"

"My allegiance?"

She said, "I have perfect command of our tongue, Cavendish. Allegiance to me means staying home and guarding the shores that Spanish boots may be treading, because such as you dispute their claims to the New World. If there be war, it shall be a fault laid on your doorstep."

He was silent for a moment.

"I'll come back, Madam," he said, and there was on his face a rare appeal for understanding.

She was not appeased. Regrets nagged her. "You have been home but a few months."

"Five," he corrected, remembering his last voyage. He had an instant's vision of Roanoke Island, with its golden sand dunes, the giant oaks dripping with moss, the pines, the gardenias, the succulent grapes. It occurred to him that she had never seen the land they had fought for. What he had seen with his own eyes, she saw only with imaginative vision. "Madam," he said suddenly, "if you could see America!"

"I?" she said.

"Yourself," he said. A flash of humor crossed his face. "If I should ever take a woman aboard, I should take you. But if you could only see America, you would understand. Do you want, Madam, to let us leave it to the Spanish?"

"The colony you established there a year ago failed," she said.

"Certainly," he said. "Because there were a hundred

men left on Roanoke, and not one wench among them. We'll try the colony again."

When he said it, like that, as though surely it were true that there would be more colonies, her fears were softened. She could see momentarily with his vision. . . . She would never lose all her doubts. But it was clear—the reasons for battle with Spain. As the risks were plain, so were the great gains, the prizes.

The uneasy peace between England and Spain was still peace, and it allowed her to let men like the one with her now sail forth on the restless seas and carry far, on their square-rigged vessels, the English flag.

"How long will it take you, this time?"

"The voyage? About two years. Look you, Madam. For the next twelve months I fight the Spanish in America, in the Atlantic and in the Pacific. After that, I am free to explore. Find the routes, chart the courses, and trade. Trade! We shall build an empire on it. And on a little force, if need be."

As if his restlessness were somehow appeased by speech, he sat down opposite her—there was a table between them—as he leaned forward. It was not often he spoke his thoughts; with her he was free to do so. The expanding world of his own age belonged to him, and it was not a vision but a reality. The horizons of the world were lifting.

"And besides that, Madam, Philip of Spain has sent Sarmiento to fortify the Straits of Magellan and thus close the entrance to the Pacific. I want to see what he has done down there. If there are forts, they must be destroyed. Else they will bottle up the Pacific more than nature herself has done."

"Aye," she said, "and we still have peace."

He laughed. He laughed as if he were truly amused. And then he said, "You believe that. It is what makes your deception so marvelous, your strategy so vastly annoying to a man like Philip."

But the hazards ahead loomed very large to her again. And the length of the voyage. "It will take you two years to round the world?"

"Because I would explore, Madam." On the table in front of her lay a parchment. She picked it up.

"Ah, well," she sighed, "I like the men about me, but somehow I like better the men who will not stay about me. Captain, here is your commission."

The parchment would hardly protect him. If he were made prisoner, he'd be hanged for piracy. But that did not make the fact of the commission any less important. He rose.

"I'll bring this back to you," he said.

The Queen's eyes were ironic.

"You named your ship *Desire?*"

"Aye, Madam."

She held out her hand. His strong brown fingers took hers lightly and firmly. She was suddenly sure that if he lost his life for her, she would avenge it.

"Who strikes at you, Cavendish," she said, "strikes at us!"

His fingers left hers.

"God go with you," she said softly.

The audience was over. He went to the door; it closed behind him. In her chair she sat for a moment; her stomach ached painfully, and she leaned her head back against the hard wood. Her face was drained of all expression. She was mother to a country, and under her hands it was burgeoning forth; under her woman's fingers it was knowing a flowering of its arts; it was ripening, big with increase. And from its island shores, its ships set sail. Set sail—and caused her fear. In her chair she sat unmoving while outside dusk fell, summer dusk, sweet and sweet smelling.

In the courtyard of the palace three men waited. Cavendish, emerging, saw each face, and the figure of his groom. Cavendish absently laid his hand on the neck of his favorite horse. He spoke first to George Carey.

"I have another errand, George," he said.

"You do, Tom?" Sir George Carey asked.

"Aye, I'll be two hours or so."

"I'll wait," Carey said, sending a sidelong glance at his companion.

Cavendish turned his attention to the other man. "I thought you were at Trimley, David," he said.

David Cavendish had obviously been waiting for his

older brother to speak to him, but now that he had, David replied instantly, "I didn't stay home, Tom."

Cavendish said one word. "Why?"

"Suffolk is dull," David said with easy defiance. Then he stopped. Both men were waiting for him; the groom was listening. David said, "Tom, I decided to see you again! I wanted to speak with you. I want to go with you."

"Now?" Cavendish said.

"Not now," David said. "I want to sail with you."

"No," said Cavendish. "Impossible, David. I want you to stay at home. At Trimley. I've told you many times you must learn to manage the estates." The last sentence he added as though to explain his refusal.

"That's a most inadequate reason," David said.

Cavendish was already in the saddle. He looked down at his brother and Sir George Carey. "Good-bye, David. I'll see you later, George."

He wheeled his horse and David and Carey watched him go. The groom followed hastily. They disappeared into a London street.

Cavendish's progress through the city was not unobserved. His great roan was a familiar sight, so was he and the scarlet sea cap perched on his dark head. The city of London knew he was leaving soon; they knew that in Plymouth harbor three ships, new built, formed the small fleet he would command and that those sturdy English ships would soon set sail. London had caught the fever of her seamen; islanders, too, they harkened to the restless seas.

Men called to him as he galloped past. They waved their caps at his retreating figure. They had seen him on Fleet Street, dressed in his heavy breeches and the seaman's leather jacket; they had seen him dressed finely at the theatres; they had seen him in the lowest of waterfront taverns, and the more he caroused ashore, the more headlong a devotion they gave him.

He reined in opposite a stone mansion of imposing size, a mansion built with Spanish gold. He dismounted, and he stood for a moment, his hands still on the reins.

"Good-bye, boy," he said.

His groom stood waiting, while the Captain bid farewell to his favorite horse. Then he was handed the reins.

Cavendish said, "Sir Francis has offered you lodging for one night. In the morning you ride for Suffolk. Have that hired nag ready for me in two hours."

"Aye, sir," said the groom, a bit wistfully. The Captain was leaving soon; the hours were passing fast.

The men who had gathered on the street to watch and hear were close.

"Good luck!" one called. "Good luck, Captain!"

Cavendish raised his hand to acknowledge the greeting.

"St. George for England!" another man shouted, just as a girl slipped through them and ran, long blond hair flying, to the stone steps Cavendish was mounting. He turned.

She looked up from the bottom of the steps, poised like a statue.

"D'ye remember me?" she asked breathlessly.

Cavendish swept off his cap and bowed. He grinned. "Your servant, mistress," he said, and was about to turn away when he swung around again, a coin in his fingers.

"Dolly," he called, and she nodded vigorously, curls dancing.

He laughed down at her and tossed the coin. It glittered, and as he went in the now open doors, she whirled and held it up for the men to see.

"Gold!" she cried.

"Jesu, what he spends," one man said proudly, staring toward the house. But the big doors were closed now; the wench was walking away with the gold clutched tight.

Inside the house, Cavendish was grasping his host's big hand.

"Hungry?" Sir Francis Drake asked genially.

"I wanted badly to see you before I sailed," Cavendish declared.

Drake, just returned from another voyage to the Indies, released Cavendish's hand. He was short and stocky. Across his ruddy cheek a jagged scar gave evidence of his profession, and he limped a trifle from a bullet wound in his right calf.

Cavendish followed him into a long paneled dining room. Drake walked over and closed the near window. Cavendish smiled.

"Are you afraid the Spanish may be listening?" he asked. He sat down, stretching his legs out comfortably. Then he yawned and rubbed his chin with his brown hand.

Drake sat down at right angles to him, and lifted the already filled tankard.

"Your health, sir," Drake said.

"Yours," said Cavendish. He drank slowly; he set the tankard down empty. Then he yawned again, deeply.

"Sleepy?" asked Drake. "Been whoring again as usual, Cavendish?"

Cavendish laughed. "I rode all night," he said. "Captain Havers sent his regards, sir."

"Where did you meet Havers?" Drake asked.

"Christ's College, Cambridge."

"Could they stomach you there?"

Cavendish said solemnly, "I stayed but two years." He was laying a chart out on the table, when Drake suddenly let forth a stentorian bellow and banged his tankard on the table.

The door flew open. As two servants entered, Drake quickly rolled up the chart. The servants brought trenchers of beef and cheese and bread, and two smoking chicken pies. Then the door closed behind them, and Drake unrolled the chart again.

Cavendish had kept his eyes on the servants, rather to their discomfiture. "You don't trust them, Drake?" he asked.

"I trust no one," Drake said. "These are Magellanic charts."

"From Portugal," Cavendish said. "But as for secrecy—I have been followed a deal lately. In Madrid they know I'm sailing."

"As long as they don't know you intend to enter the Pacific."

"They might," Cavendish said. "Their intelligence is

good." He helped himself absent-mindedly to food. The pie was very hot, and he decided to transfer all of it onto his plate to facilitate its cooling. He began to eat.

Both men ate hungrily and at ease, washing their food down with drafts from the foamy ale. They interspersed their drinking and eating with talk, questions and answers, brief and knowledgeable. They talked of the Pacific, greatest ocean in the world, swelling endlessly blue, cradling its islands, guarded by continents—the Pacific.

They talked steadily.

"You are the only man who could tell me these things," Cavendish said.

He accepted the long clay pipe Drake handed him. He drew a pouch and offered it to his host. The tobacco was softened and pressed into small cakes; it had been very lightly moistened and sweetened with molasses. Drake shredded a cake in his fingers; the tobacco spilled onto the table as he pressed it into his pipe.

"It's good, Cavendish," he said. He puffed gratefully at the pipe.

"I could have sold a hundred cargoes of it," Cavendish said.

Drake studied the younger man's tanned face. Cavendish had discovered this way of curing and readying the tobacco for sale. "Have you always been wealthy?" he asked bluntly.

"Quite," said Cavendish, briefly.

Drake knew that Cavendish had come into his estates and fortunes at nineteen, when his father had died. The story went that he had spent all his fortune in two riotous years in London, but Havers had told Drake it was not true. Cavendish had spent only half of it before he went to sea.

Havers had said, "I've seen him go overboard after a favorite cap. But don't judge him by that, Drake. He wouldn't risk his life for it, and neither did he spend his last farthing. . . ."

"You're fortunate to have Havers," Drake said thoughtfully, breaking the silence. "I hear you're shipping a great many of my men," he added. He looked sharply at Cavendish.

"Aye," replied Cavendish.

"You had no difficulty persuading them to sail once more around the world?"

"Very little," said Cavendish.

"That's rather surprising."

"Why?"

"Come, sir, that's a mad question. To say it quietly, the world's rather large."

Cavendish's blue eyes lighted a little. "Not so large, Drake," he said.

"You think not? I rounded it only because I could not return by the route I fetched the Pacific!"

"That was your reason?"

Cavendish smiled and stood up. One of his brown hands had lain protectively on the precious pieces of canvas-backed paper. His charts. Tenderly he began to roll them up.

"I've heard you are an arrogant bastard." Drake's square-beared face seemed squarer and he had planted his feet wide. "I've heard you are a good seaman too. Perhaps you're not aware that England needs good seamen now, with the Spanish mayhap ready to send their fleets to the very shores of England. You must have a magnificent reason for sailing now; much more elegant than mine!"

Cavendish frowned, his eyes level under the drawn brows. The rolled charts were in his hands, and suddenly he gestured with them, looking directly into Drake's belligerent face. "When I look at these, it's as though I see the Pacific, the New World, islands and continents! I like to draw charts. When I do, I draw in the outlines of empire. And you forget, sir—it might be best to carry the fight to the enemy!"

He stopped, and then because he saw in Drake's face a glimmer of understanding and just a hint of admiration mixed with the scepticism, he said, "You know we're building an empire! You know it, because you're doing it. Drake, it doesn't matter why you sail around the world. It doesn't matter why I do. In the end, we are both striking at the Spanish Empire so that we can build an even greater one. For England. One so great that the sun will always be shining on some part of England's world."

Drake was silent, and the silence filled the room.

Cavendish bent over to secure the leather straps that bound the charts.

"It's time for me to leave you, sir, I told my groom two hours."

Drake smiled. "And so exactly two hours it will be, eh? I have known you by repute, Captain. I know you better now. I wish you good fortune. And fair winds, sir—the fairest of winds."

Chapter 2

THE LION was the only waterfront tavern in Plymouth that David Cavendish had not visited. He walked toward the swinging sign slowly; his boots made clicking sounds against the cobblestones. The dark street was quiet. The water lapped softly against the docks. In the harbor, lights showed aboard the ships at anchor there.

It was Wednesday night. It was nine o'clock, and David knew that if he didn't find his brother tonight, he might not see him again before he sailed. He didn't know when the *Desire* and the two other ships that formed the small fleet would leave; he knew only that Cavendish expected to sail Thursday.

David approached the tavern slowly. If Cavendish were not here, he would not know where to look next. Tom must be here.

He opened the door, and a familiar scene was revealed. The tavern was crowded. Although David knew none of his brother's crew by sight, he imagined there must be a good many of them here now, for the tables were filled by lounging seamen.

Then, suddenly, he saw his brother. He edged inside the door and sat down at a small table. He hadn't even a farthing, not enough for a tankard of ale. He wished he did, but he had spent all his silver pieces in searching for Cavendish. He sat back on his stool and looked down the length of the crowded room; he could just see Cavendish's profile as he leaned across the table, talking to Sir George Carey and another man whom David knew slightly and did not like.

This man's name was Hope; he had put up some of the gold to build the *Content,* Cavendish's second ship, and he was going to sail on the *Content* because he had helped to build her. David saw that all three men were laughing, and there was a handsome wench with them,

13

at whom he stared appraisingly. He never knew where his brother found such wenches, but he always did.

Knowing he was completely unobserved, David began to feel better. He had found Tom, and he had time to collect his wits before he spoke to him. Yet, his palms sweated a little as he sat and waited for the courage to make himself known to Cavendish. He was conscious of contempt for himself. He was only seven years the younger. Rebellion rose in him; he muttered an oath. But still he didn't stand up and walk toward the far table. Strangely enough, what most disturbed him now was that if he were not successful he would have to ask Cavendish for enough silver to get home to Trimley. If he didn't ask for it, he would have to walk, unless he stole a horse. Then, abruptly, the idea was very enticing: to have nothing, to know no one, and to be free.

Two men at the next table were looking at him. David looked back and leaned his elbows on the table. Then, with determination, he suddenly rose to his feet. But when he realized that their attention had been diverted by the man Hope, he sank back on his stool and stared, too.

As far as he could discern, Hope was not drunk. But he was standing up, and he had pulled the wench to her feet, and their voices were loud and entangled. The wench hurled an insult at Hope; he bowed; Cavendish was watching and laughing. Then Hope said something low that David could not hear. After that, he turned away; but the wench, whom he had evidently insulted deeply, sprang after him and gave him a healthy cuff across the side of his face.

Hope turned back, seized the girl by the shoulders, and started to shake her. He had lifted his hand to strike her, when Cavendish said in a clear voice, "Take your hands off her." Cavendish had risen lazily to his feet, and was standing alongside of her. He reached out one hand, and his fingers fastened over Hope's wrist.

"Let her go," Cavendish said. The room was silent, and his words could be heard plainly.

Hope answered angrily, "When she apologizes for striking a gentleman, you can have your whore, Cavendish."

David rose to his feet, to see the better. He knew he ought to edge out the door before his brother became aware of his presence. But he wanted to see for himself what would happen. In only a few seconds, he realized what would occur. Cavendish hit Hope across the side of his chin, and Hope fell backward into the next table. He steadied himself against it for a minute. Then he shouted, "I'll have satisfaction for that!"

He wrenched the rapier out of his sheath and would have lunged forward with it, but two men seized him from behind. He struggled frenziedly.

"Sit down," Cavendish said to the wench; he patted her backside as she went past him. Her eyes were big as she watched him.

"Don't fight, Captain," she said, pleadingly.

But Cavendish had turned back to Hope, who had stopped struggling because one of the seamen who held him was twisting his left arm every time he tried to move. His breath was coming raggedly in his impotent anger. Cavendish drew his own sword and motioned with it.

"Push those tables back," he said to the circle of men.

They obeyed quickly. They saw that Cavendish was ready, and released Hope. The blades crossed, and the wench cried out in terror. David heard George Carey say to her, "Hold your tongue!"

Behing David, the door opened and closed with a bang, and David realized that the landlord had sent someone for the night watch. He climbed up on the table to see better, but another man tried to climb up too, and the table began to tremble under their combined weight. David had a brief glimpse of his brother's face before he jumped down again; he heard the click of steel against steel. The room was breathless; the girl cried out again, and again Carey told her to be quiet.

David could see how fast Cavendish moved in the small space. Suddenly there was complete quiet; the stamp of the duelists' feet had stopped. Outside there were cries and voices; inside David saw that the brief fight was over.

"All of my company who are here will go back

aboard now." It was Cavendish. He was not far from the side door, and he went to it and opened it. "All of you!" he cried.

In amazement, David watched the quick evacuation of the tavern. It had just been effected when he realized that in a moment Cavendish would see him, and he jerked open the door nearest him and ran out into the street. Other men were running, and he ran too. He caught up to the last one.

"What happened?" he asked breathlessly.

"Captain killed him," was the reply.

David slackened his pace; the man ran on down the narrow street. In two minutes David was alone again, walking slowly. It had started to rain a little; off the harbor came a slanting wind. David reckoned he would walk for thirty minutes and then return to the tavern, innocently. He did.

He re-entered the Lion at ten o'clock. The room was deserted except for the landlord. He regarded David suspiciously. "What do you want? I'm going to bar the doors now."

David didn't ask questions. "I want to see Captain Cavendish," he said.

"Oh," said the landlord. "Vut, sir, are you Captain Havers, sir?"

"No," said David. "I'm not a member of his company."

"Then I cannot disturb him," the landlord said.

David looked around the room. It had been tidied up a little. "May I wait?" he asked.

The landlord frowned. But David was a gentleman.

"I must see the Captain," David said. "I'll wait. I'll sit over there." He pointed to a wooden bench that ran along one short wall.

The landlord eyed him. Then he sighed. "All right, sir," he conceded. He walked over to the door and barred it. He blew out the last lamp. "Good night, sir," he said, puzzledly, wondering why David didn't ask for a room. "Good night," he said again at last. Then he paused for one last remark. "I'll be glad when the Captain sails," he said sourly.

The bench was hard. Even so, David stretched out,

waking and sleeping, changing his position, trying to get comfortable on a wooden bench. He pillowed his head in his arms and slept fitfully. When the first light of the dawn filtered through the windows he sat up and surveyed himself.

He tried to tidy his clothes. He brushed himself off with his hands, and rubbed the dust off his boots. He went out the back door and found the pump. He washed his hands and face, smoothed his hair back with his wet hands. He wished he could ask for a razor, but he had nothing with which to pay for it. He went back into the common room and saw his brother. Now he must speak.

"Good morning, Tom," he said.

Cavendish swung around in surprise. There was no one else in the room, and Cavendish had been going to sit down at a table for breakfast. He already had ale, and he lifted the tankard to his lips and drank.

"What do you do here?" he asked, setting down the tankard; and his eyes took in David's appearance. "Where did you spend the night?"

David shut the door and came closer. Both men sat down, and David said, "I had to see you Tom!"

Cavendish's blue eyes were on him, and David said, truthfully, "I spent the night on that bench, waiting."

Cavendish looked toward the bench and grinned. "Hungry?" he asked.

"I'm famished," David said.

"Go tell the landlord to bring two meals," Cavendish said.

He watched while David disappeared into the kitchen. When David came back, his steps lagged a little.

"Why didn't you bring yourself some ale?" Cavendish asked.

"I—"

"I'll pay for it," Cavendish said.

"Thank you, Tom." David was silent.

"Why did you want to see me? How did you find me here?"

David blurted out the truth.

"I found you last night, but I didn't want you to see

me, because you had a fight with Hope. So I waited until this morning."

Cavendish said nothing as the landlord appeared, burdened with food. He set it down for the two men, and Cavendish began to eat. David waited.

"Eat," said Cavendish, gesturing with his knife.

"Aye, sir," David said.

"So you found me last night? And what did you want?"

David was chewing a big piece of ham. He spoke through it. "I want to sail with you," he said.

Cavendish nodded. He washed down a mouthful with another draft of ale.

"I followed you from London."

Cavendish picked up a piece of white bread. "You'd not have this aboard for long," he said, "David, do you think a two-year voyage is a pleasant adventure?"

"No," said David. "But I think it's better than rotting in Suffolk!"

"It is useless for me to try to make you understand why I will not allow you to come."

David felt the anger, the old rebellious anger, rising. His face was white. He started to speak; then rigidly he controlled his voice. Under the table his hands were clenched. "Tom," he said slowly, "why cannot I find out for myself?"

There was no answer. David tried for calm. "Tom," he said, "I'm twenty-four years old. For twelve years—" He broke off. "Tom, let me come!"

"No," said Cavendish.

David said, low, "Is it because you think I'm not—fitted for hardship?"

Cavendish shook his head.

"Tom, let me prove I can do it!" It was an appeal he didn't want to make. And it apparently made no impression, for Cavendish said, "The men who prove their bravery usually die."

David was surprised. It had not occurred to him that he might die. "You'll be there," he said, and then Cavendish suddenly said something that surprised him even more.

"I should not ship you aboard the *Desire*," he said. "If you sail, you'll sail with Havers."

"You'll not let me sail with you?" David repeated. "But let me sail with Havers, then!" He would have said more, but Cavendish had stopped eating and was looking at him steadily. Because he suddenly realized he was hungry, David began to eat hastily, keeping his eyes on his plate. Finally he heard Cavendish say, "Very well, then. You may come."

David looked up and smiled. As always, when he won a victory, he was pleased, and Cavendish was not. Cavendish looked grim and annoyed. He stood up, called to the landlord, tossed a gold piece onto the table and started for the door. Hurriedly David grabbed a piece of bread and followed him.

On the short walk to the dock Cavendish was silent except for one question.

"Have you any gear?" he asked.

"No," said David. He shot a glance at his brother, and then he stepped into the ship's boat and sat in the stern sheets with Cavendish. David looked ahead. His eyes were fastened on the *Desire*.

Her blue and gold paint gleamed. Her gun ports were closed. There were men in her topmast shrouds; one of them waved an arm to the small boat pulling toward the *Desire*.

"Are they topgallant sails, Tom?" David whispered, not daring to point.

"They are," said Cavendish. "You'll learn to pronounce that later."

"She's very fair, Tom," David said, and Cavendish nodded. They had pulled up alongside the *Desire*, and David tried to mount the ladder with as much ease as his brother. He stumbled. He stepped onto the *Desire's* deck for the first time.

Two men were coming toward him.

"Master Moon," Cavendish said. "My brother, David Cavendish."

Moon's bearded face was almost as round as his name. He bowed briefly.

"And Master Pretty was carrying a book. David asked, "What's the book, sir?"

Pretty held out the book, riffling the pages. They

were blank. He said shyly, "I'm going to keep an account of the voyage, sir."

At this, Cavendish turned his head to look at Pretty. Pretty fidgeted. He felt impelled to say more.

"It is very important, sir. Only two men have rounded the world before you, and Magellan did not live to return."

David had liked Pretty instantly. "Aren't you from Suffolk?" he asked.

Pretty nodded.

"I thought you were," said David. "Where? We come from Trimley St. Martin, near Harwich."

"I know," Pretty said hastily. "Captain wants you, sir."

David turned. "I'm coming, Tom," he said. He crossed the deck, giving one last glance around. "What are all those pieces of wood on the deck?" he asked his brother's back.

"A pinnace," was the answer. "In pieces, lashed down to that deck. We'll put her together at sea." Cavendish opened a door, and David saw Havers.

"Captain Havers," he said, and bowed, not taking his eyes off Havers' face—the gray eyes, the honest face.

"You've met Captain Havers, David," Cavendish said.

"He certainly has," Havers said, wondering why David was there. "Captain Brule has been aboard, Tom."

Cavendish had sat down in a chair. The cabin was small. He was pulling off his riding boots as he talked. "We have our commission, Havers." He stood up and opened a small door that David saw was the Captain's personal storeroom. Neatly, Cavendish stowed the riding gear. He tossed out a pair of shoes for himself and another for David. He brought out a pair of loose canvas trousers.

"David is sailing with you on the *Hugh Gallant,* Havers," he said, sitting down again. "He's never been aboard a ship before in his life, that's all."

"I think I can learn, sir," David said diffidently.

Havers had evinced no surprise. He smiled.

"I know you can," he said. "I need you. I'm glad, sir."

He held out his hand and David took it warmly.

"You need me?" he asked, anxiously.

"Aye, sir, I do," Havers said.

"From what Tom says, I'm lucky to be sailing with you!"

Havers said, "I've heard much of you."

David's dark eyes looked into Havers' gray ones. "I warrant I'm not much like Tom."

Havers said, "Why should you be?" His eyebrow raised in a manner David was to know well.

"Tom raised me."

Cavendish had changed into a pair of loose trousers which he tucked into the top of a pair of short boots. He held out a pair of trousers to David and the pair of shoes.

"Put these on," he said.

"You may change later," Havers said. "Tom raised you, did he?"

"Aye," said David, picking up the shoes. "My mother died when I was born. Our father died when Tom was nineteen. I was twelve."

Havers had started out of the cabin. "We'll talk more aboard the *Hugh Gallant*," he said.

David was hesitating in the doorway. "Good-bye, Tom," he said.

"Good-bye, David," Cavendish said, looking up from his boots. He stood up. "Don't worry about your lack of gear. You can replenish it from the first Spanish ship we take."

"Will that be soon, d'ye think?" David asked.

"Three to five days. Probably."

They were on deck. David's eyes went past the three-masted *Content* to the bark on which he would sail. The *Hugh Gallant* was a three-master too; like the *Desire*, she slung a sail under the rising bowsprit; David counted six shut gun ports in her side. He dropped one boot, picked it up, and followed Havers over the side. From the boat he watched Cavendish's figure on the high poopdeck.

"Good-bye, sir!" he called.

Cavendish had mounted to his own high deck from which the mizzen rose. The lateen sail was furled; soon it would be heaved out. On this deck he would stand for many an hour, many a day. Below, the hammocks for the men were slung so close they could touch one another. Below were food and guns and extra sail and cordage, and nails, iron, wood, rope, tar, pitch, lead strips. Once again his mind went over what he had done and purchased in the last months.

Havers and David had left. Their boat was pulling to the *Hugh Gallant*. Cavendish saw Brule's figure as he paced across the quarterdeck of the *Content*.

The *Desire* would stand out of Plymouth first. Her anchor cables began to creak; barefooted men strained at the capstan bar; the crew were aloft; on deck the officers shouted orders; the marines watched. The ship's surgeon had joined Cavendish.

A man by the name of Fuller was the *Desire's* master. His voice was loud and crisp. Moon was in command of the gun crews. Some were at their posts; the *Desire's* guns were being loaded for a last salute to Plymouth. Moon's orders were quick and concise.

"Mind your locks! Fire!"

The salute rolled out into the morning air. The smoke billowed away and was gone, floating upward into the sunshine.

The *Desire's* main sheet squared; her tops filled; she came about with the wind. At her masthead fluttered the flag of England. The wind was stiff for summer. Running before it, the *Desire* stood out to sea, the *Content* and the *Hugh Gallant* in her wake.

PART

2

Chapter 3

IN THE MORNING of the fourth of November, Tyler was aloft. The lookout was small and high on the foremast. Tyler strained his eyes; he was looking for something, and suddenly he saw what it was he was looking for. He gave a hearty shout.

"A sail! A sail!"

Below him, on deck, there were answering shouts. Seamen swarmed into the rigging to see for themselves. Master Fuller laboriously set himself to climb the foremast shrouds, and, with the sight he saw, just as laboriously he descended.

It was seven o'clock. The Captain had had his bath under the pump, and by now he would be shaving in his own cabin. In fact, Fuller thought, he would be finished shaving and ready to eat.

By the time Fuller had thought of all this and reckoned what his Captain was doing, he was standing before Cavendish's door. Master Fuller knocked.

"Come in," said Cavendish's voice.

"We have sighted a sail, sir," Fuller said, breathlessly.

Cavendish was rinsing his face. He said, "So I heard."

"She is six points off the starboard bow. And it is she, sir! You were right!"

Cavendish nodded. He had dried his face, and he picked up his precious glass, taking it from the leather case. Fuller stood aside and Cavendish went unhurriedly out on deck. There was plenty of time.

He walked fore. The ratlines trembled as he mounted the foremast shrouds; he held the glass close under his left arm.

The men were staring up at him, he knew. He felt the wind on his face; it was a good wind. In his ears were the sibilant sounds of the rigging; the *Desire's* timbers creaked as she mastered the Pacific swells. Cavendish raised the glass to his eye.

He saw a ship, a great Spanish galleon. It was she, all right. She was called the *Santa Anna,* and she was the richest prize in the world. She was worth a million pounds to the Spanish; each year she crossed the Pacific from Manila to Acapulco laden with the treasure of China and the East. He had had intelligence of her three weeks before; for that time he had lain in wait for her here.

He lowered the glass. The motion of the ship was even. Abaft the beam the low mountains of the Californian cape smudged the horizon; dead astern was the *Content,* spray flying from her bows, her spritsail taut with wind. She had seen the Spaniard, too.

He raised the glass again. The Spaniard was as large as he expected, fully seven hundred tons, more than five times the size of the *Desire.* She was standing into the Gulf of California, running full before the west wind, the sun gleamng on her red paint. He reckoned she was not making more than five knots, for all her sails; and satisfaction welled up in him. She was slow, then, and a good and proper target. Even as he watched, she came about. She had seen the two English ships. She came about; she didn't want to fight. From the shrouds, Cavendish called, "Keep her on this tack, Master Fuller!"

"Aye, aye, sir!" the answer came singing back.

Cavendish lowered the glass again. The Spaniard was running away, and that meant that he had given the Englishman two hours or so to prepare for battle. The Spaniard, for all his size, didn't want to fight. That was good, too. He tucked the glass under his arm and started down. The figure of his brother crossed the deck beneath, but David didn't stop. Cavendish stepped out onto the deck. Master Fuller waited for him, expectantly.

"Fine morning, sir," Cavendish said, "with the wind holding fair."

"Aye, sir," said Fuller.

"My breakfast was interrupted," Cavendish said. "I

have reckoned it will be two hours before we are close enough to fire."

"Aye, sir," said Fuller.

"Therefore I will eat now," Cavendish said. Glass still under his arm, he disappeared into the crowded poop.

Fuller had had his orders. It would be thirty minutes before Cavendish reappeared, and in that time there was much to do. Most of the company were on deck, hanging over the rails. Fuller soon put a stop to that; he raised his voice in a stentorian blast.

Cavendish proceeded to his own cabin. He put the glass away in its case. He would need it again soon, but he fastened the straps of the case carefully. After that, he went along to the *Desire's* great cabin.

There was one man in the cabin—Havers, who sat at one end of the polished table, eating from a silver plate, and using gleaming silver cutlery engraved with the Captain's crest.

"I did not wait for you, Tom," he said. He was stuffing food in his mouth as fast as he could. There was a fight ahead.

Cavendish seated himself. "I'm sorry I was late," he said politely.

This understatement made Havers grin; his gray eyes crinkled with laughter. When he stopped smiling, there were tiny white lines around his eyes, for he always squinted deeply when he was in the sun.

"Pretty good eh, Tom?" he asked.

"The pineapple?" Cavendish was eating the fruit. "It's excellent."

"Are you sure you'll not have some sugar?" Havers asked, smiling again.

"It is sweet enough."

Over their heads there was a loud bump as a tub of sea water was placed at the nearest hatch. They heard Moon's voice raised in profanity because evidently one of the seamen had spilled a bucket of sand. The *Desire's* well-scrubbed and smooth decks were being sanded for battle.

Cavendish finished the pineapple.

Havers said, "It's a pity we lost the *Hugh Gallant*."

This made Cavendish look up. "Aye," he said. He knew that Havers mourned the loss of his ship. The *Hugh Gallant* had not been lost in battle. The heavy seas around the tip of South Ameica had taken their toll of her. She had had to be sunk; four weeks ago they had sent her to the bottom with a few well-placed shots from the *Desire's* heavy ordnance. Cavendish knew, too, that Havers missed his own command. The crew of the *Hugh Gallant* had been transferred to the *Desire,* which had needed men. It had been a year and five months since they had sailed from Plymouth, and in that time they had lost forty men and one ship. They had sunk eighteen Spanish ships of war, and innumerable smaller craft and merchant vessels. They had stormed and burned scores of towns. They were rich already, all of them, with plunder.

"It is a pity we lost the *Hugh Gallant,*" Cavendish said aloud, for it had brought David aboard the *Desire* and under his command. He had been a fool not to think of this contingency in England. David under Havers was a different man from David under his brother. But he could not make an exception for David when he had ordered all of the *Hugh Gallant's* crew to supplement the fifty men who formed the *Desire's* dwindling company. In England he had made a mistake. David should never have come. It was too late, now.

"I'll leave you now, Tom," Havers said, rising.

Cavendish suddenly asked a question, just as Havers was at the door. "Havers," he said, "Havers, tell me. Did David ever speak to you about the Spanish *caballero* on whom I used a thumbscrew?"

Haver's face sobered. "No," he said.

Cavendish knew Havers was speaking the truth. Havers was the most honest man he knew. "Very well," he said.

Havers closed the door. Alone, Cavendish ate quickly, drinking his ale. Then he, too, left the cabin.

His mind was occupied with the coming battle and the strategy he had laid down in detail to all officers of the *Desire* and the *Content,* the night some weeks ago when they had first learned of the *Santa Anna.* It was too bad they had but two ships, but it was foolish to think about that. He put on a supple coat of lght mail and a gilded helmet. Then he took the helmet off and brushed his hair again, setting the helmet back on his head. Thirty minutes had passed, and he went out on deck.

The decks were well sanded, and tubs of sea water stood at the hatches. He lifted his eyes and slowly he began his tour of inspection.

Preventer rigs had been run up the yardarms; they were well slung, and he was satisfied. The light guns mounted on the castles were already served with powder and shot; in front of them crouched the gunners, their naked backs already gleaming with sweat. The hot California sun burned down. The wind was holding fair.

The *Desire* was sailing six points off the wind. Cavendish mounted to his own deck; over his head the flag blew atop the mizzen. The *Content* had dropped astern; she was not as good a sailer as the *Desire*. But he could see Captain Brule's figure on the quarterdeck. He waved his arm.

He could depend on Brule. He could depend on Brule never to forget the strategy. He had been carrying the glass and now he took it from its case just as the familiar rumbling sounds told him that the gun ports were opening and the guns were being run out. Moon's voice echoed from below. Cavendish raised the glass to his eyes just as the lateen sail over his head slatted a little.

"Mind your luff, Master Fuller!"

"Aye, aye, sir!"

The sail filled; it was drawing right. Again he raised the glass, and the seamen perched precariously on the yardarms stared no harder than he did.

For he could see his quarry plainly now.

She was huge. A monster of the deep. Her red-painted galleries rose high over the water as deck after deck had been piled on each other. The colors of Aragon and Castile flew at her masthead; she showed her green bilges as she rolled in the Pacific. He could well imagine the activities aboard her now, and the size of her guns. And every minute the *Desire* was bearing down on her.

Havers came pounding up to the poopdeck. "All nettings triced, sir," he said. "All aloft is in order. The irons are ready to cast."

"Good," said Cavendish. Havers reflected he always said that.

Havers was wearing light mail and a helmet too. "The surgeon reports he is ready for the wounded."

Cavendish nodded. "D'ye want this?" he asked, holding out the glass.

"Thanks," Havers said.

He squinted through the glass, and Cavendish walked over to the rail to look down at the deck. The muskets were being issued to the soldiers. The soldiers were well armored, protected across the chest and shoulders, and they too wore helmets.

The bowmen were already mounting into the shrouds; the sun shone on the sharpened points of the grappling irons. It was eight-thirty. Suddenly he saw David.

David was walking slowly across the deck. He was wearing a heavy sword and a dagger. He was tanned as dark as an Indian.

"Good morning, sir," he said stiffly as he approached Cavendish. "I am ready."

Cavendish frowned. "You are to wear light mail," he said.

David said, "It hampers me, sir. I'd prefer not."

"The first ten men over the side wear mail," Cavendish said. "So you can hold that deck awhile."

"Aye, sir," said David, turning away; but he hurried, for there was not much time left. The *Santa Anna* was almost close enough for hailing.

Havers handed the glass back to Cavendish, who lifted it for the last time. The red stern galleries were nearer. Was that a woman's figure he saw on the topmost balcony? He looked hard; then he lowered the glass. Once more his eyes went over the ship. Rapidly they were bearing down on the *Santa Anna* as she fled before them. It was time to hail her. It was nearly nine o'clock and the two hours had passed. He lifted the trumpet to his lips and his voice echoed out over the ever narrowing stretch of water.

"Oh, ship of Spain! Whence come you?"

There was no answering hail. The *Santa Anna* rolled heavily, and Cavendish put aside the trumpet. Deliberately, in his laconic tone, he spoke the words all the company were waiting for.

"Give her a shot piece, Master Moon."

"Aye, aye, sir!" Moon's crisp voice was loud. He prided himself on being ready. The ship was silent as Moon gave his orders. The crew waited. The matches were struck. The first shot rang out.

It fell short. Cavendish had expected it to. "We do her no harm," he said. He turned his head to see the *Content*. He judged the distance between him and the *Santa Anna;* he judged the *Content's* tack.

"Helm to starboard! Run a good berth ahead, Master Fuller!"

The *Desire* leaned in the wind. Five minutes passed. The *Content* was broad on the larboard quarter now.

"Master Moon! You may fire!"

"Mind your locks!" came Moon's voice instantly. There was a minute's pause. "Fire!"

The *Desire's* first broadside was fired. She shuddered. Flame belched from her sides; smoke rose. Cavendish squinted through the smoke to see. The heavy cannon balls had hit the *Santa Anna's* side and dropped; but the smaller shot had raked the deck and found its target.

"Her decks, Master Moon!" Cavendish shouted.

The guns mounted on the forecastle roared. Below, the gunners worked frantically. The Captain was bringing the ship into position for another broadside; the *Desire* was going to run past the *Santa Anna* on this tack. Moon waited breathlessly. The guns were aimed high, so they would sweep the Spanish deck.

"Fire!" Moon shouted.

Fire and smoke came fom the guns of both ships. Cavendish waited for the shock which would tell him the *Desire* was hit. He tensed for it. A shot plowed through the sprit, cannon balls splashed into the water. The *Desire* had escaped a hit, almost miraculously; for a second he couldn't believe it. He stared at the smoke-clouded *Santa Anna,* and as he did, the *Desire's* crew let out a loud cheer. The Spaniard had been hurt.

Her mainmast had been hit. It had toppled over on itself, its sails flapping helplesely. She had sustained bad hits fore, and her bowsprit was gone. He wanted to compliment Moon but there wasn't time. He swung around and gave the order to fire to the gun crews in the sterncastles. The *Desire* was forward of the beam of the *Santa Anna* now; her stern guns thundered forth; in a few minutes she would be out of range. The first encounter had been more successful than he had dared to hope.

The *Content* was still on the quarter. Between her and the *Desire* was the *Santa Anna.* Cavendish held his breath; he heard the thunder of her guns coming almost on the heels of the *Desire's* firing. Through the sun the clouds of smoke rose; then he saw the *Content* lifting gracefully, her damage done, putting a safe distance between her and the huge *Santa Anna.* She had slipped in like a gull, her talons ready. Still on the quarter of the *Desire,* she came about, her sheeted cross jack holding her close to the wind. Both ships were safe.

The *Content* was obeying her orders almost like a live thing. She stood off, waiting. Cavendish raised his voice. "Trim all sails!"

The topmen obeyed. The great mainsail squared. Cavendish felt the wind from the west. He would run full before it; they would bear down on the *Santa Anna* before she realized the daring of the small attacker. A gust of wind filled the sprit; swiftly the *Desire* bore down on her quarry. Her fore guns spoke first; rapidly the water between the two ships narrowed. Moon fired all heavy ordnance; the Pacific swells lifted the *Desire* proudly. It was time to board.

The maneuver was so unexpected that the *Santa Anna* was caught. Her guns fired harmlessly into the water where the *Desire* had been.

"Make ready!" Cavendish shoated. He ran down to the boat deck.

There were only fifteen feet between the Spaniard and the Englishman.

"Lay her aboard!" Cavendish seized a heavy grappling iron; it swung from his hand and he felt it bite deep into the tough teakwood of the *Santa Anna's* bulwarks. All along the side the grappling irons swung outward. Like a lovely leech the *Desire* was fastened to her prey.

The *Santa Anna* towered over her attacker. Men high in the *Desire's* nettings jumped the distance to her decks. Up the ropes, fifty men scrambled, with David leading them. He jumped down to the deck of the *Santa Anna* while the drums beat.

"St. George for England!" the man next to him cried.

David knew nothing except that in front of him was the enemy. Arrows whizzed past his head. He used a heavy broadsword which he swept in circling strokes. Under his feet the sanded deck was already bloodied. Musket fire rang out; from behind their close fights the Spanish surged forward at the small group of Englishmen, but David knew he was being protected. Men in the *Desire's* shrouds were covering him with well-aimed arrows and gunshot. He and his men inched forward to meet the flashing swords of the enemy Spanish.

The man next to David fell. He was hurt, and David ordered him over the side. David himself engaged two Spaniards to protect the wounded man. But he couldn't watch him; once more he inched forward; he had killed two men, and he should kill more. That was part of the strategy. They couldn't blow the *Santa Anna* out of the water; she was too big. Besides that, she carried gold. What David and the boarding party must do was hold this deck for as long as they could and kill as many men as possible, for Tom wanted to cripple the *Santa Anna* slowly, methodically, and mercilessly. So she would wallow helplessly on the seas. He wanted to cripple her and her crew.

A slight Spaniard, rapier in hand, was rushing toward him. David raised the heavy sword and brought it sideways into his opponent's outstretched arms. The Spaniard cried out.

The Englishman next to David was killed outright. He fell almost at David's feet. Another Englishman was wounded in the arm; he was battling with two Spaniards, and David stepped to his side.

"Retreat," he said.

The man obeyed gratefully. David thought they had held the deck for about fifteen minutes, although it seemed like hours. He had learned in the last year and a half to reckon time, to reckon when he would lose more men than Tom would want. He had seen two of his men die.

"Retreat," he called out evenly, as he himself began to back to the rail, slowly, giving his men time to extricate themselves from the mass of defending Spanish. The melee of swords and men, and shouts and arrows made the English indistinguishable from the enemy.

He could not turn his head to see his men slide back to the safety of the *Desire*. A heavy stone landed on the deck beside him. The Spanish were even hurling stones. His sword found another target; he was sure he alone had accounted for five Spanish at least. Behind him he felt the rail.

He swung one leg up. His sword swept the space before him. He gained the rail; he was safe, and he was the last man to leave the *Santa Anna*. He had done a good work and he would be briefly commended. He heard Cavendish's voice.

"Lay off!"

Knives slashed at the ropes. Freed, the *Desire's* sails filled with the wind; she stood off quickly. In the Spanish stern, guns fired. The *Desire* sustained a hit, and two Spanish shots plowed through the maintopsail. David came running up to the poopdeck. For a minute he was silent, watching, as the *Desire* put a safe distance between her and the Spaniard. David was silent while the *Content,* seizing advantage of the Spaniard's preoccupation with the *Desire,* had slipped in for another broadside. Then she, too, stood off. David sighed with relief. He could speak now.

"Two men lost—Richards of Dorsetshire, and William Stevens of Plymouth. Four men wounded, sir. But not badly."

"Excellent, David," Cavendish said warmly.

"It's going just as you said it would," David said.

The Spanish were shouting derisively across the water. David said, surprised. "They think they've repulsed us, Tom. They think we're done fighting."

Cavendish smiled. Pretty appeared. "The shot hole is above the water line, sir."

"Good," said Cavendish.

He was looking toward the *Santa Anna*. Her mainmast was a stump; her forecastle had been badly damaged. The first hours of battle had gone exceedingly well; some of the tenseness had left the crew; they were more eager now. He looked upward at the sun.

It was exactly noon and the land of California had dropped away. It would continue to be running battle. Pretty had gone below to supervise the serving of a cold meal to the gunners who remained at their posts. A ration of ale was issued to the men. The top sail was mended; two leather patches were sewed on it.

Cavendish paced across the deck, restlessly. He did not intend again to expose the *Desire* to the Spaniard's heaviest guns, whose muzzles protruded menacingly from her red sides. She was tough, but she was hurt, and now he made ready for the running battle.

There were seven hours of daylight left. They should be enough. There was no necessity for hurry. The *Desire* prepared to harry her enemy.

The soldiers shed their mail. Naked to the waist, and bare-footed, the topmen clung in the shrouds. The *Desire*— she had been for these minutes under shortened sail—heaved out her sails and loaded her guns. She was ready.

"We'll go in again, Master Fuller," Cavendish said quietly.

During the next hours he did not leave the deck. During those hours they heard again and again his quiet commands, in between the guns of the *Desire,* the *Content* and the *Santa Anna*. And hours passed. Slowly the sun started its dip downward. The great Pacific rolled endlessly; farther and farther away dropped the coast of California which echoed to gunfire for the first time. Cavendish had been standing in the sun since eight o'clock. Across his cheekbones and nose, the red of a fresh sunburn showed plainly, tanned as he was. His blue eyes were squinted under the golden helmet. He was succeeding slowly; the Spanish knew it, and so did his own crew. This morning they had doubted success; even Havers had doubted it, when they had seen the galleon and the size of her.

The *Content* had been keeping up a steady firing from a safe distance. Her light shot was plowing across the Spanish decks. The *Desire* was bearing down for a broadside; Cavendish could hear the orders shouted aboard the *Santa Anna* as her officers vainly tried to bring her huge bulk about so her heavy guns could be trained on the small enemy ships.

"Hard to starboard!" called Cavendish. "You may fire, Master Moon."

The *Desire's* heavy shot plowed into the Spanish stern, the castles, the decks. Smoke poured from the wounded ship. The wind was still holding fair, and the *Desire* came about and steadied her course.

The *Santa Anna* wallowed in the Pacific swells. She was wreathed in smoke through which the sun shone. Her foremast was gone; her sprit had been shot away. Her bulwarks were crumpled; her stern galleries were gone. She was helpless now except for her size. Methodically, she had been reduced to this. Cavendish looked to the west, to the lowering sun.

There were roughly two and a half hours of daylight left. He had expected to be able to board the *Santa Anna* again and finally at nightfall. But there had been hope that it wouldn't be necessary.

The *Desire* and the *Content* numbered only eighty crew. He didn't want to spare any of those men, not one. And perhaps he wouldn't have to.

"Master Fuller," he said, "trim all sails. We'll bring her in close."

"Aye, aye, sir," said Fuller, excitement in his voice.

The wind held fair. The sails squared. Aloft the bowmen fitted their arrows; on deck the muskets were loaded; the powder-blackened gun crews worked methodically under Moon's command. Incredibly, they smelled victory. They were closing in for the kill; it was time.

The *Desire* bore down on her quarry. All heavy ordnance was fired; the great guns thundered forth, and
when the smoke lifted there came a shout from the *Desire,* a ringing shout. The *Santa Anna* had taken heavy
damage between wind and water.

"She's bad hit, sir," Moon cried.

She was.

"She's in danger of sinking," Master Pretty cried to
Cavendish. Master Pretty had a vivid imagination.

"No, she's not," Cavendish contradicted. "But she's
bad hit." He was loading his musket, for he was going
to bring the *Desire* in again. The *Content* stood off, as
she had been ordered; she stood off, ready to come to
the aid of the *Desire* should the *Desire* need aid.
Aboard her, Brule watched through his glass.

The *Desire* stood in, her guns blazing, her target,
now that she dared to come close, not the decks but the
Santa Anna's thick sides. Smallshot tore through her
rigging and sails. The cries of the wounded were plain.
There was a heavy explosion, and Cavendish heard a
woman's scream.

The *Desire* shook with the recoil of her own guns.
Smoke enveloped both ships. Arrows winged from the
Desire; musket fire rang out, the two ships were locked
now in close battle.

"Fire!" cried Moon, his voice rising above the din,
and through the smoke.

Aboard the *Desire* the excitement was wild. Sweat
poured from the gunners' blacked bare shoulders and
chests. Heat rose around them. And, suddenly, through
all the cries and shouts and orders, came a Spanish
voice crying, *"Abajo! Abajo!"*

Moon halted in the middle of a command to fire.
The smoke curled upward, the sky was red with sunset.
Against that red, at the *Santa Anna's* mizzen, the flags
of Aragon and Castile came swiftly down; more swiftly
to the masthead rose the white flag of surrender.

The *Desire's* crew let out one long yell. Tyler seized
the nearest shipmate and slapped him so hard that he
almost fell onto the deck. The already loaded muskets
were fired wildly up into the air. Master Fuller roared

for quiet. The *Content* steadied on a starboard tack, bore down on both ships, her twenty crew raising their voices as loud as they could.

In the midst of the joy with which the English greeted victory—a victory hard won and wrested from under the noses of the biggest Spanish guns afloat—into that joy a voice came across the water. It was an even voice, speaking flawless English, an authoritative voice: "We yield our goods." There was a pause. "We ask mercy for the lives aboard."

Cavendish had walked to the rail.

"Strike your sails," he said. The two men might have been in quiet conversation.

"We ask mercy for the lives aboard," once more came the Spanish voice.

"You shall have mercy," Cavendish said. There was only a narrow strip of water between the lovely swift *Desire*, her white sail gleaming in the sunset, and the huge crippled galleon.

"Hoist out a boat, sir," Cavendish said. "You may come aboard the *Desire* to parley." He looked up over his head. The flags flew bravely. He spoke to Fuller.

"Have a prize crew ready for me, Master Fuller," he said. "We have not too much daylight left."

Chapter 4

THE *Desire* was hove to alongside her prize. The seamen were in the rigging; the gunners, sweaty and black, had come up on deck. They were watching the boat that pulled evenly from the *Santa Anna.*

The boat drew up alongside the *Desire.* Hands reached out to steady her. Then the first Spaniard mounted the *Desire's* painted ladder. He stepped onto the deck. Cavendish went forward to meet him.

The Spaniard was as tall as he was. He was slender and graceful and his eyes were brilliant black in his lean face. But before the two men met, another man, slight and with terrified face, gained the deck and threw himself forward at Cavendish's feet. In the startled silence he cried brokenly, "I offer to kiss your worship's feet."

Cavendish looked down at the kneeling man and his own polished boots. Tyler looked down at his own bare feet and wanted to say something. But he did not. The Englishmen were silent so they could hear; the powder-blackened men edged closer to this scene on their deck. They stared at their Captain and waited for him to speak.

"We crave your mercy," the frail Spaniard pleaded.

The tall officer's face had frozen into a mask. He paid no attention to the kneeling man. He said evenly, "You have already pledged mercy for our company and our passengers. I am Señor de Ersola, chief pilot aboard the *Santa Anna.*"

"And I am the chief merchant," the still kneeling Spaniard cried.

"You may stand," Cavendish said to him. "Later you may provide me with a full list of your merchandise." His eyes were on the tall officer. It was this man with whom he had spoken during the battle. He could not mistake the voice.

"Captain Cavendish," he said, "and Captain Havers, Señor de Ersola."

De Ersola bowed. He drew his rapier from its sheath, reversed it and held it forth. Cavendish took it, and again the two men surveyed each other. The Spaniard wasted no time.

"I offer myself as hostage for Captain Flores of the *Santa Anna,*" he said briefly.

"I fear that is not possible," Cavendish said, just as briefly. "I desire to speak with your Captain."

De Ersola gave a glance around, quickly summing up the numbers of the *Desire's* company. Then he walked to the rail and gave an order in Spanish to the seamen in the boat. The boat pulled away. De Ersola turned slowly and walked back to Cavendish. Once more he spoke in his flawless English.

"Captain Cavendish," he said, "there are eighty passengers, including women, aboard the *Santa Anna.* For their safety, for the ship is holed between wind and water, I have ordered them onto the quarterdeck."

"Your passengers and company will have good usage," Cavendish said.

"Excellent," said de Ersola. He did not ask what Cavendish intended. He stood easily, unarmed, looking to the *Santa Anna;* he saw the stout figure of his Captain descending into the ship's boat. Then he looked back to Cavendish and Havers.

"Let me congratulate you on your splendid seamanship," he said.

"Thank you," Cavendish said. "You are out from Manila?"

"Six months," de Ersola said. He was watching the boat; he went over and extended a hand to his Captain. Flores gained the deck and de Ersola stood next to him.

"Captain Flores," he said, "let me present Captain Cavendish and Captain Havers."

Flores inclined his head. Through his dignity, he was still struggling with the incomprehensible thought that he had lost his ship. He looked hopelessly at Cavendish, but Cavendish was hardly conscious of him. He was conscious of de Ersola, for de Ersola knew that this one battle, the loss of this great ship, was not the important thing. What was important was that there were English ships here in the Pacific. Flores had fought a battle and lost it; de Ersola knew the fight was bigger than that, and he was not defeated. Cavendish had seen him mentally counting the *Desire's* company. They were far less than the Spanish. The prize crew which he intended to throw aboard the *Santa Anna* tonight would be comprised of only forty men. He said curtly, "Tonight I shall keep yourself, Captain Flores, and your pilot and chief merchant aboard the *Desire* as hostages."

"I should like to speak with you further!" Flores said. Sudden excitement blazed in his eyes. He looked anxiously toward the *Santa Anna*. "What—"

"You may surrender me your sword, sir," Cavendish interrupted.

Flores drew the sword from its sheath; silently he gave it up to Cavendish, who in turn handed it to Havers. The Spaniard spoke again, but Cavendish had already turned away.

"Are your men ready, Master Moon?"

"Aye, sir," said Moon.

While Cavendish had been talking, a boat had been hoisted out; Moon barked an order; another boat was pulling from the *Content*. There was no time to lose, for darkness would soon be on them. Without a backward glance, Cavendish slid down into his longboat. Havers and Fuller would take good care of the Spanish. He took Moon and Pretty and David with him; Brule was sending ten men and two officers from the *Content*.

Cavendish was the first over the side of the *Santa Anna*. He stumbled against something; he looked down.

Cavendish had stepped over a dead man, but David had bumped him, and then he too stepped across the body and felt himself slide forward in the blood that lay on the deck. He steadied himself. Pretty was by his side; a piece of mast lay to his right, and a heap of torn sail; there were figures on the deck—prone. Even as David watched, he saw one figure rise up, and he started.

It was the priest. His cassock flapped as he moved forward and knelt by another man who lay on his side and groaned in quick small gasps. David heard the priest's voice, low; then he took another step toward Cavendish.

"I've never seen it so bad," he whispered.

"Watch your step," Cavendish said.

A mangled ship's boat blocked their way. An eerie silence hung over the stricken vessel. Now David could see her forecastle plainly. The starboard side was torn away, and one of the guns mounted there hung crazily downward. There was a cleared space before the mast. About a hundred men were gathered there, waiting. David reckoned quickly then that about two-thirds of her crew had been killed or wounded. Under his feet the deck slanted; he slipped again on the bloody planks. And aft—he could see them now—aft on the quaterdeck were the passengers. David stared. There were many women. He knew Moon was staring too, striving to get a glimpse of a face, or the curve of a figure.

Moon muttered, "This cursed galleon is too big." He was grinning.

Behind them, the forty English prize crew had tumbled onto the deck. Cavendish motioned three men with muskets forward.

"Take up your posts at the foot of the stairway to the quarterdeck," said Cavendish.

Moon whispered, "They are lucky, the bastards."

David looked about again. He kicked aside a broken sword. The confusion was so indescribable that David stoood helpless, waiting.

He did not wait long. Cavendish's first order came quickly.

"Master Pretty!" His voice cut through the stillness. "Go below and see how badly she is hit. Those holes should be plugged."

"Aye, aye, sir," said Pretty. He started away with five carpenters from the *Desire.*

Cavendish had been walking slowly, estimating the amount of damage. He was frowning; then he turned to face the Spanish seamen. He would make a careful inspection as soon as the Spanish were disarmed. "One by one," he said distinctly in Spanish, "you will come forward to be relieved of all weapons. Your Captain and chief pilot are being held hostage."

There was no need to say more. A Spanish officer stepped forward. Moon met him and took the proffered sword.

"Gracias," Moon said, looking with some pleasure at the silver-hilted weapon.

The officers introduced themselves. The task of sorting the good weapons from the bad began. The pile of small arms, pikes and javelins grew. What was useful, the English seamen transferred immediately into the longboat; the rest, and the stones, were tossed into the sea with dispatch. In the midst of this, Pretty came running up for a detail of Spaniards to man the pumps.

"Her wells are full, sir," he said to Cavendish.

Cavendish ordered twenty unarmed men to Pretty. They disappeared below; soon there was the sound of the creaking of the pumps, the sound of hammering. Methodically, the work of disarming the Spanish went on. Nothing could be done until the task was finished. Cavendish was speaking to the priest.

"We must bury the dead and badly wounded, Father," he said. "Will you choose some men to help you?"

The priest nodded slowly. "I shall, my son."

Cavendish said, "Do not try to save those who are beyond much hope."

Once more the priest inclined his head. "I shall do my best," he said. He turned away; he called out a few names, and those men came to him gratefully.

"And after you have finished with the dead, you may attend the wounded, Father, if you wish."

"I do wish," the priest said.

He had already covered the faces of a few of the dead. The first body splashed into the blue sea. The ship had lost its silence; the victors and the defeated began their task.

Unarmed Spanish soldiers were set to work to clear the decks of wreckage. The priest moved about. Men with litters carried wounded men below. David was supervising the rigging of running lights. He worked fast; the dusk was deepening.

Cavendish himself was ordering men aloft. The stumpy mainmast still carried her square sail. He set his own men to repairing the cut rigging.

"There's nothing holding that sail but the eyelet holes, sir," one man said.

"Reeve fresh running gear," Cavendish said.

The Englishmen were casting in new shroud knots. The mizzen was heaved out; the two crews worked steadily, for all their weariness. The *Santa Anna,* after an hour, was miraculously under sail.

The main deck was cleared. Streams of water washed across it now; the running lights gleamed; the pumps creaked, and spray began to fly from the *Santa Anna's* bow. She was gathering way.

The foresail was unfurled. It held. It filled with wind. The Spanish were so glad to be alive that they talked incessantly. They had been six months at sea; it was a relief to be with another crew, other men, even though they were enemies. Occasional laughter was heard.

The fresh running gear on the mainsail had been reeved. The great sail strained in the wind. One Spanish officer was using a log line.

"Three knots," he reported excitedly, proudly, to the English Captain. They had done much, all of them.

Moon came up to Cavendish. After he had finished disarming the prisoners, and sent the good and usable weapons back to the *Desire,* he had carefully inspected the *Santa Anna,* below decks, as had been his duty many times before. Moon was accustomed to this.

He carried heavy keys. "All powder and shot is locked and guarded, sir," he said. He had stationed his men at the various hatches; all of them were heavily armed.

Pretty reappeared. "There's no further danger for to-night, sir," he said proudly. "The most dangerous shot holes are plugged. The water is not rising, sir."

"Excellent, Pretty," Cavendish said.

Pretty sighed. He was very weary. His eyes were deeply circled.

"Tomorrow you can sleep, Pretty," Cavendish said.

"Aye, sir," said Pretty. "But I don't want for sleep, sir. No more than you."

The night stretched ahead of them. There would be no sleep. And there still remained the passengers. On that upper deck was clustered the most precious part of the cargo, for all it's gold. Women. Pretty waited expectantly.

"Fetch Master David," Cavendish said. "You can both come with me."

"Aye, sir," said Pretty. Cavendish moved aft slowly. Pretty hurried; he and David joined Cavendish at the foot of the stairway. The armed men were standing stiffly. The low murmur of voices above them stopped. There was silence as Cavendish slowly mounted the steps; after him came the two officers and the guards.

The dusk was complete. Through it, the passengers of the *Santa Anna* looked at the conquerors. The silence was tense.

David stood to the side of the Captain. He stared at these people, forgetting what he himself looked like, disheveled, dirty and menacing. It had been a long time since David had seen any human being except seamen, enemy or English, and Indians. These were people like the ones he might see walking down a London street. There were a few *hidalgos,* some merchants and traders, women of quality and their servants. It had been a long time since David had seen white women.

They were looking back at him. But mostly they looked at Cavendish, with appeal. Their fate lay with him, but they were ready to be dependent on him because they had seen the order he had restored. That obvious dependence made a quick anger rise in David. But he shut his mind to thinking; all he knew now was to obey.

Cavendish said first, "You may all rest assured that there is no further danger. The shot holes have been plugged."

A rippling sigh made Pretty feel sorry for them. David looked ahead grimly.

"Tonight," Cavendish went on, "you shall be placed below hatches, with guards."

David did not expect him to say more. David knew he wouldn't, and that was the end of it. Pretty was taking these last few seconds to look his fill at a dark-haired girl in white blouse and skirt whose huge eyes were fastened on David.

"Sirs," said Cavendish, and Pretty looked hastily back at him, "you can report to me in the Captain's cabin when you have finished.

"Aye, sir," said Pretty.

"Aye, Captain," David said.

Cavendish swept him with one brief glance. He turned away, glanced at the cleared decks and decided to go below for a look at the compass. He squinted up at the sky; he would relieve the man at the helm too. He saw once more that the *Desire* and the *Content* ranged close alongside, hove to under shortened sail.

He left Tyler at the helm. The course was east northeast. As he came down the companionway aft, one of the men stationed there stopped him at the foot of the ladder.

"Captain," he said, hesitantly.

Cavendish waited.

"Sir, this door." He pointed to it. "It's locked."

Chapter 5

THE DOOR was heavy gleaming teakwood. "I know I should have noted it before, sir! I thought I'd seen to all these cabins, here, with Master Moon!"

"Where is the Captain's cabin?" Cavendish asked.

"Next, sir. I lighted the lamp for you, sir."

"Thank you," said Cavendish.

The soldier moved away to his post. He shifted his musket and listened. Fifteen feet away, Cavendish lifted his hand and knocked on the teakwood. Two sharp knocks.

There was no answer. He did not knock again. He said, in Spanish, "Open this door, or I shall have to force it."

There was a scuffling sound. He heard the bolt drawn back. But he waited, and finally the door opened. Facing Cavendish stood a slight boy, black-haired, with long almond-shaped eyes. Those eyes were full of apprehension. He didn't speak. He blocked out the rest of the cabin.

"Who are you?" Cavendish asked.

"Cosmos" was the answer. The boy hesitated, started to speak, and did not.

Cavendish smiled. "Are you of China?" he asked.

The boy shook his head. *"Japón,"* he said. Again he started to speak; again he was silent, respectfully.

"Step aside, Cosmos," Cavendish said, pushing the door open farther. His eyes searched the cabin briefly. He frowned at the three smaller boys of graduating sizes; he was sure they were Filipino children, brought back to be pages to Spanish nobility. This boy Cosmos—Cavendish had already decided to acquire him for himself, as a personal servant. Cosmos' eyes were still on him, hopefully, questioningly, and Cavendish's gaze flicked past the three Filipino boys, past a little girl and a Filipino woman who guarded her with hostile face turned to the intruder.

Cosmos could keep silent no longer. His tone was woefully anxious. *"Señor,"* he blurted, "have you seen the *señora?"*

Cavendish, puzzled, frowned at him.

Cosmos rushed on. "She is beautiful and she wears green and she was with us! She is gone!"

Cavendish said, "You shall probably see her in the morning. She is, most like, with the other women. Do not lock this door again; there is no danger."

He closed the door behind him. He called the man on guard. His tone was sharp.

"Have you had sight of a woman in a green dress?"

The guard replied instantly. "No, sir!"

"I see," said Cavendish, looking at his face. He turned, walked the few feet to the Captain's cabin, and opened the door.

For the first second he was caught off guard. He had not expected to see anyone, and the woman who stood just inside the door almost succeeded in brushing past him. Then he put out his arm to bar her way.

The door was still open. Against the paneling of the cabin, she leaned back, arching her body away from him; his mailed arm blocked her path.

She did not move. He looked down at her face; her hair was tangled. It was reddish gold, and the eyes that met his were as green as the rumpled satin dress she wore. There was dirt smudged on her cheek.

He said, quietly, "Your name, *señorita?"*

"Señorita?" she whispered. Her head was tilted back and she shook it. "I am a widow," she said. "Señora de Montoro."

She was rumpled and it suited her. She was beautiful. As Cosmos had said. Cavendish kicked the door shut with a movement of his boot. He didn't move his arm. "How did you come here?" he asked.

"I—was with my child." She spoke as though this could not be quite real. Then she remembered it was real. "Tomas told us to go up on deck, but I did not. I kept the other boys with me." Her gaze was steadily on his tanned face and the blue eyes under the helmet. She spoke more spiritedly. "I did not want the children to see—what they might. I kept them in Tomas' cabin."

He did not take his own eyes off her. "Tomas?" he asked. There was a little edge to his voice. "Who is Tomas?"

"Señor de Ersola," she said.

Cavendish saw clearly the face of the tall Spaniard. "Señor de Ersola is being held hostage aboard my ship," he said.

Her eyes were as green as the emeralds that were among his richest prizes, loot that lay in his own storeroom aboard the *Desire*.

"You hold him hostage?"

"I do," said Cavendish.

She was rather tall. She stood six inches below him. "You are the English Captain, then?"

"Cavendish," he said. "I might have said so before, *señora*."

"You might," she said. She made a little movement, as though toward the door, but he did not move. He still blocked her path.

"A moment," he said.

Her lips were parted slightly; she ran her red tongue over them. "I wanted to see what was happening," she said. "We are under way."

"True," he said, his tone almost bemused. Was she so fair, or was it a year and a half at sea that made her seem so to him? Her face was dirty, her eyes were shadowed, but there was a sweetness about her that he wanted to taste.

"You're Spanish?" he said.

"My mother was Dutch," she said, evenly, as though a great many men had asked her that question before in the same tone of voice.

"Your hair," he said.

She looked as though he were proceeding the way she had expected. She said nothing.

He wanted to touch her. He reached for her hand, letting his fingers slide down her arm. She stood motionless; their hands met, and for a second her fingers curled around his, and then her hand was small and stiff. He drew her over to the table where the lamp burned above. He dropped her hand.

"Were you afraid you were going to die?" he asked.

The hours of battle that had passed were a jumbled panorama. "I don't know," she said.

He poured two cups of wine from the decanter that stood on the table. The cabin was rich in appointment, spacious; it had a large Venetian mirror; the mirror reminded him he had his helment on. He took it off gratefully, running his hand over his gray-tinged hair. She watched.

"Drink this," he said, holding out the cup.

She took it from him. Her fingers were strong and slim; her wrists delicate. She raised the cup to her lips; she drank slowly.

"If you had stayed below, there was little danger to you," he said. "Our guns were aimed at your decks. Until we could bring the ship in close."

"Tomas had put us below decks," she said.

He said suddenly, a little jealously, "My name is Tom—"

"He is unhurt?" she interrupted.

"Quite," said Cavendish. "Drink your wine. There's more."

He watched her lift the cup to her lips. She drank it all. She held out the empty cup and once more their hands touched. The tension tightened in the cabin; the soft motion of the ship made the lamp flicker. Cavendish turned to refill the cup.

"I do not want more," she said.

"It will do you good." He straightened up.

"I do not want it!" There was anger in the green eyes, and the sight of it brought the brilliance into his own blue eyes.

"Take it," he insisted, holding out the cup.

She struck it away and it rolled over the floor. The wine splashed. The calm was broken into shattered pieces.

He caught the hand she had used; for a moment she tried to pull away, but that was useless, and she raised her other hand and struck him as hard as she could with her clenched fist.

There was no sound in the paneled cabin. He seized the hand that had struck him. Slowly his arms tightened around her. Her head lay back against his arm; the red-gold curls spilled over against his chest. He bent his head; she could not move, and he kissed the curve of white throat, the smudged cheek; her hair was soft. His grip was brutally strong. He loosened it.

She twisted out of his arms in a supple movement. Her back was to him and he looked down. Across her shoulders were the marks of the mail he wore. His voice was rough and he spoke in English.

"I apologize," he said. "I hurt you."

She came at him in English. "Does that surprise you?"

Her lilting English had been pleasant to hear. He said approvingly. "You speak English."

She swung around to face him; he saw she was still trying to get her breath. *"Je parle français aussi! Canaille!"*

Unsmiling, he bowed. *"Merci,* madam, I also speak Portuguese."

"I cannot!"

"A pity, *señora.* Perhaps I could teach you!"

Every curve of her body spoke defiance. He smiled a little; he hardly realized she was speaking to him, that the red lips were moving.

"And as for your apology, Captain, I do not accept it."

She turned, even as his eyes were on her. Her hand reached for the door.

Now he spoke quickly. Now he remembered he could not keep her here.

"Since Señor de Ersola is not here, *señora,* permit me to escort you to another cabin, where you will be more comfortable."

She had opened the door. Rapidly she was starting away. "It is not necessary," she said, over her shoulder.

Angrily, he was tempted to let her go. But he was suddenly afraid that the man who would undoubtedly catch her might lay hands on her.

"*Señora!*" he said sharply.

At the tone, she stopped. Three rapid steps brought him to her side. Strongly conscious of each other, they walked together to the cabin door. Cavendish leaned over to open it. His shoulder brushed hers.

"Bid your Filipino woman bring your child. I am going to place the three of you in a separate cabin."

Without a word to him, she obeyed. He followed easily the rapid flow of Spanish in which she said to Cosmos that she was safe. Cosmos tried to smile while she took her little girl by the hand.

Then Cavendish spoke to Cosmos, "You shall come with me, now," he said.

Cosmos said, "Si, *señor*." His voice was hopeless.

But Cavendish paid no attention. "This way, *señora*," he said. Across from the Captain's cabin was another large cabin. He opened the door. The man on guard materialized out of the shadows.

"D'ye want me, sir?" he asked, staring at the Spanish woman.

Cavendish said, "Señora de Montoro, her woman and child will remain here for the night." He bowed to her. "Do not lock your door," he said, "nor leave this cabin. This man," he inclined his head, "is on guard."

"*Sí, señor,*" she said. She lifted her hand to close the door; she had shepherded her little girl into the cabin; suddenly she raised her hands in appeal, and the sweetness of her was very evident. "Why do you want Cosmos?"

"I need a page," he said. "I shall take him back to England with me."

"England?" she said, and she looked up at him, as if he were reminding both of them, himself and her, that this meeting was one of purest chance, and that ordinarily their lives would never have crossed and they could not now entangle because they had so much between them and so little time. Their eyes met.

She didn't say good night. She closed the door, and Cavendish turned away, with Cosmos trailing after him uncertainly.

But when Master Pretty entered the cabin fifteen minutes later, Cosmos had already served his Captain with fruit and wine and preserves and biscuit. Cavendish's head was bent over the papers that lay on the table. The specie list; the manifests of the *Santa Anna*. Pretty looked at his bent head. He hated to interrupt. There was a thousand questions he would have liked to ask; this great rich prize was theirs; what was Cavendish going to do with it?

Pretty sighed. "Sir," he said, "the women have been put under hatches with guards." To Pretty, the passengers were the women.

Cavendish looked up. He grinned. "They are such a lovely problem, eh, Pretty?"

Pretty nodded. He started to speak, but Cavendish had turned back to the lists. Pretty went out the door and closed it behind himself.

Chapter 6

THE COAST of California lay drowned in mist. Mist covered the mountains, the morning sun, the cypresses along the rocky beaches. On the tip of California was the bay of San Lucas that the Spanish called Aguada Segura.

It was a small bay, ringed with low mountains, white beaches and white breaking surf. Almost at its very center, a river entered the bay; its water was fresh and clear and good to drink.

On the high deck of the *Santa Anna,* Cavendish was wet through; he brushed the drops of water off his face once again with his wet hand.

The *Santa Anna's* sails were reefed; the south wind was lazy. The galleon was putting into port like a majestic duchess, her running lights still gleaming to guide the *Desire* and the *Content*.

"Thirteen fathoms, sir," called out the linesman.

"Strike all sail," Cavendish commanded.

Pretty, who was fore, drew a breath of relief. Not because he had been worried, but because he was desperately tired.

"Twelve fathoms, sir," the linesman called out.

"You may heave out the anchors now, Master Pretty," Cavendish said.

"Aye, aye, sir," said Pretty.

"And extinguish the running lights."

The mist had come up before dawn. For two hours Cavendish had stood on the high deck; he knew these waters well. He had wanted to make port by morning. He had. He was conscious of Cosmos who had come up beside him; there was immense admiration on Cosmos' face. Even Señor de Ersola was not a better navigator than this Englishman. The mist floated past them; the wind separated it; above, the sun was shining, the California sun.

54

"Soon it will shine through, sir," Cosmos said.

"So it will," said Cavendish.

He was wearing a cloak. The officer named Moon had called him up on deck two hours ago when the fog closed in on them. Cosmos had brought a cloak to keep the Captain dry. Now Cavendish handed it back to him, and Cosmos took it.

"You want anything, *señor?*" he asked.

"Not now," said Cavendish.

The *Santa Anna* was at anchor. Four anchors moored her. The first ship's boat was slung over the side. It was full of canvas, cordage and light axes; it had been loaded in the morning. On deck, the first boatload of men was ready to disembark. They had been lined up by Moon, and one by one they went over the side. The sun came out and the boat pulled for shore. Cosmos watched.

By the time they had beached the boat and drawn it up on the white sand, another boatload of men had disembarked. On deck, the English directed the maneuver; the Spanish officers were leaving the *Santa Anna* too. Cavendish suddenly turned, and Cosmos, carrying the wet cloak, followed him below.

"Fetch your chest, Cosmos," Cavendish said.

"Aye, aye, sir," said Cosmos; for a second his eyes sparkled, and Cavendish grinned at his first English phrase.

"We go to your ship now, sir?"

"We go aboard the *Desire* in ten minutes," Cavendish said.

Cosmos scampered away. Cavendish brushed back his wet hair; a lock had fallen across his forehead. He knocked lightly on a cabin door.

There was a little pause.

"Who is it?" a voice asked.

"Captain Cavendish," he said. "May I come in, *señora?*"

There was another little pause. Then her voice came again. "Oh, I am sorry, *señor*. But you see, I am—*en déshabillé*."

Cavendish's hand dropped from the latch. Then he looked thoughtful. There had been a trace of laughter in the voice that had answered him. He would wager any amount of gold she was standing on the other side of the door, fully dressed. He started to open the door. Then he stopped, for he couldn't be sure. And he couldn't help smiling.

"Hurry, then, *señora*," he said. "I am anxious to see you with your face washed."

"I hurry," she said, in English, with an upward inflection.

"I sent you your boxes," Cavendish said.

"I know. It is most kind of you." She opened the door then, and he saw she was dressed in white. Her hair was brushed and gleaming, and fastened on top of her head. She was perfectly groomed, and she had opened the door quickly enough to let him know she had been teasing him a moment before.

She spoke demurely. "Cosmos brought us food and water. I thank you very much."

Cavendish smiled. There were footsteps on the companionway, and he said, "Pitt, will you come here?"

"Aye, aye, sir," said an English voice. Catherine de Montoro looked at the newcomer.

"This is Pitt, *señora*," Cavendish said. "He is from the *Desire*. He will be on guard here now, and if you wish something, he will be happy to oblige you."

"Aye, madam," Pitt said. He shot a look at Cavendish; then he moved away.

"And this will be your cabin, *señora*, while you are still aboard the *Santa Anna*."

"While I am still aboard?" Her eyes were suddenly questioning.

His face was guarded. "Your officers and crew are being disembarked," he said. "To the beaches. We are anchored at San Lucas. Aguada Segura."

"Aguada Segura?"

"Safe watering place. An apt name," he said. "You and the other women will remain aboard. For a while. The man on guard at the companionway will be relieved, at each watch. But he will always do whatever you wish. You understand, *señora*?"

"I do," she said. Her voice was more distant. "Then you take Cosmos with you?"

"Aye, madam."

They had been speaking English. Now she lapsed into Spanish, her face intent and serious. "Cosmos is seventeen," she said quickly. "He is—*señor*, he can read and write his own language. He is capable of intense devotion—he will be faithful always, if—"

Cavendish said, "I shall leave him here to wait on you."

"No!"

"Why not, *señora?*" He looked down at her steadily.

"Because he belongs to you now," she said. "I do not need him. Soon I leave this, too." She motioned to the cabin. "You said."

"Señora," he said, and there was a look in his blue eyes that was asking for understanding. It was there briefly, and then it was gone. But she had seen it plainly.

"I must go now," he said.

"Will you bid Cosmos *adiós* for me?"

"I shall," he said. It did not occur to him to let Cosmos say his own good-bye.

"Gracias," she said.

"Good-bye, then, *señora,"* he answered. He turned abruptly and she heard his steps ascending the ladder unhurriedly. He was gone.

On deck, there were no seamen except the English. The disembarkation of the Spanish crew was complete. The sun was shining; the waters of the bay were blue. At anchor rode the *Desire* and the *Content* and the great *Santa Anna*. The white beach was near. On it, drawn up neatly, were the ship's boats from the galleon; from the narrow belt of pine forests that stretched back from the sand came the sound of axes as the Spaniards felled small trees, and made clearings for the tents they were putting up. They were using extra sail from the *Santa Anna* for tents.

Cavendish's boat was ready for him. He slid down into it, and the men pulled for the *Desire*. Cosmos watched the ship draw nearer; his small chest containing all his worldly belongings was under his feet; he looked down at his folded hands to conceal the tears in his eyes.

The Captain's brother was watching him. The Captain's brother seemed to understand; he smiled and patted Cosmos on the shoulder as Cosmos climbed aboard the *Desire*. The seamen stared at him.

"They've never seen your like before," David said. Cosmos grinned happily.

"You're a vain monkey," Cavendish said, and Cosmos nodded.

"Aye, aye, sir," he said, and the men laughed at him.

Cosmos picked up his chest and followed his Captain aft. He felt much better. Cosmos was introduced to Captain Havers. He listened for a moment while the two men talked, quickly; there was a pause in their conversation, and Cosmos put in worriedly, "You eat now, sir?" His brown eyes were on Cavendish.

"Aye, aye, Cosmos," Cavendish said, mimicking him and smiling as Cosmos hastened out. "In gold alone, Havers, there are one hundred and twenty thousand pieces." He was stripping off his clothes.

"Lord God," said Havers, puffing on his pipe. He thought that over for a minute. He blew out a cloud of smoke. He rose to his feet. "I'll summon the Spanish Captain and de Ersola now, Tom."

"I'll be ready in fifteen minutes," Cavendish said. "I'm famished, Havers."

"Fifteen minutes, then," Havers said.

"I want David present," Cavendish added.

"Aye, Tom," Havers started out and bumped into Cosmos coming in the door. Cosmos carried a tray of food.

"You're quick," Havers said approvingly.

"I told the cook, hurry," Cosmos said. He set down the tray and took the razor from Cavendish's hand. "Eat first," he said. "I sharpen this."

He moved about the cabin, laying out fresh clothes. Surreptitiously he watched Cavendish eat. The Captain had a wonderful appetite. Cosmos was pleased with the amount he ate. When Cavendish was dressed and shaved, Cosmos looked at him critically.

He handed Cavendish a gold-hilted dagger as a finishing touch. Absently Cavendish thrust it through his belt.

"You may come with me, Cosmos," he said.

Pleased, Cosmos trotted after him. He was five feet tall and he came just to Cavendish's shoulder. Cosmos opened the door for his Captain and followed him into the *Desire's* great cabin. Cosmos looked about appreciatively.

There were four men in the cabin and Cosmos knew them all. Señor de Ersola, standing tall and graceful, greeted him with a speculative smile. Cosmos was one of the first signs of victory; he belonged to the English Captain now.

"Good morning, sirs," Cavendish said, seating himself. "If you will sit, we may be comfortable while we talk."

Cosmos stood behind Cavendish's chair and watched the other men sit. Cavendish asked him to pour some wine, and he did. He filled the silver goblets.

"Now," said Cavendish, "the terms of your surrender were simple and easy. I pledged your lives and good usuage"—he stressed the two words—"and you gave over to me all your goods, weapons, merchandise and food. All of that now belongs to us."

David looked from Cavendish to Flores. David was unsurprised by Cavendish's opening words; he was employing his usual tactics, driving forward to something he wanted by emphasizing the strength of his own position.

The Spanish Captain Flores, his plump face white, said, "That is quite true, sir."

De Ersola took a sip of his wine. His dark face betrayed nothing of what went on in his mind. Cavendish resumed. "Thus, the *Santa Anna* belongs to us. Your company, including your officers, has already been disembarked. I have given them permission, instruction rather, to build tents ashore, in clearings under the pine trees back from the beach. Those tents are to house your passengers." He looked about at Cosmos. "Will you serve us some fruit, Cosmos?" He was frowning a little; he picked the dagger out of his belt, and held it lightly in his palm, as if he were wondering if he had explained enough. He wasn't used to explaining. "It's impossible, of course, sirs, to have women aboard while we unload the *Santa Anna* and transfer her goods to the *Desire* and the *Content*."

Captain Flores made no answer. Cosmos offered him a platter of fruit; he did not even see it. Cavendish took an orange and began to peel it. David wanted nothing; only de Ersola took an orange; he too began to peel it slowly.

"And then, Captain?" he asked, looking up.

Cavendish met his dark eyes. "I reckon that we'll be in port two weeks, roughly. It will take that long to re-stow your goods, and to make ready for our voyage across the Pacific. Gentlemen, the average age of my company is five and twenty. They are healthy. Aboard the *Santa Anna* there are eighty passengers. Including women."

De Ersola kept on peeling his orange. "What do you want from us, Captain?" he asked evenly.

Cavendish said, "I want your parole."

Flores said, "You want to tie our hands! You want to make things easy for you and your English pirates!"

"That's exactly what I want," Cavendish said. He was cutting the peeled orange into eight pieces.

Flores said, "I cannot in honor give you my parole, Captain." He was trying to realize that this had happened to him. His people were being put out on the beaches, to live in tents. Yet he must realize it, and thus be able to plan ahead for the future days. He started to rise.

"Sit, please," Cavendish said.

Flores flushed; then the flush receded, leaving two red spots on his white cheeks.

Cavendish ate one of the pieces of orange, and then another. "I have the Pacific to cross," he said. "I have only eighty crew and I want to hang none of them for rape or murder. Yet, ahead of them lies the Pacific. They have fought hard and well the last months. They have endured great hardship and great danger. They have watched their comrades, to the number of forty-eight, die. Some miserably. My company are in need of play. They need to swim and hunt and fish here. They need the land. And I am not going to deny it to them! Yet I must put your company on land also."

De Ersola said calmly, "Without parole, what is your alternative? I wonder, Captain, if you'd lend me that knife?"

"Certainly," said Cavendish, holding out the gleaming knife.

De Ersola cut his orange into eight pieces also. Neatly. Then he handed the knife back. "Thank you," he said.

"Without parole," Cavendish said, "all my company go armed always. You and your officers will be held as hostages. Any act of violence against any of my men will be severely punished. But I shall punish any of my men who are guilty of rape." He laid the knife down on the table negligently.

Flores said, "Captain, have you thought what you are saying?"

"I have," Cavendish said.

"Have you thought what you are saying?" Flores repeated, hopelessly. "Punishment for armed violence will make life no less hell for our passengers and women! Are you suggesting your men go armed, and with your sanction, among our people?"

"Those are the terms," Cavendish said. "I'd suggest we live in peace. I am minded of Drake's story to me, that when he took a ship in these waters, the two crews were so glad to see other men and be on land again, they were able to work and live together in peace."

David could tell that Cavendish had won this battle of words. De Ersola seemed to know it, too. His face was inscrutable; de Ersola knew that, without parole, the Spanish had a chance to recapture the *Santa Anna,* even though the chance was slight indeed and might cost most of their lives. But de Ersola knew that Flores would capitulate. Flores was appalled at the amount of bloodshed that might ensue from a single incident, a single hot word.

Flores put his hands on the table. "I'll agree to the truce," he said. "You shall have my parole, and all of my company's."

Havers drew a breath of relief. David was conscious that he was pleased at the outcome, for the land did look sweet, and the women would live there in tents.

. . . He listened to Cavendish's voice go on, saying that there would be night and day watches on the beach, with five men from each ship; saying that Flores' officers would be paroled, and that Flores himself should stay aboard the *Santa Anna;* than no man would be armed, except the officers; saying that tonight, to celebrate the truce, he would be happy if Flores and his officers would join him aboard the *Desire* for dinner, and that on the beaches, the men could roast the hares and conies and fry the fish they were already catching.

Cavendish and Flores shook hands. Flores was to go out now and apprise his men of the conditions under which they would live and work during the coming days. It was very simple, and de Ersola knew, with regret, that the plan would work, and work well. The English would reap the benefit of their Captain's truce. He followed Flores out of the cabin; soon he would be back aboard the *Santa Anna,* as a friend to the English.

Cavendish picked up pen and ink as soon as Flores and de Ersola had left. He said to Havers, "When you escort the Spanish back aboard the *Santa Anna,* pick out fifteen of the Spanish women to dine with us tonight. Or ask Flores to do it; that might be best."

"I think it would," Havers said dryly.

"And, Cosmos, you may deliver this note to the Señora de Montoro." He was still writing as he talked. He sealed the note and handed it to Cosmos. He smiled at David. "Eight hours of sleep for you, lad," he said.

He went to his own cabin, then. His duties were done for the present; he fell fully dressed into his hammock and went to sleep.

Chapter 7

CATHERINE DE MONTORO sat between Cavendish and David at dinner. The *Desire's* cabin was crowded because besides the seven English officers and Captains Brule and Havers, there were two Spanish merchants, fifteen women, and de Ersola and three other Spanish officers. What strain there had been at first had been removed by the wonderful food and the flowing wine. The Spanish had been at sea six months. It was so good to be on land and near it—their lives had been threatened by both the vast Pacific and the English—that an odd excited festivity prevailed. Cavendish, who drank little, observed this with pleasure. The two weeks ahead could be a perfect prelude to the rigors of the long months at sea which were still to come.

"The food is marvelous," Catherine said gratefully.

"We raided Mazatlán, across the Gulf," Cavendish said. David had forgot his food at the nearness of Catherine.

"We should apologize to the *señorita* for that," he said.

At his words, Catherine smiles. "I don't forgive you," she said, "and I am not *señorita*. I am a widow. I have a girl, six."

"You have?" David asked. "How long have you been a widow, *señora?*"

Catherine looked surprised. "A year, almost," she said.

David said, "Thank God, I didn't make a widow of you. I was afraid—"

"Sir, what heavily laden conscience you have." She abandoned her food for a moment and studied his face. He was embarrassed, and suddenly she said, "Don't look so, sir. You have an interesting face. I paint, you see. I prefer portrait painting."

David's admiration was plain. "You do much of it, *señora?*"

Catherine knew Cavendish was listening. She was conscious of him beside her; his brown hand brushed hers as he picked up his wine goblet. "I paint a deal," she said. "You see, sir, to be frank with you, my husband and I came to Manila to make his fortune, as so many men did. But fortune eludes some, and when he died, I had very little." Absent-mindedly, she took a bite of roast chicken.

"But there is wealth in Manila. And we try to make life gracious. The governor wanted his portrait painted; the wives of wealthy merchants—" She flung out her hands. "You understand." Her wine glass had been filled and she picked it up. It was silver and it bore a crest. She puckered her brows at it, and both Cavendish and David watched her.

" '*Animum fortuna sequator,*' " she read. She shot a sidelong glance at Cavendish, who was waiting to see if she could translate it. "I can read it, Captain," she said. "It means 'Let fortune follow courage.' Your motto?"

"Aye, madam," he said. "But one thing. *Fortuna* means not fortune, but good fortune, good luck—'Let good luck follow courage'!"

"If you'd given me a minute more, I would have remembered," she said.

Cavendish laughed.

"Do you believe it?" she asked, seriously. "I mean, the motto?"

"It's in the nature of a toast," he said. "But I warrant I do."

David said, "Then you are both of simple minds."

"No!" said Catherine. "For we mean moral courage as well as physical."

"Can you differentiate between the two?" David asked. "For where there is one, there is the other, in proportion."

At this, Cavendish laughed aloud. "He's sharper than you thought, *señora,*" he said.

Catherine looked from one to the other. "At least you didn't steal the goblets," she said.

"Trust a wench to change the subject," David said. "Are you on your way to Spain, *señora?*"

"Yes," she said. "First to Acapulco, then to Vera Cruz, and thence to Spain. And you are right about the courage. I hadn't thought it through."

"Well, don't feel badly. Tom hasn't either. Although I must say for him he doesn't need to. He has certain tenets that he holds to and from which he never varies." He drank off all his wine. "Whereas, often I find little justification for my actions."

"I don't quite understand you," Catherine said, aware once more of Cavendish.

"Why not?" asked David.

Cavendish, who was listening, again laughed aloud.

Catherine pouted, and David chuckled. "Lord, you're sweet," he said, "to put up with both of us. Have you finished, *señora?* If you have we'll go topside and I'll explain all."

"The *señora* wants some preserves and more wine," Cavendish said.

Catherine said, in a very restrained but eager manner, "I would like some preserves." Cavendish watched her as she ate.

"Marvelous," she said, licking the taste of sugar off her red mouth. She was wearing white again, white satin brocade, with a collar of handmade lace. Around her throat was a slender gold chain and locket. She wore a plain gold ring. The other ladies, whose laughter and chatter filled the cabin, wore jewels of value. Cavendish wondered if Catherine de Montoro was clever enough not to wear jewels; he decided she probably was, and it made him smile inwardly.

"Your husband left you nothing, *señora?*" He asked, bluntly.

"Very little," she said, looking straight at him. "I paid my passage to Acapulco with a family portrait of Captain Flores' wife and children."

"Checkmate, *señora,*" he said, and he smiled. His fingers were over her hand, and he tightened his grip for a moment; slowly the strong fingers released hers. Catherine turned to David.

"I'd like to walk the deck now," she said. "If you wish."

David pushed back his chair instantly and stood up. "If you'll pardon us, sir," he said. He held out his arm to Catherine and she took it; they left the cabin without a backward glance.

On deck, the running lights gleamed. The musicians were there; soon they would play for dancing. David led Catherine over to the rail, aft, under the shadow of Cavendish's high deck. The moon was up. Its light laid a path across the shimmering water. Near, the surf pounded against the beaches; on those beaches a fire burned brightly; around it men were gathered. And a ghostly line of tents stretched under the first pine trees.

"The tide is full," David said.

"I shall live there," Catherine said. "In a tent."

"You shall," David said.

They were silent. "Why is it always so beautiful?" Catherine asked.

David said, "I do my best thinking at night, at sea. Ask any seaman. Ask yourself, for that matter."

"I suppose I dream instead," she said. "But what did you mean when you said that you sometimes found small justification for your actions?"

He said instantly, "You know. Now tonight, I asked you to come here with me, not only because I wished to talk with you"—he swung around to face her—"Believe me, *señora,* I do want to be with you! But I also wanted to bedevil my brother."

Catherine said, "So did I."

David laughed. "I knew that, but I didn't expect you to say so now. However, *señora,* you are a woman, and it is to be expected that you should want to have Tom. But—to me, it should matter little whether I annoy him or not."

"Why did you say that?"

David understood that she was thinking only of what he had said about her wanting Tom. "Because most women do, and I should think, you, especially. Give him no quarter, *señora.* He gives none, nor does he ask it."

"I was thinking of what you said about yourself," she said.

"You were not, but I'll explain. A year and a half at sea have given me time to grow and think. For twelve years previous to that, I was dependent on my brother. I still am. I obey orders. But, *señora,* I don't want to. Why?"

"Because you resent him?" Catherine asked, tentatively.

"Partly," he said, "but also because I cannot believe nor understand the things he does." He paused. "Have you ever seen a man tortured?"

"No," said Catherine.

"I have," he said, "and I still cannot condone—not Tom's action—but my standing supinely aside and watching what I believe is wrong. Wrong? More than that."

"But why?" she said. "Why did he have a man tortured?"

David said, "*Señora,* you are interested in one thing, and that is one man. He did it because he had to find out if the Spaniard in question carried letters about us. If he carried the letters, then we were safe. If he didn't, Tom had to intercept the ship which did carry the news of us to Acapulco. Tried fright, first. He pretended he was going to hang the Spaniard; the hatch was rigged, and the officer still didn't confess. So Tom used a thumbscrew. The Spaniard confessed then that he'd thrown the letters overboard when we took his bark. You see, Tom's action was justified, from his point of view. From mine, it was not. Not even through the safety of the crew was at stake. Here comes Tom."

Cavendish was walking across the deck toward them, purposefully. With him were de Ersola and a Spanish lady of quality whose name was Arabella de Madariaga. She wore a mantilla over her black hair.

David, close to Arabella, looked at her critically. De Ersola was telling Cavendish an incident of their voyage and Cavendish, leaning back against the rail, was silently appraising Arabella too.

Catherine looked angry. David said, in her ear, "But, *señora,* we are only men."

Catherine turned her head away from him. In the running lights her hair gleamed red. De Ersola finished his tale, and David said to Cavendish, "The *señora* and I talked of various things. I think she would like to see those leather paintings of yours."

"I would, Captain," said Catherine, ignoring Arabella, but bestowing a smile on de Ersola. De Ersola looked weary and drawn; Catherine knew he had gone without sleep for thirty-six hours, because he had been on the beaches directing the men; he was taking Captain Flores' place tonight, while Flores sat alone in his cabin. Cavendish was saying that he would be pleased to show her the paintings, and Catherine laid her hand on de Ersola's arm for a minute.

"Excuse us, Tomas," she said.

"I'll wait here for you," he said. "We'll dance."

She nodded, smiling, and she walked along between Cavendish and David, feeling satisfied that she had outdone Arabella, for the moment, at least. And she wanted to see the cabin where Cavendish spent so many of his hours.

As she had expected, Cavendish's cabin was scrupulously neat. The table top had a half-drawn chart affixed to it; the hammock was unslung, and the ship's clock ticked; sand tumbled steadily in the hourglass. David opened the small door that led to Cavendish's storeroom.

But Catherine was looking at the chart. As much love had gone into it as she put into her portraits; she knew that, and she looked up at Cavendish, her eyes shining with pleasure to recognize something in him that was akin to her, and yet so different, so much like him.

"It's wonderful," she said, quite inadequately, but her expressive face told him plainly that she had quite enough imagination to know what those charts meant, and what they meant to him personally.

"I knew you'd like it," he said, low.

David interrupted. He had been busily unrolling an oblong piece of fine leather. On it was painted the picture of a garden in flower.

"Look, *señora*," he said, vainly trying to hold it straight. He let go one end, and it rolled up.

Catherine caught the end of it. "It's very lovely," she

said, trying to look sideways at the leather. "You hold it, please, Captain," she said.

Cavendish obediently took hold of the leather, and Catherine stepped back to get a good view.

"It *is* lovely," she repeated. "I've never seen anything like it."

"May I let go now?" Cavendish asked. He was impatient, and he glanced at David. "Put it away now, David," he said.

"Aye, aye, sir," David said jauntily. He rolled it up neatly and stowed it in the storeroom. The storeroom door stood open wide, and Catherine was looking into it with unconcealed interest. She said, "Are those bells gold?"

David, whose back was turned, muttered from the small space, "They are, *señora.*"

But Catherine looked at Cavendish. "They were church bells," she said.

"They were," was the even answer. This time it was Cavendish who had answered.

Catherine, who felt intense anger, wanted desperately to ask why he had stolen them, and at the same time knew she was not surprised that he had. "What is in that box?" she asked.

David held a heavy box in his hands, to replace it where it belonged. He straightened up, box in hand. The lid flew up.

"Look at it," he said. "You'll never see the like again."

Catherine gasped. There was a fortune of jewels within, jumbled together carelessly, the collar of pearls only partly concealing the size of an emerald lying beneath. Slowly Catherine put out her hand; she pushed aside the pearls to see a clustered necklace of rubies. The emerald gleamed wickedly.

"Madre de Dios," she said, shaking her head and turning to look at Cavendish.

He was not looking at her. He was angry, and he was angry with David; his face was set, as if he were trying to decide what to say, and David was waiting grimly for him to say it. The emerald winked in the light, and

Catherine closed her fingers over it. It was smooth; it fitted in her palm, and with sudden fierce desire to have it she withdrew her hand from the box with the emerald clutched tightly. She flipped the lid of the box closed.

"You'd better put it away," she said.

David shoved it back in the storeroom with his foot, negligently. He closed the storeroom door. Cavendish's voice cut through the cabin.

"Leave us, David."

Catherine's eyes widened. The emerald was hot in her palm—along with her handkerchief. She sent an appealing look at David.

David answered the look. "Why, Tom," he said lightly, "must I part from the *señora?*"

Cavendish had taken two steps to the door.

"Leave us," he said.

David's dark eyes blazed with anger, and Catherine suddenly felt fear. But David was controlling his anger.

"I'll desert you this time, *señora,*" he said, as if he were warning her that the next time he would not; that there was coming a time when he would act.

"We'll not talk long," Catherine said. He could not have known she had taken the emerald; he must have sensed that she didn't want to be left alone with Cavendish.

Then David closed the door. Catherine forgot David completely. Cavendish stood in front of her, and she looked straight ahead at the wide shoulders. His voice was amused.

"What did you steal, *señora?*" he asked.

"I?" she said, catching her lower lip with her white teeth.

"You," he said.

She raised her eyes to his face.

"You steal church bells!"

For only a second he hesitated. Then his reply came. "Only if they are of gold."

He reached out his hand and his fingers fastened over her wrist. He lifted her hand; a bit of lace and linen escaped the clenched fingers.

Slowly her fingers relaxed. Cavendish picked the emerald up. "There is a chain for it," he said.

Catherine said breathlessly, "Do you wish to know why I took it?" She spoke rapidly in Spanish, slipping into her own tongue, forgetting English.

"Y por qué?" he asked.

"Because I desired it passionately," she said, "and because it gave me pleasure to take it from you!"

"Neither is a reason for theft," he said.

Defensively she said, "You steal. Why shouldn't I?"

"Señora, since we are speaking frankly, I desire you passionately and it would give me pleasure to take you."

"That is different! I am not inanimate!" In the heat of this argument she spoke first, and then she flushed a little.

Cavendish was frowning, studying her; he knew she wouldn't take the emerald if he offered it to her, but he was going to try it anyway when she said, looking up at him with her green eyes. "I am sorry, Captain. You think ill of me, and you are right."

"I don't think ill of you!"

"I value what your Captain Havers and Master Pretty think of me," she said, in a very low voice. "So I should stay here with you no longer."

Cavendish dropped the emerald on the table, and opened the door. "We talked only four minutes," he said. He hurried her along; they emerged on the deck where the musicians were playing.

"Will you dance?" Cavendish said.

She nodded wordlessly.

They were playing a French dance that had become popular long ago. Cavendish put his arm around her; they moved easily through the intricate but slow steps; the pressure of his fingers on her waist told her then to move away from him, and when to come back.

They danced in silence. When the music stopped, and when the men struck a gay jig tune, Cavendish said, "I can't dance to that, *señora.*"

They moved over to the rail. De Ersola joined them, out of the light, standing on one side of Catherine, with Cavendish on the other side. The two men began to talk.

Catherine was silent. She listened. Gradually she relaxed; between the two of them, she felt safe and secure. She listened, saying almost nothing, taking pleasure from their quick sentences and the just as quick smiles.

"I have a good friend who met you two and a half years ago, Captain," de Ersola said.

Cavendish grinned.

De Ersola went on, answering the smile, "I believe you held him for ransom aboard the ship *Tiger?* Señor Costella?"

"One thousand pounds in gold be paid me," Cavendish said. "He gave me trouble, sir. Off the Azores, we fished him out of the water—stark naked—swimming for shore."

De Ersola laughed. "I thought you added two hundred pounds more for that."

"I think I did," Cavendish said. "I had nothing but trouble with him, sir, and he beggared my officers at dice."

De Ersola kept on chuckling. "You must have had quite a company aboard the *Tiger.*"

"Jesu, I did," Cavendish said. "And twenty Spanish hostages. It was summer, *señor,* and you should have seen Costella strolling the deck, usually almost naked and smoking his pipe."

"He comes from an extremely wealthy family," de Ersola said. "He has his own command now."

"Then next time I shan't catch him so easily," Cavendish said.

"If at all, Captain," said de Ersola, and Cavendish smiled. De Ersola glanced at Catherine. "You say nothing, *señora.*"

"I like to listen," she said. "I truly do. What lives you lead!"

De Ersola said, "And you, too. Tomorrow, you shall be wakened before dawn, and you shall be moved to that beach. I'm going to take you back aboard now, Catherine."

"Now?" she said.

"Now," he said. "You are white and tired. You need sleep. For that matter, so do I." The night before, confined to quarters, he had paced the small cabin while Flores had slept uneasily.

"We've enjoyed your hospitality, Captain," de Ersola said.

"We have, *señor*," Catherine said. She held out her hand and Cavendish took it; she felt his lips against her skin. She moved with de Ersola toward the ladder.

In the boat, they waited for the others to join them. Cavendish's figure stood on deck as he said good night to the other men and women. Then the boat pulled away from the *Desire*.

De Ersola escorted Catherine to her cabin. In front of the door he said, low, "Do not forget now, Catherine, I've warned you."

"*Sí*," she said. "*Gracias*."

He took her hand; his eyes were tender, and there was a regretful cognizance in them. He had started to ask her an outright question, but he did not, for he knew the answer. Instead he said, "Sleep well, Catherine."

"Tomas," she whispered.

He smiled. He turned away slowly, and she closed the cabin door. Tina, her Filipino woman, slept on her mat; so did her daughter, on her side of the big bed. Catherine tiptoed over to the lamp that Tina had left burning. There was enough fuel left.

Catherine took her dress off carefully. She got out her needles and thread and a pair of silver scissors. From a box, she took all her white shifts, and began to pull out the hems. Once that was done, she opened her money case, and into the hems of the white underwear she started to sew the precious gold. In the lace apron of a satin dress went her pearls; in the starched collar of a ruff went a ruby ring and three pairs of diamond earrings. But it was the gold that was most important.

She worked swiftly, her needle flashing in the light. Her head was bent over the work; this was all the wherewithal she had, and she must hide it from the English. Tomorrow, de Ersola had warned her, they would search her boxes for gold and jewels; they would find nothing but these few trinkets, and ten pieces of gold. She had told them she was poor. They would believe that this was all she had. They must, else she would be set down penniless, and she would never get to Spain.

Did she need to leave ten pieces of gold for the English? But less would arouse curiosity. She had only one hundred pieces; it hurt badly to leave ten of them to be found.

The lamp was going out and she was almost finished. She looked up once again to make sure neither her daughter nor Tina had awakened and seen her. They must not know. Both were asleep.

She took the last stitch, snapped the thread in her fingers, and picked up the case of jewelry again. There was nothing left in it now but the locket that she had worn tonight, and a few almost worthless trinkets. Quickly she emptied her ten pieces of gold into the bottom of the box, and locked it. She must dispose of the other box that had held the money. She turned out the flickering lamp.

On deck all was dark and silent. She dropped the empty box overboard. It splashed into the water and she took to her heels, flying back across the deck, gaining her own cabin, now dark and close.

She had done it, and she pulled a quilt over herself stretched in the bed. It was the last night she would have this luxury. She reached out a hand to touch little Catherine tenderly; the child stirred sleepily. "Good night," she whispered. "Good night."

Chapter 8

CATHERINE was awakened the next morning at five o'clock. There was a knocking on the door; it was still dark, and there was no fuel left in the lamp. She wakened Tina and Catherine, and they had just finished dressing when the door burst open and two English seamen walked into the cabin. It was now barely gray with daylight. They stared at her openly, not speaking.

Catherine took her daughter's hand in hers. "What do you want?" she asked in English.

One pointed. "Your boxes. Captain's orders."

"Oh," said Catherine. "Take them, then."

"You'll come up on deck, madam," the other said. "The Captain's in a hurry, and your boats are ready."

Catherine motioned to Tina to follow, and hurried up on deck after the two men who carried her boxes. They set them down on deck in front of Master Pretty.

"Good morning, madam," he said stiffly. This morning he was not the shy man to whom she had spoken at dinner, but an impersonal enemy first officer. He was opening the first box.

"That contains my child's clothes, and my petticoats, and such," Catherine said evenly.

"I see it does," said Pretty, closing the lid and waving his hand. The box was packed up and Catherine watched it disappear over the side.

"And that contains my own clothes, sir," Catherine said, trying to be calm. "Are you looking for gold?"

Pretty nodded. He pushed aside dress after dress. He was satisfied. That box also Catherine watched, as they picked it up and took it away. The next box contained the jewel case. It was buried down beneath Catherine's linens. Pretty found it and hauled it out, snapping open the lid. This box he handed without a word to Tyler, who was on the other side of him.

"There is nothing else in there except my linen, some

75

material and and, in this box," she pointed, "a few bits of silver from the East."

Pretty, undiverted and thorough, opened it and looked through it. "You may keep all silver," he said.

"And that contains my painting," Catherine said, "my oils, brushes and pigments."

Pretty saw that it did. Small Catherine was watching him with interest. "You may leave now, madam," he said.

Catherine said, "Thank you, sir." She had not released her child's hand, and she started across to the narrow ladder and the boat waiting beneath it.

Pretty turned to the next woman who waited alongside her belongings. Catherine had a last look at him, bending over another box, and pride went through her, for on that deck the Spanish women waited impassively, while around them were English seamen watching. More women had come up on deck; their eyes went from the English to the lonely strip of sandy beach and the line of gray-white tents. Catherine went down the ladder slowly; she heard Pretty's voice coming sharply, and she said to the seaman who was staring at her ankles, "Will you lift my little girl down, please?"

When Catherine sat at her side, she put her arm around her and held her close. Tina came down gingerly, and they waited. The boat bumped the *Santa Anna*.

Arabella came next, with her mother and servants. Then a family—mother, father and two daughters. No one spoke. Once, the father, a merchant, whispered a word to his wife. The boat pulled evenly to shore.

The beach onto which Catherine stepped was white and smooth and hard now, at ebb tide. About a hundred yards away the river tumbled into the bay, and the sun was coming over the low mountains to the east; the sky was turning blue, and the waters of the bay had lost their grayness and were the singular color of the sea, an opaque and almost cobalt blue. The air smelled fresh and sweet.

The line of tents was back from the beach, under the pine trees, in clearings which had been made by felling the smaller trees for tent poles; there were about thirty tents stretching between the river and the spot where the boat had landed Catherine. Just beside her feet was a big fire pit; she skirted it and started down the beach after the two seamen who were carrying her boxes.

She looked back as she followed after them. Past the spot where she had landed on San Lucas, the Spanish were putting up more tents for themselves, apart from those for the women. Two hundred yards of white beach stretched between the two colonies of rude tents. Catherine stopped short, as the men in front of her did.

"This is my tent?" she asked.

One nodded. "This, and the next one, madam."

They were the last two tents in the straggling line.

"Where do you want these boxes?"

She indicated two boxes. "Please put thim in the first tent, and my things in the smaller one, at the end."

They left her then, in the bare tent. The sand was trampled with footmarks of the men who had put it up. She sat down on one of the boxes, weakly. She still had her gold and jewels. Then she got up and flung open the lid of a box, extracting a blouse and skirt that she often wore while painting. She put them on quickly, kicked off her shoes and went outside.

Master Pretty entered Cavendish's cabin at eight that morning. He said good morning to David, who had evidently been helping himself to some food left on Cavendish's tray; David's mouth was full as he answered Pretty's good morning.

"All jewelry and gold were taken from the passengers before they were disembarked, sir," Pretty said, as he laid down a small box.

Cavendish nodded. Cosmos knelt at his feet, putting on his boots.

"Only royalty have oriental pages, sir," David said, chewing lustily.

Cosmos rose to his feet, taking the tray from under David's nose. David made one last snatch at an orange, and began to toss it in his hand.

"Well, Pretty?" Cavendish asked, as the door closed on Cosmos.

"And this box, sir," continued Pretty, who had been

diverted as usual by David, "contains all of the *Señora de Montoro's* effects—ten pieces of gold and a few trinkets."

He and David, both standing, looked at Cavendish as he opened the box and drew out the gold locket. Cavendish snapped it open.

"She is most clever," he said, as he studied the miniature inside. "Her daughter," he said.

"May I see it?" David asked.

Cavendish handed it over. His eyes went over the contents of the box, as his fingers moved the pieces of jewelry. They were few.

Pretty said, "I felt sorry for the *señora.*"

Cavendish said, "It never hurt your conscience before to take Spanish gold. You're developing quite a tenderness. That's all, Pretty."

Pretty went out, and closed the door. David said slowly, "I've always had a conscience."

Cavendish held out his hand for the locket. David closed his fist over it. "Let me purchase the *señora's* things, Captain," he said.

"No," said Cavendish.

"I want to make her a gift of them," David went on. "You do not."

"Give me the locket, David," Cavendish said, getting to his feet.

The two men stood eye to eye. Cavendish was heavier than David across the shoulders and in the powerfully muscled arms. Faced with him, David felt the uncertainty closing in on him.

"I want nothing from her! She has so little!"

Cavendish looked amused. "Surprisingly little," he said, his eyes on an emerald that lay carelessly on the table. "Is she saint or mother to you, David?"

David dropped the thin locket down beside the gleaming emerald. "I'm going to—" he began and then stopped, for it was always the same. His brother had seemed to forget that he was talking at all. Cavendish was busy buckling on a sword belt.

"Do we go ashore now, sir?" he asked, distantly, matching Cavendish's dismissal of the subject, looking down at the locket as though it were far away.

Cavendish nodded. "And wear a sword," he said. "We've put their women out on the beaches; tension may be high this morning."

David asked grimly, "Just this morning?"

"They'll get used to it, in time," Cavendish said.

"Aye, aye, sir," David said.

He joined Cavendish in the stern sheets of the Captain's own longboat. It pulled toward shore, with both of them silent, Cavendish looked ahead at the beach. He stepped out onto the sand. David and Moon jumped out behind him, and then fifteen English seamen. Cavendish stood looking around, while the whole camp grew silent and stared at the English Captain.

Cavendish appeared not to notice that the group of Spaniards, who were unloading the latest boat from the *Santa Anna* with its cargo of hammocks for the women, had stopped working; he turned to look at them and they began again to unload the boat. Then he looked up the beach where fifteen Spaniards were putting up more tents for themselves.

Cavendish started away, at a walk, going forward to look at the tents for the women. Moon followed him with his eyes, tense, as Cavendish brushed past Spanish seamen who stood aside for him. David stayed where he had been left, at Moon's side.

Cavendish stopped short, his arms hanging loosely at his sides. Then he turned back to David.

"Take charge of unloading the boats, as they beach, sir," he said, and started to walk up the beach toward the line of tents ahead of him.

The thirty tents had been neatly put up. He passed close to them, close enough to hear a woman weeping, and the murmur of a man's voice as he tried to comfort her. Cavendish walked past; he entered the last tent in the row.

He found Catherine bent over a heavy box. And she, startled by footsteps, whirled to face him, and the first emotion she knew was joy.

He was wearing soft leather boots, and a broad gold-studded belt around his waist. His white shirt was unlaced at the neck, and he dominated the small tent. His eyes took her in.

"You look like neither saint nor mother," he said.

She was conscious of her bare feet. She held a pearl-handled short knife in her hand. She stepped back a little from him.

"You knew where to find me?"

"I did," he said.

She was aware of aloneness with him—the awareness was sharp. And she knew that he was responsible for her being alone. Other women had to share tents.

"What are you going to do with that knife?" he asked, lazily, coming closer.

She stood her ground, digging her heels into the sand. "Cut pine branches for beds," she said.

"No," he said. "Use the hammocks. Don't sleep on the ground. And don't stab anyone with that knife."

Catherine hardly heard what he said. He was near enough to touch, and his blue eyes met hers. It was quite clear to her that she was falling in love with him; perhaps it was clear to him too, and he was expecting a quick conquest. It flashed through her mind that he most likely intended to share this tent with her tonight. She said lightly,

"If I had a duenna, I should call her to put you out, Captain. I have a deal to do and I cannot receive you here."

He looked impatient, as if she were putting him off needlessly. "Why have you no duenna, then?"

"Because I cannot pay her," Catherine said.

" 'Tis most unusual, *señor*," he said.

She raised one eyebrow. *"Dios, señor,"* she said, "do you think I am a loose woman?" She laughed. "I am but poor."

"Give me your little knife," he said.

She drew a long breath. She thrust it out at him, in a sudden gesture, shining blade first. He took light hold of the sharp blade.

"My hands are dirty," he said, casually. One box stood open. He used the haft of the knife to lift a thin white shift edged with lace. He held it on the knife for a moment; then it slipped off the knife, back into the wooden chest.

"That was a trifle heavier than it should be," he said.

"I imagine there were at least three gold pieces in it."

"I'm sorry you found it," she said, steadily.

"Are you? Certainly you expected me to find it."

"No," she said, and pride helped her face him. "I have only enough to pay for passage to Spain. I had no recourse but to hide it."

But she had not concealed entirely the hurt he had caused. In her bare feet, she looked small and defenseless as she stood before him.

"You have paint on your blouse," he said.

"I know. I use it to work in. And the skirt."

"*Señora*, if you have need, certainly you know I will help!"

She struck back now, eagerly. "Señor de Ersola will help," she said, "but I want none! May I have my knife?"

"Aye," he said angrily.

She took it from him, carefully avoiding his fingers.

He surveyed her for a moment. She was withholding from him what he wanted. He thought of the black-haired Arabella; he turned to go. Then he saw a portrait that was leaning against the canvas of the tent. He inclined his head in the direction of the portrait.

"Who is that?" he asked.

"The son of the Alcalde of Manila," she answered. "In command of the soldiers there."

Cavendish turned for a look at the portrait, at the strong face, the lips upturned and ready to break into laughter. "A friend of yours, *señora?*"

"Yes," said Catherine. He was jealous—she knew it. Her eyes were bright. "An interesting and masculine face, is it not?" she asked.

"Very," he said.

"And once again," Captain, I shall have to remind you that you cannot stay here longer." She picked up the portrait and put it in a box, while he watched her. He shifted from one foot to the other.

"Come watch us build a bark," he said gruffly, to her back.

"Where?" she asked, closing the lid of the box, and turning.

"On the beach." He didn't move.

"I shall, then, Captain. Later."

"Later?"

"When I finish. You must go now."

"It's important that you do not stay in your tent and mope."

Catherine started to contradict that statement, but he went right on.

"I want you to mingle, and the other women to come out and make friends with us."

"Oh, you do?" she asked, angrily. "You do, do you?"

"Aye. And one more word, *señora*. Do not walk back into the forests. Stay on the beaches. You will be safe on the beaches."

"Safe?"

"Aye. You would probably be unmolested, in any case, because they know that I—" he broke off; his quick grin was guilty. He could not leave, yet. He put his hand on her head, fastening his fingers in the red-gold curls. "Stay on the beaches, wench," he said. "Good-bye."

Chapter 9

THE SUN was hot on David's head. The sweat rolled down his face and gleamed on his bare back and chest. His boots sank into the sand, as he braced himself to hoist the heavy plank.

"Heave her up, lads!"

The two men working with him heaved hard. The plank rose to their shoulders, and they carried it from the boat thirty feet up the beach. They laid it down and David straightened gratefully. He wiped the sweat off his forehead with a dirty hand.

"One more," he said, "and we'll be done."

He walked down to the ship's boat that they were unloading. He had forgotten this morning's brief quarrel with Tom. Tom stood near, with Havers and de Ersola; Tom was directing and watching the building of a crude cradle in which soon the keel of the bark he was building would be laid. That keel, taken from the *Santa Anna*, had been a damnably heavy piece of timber.

"Lanang wood," David heard de Ersola say as he went past the three men. "Lanang wood from the Filipinas."

The air rang with the sound of hammers and the steady sound of the saws. The air was full of voices, curses and laughter. For a minute David stood at the water's edge.

It was nearing midday. The water of the river sparkled in the sunlight; a boatload of men was fishing there, and their voices echoed over the water. The whole colony was busy. Over the firepits great pots had been slung, and the smell of stewing hares tickled David's nostrils. Here, where he worked, the tides had sucked out a small basin; farther up the beach was a fat tongue of sand that stretched into the bay; this was used as the colony's dock, and ship boats were drawn up there neatly. There, too, the Spanish were building a long table and benches for their officers and highborn women to eat from. And a hundred feet from where David stood, began the row of tents for the women. Already they had come out of the tents to watch the men.

David laid hold of the last plank. It was good to work. He heard Cavendish's voice; he felt Cavendish's eyes on him as he went past, one end of the plank on his shoulder. Satisfaction filled David. It was good to work and make things, under Tom's direction. Pride and accomplishment followed such labors, from the mending of a sail to the careening of a ship.

It was marvelous what men could do. It never failed to fill David with wonder, what these men could achieve. Set them down anywhere, and with their simple tools they could do anything. To be a part of it was deeply rewarding.

"That's all then," David said. He walked over to Cavendish; he was looking for the shirt and jacket which he had carelessly flung down on the sand. He didn't see them, and he came up to Cavendish and Havers.

Cavendish held out the shirt and jacket.

"Thanks, Tom," David said. He looked over his shoulder at the figures of some women who had gradually come closer, drawn by the activities of the men. "I can't have a swim now," he said, grinning. He slipped the shirt over his head.

"Too bad, boy," Cavendish said.

"Christ, those planks were heavy," David said. Absently, he started to pick at his palm, where a ragged splinter had dug deep into the flesh. His hands were dirty with pitch.

"Here," said Cavendish.

David held out his hand obediently. Cavendish had a slender dagger. He slit the skin quickly, lifting the splinter out.

"Wash it," he said, "in the sea."

David laughed. "Tom thinks the sea cures everything," he said to de Ersola.

"Wash it," Cavendish repeated.

"Aye, sir," said David. He felt very happy. He washed his hands carefully, opening the slitted skin to get the dirt out. Tom had been deft; Davd's hands were deft now, too. Sometimes he remembered his first nights at sea, when he had practiced tying knots. He had worked so hard that he had dreamed of knots—shroud knots, running knots, timber hitches.

"So you are building a bark," de Ersola was saying as David came back. "For the Pacific?"

"Possibly," came Cavendish's easy voice.

David was pleasantly tired and hungry. The sun felt good. The women's clothes were gay; their laughter came to his ears. Havers' chuckle sounded, and the murmur of Cavendish's voice. David yawned. Out in the bay the three ships rode at anchor, like guardians of the colony ashore.

"Cortes tried a colony here some years ago," de Ersola was saying. "It failed miserably."

"Aye, the soil's poor," Havers said.

"Thin," said de Ersola. "Back in the pines are the remains of two houses. We're rebuilding them to store goods and food."

"I think I'll walk back and see them," said Cavendish. "D'ye want to come, David?"

David, in the middle of another yawn, nodded. He had expected de Ersola to come too, but the Spaniard did not move. His dark eyes were on the shape of the *Santa Anna*. David walked along at Cavendish's side.

There should be no more trouble between them, now. He felt sorry he had talked at all to Catherine the night before. She might have thought he was condemning Tom, when he had meant only to show her the resentment he found in himself. He still didn't know why he had told her about it, except that he had felt instantly free to talk.

This morning he had known Tom's eyes had been on him with pride and affection, when he had shed his jacket and shirt to help his crew move the planks. He knew that he wasn't a court versifier any longer, but an officer aboard Her Majesty's ship *Desire*. He was a good officer. He was rich, in his own right. Not as rich as Tom, certainly—for Tom, David was sure would be the richest man in England when the *Desire* fetched Plymouth again. And David knew, too, that what he had written aboard the *Desire* was good. The description of the twenty-two days they had spent in the navigation of the Straits of Magellan was good writing. No one had seen it, but he carried the knowledge of it within him.

"What are you building the bark for, Tom?" he asked suddenly, as they came in sight of the two houses.

Cavendish was looking at the houses. The porches were sagging, and the Spanish carpenters were busy on the roofs. Newly cut timbers to support the sagging porches were lying on the ground. Clearings had been made here some years ago, and only scrubby small pines dotted these clearings.

"They'll be useful," Cavendish said.

"The houses? I warrant so," David said. He was not very interested. "What are you building the bark for, Tom?" he repeated.

"For use," said Cavendish.

"Use?" David said, puzzledly.

"Aye," said Cavendish. He had turned away and David looked at his face, sideways.

"But—" he said, when a woman's scream cut short his words and thought.

It was what Cavendish had feared. It was a muffled scream an appeal for help. Cavendish sprinted in the direction of the sound and David plunged after him, their booted feet making no sound in the sand.

David pounded along behind Cavendish, not bothering to avoid the branches of small trees. When Cavendish stopped, David bumped into him. Then he moved up alongside his brother.

All David saw was the figure of a girl in a white blouse and skirt. But Cavendish had seen the culprit.

"Rogers," he said.

The crackling of a branch told David that Rogers, one of the *Content's* men, had not fled far, and that he was returning slowly. Very slowly. He came into view, carrying the bow which he had stopped to pick up in his flight, and which had betrayed him to Cavendish.

"Captain," he said.

Rogers' cheek bore a long scratch. He stood before

Cavendish, eyes on the ground, Cavendish said nothing, and finally Rogers lifted his eyes.

"Rogers," said Cavendish, "I made clear what the penalty for violence would be, did I not?"

Rogers said, "Aye, sir." He knew then there was no hope for appeal, not when the Captain reminded him what his orders had been.

"Have you anything to say to me, then?"

Rogers wished desperately that he had, but he had no faith in his ability to lie when Cavendish's blue eyes were on him.

"No, sir," he said.

"Then you may convey to Captain Brule my decision and my respects."

Rogers winced at the thought of telling Brule.

"Aye, sir," he said. He started away.

David felt intensely sorry for Rogers; he watched him go. Rogers had shot three hares which hung from his belt, but he wouldn't care about eating them tomorrow.

David looked at the girl. She was small. Her dark hair fell to her shoulders. Her skin was startlingly white. He remembered her from the first night aboard the *Santa Anna*. She smiled at him tentatively. Cavendish cut short the smile.

"What were you doing here?" he asked, curtly.

Her eyes were deep, deep brown. "Walking, *señor*," she said, low.

"Your name?"

"Lola, my lord."

Cavendish, angry, frowned at her, and she straightened, lifting her shoulders high.

"I did nothing!" she said. The jade pendant around her neck rose and fell. Under Cavendish's eyes, she repeated, "I did nothing! English pig!" Her gaze shifted to David. "I did not mean you, *señor,* or the Captain."

David grinned.

Cavendish, unappeased, because this incident marred the camp's first day, said, "You will stay on the beaches."

She stood proudly, facing him. *"Sí,* my lord."

It occurred to David that Cavendish had made no apology for Rogers. David said, "Why, *señorita*, I— are you hurt?"

"No," she said. "But the English was." She lifted her hand and surveyed her pointed nails. "Blood," she said, raising two fingers for David's inspection.

"I see," said David.

"No, you did not," she said. "Look!"

David transferred his eyes from her face to the fingers she held up.

"I see now," he said.

"*Sí,*" she said; "my lord," she added. She dropped her hand, and sighed a little, waiting for her dismissal.

David knew that Cavendish had been angry because he had had to punish one of his men. Cavendish said aloud, in English, "Well, at least Rogers will have recovered by the time we set sail." Suddenly he smiled at Lola, and he looked her over carefully. David was conscious of a sudden fear.

"Tom," he began, when Cavendish cut him short.

"Escort the *señorita* back to the beaches, David," he said in English. He turned on his heel.

"Aye, sir," said David grimly to Cavendish's back. This was what he had wanted. He had obtained it without asking. As a favor, and because it might cure hotheadedness. He took a deep breath, and wondered why his rebellion had been so quick and resentful. He muttered an oath.

"This way," he said, forgetting that Lola had not understood Cavendish's words.

Her brown eyes looked up at him questioningly, but she took her place at his side. For a minute they walked in silence. She studied him covertly, now she was alone with him. She waited for him to speak first.

"You're to cure me," he said, finally.

"Of what, *señor?*" she asked, with interest.

"Never mind," he said, looking straight ahead. Absently, he held a branch aside for her.

"I saw you this morning," she said, tentatively.

"Did you?"

"I was watching you haul planks."

"They were heavy," he said. He remembered the

morning—the light-hearted and even repentant morning. Now the impatience and anger and resentment were strong.

She said, "You are very strong."

"Sí, señorita," he said. "I'm a man—but I must be a baby. Do I look like a baby to you?" His voice was rough, and he stopped walking. His hands reached out and fastened around her waist. Her ribs felt brittle enough for him to crush easily. He pulled her nearer to him.

"Scream, wench," he said, "and my back will be raw tomorrow, too."

She shook her head slowly. "I shall not scream." She was looking at him intently. "But you are the Captain's brother."

His hands dropped from her waist. "How did you know that?"

"Everybody knows it," she said.

"Well, it would make no difference whether I were God Almighty—as far as punishment goes, for a disobeyed order. I do not complain of that, *señorita,*" he added.

"I knew that," she said.

"Did you?" he asked, uninterestedly. He stopped again, judging how far he had penetrated into the woods. She knew, of course, that he was not taking her back to the beach, and she had made no protest. Fifty feet ahead was a place where they could lie beneath low hanging pines.

"Are you alone, here, on San Lucas?" he asked.

"Sí," she said.

"Why?" he asked.

She walked fast to keep up with him. She walked lithely, barefooted. "My mistress was killed," she said.

"Oh," David said.

"In the battle. She was the only woman hurt."

"You weren't born out here? In New Spain? How old are you?"

"Eighteen," she said. "I was born in Barcelona. I came with my mother and my father to Manila."

David said, "We can sit here." He was taking off his jacket, and he laid it down.

"For me?" she asked.

"For you," he said.

She shot him a glance. "It is very fine, to sit on." Then she smiled, and sat down. Once more she changed her mind. "I don't need it, *señor,*" she said, and pulled the doublet from under her, folded it neatly and laid it aside.

"You're a disobedient wench," he said. He dropped down beside her, and stretched out full length.

"You worked so hard," she said, remembering him as she had seen him this morning; she had spent two hours watching him, hearing his voice, and seeing his laugh. He was difficult, this man. Now he was curt and miserable. She ran her fingers through her hair, and lifted it back over her shoulders.

"*Señor,*" she said—and then she stopped.

"You may call me David," he said.

She said the name experimentally, lengthening the two syllables. "David."

"Well?"

"David, how old are you?"

"Six and twenty," he said. He raised himself on one elbow.

"Look, wench"—he was hunting for her name—"Lola, you are alone here."

"*Sí,*" she said. She wet her lips.

He continued with the easy arrogance of his class. "Then I will take care of you."

Her hands were clasped. Her dark eyes were thoughtful. But he was not waiting for her answer. His arms were around her and he wanted the first kiss.

"*Sí señor,*" she whispered.

Chapter 10

SHE THOUGHT he was very handsome, this Englishman. She lay beside him while he slept, exhausted, on the sandy pineneedled floor.

The sun was setting. It was cooler; she had put his shirt aross his bare back. He moved a little in his sleep, and she covered his shoulders again. He stirred.

He opened his eyes and saw her. He reached for her, drawing her closer to him, wrapping his arms around her.

"I'm cold," he whispered.

"Your jacket," she said.

He made a dissenting sound. His head was buried in the curve of her throat. "You keep me warm."

"*Sí*," said Lola. She sighed a little. Perhaps he would talk to her now; there was much she wanted to know.

"Where do you live in England, *señor?*"

The answer was muffled. "Suffolk."

Lola frowned. "Where is that, my lord?"

He grunted. "I live in London too."

"Is your house big?"

The answer was intended to be "yes."

"Does your mother live there?" Lola asked. His mother must be very proud of him. In Suffolk?" She stumbled over the name.

"I never knew her," he said. "She died long ago."

"Oh," said Lola. "I'm sorry, *señor.*"

He raised his head to look at her. "Are you, wench?" He smiled, then he yawned.

"But you have your brother," she said.

"I certainly do," he said.

"What is it?" she asked. She kissed the side of his face. "My love," she whispered.

He said, wonderingly, "Lola, you are most fair. Truly, you are. Your body is perfect."

"I dance," she said.

He laughed. "However you explain it, you are a work of nature in which nature scarcely failed. Wench, what time do you suppose it is?"

"Time?" she said.

"Not a pleasant word, I admit." He sat up and looked at the bit of sky he could see through the trees. He judged it to be six or thereabouts. "I have a little time," he said. But he picked up his shirt and shook the sand from it. He slipped it over his head.

She was watching, and when his head reappeared, he noticed her steady gaze on him.

"When I come tomorrow," he said, "what would you like me to bring you?"

She said slowly, "You do not think, *señor,* that I—"

"Christ, no," he said.

"Let me fasten your shirt," she said, her face eager. She tied the lacing deftly, concentrating on her task. "There."

"Thank you," David said. "You haven't told me what you would like."

"A jewel?" she said. "Or a bottle of wine?"

"And a fresh fish," David said, smiling. Later, he would bring her gold, but not yet. He studied her clear white skin; she was vividly beautiful. "Pearls for you, Lola," he said. "Stolen pearls. Wear them like a duchess."

"I?" she asked.

"You," he said. He put his arms around her and began to kiss her. "Have you ever seen a duchess, Lola?"

She found it hard to answer while he was making love to her. "Once," she whispered. "In Spain."

"Was she haughty?"

"She was fat," said Lola. "Very fat, *señor*. Oh, David!"

" 'Oh, David,' " he mimicked, " 'oh, David'!"

At that, she tried to avoid his kiss, turning her head. She fought him a little for a moment.

"Oh, David," she whispered.

The sun had set when he took her back to the beach. In the evening light, the row of tents looked settled, and in place under the pines. The remains of the fires smoldered in the pits; the bay looked just the same. The keel of the bark had been laid, but the men were gone, and the little cove was silent and empty. Waves lapped at the shore; the tide was going out.

"You've missed your evening meal," David said, absently, looking at the bark.

"Could I make your dinner?" Lola asked. He had said little on the way back to the beach.

He shook his head. "I must be back aboard."

Around the large fire on the beach, men were gathered. David saw some familiar figures. "They're changing the watch," he said hastily to Lola. He raised his voice. "Avast there, Tyler!"

He had a last word for Lola. "Come no farther, wench. *Hasta la vista!*"

"Hasta la vista," she repeated wistfully, standing where he had left her, near the tents for the women, watchng him run across the beach and to the waiting boat. He jumped in, she waved to him, but he mustn't have seen her, for he did not wave back.

He was preoccupied. He had enough time, too. It had long since ceased to occur to him not to be on time. Back aboard, he went straight to Cavendish's cabin. He found Cavendish bent over the chart he was drawing. David wasted no words.

"That's what I wanted to see, Tom," he said. "California."

"Here it is," Cavendish said, raising his blue eyes to David's face. He sounded very eager, but that was all he said.

David looked at the lines and latitudes that imprisoned California on paper.

David said, "How far is it from here across the gulf?"

"To Mazatlán? About seventy leagues, roughly."

"And by land?"

"Impossible," said Cavendish flatly. "Hundreds of leagues. Look. All you need to do is look."

"Women could never stand that journey," David said.

"No," said Cavendish. He picked up his pen and marked in a sounding. His print was tiny and neat.

"But two hundred people cannot get aboard the bark you're building," David said. "Not more than twenty could, and that not with safety."

"Of course not," said Cavendish.

"I see," said David quietly. He turned; he bumped into Cosmos, brushed him aside, and went up on deck. It was his watch soon; he had about twenty minutes. He had missed dinner, and he was hungry, terribly hungry.

But he didn't move. He stared down at the darkening water; the ship was still; he heard men's mutted voices; he could pick out their owners. He thought of Lola; he thought of Catherine. And then he heard Havers' tread behind him.

There was no need to turn; he was sure it was Havers. He felt himself relax, as Havers leaned against the rail, too, and looked down into the water.

"You're relieved, Havers," he said.

"I didn't know it was your watch," Havers said.

"For the next week it is," David said.

Havers said, "I hear the men are envious of you."

David grinned. The two men were silent.

"If you're wanting your pipe, you're relieved," David said.

"No," Havers returned.

They had talked so much this way. Aboard the *Hugh Gallant.* David thought of her now, sunk deep beneath the Pacific swells. "God bless her, Havers," he said.

Havers nodded his recognition.

"I shall never remember her with any but the most sincere affection," David said. "D'ye realize, Havers, how much I learned from her?"

"I do," said Havers.

"Havers, you're far from a simple man. You think too much. We have a motto, Tom and I, 'Let good luck follow courage.' What do you think of it?"

"I like it," Havers said.

David said, "I like it too. There's something I'm wanting to do, Havers. Something I'm wanting to do very much."

Chapter 11

THE HOLD of the *Santa Anna* stank of bilge. Cavandish was used to the stink, but he was glad that he had finished there, this morning, for it was almost twelve noon.

"Master Pretty," he said, "open me up these eight chests here, and I'll have finished for today."

"Aye, aye, sir," said Pretty, unlatching the first chest and throwing open the lid. He had been with Cavendish most of the time that they had inspected the five hundred tons of merchandise in the *Santa Anna*, choosing carefully what was most valuable, because they could take only a part of the huge cargo.

The chest stood open. "Chinese damask," Cavendish said. He felt the heavy silken material in his fingers. "Heavy and strong," he said speculatively. "Very strong."

"Aye, sir," Pretty said automatically.

"The tally shows hundreds of yards; the exact amount excapes me," Cavendish said, thinking aloud. He paused a minute. "I want all this stowed where it will be least likely to get water-soaked, sir. Now open me those others."

Another lid flew back. A loud bump from above made Pretty jump. "Cloth of gold, sir," he said. "And this one, too." He worked swiftly. "Nine chests of cloth of gold, sir."

"Well stow them aboard too," Cavendish said, coming to stand by Pretty and looking into the chest. "Jesu, that's lovely."

"It is, isn't it? asked Pretty appreciatively.

The cloth was lustrous and shimmering. It made Cavendish think of Catherine.

"Cut me off a length of that cloth, sir," he said.

Pretty obliged; he started to unroll the cloth, pulling out his dagger to cut it with. Then he rolled up the length of cloth neatly and handed it to Cavendish.

"Thank you, Pretty," Cavendish said. "Now, when you have these chests hoisted out of here, you've finished for the day."

He stepped out of the glow of the lamp and made his way through the half-open chests. He heard the lids close back as Pretty got them ready to be stowed aboard the *Desire*. In the darkness, Cavendish found the narrow ladder; above him were voices. He heard plainly: "If Rogers had been from the *Desire,* he wouldn't have had it so bad!"

The denial was short and foul. Words flew. Cavendish listened.

"You bastards have more gold stowed aboard than we have!"

Cavendish started noisily up the ladder again. By the time he reached the top, the owners of the voices had disappeared. But he had recognized them. He went out on deck.

There were ten men from the *Content* working among his own crew this morning. He watched the neatly lashed chests swung over the side and lowered into the waiting boats. He watched the men closely. How many of them thought they were not getting their rightful share of the gold, to stow aboard their own *Content?* Ahead was a long and arduous voyage. Three oceans lay between them and England. Already they were a year and a half out of England. But his command had been held as tight and rigid as one man could hold. He frowned. He walked over to Brule, who stood alone.

"Brule, how's the morale of your company?" The question was put, plain and unexpected. Brule looked amazed.

"Splendid, sir," he said. "There's naught on their minds save the Spanish fish dinner ashore tonight."

Laughter sounded suddenly from the group of men. Brule thought it proved his words. He smiled at Cavendish. "Why did you ask?"

Cavendish prevaricated, because he knew only too well that the reason for discontent was often not the reason voiced, and because he had overheard and eavesdropped. It would scarcely be fair to tell Brule that a certain William Byet, who worked just a few feet away, had complained that the *Desire's* company was favored.

"Brule," he said, "I am never unaware of the possibility of mutiny."

"You, sir?" Brule asked, amazed again. "I know the danger, sir—I've seen it happen."

"There is temptation here, in the New World," Cavendish said. He believed it truly. "To stay here, I mean, Brule."

"Aye," Brule said, sighing a little. But he was obviously unworried about his crew.

"Good-bye, then," Cavendish said. He left Brule. He let himself be rowed back to the *Desire* and he climbed aboard and mounted up to his own high deck.

"Good morning, Havers, David."

Havers was puffing on his pipe. "Good morning, Tom," he said. He had not seen Cavendish earlier. He recognized that Cavendish was in no mood to talk, and he and David were silent for a minute. Cavendish leaned against the rail and looked toward shore. David and Havers resumed their lazy conversation. Tobacco smoke wisped past Cavendish's nose.

"David, tell Cosmos to fetch me my tobacco and pipe."

"Aye, sir," David said.

Cavendish still looked toward shore. The colony was settled, now. It was five days old. Washing hung outside the tents on lines stretched between the pines. Caldrons swung over the fire pits. The Spanish were having their midday meal, and the women's clothes made bright bits of color against the beach.

Nothing had marred the truce. Amity, real friendliness existed between the English and Spanish. Cavendish's men went ashore with gold in their pockets; they bought their favors.

During the days they worked, fished, swam, and hunted. The *Santa Anna's* most precious goods, spices and gold, were being stowed aboard the *Desire* and the *Content*. The water casks were being cleaned and filled. They were revictualing, salting fish and game. The *Content* was already wearing a new suit of sails.

"Your pipe, sir," Cosmos said.

"Thank you," said Cavendish.

"Your tobacco."

Cavendish carefully pressed the tobacco into the bowl of his pipe. There should be no reason for trouble now. He was probably a fool to worry about the words he had overheard this morning. Just as he was a fool to worry about David.

Cosmos, who was watching his Captain, held a light ready. Cavendish sucked on the stem.

"Your dinner is ready soon, sir," Cosmos said.

"I want none," Cavendish said.

Cosmos looked troubled. The Captain always ate heartily. "None?"

"None!"

"Aye, aye, sir," said Cosmos hastily. He drew back.

Cavendish sucked in the smoke. It tasted good. He sighed. The *Desire* rode close enough to the beach so that he could distinguish the men and women who came in and out of their tents, who walked and ran, laughed and worked along the narrow strip of sand. While he watched, the woman for whom he looked detached herself from the group of men and women eating at the long table. She started along the beach, walking slowly, her little girl with her.

The color of their hair was exactly the same. They passed the fire pits, and were going toward their own tents. Cavendish watched until they disappeared into the next to the last tent.

Cavendish stared at the gray-white tent. Within it, she was probably putting her little girl to sleep for an afternoon siesta. Perhaps she would take one herself; sometimes she did.

He swore under his breath. For five days now he had not seen her alone. Always she was with Havers, or de Ersola, or David. Master Pretty, gentleman from Suffolk, followed her everywhere, she had given him a small sketch of the *Desire* that she had done the second day they had been here at San Lucas.

De Ersola's eyes were always on her. De Ersola—he was virtually the Spanish commander; Flores left everything to him. Flores stayed aboard the *Santa Anna,* shut in his cabin. Cavendish had heard that he spent his days in prayer.

De Ersola had made friends with the Brule. Cavendish had watched the friendship progress. Brule was simple seaman, and a good seaman; he thought de Ersola the most proper gentleman he had ever met. And Cavendish knew that de Ersola was clever and wary. De Ersola probably was after the *Content*. Could he possibly have sensed the discontent aboard her? De Ersola was an opponent worthy of the name, and Cavendish respected him; he would bear watching, always.

His pipe was almost out. He drew on the stem until a cloud of smoke regarded him. Near, some men from the *Desire* were fishing; it was almost noon, and they were hauling up their anchor; they were coming back aboard for dinner. They had a good catch; fish after silver fish had been swung into the boat.

Suddenly Cavendish spoke to Cosmos, who was still standing near.

"Tell Tyler to hoist out my boat," he said.

"Aye, sir," said Cosmos.

"I'm going fishing," he said. "I want lines and tackle and bait. And a bottle of wine."

"Aye, sir," said Cosmos, and he darted away. His Captain was in a hurry, Cosmos knew.

Cavendish waited only a few minutes. His own longboat was hoisted out; he left his own deck and settled himself in the stern sheets while Pitt hoisted the sail. Then Pitt climbed aboard the *Desire* again. On a larboard tack, the longboat slowly sailed to the river, with Cavendish's figure alone in the stern.

The wind was offshore. Suddenly he veered his tack; he could sail close along the shore, along the deserted beach; the women were in their tents for their siestas. The tide was coming in; he scanned the beach.

He saw her come out of her daughter's tent. He lowered the sail, letting the current take the boat into the beach.

"Ahoy, *señora*," he called, across the narrowing strip of water.

She stopped. She looked out to him. "Ahoy," she said.

The longboat ran aground. "Will you come for a sail?" he asked.

Her hair was shining in the sun. She was tanned, her cheeks were bright. He waited for her answer, but she could not come, he was sure of it. Therefore it was with real surprise that he heard her say, "I would love to sail, Captain."

The boat, bow in sand, rocked in the little waves. She didn't wait for him; she waded out, picking up her skirts, climbing into the bow and seizing a long oar.

"I'll push off," she said.

He laughed. "You cannot," he said, reaching for an oar himself.

"I'll help, then," she said, her back to him. "See?"

The longboat, freed, danced a little. Cavendish hoisted the sail quickly. "Come nearer, wench," he said gaily.

She boated the oar and scrambled over the thwarts, coming to sit beside him. She dropped her hand over the side, but she could not reach the water; she leaned back.

They had been eying each other covertly. Then their eyes met.

"Buenos dias, señora," Cavendish said. "I wanted to be away for a while."

"You should not leave?" she asked, seriously.

"No," he said, declining to say more, but she seemed to understand, for she smiled at him in such a way that he felt she must.

"You have the most beautiful smile," he said.

"Thank you, Captain," she said.

"We're going up river," he said quickly. "I was going to fish."

"Could I? Too?"

He grinned. "Certainly."

"We're sailing so slowly," she said. "Could I fish now?"

"I'll bait you some hooks, and you can."

"I'll take the tiller," she said, and he raised his eyebrows in amazement.

"A friend taught me," she said.

"Go ahead," he said, laughing. He watched her for a

minute, then he set to work to bait two hooks; he let the line gently over the side.

"Trail them," he said, as Catherine released the tiller reluctantly. "I'll let you sail back before the wind," he promised.

"That would be wonderful," she said, curling up on the seat beside him, watching the trailing line. She was silent for a minute, her fingers on the line, firmly but lightly, letting it slip out gently. "I've something," she cried, and she jerked the line and felt it tremble. She started to haul it in hand over hand, swinging a silver fish into the boat with enthusiasm.

"Lord," said Cavendish, who ducked his head. He put his boot on the wriggling fish. "He's off the hook already, mistress. Next time you must do better than that."

"I'll take the tiller again," Catherine said.

He burst out laughing. "You can bait your own hooks," he teased her, but he let her sail the boat while he snapped the fish at the gills and put it into the basket. By the time he had baited the hooks again, and unsnarled the line, he said, "I think we'll anchor here."

She looked disappointed, and he smiled. "I can't be away too far, you see," he explained.

Catherine nodded. She watched him heave out the anchor, pay out the rope and fasten it around the cleat. He took off his doublet; then he fixed a line for himself. He was sitting opposite her. He tossed his own line overboard.

"Would you care for wine?" he asked.

"No, thank you," she said. There was silence between them. For the first time in five days they were alone. Catherine looked over the water toward the shore; then her eyes came back to him.

"Would *you* want wine, Captain?"

"Aye," he said. "Thank you, *señora*. It is—"

"I see it," she said.

While she poured the wine he could look at her and her bent head and her slim hands. He took the cup from her.

"Thank you," he said again. He drank the wine off. She put out her hand for the cup.

He gave it to her, leaning forward. Under his eyes, she put it back in the basket. She looked up at him.

"When did you get gray?" she asked.

"On my first long voyage," he said.

"Oh," said Catherine. "Was it bad?"

He said, "Very bad." His profile was turned to her as he said the words. "One of your officers, the Portugal Roderigo, reminds me of a very good friend I made on that first voyage."

"Roderigo?" she asked.

He felt the words coming to his lips, in short sentences. "My friend was Portuguese too. He taught me much. We landed in America, and he had been there many times before. He loved America.

"You see, Grenville left me aboard. They—Grenville and the Portugal—went ashore, and my friend borrowed a horse. He was such a small man. I never saw him again. He was thrown, badly. And he asked Grenville to bury him there, in America. I never saw him again."

He raised his eyes from the hook he had been baiting, to look at her. She was silent, but he realized that he had never told this to anyone before, not even to Havers.

He felt no need to say anything further. He flung his line over again. He felt the warm sun on his head and through the thinness of his lawn shirt. The boat rocked gently; he stretched his legs out comfortably, his eyes half closed against the glare of sun and water.

"When did you first go to sea?" she asked softly.

He said, "When I was fourteen. We lived near Ipswich. I used to spend my time at the docks. I stowed away and sailed to Holland."

Again he noticed the beauty of her smile; it was warm as the California sun.

"You want to sail around the world?"

"Aye," he said. "Why did you come to New Spain, *señora?* Because of your husband?"

She used the same short sentences he did. She used them honestly, as he did. "My husband and I came together. I was strictly reared. My parents regretted my marriage. So we came to New Spain. But—" She paused.

"My husband did not want to stay. He was not successful here. He wanted to go to Manila; his uncle had gone there two years ago. So we sailed the Pacific. Within six months he died. Of a fever."

He regarded her steadily. "And now you are going home."

"Yes," she said, low. "With my daughter."

"And Tina," he said. "You know, *señora,* you could sell Tina for a deal of gold, in Spain."

Her face grew stormy. "I never shall," she said determinedly. "Captain, what do you think I am?"

He laughed, throwing his head back.

"I love Tina," she said.

"Transfer it to me," he suggested, his blue eyes alight.

"You hardly deserve it," she said. "Tina does."

"I would not want the same kind of love, though." He hauled a big fish into the boat.

"Oh, that's a huge one!" Catherine exclaimed.

He thrust his fingers into its gills and held it up for her to see.

"A nice one," he said proudly, dropping it into the basket. He washed the blood from his hands in the water. The lines and hooks were under his feet.

Catherine said quickly, "You have been very successful with the camp."

He leaned forward, looking at her, resting his chin on his hands.

"Jesu, *señora,*" he said, "you are a wench to love. Why do you put me off?"

"Fish," she said.

"That's a splendid answer. You're paying no more attention to your line than I am." He reached forward, and took the line from her fingers, hauling it in the boat quickly. In a tangled heap, he tossed it under the thwart. She sat stiffly, facing him.

"I want to say something to you," he said. "Listen."

"I want to say something to you! And if you were polite, you would listen."

"I am," he said. "Speak out."

"I worry over David," she said. "He—"

"Is that what you had to say?"

"Is it not enough?" She was breathing quickly.

"No," he said.

She struck her hand on the boat's side, angrily.

"Then what do *you* wish to say?" she asked, her chin set. "I'm ready!"

"I've changed my mind," he said, roughly. He got to his feet and sat down beside her. His arms reached for her, deliberately.

She tried to move. She twisted her head away.

"No!" she said.

He hardly heard her, only the sound of her voice. He pushed the blown curls back from her ear; he looked down at her profile, tightened his arms around her and began to kiss her ear, her throat, and the curve of her cheek; as she tried to turn her head away from him, he followed the movement with his lips, and then, as if he tired of that, he put his hand on the back of her head and found her mouth with his, pulling her across her seat, his heavy shoulders pinning her back.

Her hands were crushed up against his chest. He felt her try to move her body, and he shifted his weight until she was lying back against him, imprisoned easily. Holding her, he took his mouth away for a second, then brushed it across her, drawing back, and when he bent to kiss her again, the first sound of gunfire echoed out over the bay.

Even then he did not release her instantly. For a long second his mouth drew from hers a yielding sweetness he knew he would get; then, abruptly, he let her go. He sat up, his hands still on her; at last he dropped them.

He moved to the anchor rope and began to haul it in, hand over hand, evenly. By the time he had heaved it aboard, Catherine had hoisted the sail, and the longboat leaned precariously as the wind caught the unfurled canvas. But she brought the boat around and he took the tiller from her hand.

"Thank you," he said.

She was silent. She felt his arm against her side, as they sat in the stern sheets together.

"No more shots," he said, after another minute. He turned his head to look at her.

"No," she said, remembering. And then she moved to the opposite thwart, sitting down facing him.

The wind blew her hair. Her blouse had been pulled awry; she straightened it, under his gaze, tucking it into the wide band of her skirt.

"You have very little respect for me," she said equably. "I don't like that."

"Nonsense," he said.

"Not nonsense," she said, and she folded her hands in her lap and her lids shadowed her eyes. He could not see the clear green color of them.

He said, "Why should you pretend?"

She didn't raise her eyes. "I try to be truthful," she said, slowly.

The wind bellied the sail. "I do not lie," he said.

"I know you do not."

"Why did you come with me today?"

She raised her eyes. The truth could not be told. "Because I wished to sail with you, and I thought—"

He was looking toward the bay. They were near enough to see a boat pulling from the *Desire,* toward the river, toward them.

"You thought what?" he asked.

The longboat sailing before the wind was fast. Already he could discern Havers' figure.

"I cannot talk to you now," he said impatiently. "I shall see you this evening."

"No," Catherine said. "I don't want to see you tonight."

The quiet answer made him glance at her.

"Do not bother to come," she said.

His own anger rose. "You refuse to see me?"

"I do," she said.

They had come out into the bay. Cavendish could see men on the deck of the *Content;* the boat with Havers' figure standing in the stern, was very near.

"You refuse to see me?" he asked again.

"I do," she said. "I can sail the boat to the beach. You may leave me."

He looked at her face; her hair was blown by the

wind. "I cannot do that," he said, thinking of the stretch of water between them and the beach.

Havers called out, and Cavendish brought the long-boat up alongside; hands reached over to steady the two boats; and Cavendish saw Tyler.

"Take Señora Catherine back to the beach," he said, and stepped into the other boat. She did not say good-bye to him; in a second her bright head would be lost to his view unless he turned to look—and he could not do that. He stared straight ahead toward the *Content*.

Chapter 12

DAVID HAD ARRIVED ashore at two o'clock. He knew Lola was waiting for him, but he spied Brule and de Ersola talking together and watching the progress of the bark. He walked over to the two men.

"She's coming along," he said, over the noise of hammering.

"She certainly is," said Brule.

David said, "In fact, she is almost finished. God grant she'll be sturdy." He paused. "She'll need to be," he added. He watched de Ersola's expression.

But de Ersola's expression did not change. "Is your brother well?" de Ersola asked, politely.

"I have not seen him this day," David replied, "except to tell him good morning. Excuse me, sirs."

He met Lola at the edge of the tents.

He started right off down the beach with such long strides that she scampered along at his side, looking up at him to see his face. Presently she reached over and took his hand.

"You walk so fast," she murmured.

"I forgot," he said, slowing his stride.

"You were in camp last night," she said, clinging tightly to his hand.

"I know it, little one. How did you know it?"

"I was watching," she said. "I heard what you said."

"What?" He frowned.

Lola was silent.

He stopped walking and faced her. "What did you do? Listen outside the tent—Señora Catherine's tent?"

"Are you angry?" Lola asked.

"I am," he said.

"I wanted to hear what you said," Lola confessed.

"You should not spy on me, though," he said, firmly, as to a child. "I mislike it very much."

"Oh," said Lola. "But I was not spying. I just wanted to hear your voice, and how you talk to Catherine."

He laughed. "Can I believe you?"

"This time," said Lola. She was pleased that he was so amused, for his laughter rang forth. She smiled at him.

"Your face is as vivid as a flower," he said.

"What flower?" she asked.

He studied her. "Not an English flower. You are as much unlike a primrose as anything I've ever seen. But perhaps you are as vivid as a white rose, at morning, with drops of dew and deep green leaves. With thorns."

"I have no thorns," she said.

"I fear you do."

"But why did you go to see Catherine last night?"

"Ah," he said, "here come the thorns we were speaking of so blithely. I wanted to speak with her, Lola, because I like her very much."

"You like her better than me?"

He sighed. "No. I like her differently."

"Why did you not take me with you?"

"Because I truly did not think of it."

"Oh," said Lola. They had come out of sight of the camp by now. "I think of you all the time."

Smiling, he said, "Do you?"

"And I know the *señora*. She painted a picture of me. So." She stopped walking and struck imaginary castanets up in the air. "I am a good dancer," she added proudly, the earrings he had given her swaying as she moved her head. "I dance for you tonight, *señor*."

She stood before him and he reached for her. "Will you?" he asked, looking down at her upturned face.

She arched one slender eyebrow. "For the others, too, I dance."

He lifted his hand playfully.

"The Señora Catherine," said Lola, "painted on deck, and I would weary of posing and then we would go under the awning and drink a little wine and talk. So much talk! Not like you."

He laughed.

"You talk to me, a little every day . . . If you should see the *señora* tonight will you take me, then?

Please, David." She drew out his name the way she always did.

"I might," he said. "I might."

They had walked toward the river and up its beach when the first shot sounded.

David stood stockstill for a moment, and then he started to run, dragging Lola behind him, then slowing a little to allow her to keep up with him. Cavendish and Catherine passed them in the longboat, and by the time David got to the tents, Catherine had been in her tent for a few minutes. He stopped in the doorway.

"What happened?" he asked, breathlessly.

"I don't know, David," she said.

David said, "I'll be off, Catherine. Good-bye, Lola." He strode off, and Lola went, as usual, to the tent flap to watch him go and to watch until she could see him no longer.

Back aboard, Master Fuller told him he was wanted on the Captin's deck.

David didn't have time to ask what had happened. Cavendish said, "You'll accompany me, sir."

"Aye, sir," said David, glancing at Havers, who was silent and grave. David followed the two men down to the lower deck and into the waiting boat. Moon was there too.

Brule was waiting for them on the *Content*. David peered curiously around as he stepped aboard. The crew was lined up, and Brule and his officers stood a little apart; Brule came forward to greet Cavendish, and David, behind them, saw then the two shrouded figures on the deck.

As if Cavendish's coming were a signal, Brule stepped before the mast and said a short prayer, and the two bodies were heaved over the side. One of them was William Byet. In the quiet, Cavendish took a step to stand at Brule's side. He replaced his cap; he was facing the late afternoon sun, and his eyes were squinting a trifle in his tanned face as he soberly surveyed the twenty officers and men who made up the *Content's* crew. David watched his brother's face as he started to speak.

"This afternoon two of your number engaged in an armed quarrel about the *Santa Anna*. One Lawrence

Gamesby, of Newcastle, was killed by musket fire. William Byet died instantly, his skull crushed with a belaying pin. They both saved me the trouble of hanging them."

Cavendish pushed his cap sideways to shield his eyes.

"These two men started the quarrel with men from the *Desire* by complaining that the gold aboard the *Santa Anna* was not being properly divided, and, further, that the company of the *Desire* was being favored. It is a pity that two men should lose their lives through a lie, and, worse, endanger other lives. It is even more of a pity that our number should be reduced by two when we need all hands."

He stopped for a moment to let his eyes sweep the men facing him.

"Now about the gold," he said. "It comes to the amount of one hundred and twenty thousand pieces, as you well know. That gold shall be divided in England by an Admiralty court, but—the amount you will each be awarded is already aboard the *Content,* stowed below."

Again he paused. "It shall not, under any condition, be divided and put into your hands yet. Your first task is to sail that flag—" he gestured to it—"back to England, and under my command. The flag that flies there also flies on the *Desire's* mizzen. Look over and see it."

The reaction he hoped for was very apparent. He was conscious of extreme relief. There was no real trouble aboard the *Content.* Now he could say more, and say what he wanted to tell them.

"You shall be able to boast that you took that flag around the world. For let us ask ourselves an honest question: was it gold that sent us forth? Only gold? It comes to me, as we stand here, on this ship, under the shadow of a great continent, that, then, it was a quite unworthy cause for which to dare the life you were given.

"Look at the land. Over those mountains, up that coast, is gold, lying in the soil. I saw it. You could put your hand in the soil, and in the rocky creek beds, and pick it up. But that is not half so wonderful as the land itself. Those towering mountains, the deep wide valleys, the rich soil, the magnificent harbors. Do you realize, do you know, that because you've sailed here, because you've proved that it can be done, other men can come, and that some day men and women shall live in that valley and on that coast, and till the soil, and build cities—because you dared to sail a ship? In my cabin are charts that you helped me draw. You know our seamen need them. This great land needs them, for it is waiting for birth. Never have you or I seen, nor ever again shall we see, a land so mighty and marvelous as this land of America. You should thank God that you had courage enough to help it begin to grow, even though the part we do is small."

David heard Cavendish's voice stop. This was his creed, then, this the single motive that drove him on. His expanding age had made him to measure for his times, and fitted him for its needs. Then David realized Cavendish was not finished.

"The seventeenth of this month is Coronation Day. We are far from home, but not too far to celebrate Her Majesty's accession to the throne of England. I believe that our Bess will like to know, some months from now, that here in California we toasted her with Spanish wine, and with the guns of the *Desire* and the *Content;* that, for the first time in California, rockets burst up into the skies. We will celebrate on the beaches, with freshly roasted pork, and we shall ask the Spanish to join us. It shan't be the last time for fireworks in California, I warrant, but it will be the first time, in the honor of your Queen and mine. In honor of England!"

The men cheered. David found himself smiling. He was standing near Brule and Cavendish, and he heard his brother say to Brule, "They're glad this business is over with and they can look forward to going ashore tonight." He laughed, and Brule shook hands with him, and Brule didn't dismiss his crew until Cavendish was in his own longboat again, pulling back to the *Desire*. Then Brule left the rail, conscious of extreme relief, too.

David was silent during the short row. He was sitting alongside Havers and he wanted to talk, but he couldn't, and he watched the muscled arms of the crewmen who handled the long oars like toys. He waited impatiently for Cavendish to go up the ladder, and he waited for Havers; then he clambered up himself, and saw Cavendish's figure aft.

By the time David caught up with him, Cavendish was in his cabin. David heard him pacing inside the small space. He wondered why, for now everything was all right again. He knocked. When he came in, Cavendish was in the act of drinking a cup of wine; he set down the empty cup.

"What is it?" he asked.

David said, "Is there something the matter, sir?"

Cavendish said, "No."

David said, "I didn't know, you see. I didn't understand."

"A long voyage is hard," Cavendish said. "They quarrel over nothing, because—" He made a gesture.

"I wasn't thinking of that," David said. "I was thinking about what you said. I wasn't here when it happened; I was on the bench; I saw your boat."

"Oh," said Cavendish. He looked at David searchingly. "Did you see Señora de Montoro?"

"Aye," said David.

Cavendish had stepped to the door to open it, and Cosmos entered with a tray of food. David hesitated. He asked, "Aren't you going to join the Spanish in the fish dinner ashore?"

"No," said Cavendish.

"Shall Havers or I take your regrets to de Ersola, then?"

"The Señora Catherine—was she—"

David said, "Why, she was as usual, Tom. Excited about the shots. As beautiful as ever."

Cavendish said suddenly, "I may go. Aye, perhaps I shall. I'll join you."

"It's time, then," said David, a bit uncertainly.

"I'm coming." Cavendish picked a brush and brushed the thick short hair vigorously. He settled his cap on the side of his head.

"Where's my gold-studded belt, Cosmos?" he asked. He buckled the belt.

"I'm ready," he said.

Chapter 13

DE ERSOLA MET CAVENDISH on the beach. The tide was coming in; it would be full within an hour. Cavendish sank into the soft sand where the boats were beached. To his right, opposite the small cove, was the completed bark. She would be launched at flood tide.

De Ersola walked with Cavendish toward the long tables set in the sand, under the trees.

"A rude way of entertaining, Captain," he said. "But this is the best we can do, to celebrate the launching of the bark."

"It'll be almost dark by then," Cavendish said. He smelled frying fish; there was an enormous amount of chatter around them. He was conscious of the easy gaiety; he was also conscious of ravenous hunger. He had missed his midday dinner.

"It will be a lovely sight, at evening," said de Ersola, looking at the steady procession of white breakers; they were even and strong against the offshore wind, and the bay was smooth and unruffled past them, dyed with the silken colors of sunset.

"We've abandoned formality," de Ersola went on, showing Cavendish to a place at his right. "Our ladies are helping to manage."

Down the table, Moon and the Portugal Riderigo were already throwing dice, as they waited for their food. The wine cups were filled. And Cavendish kept looking for Catherine.

He saw her down by the nearest fire, with other women and men, and then she came walking toward them, carrying two plates piled high with fried fish.

"I hear you had an untoward incident today," de Ersola sad, his brown eyes speculative.

Cavendish did not answer for a minute. He was watching Catherine come closer. "So we did," he said, finally.

113

Catherine put a wooden plate in front of him.

"Good evening, Captain," she said. She put the other plate down before de Ersola.

"Lord," de Ersola said. "Are you helping too, Catherine? You shouldn't."

"Everyone is," she answered. "Everyone!" She smiled.

"Thank you, *señora*," Cavendish said. "Would you—"

"I cannot stay to talk, sirs, I'm working."

"Please begin, Captain," de Ersola said.

"I shall," Cavendish said, angrily.

He ate quickly. He finished the last morsel of fish while he watched for her, moving around the fire. When she finally came back to the table where he ate, he indicated his empty plate.

"Would you fill it for me?" he asked.

She stood at his side. "You want more?" she asked, remembering how much she had given him—the best pieces, browned right, and thick. She picked up the plate. "Do you want more, Tomas?" she asked de Ersola.

"Even with you to wait on me, *señora*," he said, "I could eat nothing more."

She looked down at Cavendish. "As much again?" she asked.

"As much," he said. "I'm very healthy, *señora*.".

She met his eyes. "I'm healthy, too," she said. "And I have not eaten yet." She walked away, with the full intention of letting someone else bring his plate back. But she didn't. She selected the fish for him carefully, and brought it back to him. Then she left him again.

The cove where the little bark had been built was full now. It was almost dusk, and the bay was shimmering gray with the faintest tint of pink left in it from the dying sun. The men had gone down to the cove; they were finished with their food, and the plates had been stacked in wooden tubs full of sea water. From the table, de Ersola and Cavendish watched.

The men strained and shoved to move the bark on her rude wheels and carriage over the soft sand. They had laid planks down to ease their task. English and Spanish worked together; the women crowded around.

The first waves slapped her bow. The men pushed her farther into the water; they were standing waist deep in it now; the breakers rolled in, lifting her.

"Here she goes!" came the cry.

She was afloat. She rode daintily. Men had followed her into the sea; they pulled themselves aboard, dripping and everybody cheered and crowded close to the water's edge to watch. Her carriage came to the surface and floated in the surf; then her sails were hoisted and for a few minutes there was silence while she made her short maiden voyage. Her anchor splashed overboard less than a half cable's length from shore.

De Ersola raised his cup. "We'll drink to her," he said.

Cavendish said, "Aye." He downed his wine. De Ersola said nothing else, and after a minute Cavendish forgot him, and the bark. The men who had sailed her were already stepping from their boat onto the beach, and the fires, with fresh logs, burned brightly.

Both men and women had gathered in a big circle on the sand. The officers and gentlemen and ladies grouped a little apart from the rest of the company. Near them were the musicians, and the first strains of a Spanish dance came to Cavendish's ears. He rose.

"Shall we go down and watch?" he said to de Ersola.

The Spaniard got to his feet with his easy grace. Side by side they walked down; the firelight lit the scene. Catherine was sitting on the said between David and Havers; Cavendish came to stand behind them. Lola was dancing.

She was in the center of the circle, barefooted, her long hair falling down her back. She moved slowly as yet, savoring the music. The click of her castanets sounded. Cavendish looked down at Catherine's head; he leaned down and put his hand on her shoulder.

"Señora," he said, low.

She turned her head. Havers turned, too, and then looked back to Lola.

"Señora," Cavendish repeated. He held out his hands to her.

She did not take his hands. "I told you before, Captain," she said, "I want to watch the dancing."

Cavendish straightened up. He kept his eyes on Lola as long as he could. He looked over at the ring of people opposite him; they had begun to clap their hands in time to the music, and one man jumped up and tried to partner Lola. The two of them went through a pantomime until he left her alone again.

The music stopped.

"More!" the men shouted.

"In a minute," Lola said. he came toward David, clicking the castanets.

Again Cavendish leaned over, and this time he lifted Catherine to her feet.

"The dance is finished," he said.

She said, "They will dance together, that man and Lola. In a minute."

"Then talk to me for that minute." His fingers fastened over her wrist. Havers had not looked up. Cavendish drew her slowly from the circle, just fifteen feet away, in the shadows.

"What did you want to say?" she asked, evenly.

"I want you to walk down the beach with me."

"I cannot."

His grip on her wrist tightened. "Why?"

"I do not wish to!"

"You'll come," he said, liking her arm with his, his hand still around her slender wrist.

"I shall not!" Her whole body was stiff and tense, braced against moving one step forward. "How dare you?" She was trembling with anger.

His blue eyes swept her. He said, harshly, "Why be coy with me, *señora?*" The picture of the handsome Spaniard whose portrait lay in her tent was plain before him. "Surely," he said, "you've known other men."

It was not true. She started to deny it. Instead, she said, "And if I have, Captain, they have been of my own choosing."

"I see," he said.

"And now that you understand me, I shall return to the dancing."

He released her arm. Catherine turned from him and went the few feet that had separated them from the circle of men and women. She sat down in her place beside Havers. David had moved away.

Havers watched her. Her head was bent. She dug her fingers into the sand, picking up a handful and letting it trickle through her fingers. She dropped her hand.

Havers put his big brown hand over hers. "Catherine," he said, "Do you—"

"I'll not cry," she said, and she looked at him with a small smile.

He said nothing.

"You knew before, didn't you, Havers?" she asked. He nodded.

"I love him so very much," she said, with complete relief at telling someone, especially Havers. "Do you think—"

Havers had been staring grimly ahead, not seeing the dance, not hearing the music.

"I'm afraid he knows it, too," she said. "He is so used to having women in love with him."

Havers said, "He is not sure, Catherine."

"How do you know?" she asked eagerly.

"I know," he said. "I know him well."

"Do you think, Havers," she asked, wanting to ask this so much, but hesitating, "do you think that he might be falling in love?" She gathered courage. "Sometimes, Havers, I feel that he does love me."

Havers said, "Something has happened to him, señora. But whether—"

"I see him," she said.

Cavendish was sitting not many feet away, alongside the black-haired Arabella. His shoulders were turned away from Catherine, but she could see the gleam of gold studs in his belt, and she could see his hands, loosely clasped over his booted legs.

Suddenly he stood up and pulled Arabella to her feet. He walked beside her, his head turned so Catherine couldn't see his face. She jumped to her feet and started to move past Havers. He didn't move.

"Where are you going?" he asked.

She stood there watching, and finally she said, "I'm not going anywhere, Havers; I'm staying here."

Chapter 14

THE *Desire* rode closest to the beach. Cavendish leaned against the rail; he was almost opposite Catherine's tent, and he was watching for her. She came out of her tent; she went to the water's edge, and she bathed her face and hands and dried them with a white towel.

For three days she had avoided him; for three days she had punished him well for Arabella. He stared across the water, squinting his eyes to see better.

She was kneeling at the edge of the water. He heard her laughter; it floated across the water to him. There was no sound of surf; the tide was at its ebb, and the bay was like a wary pool, so quiet was it with the off-shore wind.

He even caught the clear sound of her voice as she said, "No, *señorita*. Not now." She was tying a ribbon in her little daughter's hair. She finished quickly; her hands were sure, he knew. Then she picked up the towel and hung it over a tree branch. She turned and left, and pretty soon there was nothing to see but the white towel, hanging there disconsolately.

He never saw her alone. She was always with someone—Lola, or de Ersola, or David. She was making a sketch of Havers; he had come over to watch her, and she had looked up at him and said, "Captain Havers is a restless man to paint, sir."

Cavendish had asked, "Is that canvas?"

Havers said, "Yes," and Catherine told him please to be quiet for just a minute. Then both of them laughed together.

"I'd like to see the picture of the *Desire*," Cavendish said angrily. "Havers told me about it."

"Oh, did you?" Catherine asked, raising those green eyes to look at Havers. "Did you, Havers? But what did I tell you about it?"

Havers grinned. "I know, Catherine. I told the Captain it wasn't for sale."

She seemed to notice Cavendish then, for she said, "Oh, I'm sorry, Captain Cavendish. You may see the picture later. I'll—I'll be finished in an hour or so."

"I don't have time to wait."

"A pity," she said. "Perhaps tomorrow, then."

He looked down at her and wanted to pick her up in his arms. "Tomorrow?" he asked, taking a step toward her. Then he glanced at Havers, and he turned away abruptly. . . .

Now he was leaning against the rail, and watching. He heard David approach him; he didn't turn. David was always with Catherine.

"Sir," David said from behind his back.

"What is it?" Cavendish said, sharply. There was no sight of her yet, and she had been in the tent five minutes.

"What is it?" he asked again.

"I wanted to ask if I could go ashore," David said.

Cavendish turned. "Why ask me?" He stared out to the tents again.

"Because, sir," David said, trying to keep his voice even, "Captain Havers is ashore."

"Oh," said Cavendish. So that was where Catherine was. With Havers.

"And," David continued, "Master Fuller is aboard the *Santa Anna* with Moon, to look over the last stores of powder and weapons."

Cavendish turned again to look at David. "What is that?" he asked, pointing.

David held up the object. "A toy boat," he said. "I made it for Kate."

"Kate?"

"Catherine's little girl. Havers and I call her Kate to keep her and Catherine separate. A good English name, we tell her," David explained. "I want to take it to her now, and—"

Cavendish said, "Havers, Moon and Fuller are not aboard, sir. I think you had better stay aboard. You can take your toys ashore later."

"Aye, sir," sad David stiffly. "But it is a holiday, sir!"

Cavendish's eyes went over David's dress. "Is that holiday attire you're boasting? Change it." He turned his back on David.

David regarded his shoulders for a moment. Then Cavendish heard his retreating footsteps. Once again he leaned on the rail and looked toward the last gray-white canvas tent.

There were only three days and two nights left. Already the first day was being swallowed up as time ate away its hours hungrily and the sun continued its impassive course across the heavens. The day was beautiful. It was calm, with little wind, and that from the pine-scented land. The slight wind carried the sounds from shore to his ears—the sound of voices and laughter, as women came in and out of their tents, as the Spanish poked up the fires for the midday meal, as a boatload of English sailors pulled for shore, carrying in the boat the first pig to be slaughtered. A few women had come down to the water's edge to see the pig wade ashore. They laughed and squealed.

Soon he would set sail, soon this colony would be a place in his memory, a white-washed beach, clean and sharp with bright sun; soon it would be gone, or rather, he would be gone. But it would stay here, this, the New World, this beach on the tip of California. He would be gone, but it would be forever here, under the sun.

It was mid-morning. It was Coronation Day. The seventeenth of November. Cavendish saw Havers and Catherine, walking side by side, talking fast; he saw Catherine's face turned up to Havers, and she was speaking eagerly, her hands raised in a gesture, and she smiled. At the water's edge they stood talking, and then Havers got into his boat. Almost impatiently, Cavendish waited for him.

"Ahoy, Havers," he said genially, leaning over the rail.

"Ahoy, Captain," returned Havers. He swung aboard and mounted up to Cavendish's deck. "How are you this morning?"

"Well," said Cavendish. He waited.

But Havers said nothing; he was going to say nothing about Catherine. Cavendish asked, "How is the *señora* today?"

"Muy bien," said Havers. He smiled. "We talk in Spanish and English, all mixed up."

"Is your picture finished?" Cavendish asked.

Havers said, "Oh, it's just a charcoal sketch, and Catherine wants to keep it."

"In memory of you?"

Havers looked out to sea. "If you wish it that way, yes, Tom."

"What does she do? Keep a gallery of the men she carries a tender fondness for? You'll be keeping company with a handsome Spanish bastard whose picture I saw."

Havers straightened. His bushy brows rose a little; his eyes crinkled and he looked amused. "Jealous, Tom?" he asked. He had been carrying his pipe; with one hand he shook some tobacco into the bowl and pressed it down with his long forefinger. Then he put the unlit pipe in his mouth. His gray eyes came back to Cavendish's face.

Cavendish grinned ruefully. "Give it right back to me, Havers." He shifted restlessly. "Here comes Moon," he said, "and I have to see him."

Havers followed Cavendish slowly. Havers saw David, he spoke, and David came over to him. The three of them stood there as Moon came up the ladder.

"There is plenty to leave them, sir," were Moon's first words.

Cavendish's face was inscrutable.

"One day will be ample time to give them," Moon continued.

Cavendish nodded and Moon continued, "You said no weapons were to be transferred tomorrow, but only on the morning of the nineteenth, the day we sail."

David heard Moon's words. He looked toward Cavendish. David was carrying the toy boat.

"What do you mean, Moon?" David asked.

There was a moment's silence. Moon hesitated,

frowning at David; he started to speak, and then fell silent again, because Cavendish said, "I'll answer that question, Moon."

He regarded David levelly. "Moon means," he said, "that the Spanish will have all day tomorrow, the eighteenth, and the early hours of the nineteenth, to unload the *Santa Anna* of all usable goods. And tomorrow will be time enough." He stopped.

"Time enough?" asked David, his tone low.

"Aye," said Cavendish, "time enough."

David was conscious of Havers and Moon. He heard vaguely the sound of the other men's voices. The smell of cooking went past his nostrils. It was all so familiar, and so was the beach nearby and the people who lived there. For days now he had known this was coming. Days? Perhaps months.

"Tom," he said, "that little bark there, that you built." He pointed to it with the toy boat he held in his hand. "She is a concession to mercy, is she not?"

"If she is," Cavendish's voice came slowly, "I do not want it known until tomorrow, David."

"Because you know it could spoil our celebration tonight? Spoil Coronation Day, and the feast and the friendliness?"

"Exactly," said Cavendish.

David laid the toy boat down on the deck. "If the little bark is going to be the only means of communicating these people's plight to the mainland—tell me, Tom, what are you going to do with the *Santa Anna?*"

David's tone had been low. The men unloading the last stores of powder and shot from the *Santa Anna* noticed nothing amiss. Their Captain and his brother were talking, and Havers and Moon stood near. But David could not keep his voice low.

"What are you going to do with the *Santa Anna?*" he repeated, spacing the words evenly.

It was Cavendish's reply they couldn't hear. But David heard it, plainly; the answer he knew was coming.

"I'm going to burn her," Cavendish said.

"I see," David said. "You're going to sink her. Why not use powder and shot, Tom? In a thundering farewell of guns for these people you're leaving helpless here?"

Cavendish's blue eyes were ice cold. "Because I don't wish to spare powder and shot. It would be folly. And for you, sir, confinement to your quarters immediately." He turned away.

"Don't go, Tom," David said. "I'm not going to my quarters like a good boy. I'm taking orders no longer."

Havers started to speak, but he didn't. Moon's round face was white under his tan. Slowly Cavendish turned around.

Cavendish didn't speak. He waited. His arms hung loosely at his sides; he took a step toward David.

"You," said David, "are going to leave these people here helpless. You are going to abandon Catherine and her little girl."

David had been calm. But the sudden blazing anger that he saw in Cavendish's eyes roused his own anger. He felt it rising in him like hottest fire, clouding the brain, pounding the blood through his heart and chest and head.

He had put the toy boat down. In front of him was Cavendish, and with vicious pleasure David raised his fist and hit hard, following the blow through with all his strength, hitting hard to the midsection with his left fist and cutting to Cavendish's chin with his clenched right fist.

The second blow knocked Cavendish off his feet. It slid him backward into a boat slung amidships. David had bounded after him, and was waiting for him to rise, when he felt his arms seized on both sides.

He had forgotten Havers and Moon. They did not hold him tightly, after the first quick grasp. But they held him, and David thought Havers said something to him but he didn't hear it.

"Let me go!" he said.

"No," said Havers quietly. The grip on his arm tightened, and David realized what he had done.

Slowly Cavendish got to his feet. His face was marked with blood. Aloft, the lookout stared down at the deck. The men who were unloading the boat stopped all pretense of work. The ship was silent. But David noticed nothing but his brother's face.

Cavendish was wearing no doublet, no sword. With deliberateness he started to roll up the sleeve of his fine linen shirt with the loose cuffs. He said to Havers, "Give me his sword."

Havers obeyed, quickly. He handed sword and belt to Cavendish who tossed both aside onto the deck. They made a clatter.

"Take off his jacket," Cavendish said. He was rolling up his other sleeve."

Havers pulled off one sleeve of David's jacket. Moon completed the job. He handed the jacket to Tyler, who stood near. "Jesu," Tyler muttered under his breath, his eyes on Cavendish's face. The Captain, who was always controlled, was so now; and it made him more fearsome, for this time he was coldly indulging his violence.

Cavendish glanced at both sleeves. They were neatly rolled. A lock of unruly hair had fallen over his forehead. He brushed it back. He looked about at the space he had.

"Now let him go, sirs," he sid. "And stand away, a little."

In the one second before his arms were released, David was conscious of fear. The old fear and uncertainty. Always before, this violence was what he had provoked but what he had never faced. Always before, it had been checked. Now it was unchecked. And David's brain, in one clear flash, told him it was Catherine's name that had loosed this anger.

Havers and Moon had let go his arms. They had stepped back and he faced Cavendish alone. He saw the first blow coming, and he put his arm up to ward it off, but Cavendish's left fist struck him clean between the ribs, and the next blow knocked him backward.

He was still on his feet. The ruthless anger he faced made him wonder if Cavendish would kill him. Two smashing blows to his face, coming right on top of each other, drove him back into the rail, and he hooked his arm over it and stood again.

In a second he was knocked down, parallel to the rail. He got up slowly; Cavendish was not bothering with strategy; he was driving a rain of steady, calculated blows to David's face. David took a succession of them, swaying, until the last one, to the side of the jaw, crumpled him up at Cavendish's feet.

Cavendish stepped aside as David fell. Blood marked the well-scrubbed deck. David lay prone, face down, and Cavendish turned his head to see Havers.

"Captain Havers," he said.

"Aye, sir," Havers said steadily, his square face somber.

Cavendish looked down at David. "Double irons," he said, and then he started away. David's sword and belt lay on the deck. Cavendish leaned down and picked them up.

"Will you hand me his jacket, sir?" he asked Moon.

Hastily, Moon came forward with the jacket.

Cavendish took it. "Thank you," he said, and he walked aft, into the crowded poop, carrying David's jacket and the sword with its dangling belt.

Chapter 15

LOLA'S EYES were dark and huge. "They're going to hang him," she said levelly.

Catherine faced her. "No, they will not."

"They will," said Lola, her breathing quick. "Everyone says it, *señora.*" She made a sudden helpless gesture, losing the poise that she had tried to keep. *"Dios, señora!* Do you think I want to believe it!"

Catherine said, "You are sure it's true? That David—"

Lola said, only, "It is quite true. It happened this morning, and it is now three o'clock. I have come to you."

Catherine was dressed in a thin white shift. Her hair was loose; on her feet were heelless slippers.

"You find it difficult to believe, *señora?*" Lola said. "I wakened you. I do not know what you can do, *señora*, but I came because you are the only one to help. I will help you dress."

"You do not need to," Catherine said, unsteadily.

Lola said, "You wear this dress? This white lace? And these petticoats? Here." She lifted one up and slipped it over Catherine's head. "Now this one, *señora,*" she said. "I fasten it."

"Thank you, Lola," Catherine said.

Lola fastened the second petticoat. Standing in front of Catherine, she said, "And certainly you know what I want, *señora.* You do, no?"

Catherine nodded. Her bright head made assent.

"You are the one," Lola said. "Only you."

Catherine, struggling with two main currents of thought, exclaimed, "Lola, you do not understand him! I do."

Lola picked up the dress.

"Even, Lola, if he should come, the Captain, and talk

to me, even then, with him it is no use to plead for David!"

Lola said evenly, "It is better than nothing. Now we do nothing."

Catherine said, "It is no better than nothing, for you are forgetting that David is his own brother."

"Your dress, *señora,*" Lola said.

"Madre de Dios; I tell you it is folly!" She flung her hands out. "It will only make him the more angry!"

"Listen!" Lola said. "Perhaps you accomplish nothing. Let it be so. At least you can learn what the Captain intends, and if David is to die, then learn when."

"I'll write to the Captain," Catherine said.

Lola looked over her shoulder as she wrote a single sentence, in charcoal: "Sir, I would wish to speak with you on a matter of gravest importance." She signed her initials, folded the paper, and Lola took it.

"I shall return," she said, as she left the tent. "Dress, *señora*, for he will come."

Catherine picked up her dress and put it over her head. She brushed her hair and secured it on the top of her head with a few polished wooden pins. Tiny curling tendrils of hair escaped the heavy silken mass. She used no powder; her skin was a golden tan. She changed her slippers for flat-heeled sandals of China silk.

Perhaps he would come. But if he did there was little to say. This minute, almost, he would be reading the note, the few words, standing in his cabin or on his high deck. Would he come?

She paced to the crude doorway; its flap was tied back with knotted rope. The *Desire* rode near. She saw Lola coming, running toward her from the beach. But Lola would know nothing yet. Still Catherine waited for her, tense.

"I sent the note," Lola said. She came into the tent and looked at Catherine. "He will have it now."

"Oh," said Catherine.

"He will come," Lola said. "Last night I see him look for you always with his eyes, while he was on the beach. I think he wanted you to know he was not with the Señorita Arabella."

Catherine sank down into her hammock, but she couldn't stay there and she got up again.

"Señora, learn what you can."

"That is all I can do," Catherine said. "Lola, tonight is the celebration. If we could get aboard, would you go?"

"Sí," said Lola. "How?"

"With Cosmos," Catherine said. "He would take me. After dark."

Lola could not answer because this was more than she dared hope.

"There will be hardly a man aboard," Catherine said. "We might—Lola, we might even free David!"

Lola said instantly, "You forget David when you say that. You forget him."

"Why?"

"Because, *señora,* he is a very stubborn man, and he may not want to be freed. He may—"

She had gone to the tent flap. Across the beach, a man was striding fast. Lola whirled.

"He comes!"

"Run!" said Catherine. "Quick! I'm going to tell him you are ill!"

"Sí," said Lola. She fled like a shadow, around the corner of the tent. Cavendish was walking fast, toward the tent, and Catherine turned from the open flap; she turned her back and waited.

It was only a minute before she knew he was standing in the doorway. Slowly she turned; he took a step forward.

"Buenos días, señora," he said.

He had come, then. He was here. The blue eyes were just as blue; there was a red welt on the side of his face where David had struck him. It made Catherine realize anew that David himself would not walk into the tent today, that probably he would never come again, and that she would never see him again unless Cosmos could help her tonight. But even the thought of David was not as compelling as the fact that she and Cavendish were together again.

"You came," she said, low.

"You wanted me to," he said. "You wrote me."

"I know. But I didn't know you would come."

He hesitated. "Perhaps you were justified to doubt."

"I learned about David this afternoon."

"Did you?" His tone warned her.

She saw the badly bruised knuckles of his right hand; she raised her eyes to his face and was afraid to ask him if David was badly hurt.

"So it is all true?" she whispered.

"Quite true," he said.

"It is done?"

"Done, *señora*."

She was breathing lightly between parted lips. She spoke what was the truth because she understood him so well. "You cannot save him now?"

"No," he said.

"But when?" Catherine asked. "Not—today?"

"No, not today."

"Tomorrow, then?"

The blue eyes looked straight back at her. "Why do you ask?"

Catherine said quickly, "I ask for Lola! She is—she loves him!"

"Oh," said Cavendish.

His tone had been softer. "Lola is sick now," she said. "If you would send Cosmos with a bottle of light wine, perhaps she could keep at least a little wine down."

He said, "I'll send the wine with Cosmos."

"Thank you," she whispered. But the memory of David—his warm brown eyes, his quick wit and the restless exuberance—was too strong. "He will die? He cannot! Is there nothing to do? Nothing? I would do anything to save his life!"

He took a step toward her; he took her hand in his, lifting it, palm up. "Would you?" he asked.

"Please," she whispered, forgetting it would be no use.

"You are so sweet and willing, *señora,* when it is something you want. But I cannot make bargains." He dropped her hand.

"I did not mean that."

"Don't bother to lie to me!" he said. "I thought you had something important to tell me."

"What else is important?" she cried.

He said, dryly, "An emerald, perhaps. To a woman, a man can be most important."

"True," said Catherine. "The most important thing in the world! And to a man, then, could a woman be that important?"

It was almost a minute before he answered. "I don't know," he said.

"There are so many women, always," she said tensely. "Like Arabella!"

He was silent.

"I did not mean to plead with you, to save David. You don't have need of me, when there are so many women out there, and when we shall never see each other again. After a few days, there won't be any colony at San Lucas!"

"Two days," he said, evenly.

"You leave the nineteenth, then," she said, just as evenly. "And I suppose David will die that day?"

"Suppose nothing," he said. "I'll do the deciding!"

"You won't even tell me when it will be?"

"No!"

"You are being childish," she said.

"I'll send the wine for Lola," he said, and the tension between them filled the little tent. Cavendish looked at her; he started to leave, but he couldn't. "Arabella is nothing beside you, madam," he said, and the taunt brought the blazing anger out into the open.

"Dare you speak her name to me!"

"Pick up your little knife!" he said. "It would suit you better than sweet words!"

She said desperately, "It's not that I do not feel sorry for you, too! I know how you—"

She stopped. "Oh, please—" She looked at his bruised hands. She tried to forget him and to remember David. She was the only one who could help David, and there was something else she must know. Tears of anger stood in her eyes.

"Did you hurt him badly?" she asked.

"Deservedly so," he said. "You weep for him already? Too bad I'll not see him to tell him about your sorrowing! But you can see Havers tonight, and weep then." He turned and left—and Catherine put her hands over her face in a helpless gesture—for if she did not stop herself physically, she might cry out to him. Pride kept her; pride, and also the love she bore him. Anger and hatred were mixed up in her heart, along with this love, and hurt too, for he had hurt her badly, and she was willing to see him suffer; fiercely, she hoped he was suffering.

There were only two days left—not even two whole days. Tonight, no matter what, she must try to help David escape. It was a frail hope. She must remember to carry her little knife. She hardly realized she was crying. She stood in the center of the bare tent.

"Oh, my darling," she whispered, "I love you. Please send Cosmos with the wine for Lola."

She knew he would, because he had said so, and because she had asked it. "Oh, my darling," she said again, because it helped to say the words aloud, "I love you."

Chapter 16

DE ERSOLA came down onto the beaches at five o'clock. All day long he had wrestled with the problem confronting him, and all day he had questioned his decision to keep secret until tomorrow the news that Cavendish was going to sink the *Santa Anna* and leave them abandoned here on the lonely cape of California. He had made his decision, but even as he walked toward the now crowded beach, he went over again in his mind the possibilities.

He noted the armed guards which Cavendish had carefully provided. Even tonight, then, there would be a watch on the beaches. It was just as well then that he had given up the idea of trying an attack on the English, unarmed as the Spanish were; the very weight of numbers might succeed, but he had doubted it so strenuously, he had perforce abandoned the idea.

He noted the casks of wine. Swiftly he judged that there were too few to allow any of the English to get drunk; Cavendish would be too clever for that.

He was an able opponent, de Ersola ceded, ruefully. He considered himself Cavendish's opponent because Flores was being faithful to his parole, and therefore he was out of the battle until Cavendish had sailed away. Then, thought de Ersola ironically, he would come out of his seclusion and take the reins of command into his own hands again. Now Flores saw de Ersola each morning, to inquire about his crew and his passengers; he seemed satisfied each morning with de Ersola's report, and de Ersola usually did not see him again until the next day, when once more Flores would be eating his breakfast and drinking his wine in sparing sips.

Tomorrow, then, would begin the task of unloading the *Santa Anna* of all her usable goods. Tomorrow had, like every day, twenty-four hours, and de Ersola was content to wait until then. Much had happened today, already. He saw Brule on the beach, and he walked down to join him.

"It smells good here," de Ersola said.

Brule frowned a little, as if he had been thinking of something quite different, and de Ersola's remark had recalled him to the present.

De Ersola said, "We hear the Captain's brother is confined under a charge of mutiny."

"Aye," said Brule. "I have had my discipline problems too, as you've also heard."

"Disaffection is common enough, in a situation like yours, sir," de Ersola said, with such simplicity that Brule responded gratefully.

"Aye, that it is, sir, with the Pacific to cross, and with such moneys aboard."

"It will be over, sir. Soon you will leave the New World behind, and they will feel, instead of its pull, the pull for home."

Brule looked up at the western sky. "Home is very far away," he said softly.

There was a great deal of laughter in the air; the women's clothes were bright and gay; and odd bits of accented English came floating to Brule's ears as he listened to their chatter with the English sailors. Brule knew what tonight would be like. There would be plenty to eat, and there would be companionship and music and dancing, and he felt a kinship with these people, who were after all like him, or they wouldn't be here at all.

Brule said suddenly, "I hope all goes well with you!"

"You've no need to equivocate with me, sir. Certainly now, between us, there can be truth. I know what Cavendish intends. The little bark rides there, and I am a good pilot."

Brule looked concerned at the understatement; he looked very much concerned, and his eyes were eloquent. De Ersola noted it with dismay, almost, and realized suddenly he had been quite wrong about Brule. Brule was not soft, instead, he was tender-hearted. De Ersola had met Englishmen before who were so tender-hearted and sentimental. But the Spaniard was going to speak out anyway, because he had planned this.

Out in the bay rode the *Content*. The *Content* could mean freedom for de Ersola and his company. And the loss of the *Content* would be a great blow to Cavendish. Without her, he would have a great ocean to cross, alone. Without her, he would enter Spanish waters in the Philippinas with a small force, but one ship and sixty men.

De Ersola said, "If we're being honest, let me ask you something. Why don't you throw in your lot with us? And taste Acapulco, and all the gold that is to be had there?"

Even as he said it, he knew it was useless. Brule was offended. He frowned; then he smiled a little.

"No," he said.

De Ersola smiled back. "You don't change course, do you? Tell me, what's the Captain going to do about his brother?"

Brule said, "He'll hang him, sir. You mark my words."

"What else can he do?" de Ersola asked. "I've no sympathy for Master David."

Brule said, "David is—I can't quite explain—but he has changed a deal since he sailed with us," he ended inadequately.

Again de Ersola felt Brule's tenderness; he changed the subject. There was no use pursuing it, and he knew Brule would report his words to Cavendish. Cavendish would not be surprised.

"Look," he said, "they're going to carve up that pig."

"I fed him myself," Brule said. "That pig, *señor,* sailed with me from Mazatlán." Brule grinned. "Come and have a piece of him."

The Spanish cooks were helping to carve. The two crews and the women had divided into groups around each fire. Later they would gather together to watch the fireworks, and to sit in a huge circle to watch the dancing, and to hear the music and to sing.

Havers was presiding over the carving of the pig. He was standing, laughing and talking to the men, interspersing his English with Spanish.

"The first piece goes to the Captain," Tyler said, as

he started to cut huge slices from the leg. He laid them on a silver plate.

"He's coming now, sir," another sailor said, looking at Cavendish's boat as the men pulled it onto the beach.

"And a couple of chops for the Captain," Tyler continued. "He favors the chops."

Cavendish came walking up to them, with Cosmos trailing behind him.

"I take the Captain's plate," Cosmos said, and Tyler grinned at the Japanese, and handed him the silver plate.

"It smells marvelous, Tyler," Cavendish said. "Havers, you're going to join me, are you not?"

"Certainly, sir," said Havers; but he saw Cavendish was not looking at him, and that his eyes were searching the group of men and women just twenty feet away, at the next fire.

"I see Master Pretty is enjoying himself," Cavendish said.

"He's with Señora Catherine," Havers said, his grey eyes bland.

"She is coming this way now," Cavendish said, stepping forward.

Catherine was carrying a plate of food, and Pretty had a full cup of wine in his hand. They were talking together, busily, and they stopped when they saw Cavendish right in front of them.

"Good evening, sir," Pretty said, stopping so suddenly that the wine slopped over across his white cuff.

"Good evening, Pretty," Cavendish said. Then he abandoned Pretty and looked at Catherine.

Her face was bent a little to watch the plate of food she was carrying. An escaping curl fell over her forehead; she pushed it back with one hand.

"We're taking some food to Lola," she said. "Perhaps she can eat a little."

"Is the wine for Lola, too?" Cavendish asked. "I sent her light wine with Cosmos."

The heavy lashes that shadowed her cheeks flew up. Catherine's face was very white. She moistened her lips. "It did her good, sir," she said. "Now she is feeling a little better. Will you pardon me, Captain?"

"As you wish," he said.

Catherine brushed by Cavendish, her brocade swishing. Cosmos' voice said in his ear, "Captain, your meat will grow cold."

"Aye, and I don't have much time," Cavendish said.

Cosmos pulled out a stool, and Cavendish sat down at the rough table the Spanish had made. Other officers were coming toward the table to join him. Cosmos had put the plate down in front of Cavendish.

"You are not staying on the beaches, sir?" he asked, his singing tones breathless.

"Not for long," Cavendish said.

"Aye, aye, sir," said Cosmos.

Cavendish frowned and looked up at him. He eyed him for a minute. Then he said, "Cosmos, I warrant you are disappointed, but you needn't be; you may stay and watch the fireworks."

Comos smiled tentatively. "Thank you, sir," he said, still breathless, and moved away.

Cavendish stared after him a moment. Then he shrugged and applied himself to his food.

The dusk deepened. The bay turned the palest color of rose; then the color faded and the sky began to darken. Down by the fire, Cosmos was trying to eat, and his stomach turned over every time he washed his pork down with a sip of wine. He went over to Tyler to ask for more wine, and got another half cup.

"What's the matter with you?" Tyler asked. "You sick?"

"No, no," said Cosmos. "I eat."

"Not much, you're not," said Tyler.

Cosmos took another chop from the big platter, and walked away with it. It was getting quite dark, and he stood on the edge of a circle of men and dug into the soft sand with his foot. He dropped the chop into the hole, and smoothed the sand back evenly. He drank the rest of his wine.

Half an hour had passed, he reckoned. He watched the scene, unsmiling, although there was much contagious merriment that ordinarily would have left him giggling too. His almond eyes were fixed on Cavendish, and finally he saw the Captain come down to the water and get into his own boat. The boat pulled away, and it was so dark that the outline of the boat disappeared very quickly. Cosmos took his wine cup back to the planks laid under the cask. Then he edged slowly away to the tents.

Once outside the firelight, he started to run. He ran past the whole line of empty tents, past Lola's, past the next one, where he slowed his pace and moved silently, for he could hear Catherine's daughter and Tina. He slipped inside Catherine's tent, and the flap closed behind him. A lamp burned.

Cosmos clasped his hands together. "It is time," he said. *"Señora,"* he added, pleadingly.

Catherine had been sitting in her hammock. She was barefooted and ready. "Good," she said, standing up purposefully. She felt at her breast, to make sure the little knife was secure.

Cosmos was staring at Lola. "She comes, too?" he asked, fearfully.

Catherine nodded, and Cosmos started to speak.

"Sh," Lola said. She wore a heavy sash around her waist. She reached up and unfastened her earrings, laying them down on Catherine's table. "I am ready," she announced.

Cosmos said, "Oh, *señora,* please do not go!"

"I am *señorita,"* Lola said. She blew out the lamp.

"No, no." Cosmos' voice came through the darkness. "I mean both of you. It is madness to go! He is aboard himself!"

Chapter 17

THE TENT was inky black; Cosmos could see nothing since Lola had put out the lamp. "This way then," he said. He had promised the *señora;* she would not listen; with reluctant fatalism he turned.

Outside he could see more. He had left a light boat as near the tents as he could. Silently he moved toward the boat, feeling, not hearing, the two women coming behind him. He moved as fast as he could; he pushed the boast out into the water and stood holding it.

"Lie down in the botton," he whispered fearfully. There was no real need to whisper, for the men and women on the beach were noisy. He pushed the boat deeper into the water, and climbed in.

"I could help you row," Catherine said, from under his feet where she crouched.

"No, no," he said breathlessly. "The rockets. They may go off soon, and they will light the bay."

"*Sangre de Dios,*" Catherine muttered. "I had not thought of that!" She glanced at Lola beside her, and put out her hand to touch Lola. "Are you frightened?" she asked.

"No," said Lola evenly. "Only for him. He may have only tonight."

"If they see me rowing out to the *Desire,*" Cosmos said, "they will think nothing. Perhaps they will think I am fearful of rockets."

"If you are caught, you must say that," Catherine said eagerly. "Remember, Cosmos."

"Stay down, *señora,*" he said. He pulled evenly at the oars.

"Where are we?" Catherine asked, her voice muffled in her dress.

"Near," said Cosmos. "I row fast."

"There are no rockets yet," said Lola. "That is good, for it means we have more time."

"After the rockets, there will be music and dancing," Cosmos said. "We have hours, *señorita,* but it would not be wise to stay long."

"No," said Lola. "We know that. We wish only to see him, Cosmos."

"Sí," said Cosmos. The shape of the *Desire* loomed up dead ahead. Lights from her shone out on a patch of dark water, and he avoided the light, banking his oars. The boat slid alongside the *Desire;* Cosmos reached out and caught up the painter, his fingers deft. He leaned down and spoke in Catherine's ear; there was need for quiet now. Cosmos shut his eyes in terror when he thought of Cavendish.

"You see the ladder, *señora*?"

Catherine didn't answer. She stood up and climbed aboard, her bare feet making no sound. Her wet dress clung to her legs. She waited quietly on deck.

Lola suddenly stood beside her. She took Catherine's hand, and put her other hand on Cosmos' belt. No word was spoken.

The *Desire* was very still. No sound came from below. But the sound of voices from the beach was plainly to be heard; there were shouts, and Catherine knew that the first of the fireworks would explode in a moment. She was trembling.

But there were fifteen feet of deck to cross before they entered the main hatch, and would be lost to the sight of the people on the beach. And there were men aboard. They crossed the deck. The heavy doors creaked. Cosmos opened one of them, and Catherine slipped in after Lola and Cosmos.

Now there was no sound at all. Lola released Catherine's hand. Catherine turned, for in the pitch dark it would be safer to go down the ladder backwards. At the foot of the ladder she bumped against Lola; in the silence she could hear Lola's quick breathing. She felt for Lola's hand again.

They went on, through the silent ship. Catherine heard little sounds, and finally she heard Cosmos open another door; it squeaked a little. She went through it, the door closed, and she realized that Cosmos had closed it.

The air was very stale, but it was not so foul as she had expected. Flashing through her mind were Havers' words to her; "We made clean the *Desire* before we stowed our goods." Catherine put her hand out again to Lola; but before she could grasp it, she heard Cosmos say, "I am lighting the candle now, *señora*."

The thick candle in his hand suddenly illumined the place where they were. Cosmos held the candle high, and Lola let out a little gasp. Then she ran, as though she would hurl herself forward, but she did not; she stopped and, standing over David, she looked down at him.

His eyes were black with the sudden light. Lola saw that he had been asleep. She stared at his face, at the bruised lips, at the blackened eye and cut cheek. His shirt was torn and blood-stained. His tousled hair was over his forehead; he shook his head to try to get the hair out of his eyes. He swore roughly, his tones tinged with amazement.

Lola knelt in front of him, running her hands down his arms as they were fastened back against the wood, until she touched his wrists and she felt the heavy irons that pinned him back.

David, in his sitting position, was almost unable to move. Lola put her fingers under the iron rings around his ankles.

"Double-ironed," David said. "But will you tell me why in the name of God you are here?"

Catherine stepped out of the darkness. "I'm here too, David," she said.

"Jesu," he muttered. Then he frowned. He was trying to pull his wits together, and for a moment he felt only annoyance that they—all of them—had thrust this additional problem on him. The first problem was Cosmos.

"Get out of here, Cosmos," he said. He hadn't the faintest notion of the time; he had slept heavily. "This is insane."

"I told them, sir! They didn't heed me!"

"Aye. Well, you go up on deck, where you left the boat you must have used. Wait there and look at the fireworks, if it's time for them yet."

"Aye, sir," said Cosmos.

"Leave the candle," David said. "Put it there, spill some wax over, Cosmos."

The hot wax dropped on the floor. Cosmos stuck the candle in the hot wax. He went silently from them; they heard the door close.

"Now," said David, strongly, "I'll give you two minutes to explain this mad behavior, and then you'll both go."

Lola had been undoing her belt. She untied it, drew out a chisel. "You see?" she said.

David laughed.

Lola stuck the end of the chisel under the heavy black piece of iron to which the rings around David's legs were fastened. She pushed on the end of it.

"Don't do that," David said sharply. He looked at Catherine, who was kneeling on the other side of him. "I'm amazed that you consented to this folly, *señora*. Lola, stop digging into the wood."

Catherine said, "I thought—" She stopped.

"You had some idea you sould free me with that chisel?" he asked. "So I could drag these clanking irons up on deck?"

Then he said gently, "*Señora,* even if you could free me, d'ye think I'd consent?" He smiled a little; he turned his head again to see Lola, who was crouched at his pinioned ankle, her chisel still poised to dig under the iron. "Put that away, little one," he said. "Wrap it up in your sash again."

Lola picked up her sash, and tied it, thrusting the chisel through it. She knelt alongside him, smoothing his hair.

"Forgive me, Catherine," he said. "You are foolish, too, then, sometimes."

"Very foolish," Catherine whispered, her eyes filling with tears.

"It was so marvelously foolish to come. But it makes me feel very wonderful," he said "and much more clever than you two."

"But," said Catherine, as she looked at the heavy irons, "but, David, what . . ."

"Consider, Catherine," he said. "I haven't even had time to think—I've been asleep. But I do know this. You can leave this to me from now on." Then he remembered. "And to Tom," he added.

"Tom?" Catherine said, and in the quiet she listened for any sound.

"Aye, Tom. After all, it's our quarrel."

Lola said, "He is so stubborn a man, *señora*."

The grease from the candle spluttered, a bit of it flaring up with a hissing noise. David glanced at it; it was dangerous. He tried to move his hips a little, but the heavy irons around his ankles made moving difficult.

"If you had brought me a knife, it would have suited me better," he said thoughtfully.

Catherine said, "I did. I carried my little knife." She reached inside of her bodice and drew out the small pearl-handled knife.

"Put it down under my shirt, against the belt," David said.

Lola took the knife from Catherine's hand. "I do it, *señora*," she said. The knife was folded. David's smooth flesh, under his shirt, was warm to her touch. "I shan't tickle," she said soberly. His belt was tight, and she slid the knife under it, and let her hand rest flat against the hollow between his ribs for a moment. She felt the strong beating of the blood in the artery there. "I love you, David," she whispered.

"Do not worry about me," he said.

"I shall not," she replied proudly, looking at Catherine.

"You may leave this to me," he said.

"*Sí*," said Lola. "I will wait."

Catherine got to her feet. "I'll leave you, for a minute," she said, moving out past the light to the barred door. She stood close to it, and suddenly she said, "There's someone coming!"

For a second she stood motionless. Then she whispered, "I'll go now. You stay here for a few minutes, Lola! Then find Cosmos."

David said, "No!" He heard the door open, and then he heard it shut again. The candle had flickered in the draft.

Catherine moved forward in the darkness. At the foot of the ladder she waited, listening, for the distant footsteps that were coming slowly closer. She seized the rung of the ladder and climbed up.

The passageway was dark. There was no sound. The footsteps had stopped, and she leaned against the wood for a moment to catch her breath. Then she felt her way forward.

There was a burst of sound that tensed her whole body. Dimly she remembered the rockets. She went on. Now she could hear nothing, but ahead of her was a light, she realized that it had not been there before.

"*Dios*," she said under her breath. She had come the wrong way; she was aft.

A door banged; she heard a man's tread. She went ahead; she stopped, and did not know which way to go. Then there was another burst of sound, and the light from the rockets.

"*Dios*," she said again, helplessly, for she realized that someone must have gone out on deck, after she and Cosmos had walked through, and that this person was between her and safety. She heard the footsteps coming toward her, and there was nowhere to go except back. She turned and fled.

But the footsteps behind her were swift now. There was no excape, and she whirled around, leaning back against the wood, almost as she had been the very first time he had seen her. And like that time, he put his arm out to bar her flight. He put one hand against the wood behind her, not touching her; he stood over her, his white shirt making a spot in the darkness, not moving, not speaking, his breath coming a little swiftly. She smelled the tobacco on his breath.

She raised her eyes to his face. Her eyes were accustomed to the darkness; she could see that his shirt was open at the neck, the sleeves rolled up to expose the heavily muscled arms. A bursting rocket flared light into his face, briefly, from the doors he had left open.

She put her hands against his chest, flat. She felt his arms go around her; she bent back from him, but he gathered her closer, his mouth on hers, seizing now what he had wanted ever since he had first taken her into his arms that night on the *Santa Anna*. Even as she struggled against him, he lifted her easily and carried her to his cabin.

Chapter 18

CAVENDISH turned his head to look at the clock. It was ten. Two hours had passed. It had been two hours since he had carried her into his cabin, her hands balled up into two little fists against his chest.

She had fought him desperately. Now, as she lay beside him on the narrow bunk, his conquest was complete.

He smoothed her hair.

"I cannot keep you here longer," he whispered.

Her eyes had been closed. The long lashes went back; her eyes were shadowed; her parted lips fresh from his kisses. There was a bruise on her white shoulder. He laid his fingers on it gently.

"You're the first wench I've broken a rule for," he said.

There was hostility in the green eyes. He smiled.

"I forbid women aboard."

She ran her red tongue over her lips. "*Dios,* I hate you sometimes," she said.

His hands caressed her. He kissed her. "Tell me you love me," he said insistently. "Tell me."

"No," she said. "No." She tried to escape his kiss. "You've no right!"

"No right?" he asked.

"But you are a man of honor and will not betray me," she said.

"I swear I'll beat you," he said.

"Not now, Captain," she said. "Let me go, Tom."

He shook his head.

"Tom." She was suddenly pleading with him; her hands on his head. "Tom, you'll not punish Cosmos? He did it for me."

His brows drew together. "I'll not need to punish him. He is probably in a sweat of fear. He'll not repeat this."

She said, "He'd do it again for me!"

He laughed then. The pure amusement, the real laughter in his eyes and on his lips, she studied. It went through her mind that she must later, some day, catch that expression on canvas, and the idea of it sent a quick joy through her.

"And if I punish him, everyone would know you'd been aboard."

She sighed. "I care not why you don't punish him. I was afraid you would, because you——"

"What?" he asked levelly.

She said simply, "You are going to try David on charges of mutiny, whether or not he's your own brother."

"Aye," he said. There was the look in his blue eyes that she had seen before—the look that asked for understanding but was willing to forgo it, anyway. "Listen, Catherine," he said. He drew her close and buried his head in the shining hair. He spoke softly. "I must sink the *Santa Anna*. I cannot leave the largest Spanish ship in the world afloat. That is why David rebelled. But there can be no mutiny aboard. None."

He continued. "I built the little bark for you. She will carry word of your plight to the mainland. I'm leaving food. Plenty. And weapons. This is a war, Catherine. Even for you, I cannot leave the *Santa Anna*. Did you see David?"

"Yes," she whispered.

He frowned a little. She had seen the results of his violence. "I was extremely angry," he said. "Look at me, Catherine." He raised his head, and she looked into his blue eyes.

He muttered an oath. It puzzled her, for she had never heard the expression before.

"Forgive me," he said. "That's no language for your ears. What did David say to you?"

"He told me he would not consent to be freed even if Lola and I could aid him. He said, 'This is between Tom and me.' Then I gave him my little knife."

"Good," Cavendish said "I was going to get a weapon to him, but it is better that you do it. David has three choices, under the law. None of them is pretty.

You must depend on me. The responsibility is mine. And David's."

"I depend on you," she whispered.

"You shall, from now on. You shall come to me, in England."

"We cannot marry," she said. "But I could live in London."

His hands tightened on her arm. "What are you talking about?" he said.

"I cannot marry you," she said. "You are wealthy, are you not?"

"Aye," he said. "Very wealthy."

"You have estates. An old name."

"True," he said. "Why?"

"You should have children. An heir. I have difficulty bearing children. I lost my second child."

"Jesu," he said, with relief. "I didn't know what in God's name you meant!"

"What did you think I meant?"

"How many men have supported you?" he asked.

Her green eyes blazed. "You dare say that to me? After you—after you spend your nights with Arabella!"

"I?" he asked. "Oh, well, that is quite different. You hardly expect me to have lived like a monk."

"A monk? You?"

"Jesu, wench, you are angry with me." He grinned. "But you shan't live in London, by yourself. The next time I leave you, you shall be tucked away safely in Suffolk."

"Oh," said Catherine. "Aren't there men in Suffolk?"

"How many duels do you want me to fight?" he asked.

She said soberly, "You do not trust me."

He looked down at her face. "You are too fair."

She said, "You are so selfish. I wish I were still fighting you. I wish—if I had not come tonight—if—"

He said roughly, "I was coming ashore later."

"You may take me ashore now," she said.

"May I?" he said. "Not yet, Catherine."

"Have you forgotten, Captain, you are breaking your own rules?"

He paid no attention. His blue eyes went over her possessively; his hands reached for her. Her anger would disappear in a minute.

"I want to hear you say you love me," he whispered.

Chapter 19

COSMOS MOVED SOFTLY about the small cabin. He moved softly and swiftly, taking away the bowl of soapy water, wiping the razor clean and putting it away. He picked up the white shirt Cavendish had worn the day before; sand sprinkled down as he lifted it, and he glanced over at his master. He filled an ale tankard and set it before him.

"I have told Master Moon, sir," he said.

Cavendish didn't answer. He glanced at the clock. It was twenty minutes before eight. Twenty minutes before David would be brought before him and his officers; forty minutes since he had left Catherine on the beach.

There was a little time to remember—to sit here, and to remember. Later he could sort out the memories, but now they were not yet memories but realities, and he could not believe that he would not see her again, and that the day and night they had had were gone.

She was near; he could almost hear her voice, touch the shining hair. In his ears was the sound of the surf. He recovered the smell of hot sand, as she had brushed it off her bare shoulder and sat up to look down at him.

He heard her say again, "I wish I had a clock. When I was little, I used to think the time passed slower if I could keep my eye on it and not let it go by without knowing."

He had sat up, too, smiling. "I'll make you a clock," he had said. "Hand me that little stick." He could feel the rough stick in his fingers as he drew a circle and notched the twelve hours of the day. He drew a line from north to south, and stuck the stick upright into the center of the circle. The stick threw a narrow line of shadow across the third notch in the circle. "You see, my love," he said, "it is three o'clock."

Now the improvised sundial would be washed away

by the tide. It had been gone when together they had
pushed the longboat from the sand, hoisted her sail, put
the hamper back under the seat, and come back to the
beach at San Lucas.

Catherine had wanted to sail the boat. In the early
hours, it had been a setting forth together into the mag-
nificence that only dawn and the sea can show to man.

"You shan't be afraid?" he had asked.

"No," she said, "I'm not afraid."

He had given her, before, the length of cloth of gold.
She said, "I'll wear that dress to court, with you."

He took the tiller because the freshening wind seized
the sails. "You are not looking," he said softly.

"I was sailing into the sun," she said.

"On purpose?"

"If I cry, it is because it is so beautiful this morning.
But I am not afraid."

His arm was around her. "You sail," she said, settling closer to him, knowing this was the last time for
many months that she could. He had told her about his
home, his estates in Suffolk. "Some day we shall leave
Trimley before dawn," she said, "and sail out together
again."

"Some day, my darling," he said, his eyes on the water. "Some day."

He knew she tried to keep back the tears. "Weep,"
he said. "It might help."

"I love you so much," she said, and he felt the movement of her lips as she spoke with her head pressed into
his shoulder. Then she lifted her head. "Every dawn I
shall be with you," she said. "The sunrise you watch, I
shall have seen too. When you are gone, I shall paint
you. When you are gone—"

The colors of the sunrise had faded. They were back
at San Lucas, at the edge of the row of tents. He
jumped out and pulled the boat into the shallow water,
and held out his arms to her. He set her on her feet.

There was nothing to say. All the words had been
spoken. They stood together, silent, close, tasting wordlessly their nearness to each other, suspending time,
thrusting away everything except this moment when
they were still together.

They were here, on this sandy beach. The ocean, the bay, were rough with restless waves and tumbled water. The sun was up. The wind was colder than it had been wont to be, these last days; the sky was patched now with bits of blue and ragged white clouds. The time was going by, and yet it would stand still and let them hold this moment long, just because they were still together.

She raised her head to look up at his face, searching the blue eyes and the hair at his temples thickly sprinkled with gray, and she lifted her hand to touch it once more. Her hand dropped down, and she felt a moment's sharp anguish; her fingers felt for his.

"Good-bye," she said. "Good-bye."

"Good-bye," he said.

There was no time to think—only to feel the severance that was coming between them.

"Good-bye," he said again. He turned away; he raised the sail, the sun shone on it, and the gusty wind made the ropes creak a bit. Before her rolled the water; it was the pathway over which he would leave her, and it was at the same time the way to home, the way to England, the way to a place called Trimley. He turned and raised his hand in a last farewell. And, alone on the beach, she waved back.

Moon knocked on the door.

"Good morning," Cavendish said. He began to speak rapidly. He spent only two minutes explaining to Moon the task he was to do this morning, later. Then he rose. "You understand? Then we'll go now."

"Aye, aye, sir," Moon said following Cavendish. He entered the great cabin at Cavendish's heels, watched his Captain sit down and speak to Havers; then Moon sat down himself and waited. Master Pretty and Fuller sat quiet; there was no sound in the cabin until the door opened again. Cavendish looked up as they brought David in.

David stood easily. He wore no doublet, only the bloodstained shirt; he was unshaven, and the ragged cut along the side of his jaw would obviously some day be a

ragged scar. He looked like the renegade that his mana-
cled wrists pronounced him.

In the silence, the door closed. The two seamen who
had escorted David had left the cabin. There were six
officers at the table besides Cavendish. There was no
one else but the man who was standing trial on the se-
verest charge that could be brought. Cavendish spoke,
and at the sound of his voice Havers felt the terrible
tenseness rise in his body. He kept his eyes on David.
This trial would be short and quick, and there could be
only one outcome.

Cavendish said, "Master Cavendish, first I must say
that, if it is your wish, I shall have brought here ten
other members of our company, as a jury. If you wish.
They are ready to be called."

Havers waited for the sound of David's voice. It was
even and strong. "There is no necessity for that, sir," he
said.

There was no necessity. Cavendish knew it. Yet as
many as forty men had sat in on a trial like this, rough
as it was. He looked straight at David. How many times
had he himself sat like this while David had stood
trial—but when there had been no witnesses, when it
had just been a matter of discipline, and the exertion of
his will over a younger brother?

He frowned a little. He had been silent, and they
were waiting; and David was not only his brother,
younger, but another man, and it was his fault too that
this had happened. They were both guilty.

"Master Cavendish," he said, "you are brought before us today on a charge of mutiny."

David's dark eyes met his. "Aye, sir," he said.

Cavendish said, baldly, "You plead guilty to that
charge?"

"Aye, sir," David said.

The tension between them was gone.

"I am guilty," David said. But there was no apology
in his voice. It was a statement.

Cavendish leaned forward and put his hands on the
table. "Sir," he said, "you and I are related by blood.
If you feel that this trial is insufficient, you may ask to

be taken back to England for retrial. That is your right, according to law."

David shook his head, and Cavendish saw he was seizing on his own responsibility now, taking it as his right, because it had always been withheld from him before. "No," David said, "I prefer your judgment and the judgment of the men here."

"Very well," said Cavendish. There were only a few sentences to speak. "Then, as an officer aboard Her Majesty's ship *Desire,* you are well aware that it is customary to offer any man under a charge such as yours, two choices of punishment. The first is death by the sword." Cavendish paused. He looked directly into his brother's eyes. "The second is abandonment. We should set you ashore, without a weapon, without accoutrements of any kind except the clothes you wear."

Memory flashed back through David. A year and a half ago he had first set foot on the *Desire's* deck. Without accoutrements of any kind. Now he would go forth again, this time alone.

"I shall take the latter course, sir."

"You are fully aware of the dangers of such a course?" Cavendish spoke earnestly, directly to David. "It is my duty to warn you. This is an unusual situation, for, should you choose abandonment, you will automatically become a prisoner of the Spanish. You bear the name of Cavendish. It is quite unthinkable that the Spanish authorities will allow you freedom."

His words were an understatement. He decided to amplify them.

"It is a choice few men would wish to take," he said. "Nuño da Silva, even though he was a Portugal and a prisoner aboard the *Golden Hind*—even then, after Drake released him, he was taken by the Spanish and returned to the Inquisition for questioning."

David spoke steadily. "I shall take the latter course, Captain," he repeated.

"Very good," Cavendish said.

"And," said David, "one question, if you please."

Cavendish nodded.

"If I should be able to accomplish it, if I should return some day to England, would I then still face the charge of mutiny, to which I have already pleaded guilty?" As he said it, he realized that only a few days ago he would have been afraid to confess aloud an almost foolish hope. Now he wasn't afraid; and strangely enough, no one smiled. He felt a flashing sort of triumph that he wasn't afraid to say openly what he had been thinking and planning.

"There's no precedent," said Cavendish. "No one has returned."

David looked from his brother to Havers. "I want to say good-bye to you, sir," he said, "and to thank you."

Havers stood up; he held out his hand. "Good-bye, David," he said, simply.

Cavendish's voice cut in. "Captain Havers is expert on naval and civil law. I should like to know what Captain Havers thinks of your question."

Havers turned to face Cavendish. "It is my opinion," he said slowly, "that Master Cavendish is freed on the charges as soon as he steps from the *Desire*. The law looks upon abandonment as death."

David said, "Thank you, sir."

"Then," said Cavendish, "you shall be set ashore, on this beach of San Lucas this afternoon, just before we weigh anchor." He stood up, and walked over to David.

The two men stood apart from the others.

"Good-bye," he said.

"Good-bye," David said.

Their hands gripped hard. Cavendish said, low, "I leave Catherine with you."

"Aye, sir!"

David turned, and in the silence after his going, Cavendish swung around.

"I'll need all of you, within a few minutes. We have business aboard the *Santa Anna*." Then he spoke directly to Moon. "And, Master Moon, if anything should go wrong with the job you are to do, and with the prisoner I expect you to bring back aboard—if anything should happen and that prisoner escape—I'll have you in irons, Moon."

Chapter 20

AT EXACTLY TEN O'CLOCK two boats pulled from the *Desire* to the *Santa Anna*. The wind was strong today from the north northwest; it flung spray from the choppy waves into the faces of the oarsmen.

"A good wind for our job," Cavendish said to Havers, as he clambered aboard the *Santa Anna*.

Captain Flores received him on deck. His face was remote, grave. His eyes seemed to look beyond the faces of the English. He bowed a little. Over his head, the colors of Aragon and Castile flew defiantly, for the last time.

Cavendish said, "Today our truce is ended, Captain."

"Sí, señor," said Flores, looking rather surprised at the number of English who tumbled onto his deck.

Cavendish glanced around to see Moon with ten men, all of whom carried loaded muskets. He almost smiled. Moon was taking no chances on those irons. "I believe, Captain Flores," Cavendish continued, "that you have removed, according to my instructions, all usable weapons, victuals, wine, and so forth, that will be helpful to you during your coming sojourn on San Lucas."

"We have," Flores said stiffly, his eyes full of remoteness.

Moon edged sideways, coming to stand by a Spanish officer; Tyler moved over behind Moon, the loaded weapon in his hand. Tyler was the best shot aboard the *Desire*.

Cavendish said, "Then, sir, it is my order now that you abandon ship. We have not too much time. Nor do we have powder to spare. I want to thank you for your co-operation. I want to congratulate you on the gallantry of your crew, and your women."

Flores said, "Our truce being ended, I see no reason, Captain Cavendish, that I should answer you with polite words. Your action of sinking the *Santa Anna* may mean death for our people. It shall certainly mean it for me, when I return to Spain, if God should ever will it. I have failed in my duty, and I shall never forgive myself. It is asking too much of mortal man—and my God will understand that it is, then, not possible for me to forgive you. I hope that some day we shall have the pleasure of taking you prisoner, to meet your just deserts."

Cavendish said, "I hope not. I regret, too. But I have two more requests. The first being the Portugal Enrique Roderigo."

Roderigo stepped forward.

Cavendish said, "You have asked me, sir, personally, if you might sail with us. The request was granted. We are happy to welcome you aboard the *Desire* for our return voyage to England."

Flores glanced at Roderigo with hatred. But Roderigo smiled and bowed, and then, briefly, Cavendish wondered at the wisdom of taking Roderigo with him. But it was done.

"Thank you, Captain," Roderigo said.

Flores was silent, so Cavendish went on. "My second request is that your pilot Señor de Ersola, also accompany the *Desire* on her voyage across the Pacific."

At the words, Tyler lifted the loaded musket. De Ersola did not move; he stood still, and then finally he stepped forward to face Cavendish.

"I shall not consent, sir," he said, his breath coming quickly.

Moon stiffened. His hand dropped to his sword. De Ersola glanced around; he saw Tyler, he saw Moon's face. He understood. Should he make a dash for freedom, and plunge over the bulwarks, he would be shot down like an animal. He said, calmly, "Why are you doing this, Captain Cavendish?"

Cavendish's face was inscrutable, since he was lying. "I need a pilot," he said. "You are an uncommonly good one."

"And you are also aware, quite, sir, that you cannot look to me for help. I shall not be ready to help."

Cavendish said, "You may change your mind, sir." His eyes were mocking.

De Ersola hunted vainly in his mind for the real reason for this action. Flores spoke up.

"This is kidnapping!" he said. "Certainly you are aware of that!"

"I'm quite aware of it," Cavendish said.

De Ersola stared at Cavendish in surprise. He said, "Think you, Captain Cavendish, that under any circumstances, I would help you navigate through the Filipinas?"

Cavendish smiled. "Circumstances?" he asked. "I can arrange circumstances so that you will beg to offer your assistance."

Flores' eyes burned; he cried, "I'll not allow you to seize this officer!"

"You have little choice," Cavendish said. "Moon, take this man into custody. Confine him. We'll allow him to have his sea chest. He might want it later . . . and we can use his maps."

Moon ordered two men to fetch de Ersola's sea chest. He never took his eyes off de Ersola. But Flores could not contain himself. "Yesterday," he said, "we learned that you beat your brother with your fists because he rebelled at your inhuman actions. Now I see why."

Cavendish reached out a leisurely hand and slapped Flores across the mouth. "I dislike you, Spanish," he said.

Flores drew up. He licked the trickle of blood off his lips. "May God curse you," he said evenly.

"And may He help you," Cavendish said. "And as far as my brother is concerned, I am abandoning him, here. You may do as you wish with him."

"So that is it!" de Ersola cried. "Captain Flores—"

"If you speak, I'll have you shot dead," Cavendish said. "Tyler!" He went on, "I am weary of this. Take him, Moon."

De Ersola was seized by the arms. His hands were bound quickly. He was hoisted over the side, and all but tossed into the waiting boat. Moon scrambled down after him. He sighed a little. His job was almost done. He took a loaded musket from one seaman and held it until de Ersola was safely aboard the *Desire*. He carried it until the irons were locked around his arms and legs.

Then he went back on deck and watched the *Santa Anna*.

The figures Moon saw on the *Santa Anna's* decks were now only the figures of the English. Flores and his officers had left. The sound of axes came across the strip of water. Moon saw Cavendish himself walking across the poopdeck. It was but a few minutes later that the first wisp of smoke curled upward from her main deck.

The men moved automatically about their task. They had done this many times before. The stiff wind from the northwest would aid them, fan the flames they were kindling; the fires crackled. Not yet could they be heard on the beaches, but soon.

Fires had been set fore and aft. Amidships, another fire was blazing already; it was this smoke Moon saw from the deck of the *Desire*.

Cavendish stook on the highest deck of the *Santa Anna*. Below him, in her poop, another fire already burned. He looked down at his men, and the fires.

"Abandon ship!" he shouted, and he ran down the narrow stairs to the lower deck. Havers came walking up to him.

"The fires below are well started, sir," he said as he and Cavendish crossed the deck together.

"Good," said Cavendish, absently. He swung down into his waiting boat, with Havers after him. "We'll stand off a little and wait until we're sure she's gone."

The wind blew strong. Aboard the *Desire* the men were already aloft; Master Fuller's voice echoed over the decks. The *Desire's* foresail filled; she came about a little, and put a safe distance between herself and the luckless *Santa Anna*. Astern, the *Content* did the same.

"Jesu, Brule has a voice," Cavendish said to Havers, for they plainly could hear Brule's commands.

"That's good seamanship," Havers said, watching the *Content*.

It had been only twenty minutes since they had left the *Santa Anna*.

"Look!" said Cavendish. Flame spiraled up from the *Santa Anna's* decks. Fire suddenly shot from the port holes astern and the wind blew a sheet of flames across her main deck.

"Her mainmast will topple soon," Cavendish said. "But that teakwood is tough."

"Any wood will burn," Havers said. "I don't see Captain Flores on the beach."

But at this distance it was hard to make out the figures on the beach. Cavendish turned away from the sight of the beaches, and watched the *Santa Anna*. The ship's bells rang out. It was time for mess. The men disappeared below. Cavendish saw Tyler cross the deck, pulling out his pocket knife, and wiping it off against his leg as he walked. The blade shone in the sun; Cavendish knew Tyler kept each edge razor sharp.

The knife. It was just such a small and deadly weapon that David carried beneath his shirt, or under his sleeve, or wherever he had hidden it. The knife Catherine had given him.

Cavendish swore under his breath.

"There goes the mainmast," Havers said, soberly. The crash of it echoed over the water, sparks flew high into the air. He, too, was leaving Catherine here.

"Christ, she's really aflame now," Cavendish said. She was a mass of fire; smoke rose in billowing clouds, but no longer could the smoke hide the flames.

"The funeral pyres of old do not match this." Havers' tone was low; he glanced at Cavendish.

Cavendish was silent. Should he relieve David of that knife? Where had David hidden it? Valuable as it would be to him, its possession was dangerous. Should he be tempted into using it as defense, the Spanish would kill him outright.

"I would like to see David," he said truthfully to Havers.

Havers said abruptly, "Leave him alone, now, sir! For God's sake, leave him alone!"

Cavendish looked out at the *Santa Anna*. She was wreathed in flames, her mizzen was gone, her upper decks were burning brightly; the smoke from her cast a pall over the water and way up into the sky. The fires licked upward, and played in and out of the smoke.

Cavendish said, "Another hour should see her burning to the water line."

"Aye," said Havers. It was almost done, now.

Another hour, and then David would face the Spanish sailors alone. They would set him on the beach, and then they would sail away.

"I don't want food," Havers said, lighting his pipe, tamping down the tobacco with his forefinger.

"I'm not hungry myself," Cavendish said. "I ordered a hearty meal for David."

"Thank God for that," Havers said. It was the only time he had allowed himself to reproach Cavendish. In a few moments, in the silence that followed his remark, he added, "Sometimes even I find it difficult to understand you, Tom."

Dense smoke billowed upward from the burning *Santa Anna*. The flames licked upward through it; now all her upper decks were gone. She looked like a floating walnut shell.

Fuller came striding across the main deck of the *Desire*. Moon was on the gundeck, and his orders were plain as six of the heaviest guns were run out. Cavendish wiped the sweat off his palms; he rubbed his hands on his breeches, and Havers stood silent, watching.

They were bringing David out. He walked along between two men, blinking his eyes a little in the sunlight; he looked over toward the quarterdeck, and saw his brother and Havers. He raised his hand a little, he smiled at Havers; and Havers knew it was the last time he would ever see him. Havers' eyes stung. He tried to smile back. Even at the distance, he thought David understood, because David slid easily down into the waiting boat and settled himself jauntily in the stern, as though there was nothing for Havers to worry about at all.

Havers watched the boat. He was not conscious of Cavendish beside him. It was a short row. The boat beached. And at the same moment Master Fuller told Pretty that they would weigh anchor now. David jumped out of the boat just as Pretty's voice rang out.

"Heave 'round!"

The men at the capstan bar went around once. The anchor was free.

"Heave her up!"

The cables creaked. David stood alone on the beach. The boat was pulling away. The topmen were aloft. Cavendish struck his hand on the rail.

"Jesu!" he said. "Why doesn't he make for the forests?"

Havers said, "Would you, Tom?"

Cavendish turned to look at him. "No," he said, quietly.

Havers smiled.

The boat was back at the *Desire's* side. Quickly it was hoisted on deck.

The guns spoke.

The salute to San Lucas rang out. Men clung in the shrouds, in the rigging. The tops filled, the mainsail squared, the flags flew bravely in the northwest wind. The sun shone fitfully on the *Desire's* blue and gold paint. The new sails glistened.

"South southeast," shouted Fuller, and below decks the helmsman swung the whipstaff hard to starboard.

The *Desire* was running full before the wind. She was low in the water, her hatches battened over a bursting treasure. Broad on the starboard bow the Cape of San Lucas went up its eight hundred and fifty feet; beyond it to the west the sun would soon be setting to throw the great ocean into a blaze of color. Night would almost come before the *Desire* rounded the Cape.

At the rail, Cavendish watched the curve of the beach, the darkening mountain. Sunset flamed across the sky, but he did not see it. The colors faded, the sky paled. Night had almost fallen when, with the *Content* astern, the *Desire* stood out on the broad Pacific.

PART
3

Chapter 21

DAVID WALKED toward the tents. Three hundred yards lay between him and the first tent. But he had walked only ten feet before he heard Lola's voice.

"David!"

He looked around in the direction of the sound. She was standing just within the shelter of the scrubby pines, a small gay figure. He started toward her.

He felt her hesitation, as though the trees meant safety to both of them. Then she ran to him, through the soft sand.

"I knew you were coming!" she took his hands. She grasped them firmly, pulling. But he stood still.

"No," he said, "I'm not running away."

Again she hesitated. "We could hide, together."

"No," he said. He could see figures of men standing down the beach, watching them, waiting.

"There is still time," she said quietly, following his glance.

He still held her hands, and he squeezed them tight. "Look," he said.

The *Desire* was under full sail. Her blue and gold stern, high over the water, left a churning white wake. Already she was too far away for David to make out figures on her decks. He looked back to Lola, and then to the beach ahead. More men were clustered before the line of tents.

"Lola, listen," he said quickly. "If I ran into those woods now, it would be good sport to catch me. And there's no living in those forests either. Not for long. But if you want to walk with me toward those tents, you may come. And—have faith in me, Lola."

"But I do," she said simply.

He released her hands. He thought she possessed the grace of a panther, and the pride of one, as he paced his steps to hers. Absently, he reached one hand to his torn sleeve, to tear it free; it was dangling. But she stopped him with a quick gesture; she started to roll up his sleeve.

"I can fix it later," she said. "I can mend it."

David nodded. "It's the only shirt I have."

"It is linen," she said. "Where is the little knife?" Her eyes were on the men ahead.

"Under my shirt, in my belt, where you put it," he said. "But I shall not use that yet."

They walked on.

"Do not hurry, and do not lag," he said warningly.

"*Sí*," she whispered. "Ah, my love, there are so many! But mayhap it is better that way."

"It is," he said, glancing down at her. "Five or ten men would be worse than fifty. The odds will be so great against me, Lola, that—" There wasn't time to say more. There were more than fifty men only twenty feet in front of them. Five steady paces decreased the distance to less than fifteen.

The tide was almost at its ebb. The beach was wide, but still David could not pass around the group of men without going down into the water. He walked forward, not changing his stride or his direction.

At ten feet, one man spoke, stepping forward a little. "Did you come back for Lola?" he asked. He met David.

David stopped. The men were staring at him speculatively. He saw he had surprised them; they were wondering what he was going to do. Lola stood calm and straight by his side. But other men had come to them, a semicircle of them.

The first man grinned mockingly. "It's the Captain's brother!" His voice pretended great surprise.

"Curse me if it isn't!" The answering seaman was a big bearded Spaniard who boasted a pair of boots. His black eyes fastened on David, and his smile disappeared. "I'd like to kill you with my bare hands," he said.

David answered in his fluent Spanish. "I doubt if you could," he said.

At David's words, two other men took menacing steps foward. The big Spaniard shoved one away with a rough push. Again he faced David; he started to speak, but David interrupted.

"If we're going to fight," he said, "then let the *señorita* leave us."

Lola raised her head high. She stood proudly at his side, waiting for the reply. But the big Spaniard said nothing; he kept his black eyes fixed on David.

"In any case," David went on, "it would be best that the *señorita* leave."

Lola swept David a curtsey. *"Adiós,* my lord," she said.

"Adiós," he said, turning his head to see her go. He waited while she walked away unhurriedly. When she was twenty feet away, he turned back to the Spaniard.

"Now," he said.

They had edged closer, all of them. "Let's hang him!" one man said, from the rear, and one very young boy said, "Maybe we ought to take him to Captain Flores, Sebastian."

The big Spaniard said, "Shut your mouth! I'll take him to Flores. Later. Look out there, Englishman!" He jerked his thumb in the direction of the *Santa Anna*. "Look at her! You dirty whoreson English!"

"I am looking," said David calmly. "Your name is Sebastian? Well, Sebastian, I'm thinking we can do something about her."

Sebastian was too amazed to answer.

"Have you been out there?" David asked.

Sebastian looked again at the *Santa Anna*. She was burning almost to the waterline, and thick smoke curled from her.

"Have you been out there?" David repeated. He, too, stared out at the smoking ship. "It might be possible," he said. "Take me out there."

"Go out there?" Sebastian asked. "Aboard her?"

"Take me out, and I'll go aboard."

"What'll you do?" Sebastian asked.

"I'll show you," David said. "I want to go aboard."

Sebastian looked at him the same way David had seen men look at Cavendish. With an incredulous, hopeful belief in their eyes.

"Sí, caballero," Sebastian said. *"Inmediatamente!"*

There was a ship's boat pulled up on the beach. Sebastian ran to it, calling out a jumble of names. One was the name of the young boy who had spoken in defense of David.

David waded out into the water and climbed in the bow. "Give way," he said to Sebastian.

"*Sí.*" Sebastian pulled at the oars. His wits were working as fast as his arms. "You were right, *señor,*" he said. "We did nothing. We watched!"

"There may still be time," David said, over his shoulder. He was standing in the bow; behind him the Spanish pulled steadily at the oars, ten men, one to each oar. David reached inside his shirt and pulled out the little knife.

The *Santa Anna* was coming nearer. Smoke obscured her; the wind dropped a little, smoke hung over her sides, and then blew away, and then curtained her again. David heard the ominous crackle of her woods; he saw flickering tongues of flame shooting up through the dense smoke. He made out her shape. He saw her bows clearly.

"Sebastian," he said.

"*Sí señor.*" Sebastian's answer was slow. Despair clouded his face again as he saw the wreck of his ship coming nearer. "She is gone!" he said.

David paid no attention. The blackened remains of the sterncastle were like a piled jumble of sooty ruin, but the bulwarks were still there.

"I see a ladder," said David. "Was that ladder iron?"

"*Sí,*" Sebastian said.

"Good," said David. "Pull to it."

A gust of wind blew smoke at them. David squinted his eyes. He was still standing, and he was conscious of his height; he was glad of it. He looked down at the knife in his hand; he saw the muscled bare arm with satisfaction, and out of the past he heard Cavendish say, "By God, David, you're as tall as I am, if you'd stand straight." How many years ago had that been? Eight, probably. How fast the time had gone. Now he was alone. The *Desire* was gone. David put the knife in his belt. The *Santa Anna* was dead ahead; the ladder was only a few feet away.

The men lay on the oars. Silently, slowly, the boat slid toward the *Santa Anna;* the wind blew the smoke away, and David reached out to touch the ladder. He drew his hand away again quickly. He had forgotten the iron would be too hot to touch. He swore silently. But he had been glad the ladder was iron. He steeled himself for the pain.

"Now," he said to himself, and he grasped the hot rungs with his left hand. He stepped onto the ladder, his hand reaching out for the third rung.

He almost let go. When he moved up, the skin tore away from his hand. Below him the boat rocked gently; now he could grasp the bulwark, and he pulled himself aboard the *Santa Anna.*

Ten feet from him the fires smoldered fiercely. The flames darted along the wooden planking. He edged forward, along the bulwark.

"Lay out!" he called back.

"Sí, sí, señor," came the singing answer. It sounded good in David's ears. He felt like Tom, yet he felt different; he knew, because he and Tom were different. Ahead of him was an open hatch. From it, smoke billowed, curling upward. He set his boot on the hot planking, gently. It was firm. His heavy boots protected his legs. He walked forward to the hatch.

The smoke obscured the interior. He drew a deep breath. He started down the hatch. Its ladder was still intact, and it was wooden. Foot by foot David descended.

At the bottom of the ladder he leaned down and felt the flooring with his hand. It was cool. He swore aloud. He climbed back up the ladder, made his way along the deck.

"I'm going fore!" he called to Sebastian.

He could walk only along the bulwarks. He noted that they were still high and strong enough. The masts were gone entirely, the upper decks were gone; nothing but a shell remained above the gundecks, but a shell would be enough, if they could save it. Excitement poured through him.

He had been walking fore, but the fires loomed up ahead of him. They were burning, almost merrily, and even while David walked, he saw a tongue of flame lick from the hawsepipe and go running down the anchor cable. He ran forward, heedless of the fires; he leaped a seven-foot section of ten-inch flames. Then, even as he watched, the anchor cable parted; the rope smoldered a little and the *Santa Anna* moved. She had been freed of one anchor; she had three left.

She moved a little, and David remembered the tide. It had turned, then; it was beginning to come in. He looked toward the larboard anchor cable. He called to Sebastian: "Bring her here!"

He ran to the ship's side and looked down. Sebastian was pulling at the first oar; the other men were pulling as hard. David jumped down into the boat.

"I'm going to cut that anchor cable," he said.

Sebastian didn't question him. The boat slid under the cable. David grasped it, sawed at it with his knife; the cable parted.

"Look out!" David shouted. "She's coming about!"

She was. She had been freed of both fore anchors; her bow was drifting around.

"She's pointing toward the beach," David said. "You see!"

Sebastian nodded. David, standing in the bow, looked down at the faces of the men with him.

"We can save her," he said bluntly.

The boat danced on a wave thrown up by the movement of the huge *Santa Anna.*

"We must beach her," he continued quickly, "else she'll sink. As soon as the bulwarks go, the water will pour in and she'll sink. Here. And we can never raise her. But if you can beach her—"

He looked at the *Santa Anna.* Her bow was pointing toward the beach; the tide was coming in.

"We can go aboard at the stern," David said. "We shall have to pay out the anchor cables. I don't want to cut her free of them. We'll need them later."

"Sí, sí, señor!" Sebastian cried.

"We can douse the fires when we beach her."

The boat once again slid under the ladder David had climbed before.

"Sí, sí, señor!" Sebastian said again—loud to the men: "You hear? You hear the *señor?"*

David, in the bow, hitched the painter around the rung of the ladder. He sprang aboard, and the ten men followed him.

"Now," said David, "get below and get those bilge pumps working!"

Sebastian said, *"Sí, sí, señor!"*

"You stay with me—I need you." He swung around and scowled at the ten Spaniards. "Get below!"

"Sí, sí, señor," Sebastian said—and: "You hear? You hear the *señor?"*

David was already at the capstan. Sebastian seized the bar. "Heave!" he cried.

The anchor cable payed out slowly. The *Santa Anna* moved, sluggishly. David and Sebastian worked steadily. Below, water began to pour from the pumps.

The *Santa Anna* had moved. Minutes had passed. David lifted his head. "We'll rest a second," he said.

There was not much time. He looked aft; the bulwarks were almost gone, and the sea was lapping the edge of the charred wood. The wind blew gustily, from the land, still from the northwest. But the current of the incoming tide was a trifle stronger.

"Heave," cried David, heaving on the heavy bar with all his strength.

The precious minutes fled. The anchor rope was slack, yet the *Santa Anna* hesitated between the current and the land wind; then she moved toward the beach and the slack disappeared. Again she strained on the anchor ropes.

"We may have to cut them," David said. "But not yet."

Sebastian dripped with sweat. The water lapped at the sides of the ship, eagerly, ready for its prey. The anchor ropes hung slack again, and David straightened up for a minute.

The *Santa Anna* moved. She moved a little faster. Again David measured the distance to the beach. He wiped the sweat from his face with his sleeve. And suddenly he saw why they had moved farther.

"Oh, Lord," he cried, "the wind is shifting!"

The wind was changing. The air was very still. A last furtive gust blew from the land, and then off the sea, like a miracle, came the south wind, lazy, fresh, ruffling the surface of the bay with its first draft of salt air. The wind was with them, and the *Santa Anna* heaved toward the beach. In ten minutes, her bows felt the sand; she trembled a little, and was quiet, like a wounded animal that had found safe harbor.

David straightened up. "So!" he said. "Now we'll pray these anchors hold."

David ran to the hatch. Suddenly he stopped. He bowed. A man had climbed up over the side and was running toward them.

David said, "Captain Flores, we've beached the *Santa Anna,* and I believe we can save her!"

Flores said, "I see you have, sir. I see you have!" There were tears in his eyes. David saw he was trembling. Then he went back to what was left of the rail. David heard Flores' voice raised in thunderous orders; David saw there were boats hovering all about the newly beached ship. He could reach out and touch them; he could lean over and touch water.

A bucket was thrust into his hand. He dipped it into the sea and brought it up; the water hissed as it hit the deck, but David didn't stop to watch. He dipped the bucket into the water again and heaved it across the planking.

All pumps were manned, in shifts. Water. It ran over the planks, and smoke so dense no man could see through it poured from the stricken ship. Into that smoke more water poured. There was no thought to this; it was labor, and long labor, and hour after hour passed by. One hundred and thirty-five men labored together. No order was needed. Only water, precious, lifted from the sea, to save a ship.

The sun had long since set. The wind still blew gently, lazily, off the south. The mists came; indeed they had come long before, on this lazy wind. Mist mingled with the smoke and the smell of burning pitch. The wind had changed. The night was almost still. The wind had changed, and the miracle was wrought.

Chapter 22

"THE WIND is changing." Cavendish said, suddenly, to de Ersola. He got to his feet. "Perhaps not," he said, looking at the clock. He paced across the tiny space. "I've told you, sir, that all I spoke, and did, aboard the *Santa Anna* this morning was lies. I want nothing from you—no aid, no maps, no service as a pilot. I'm going to ask you to forgive me, but it was my brother."

De Ersola said, "You know I would not have allowed him freedom, and you feared I should exact the penalty, did you not?"

"Aye, sir, I did. Flores is different from you. With Flores, my brother has the barest chance of life. With you, he had no chance. I gave Flores ample reason to hate me—and to sympathize with David."

"True," de Ersola said. "Your slap at Flores fooled him, but not me."

"I did not expect it to." Cavendish turned to face the pilot. "And I'm guilty of kidnapping; I'm guilty of making you a prisoner, undeservedly, and I hope you will allow me to make proper restitution to you. I offer you passage to England, and sanctuary there, or I shall set you ashore on Luzon, not far from Manila. I shall ask of you only your parole."

De Ersola hesitated.

"Aboard the *Desire,* I'll need your parole, sir. You can understand that."

"I can," de Ersola said. "Unless I want to spend the voyage below." He glanced at Cavendish thoughtfully, and took another gulp of his ale. His eyes seemed suddenly amused. "Tell me Captain," he asked, lazily, "do you play chess?"

Cavendish grinned. "I do," he said.

"Well, then, I demand another honest answer. Do you play well?"

Cavendish chuckled. "Better than you."

"Impossible," said de Ersola. "I'll give you my parole." He got to his feet and held out a brown lean hand, and Cavendish took it. Both men were smiling.

"Thank you, sir," Cavendish said. Then his face sobered. "The wind is changing," he said. He heard the slatting of the sails. Without a word he went through the cabin door. He went out on deck.

"Master Fuller!" he shouted.

"Aye, aye, sir," came the answer.

"Three lanterns in the stern!" Cavendish ordered. "Strike the tops!" Mist blew in his face. He swung around and peered into the mist and the dusk. He could not see the shape of the *Content*. He watched the lanterns hoisted, as a signal to her. Three lanterns meant shortened sail; three lanterns meant change course to due south.

Havers appeared on the poop deck. He saw the gleaming lanterns.

"The wind changed in a minute," he said. "Look at that mist."

Captain Brule was on deck when the wind changed. He gave the order to shorten sail, and he hurried into his cabin to look at his charts. He had to light his lamp, and he bent over the charts, reassuring himself again that he knew them well. He put out the lamp and went back on deck.

He could not see the *Desire*. There was only mist to see. He frowned.

The wind was too light. He glanced upward at the sails. He paced the deck restlessly. He peered ahead. No lanterns shone through the mist. The mist was thick now, it lay on the backs of his hands and his hair. His leather jacket was slippery to the touch.

He peered ahead. He went down to the boat deck, crossed it, and mounted into the head. There was nothing to be seen. Had it been only five minutes ago he had seen the two lanterns winking? Two lanterns hung in the *Desire's* stern to guide him?

"I see naught, sir," the lookout called down. "I can see no lights"

Brule stayed in the head. The mist floated past him.

"Lay aloft!" he roared suddenly. An officer came across to join him.

"I don't want to lose the *Desire*," Brule said. "The wind's light. I'm going to hoist the tops."

"Aye, sir." The two men stood together, looking ahead in the darkness.

The ropes creaked; the tops filled slowly; the *Content* leaned gracefully, her bow throwing up a fine spray as she dipped.

"I'm going to stay on deck, sir," Brule said, mopping the wet from his face with a wet hand.

"Can I fetch you something, sir?" the officer asked.

"Aye, you can. Fetch me a cloth," Brule said. "Fetch me two cloths."

The officer moved away. He was back quickly, and Brule wiped his face and head gratefully. "That's better," he said. "Curse this mist."

"That wind changed so suddenly," the officer said. "One minute I could see the *Desire's* lanterns, and the next I could not."

An hour passed. Brule had used two more towels. He turned to the officer with him.

"We'll change course," he said. "Change course to due east. Sir, I'm going to have something to eat."

He strode away. While he ate, he studied the charts again. He went below and watched the compass. He stayed by the helmsman about fifteen minutes. Then he climbed back to his own quarterdeck again.

He was there when the dread cry came from the lookout. Twice it was shouted, and even then Brule could hardly believe it.

"Breakers ahead! Breakers ahead!"

Chapter 23

"IT WAS A MIRACLE," Captain Flores said. He sat down heavily on the bench beside the rude table on the beach. He was almost overcome with exhaustion. "God sent us the wind."

Catherine said, "Drink this, sir." She held out a cup of wine, and Flores took it gratefully.

"Tonight I shall drink this right down, *señora*," he said.

"Bless you, sir," Catherine replied gently.

He smiled at her. "I expect you want to ask mercy for the Englishman."

"I do," Catherine said.

He said slowly, "There are orders from Philip."

Catherine said, "But you have not received them yet, sir. You know of them only through hearsay."

Flores looked surprised. "True," he conceded, "and yet—"

"You have not received them, sir! He saved us. Mayhap he was the miracle!"

Flores lifted his eyes from his cup of wine. It was empty.

"A little more?" Catherine asked.

"No, no, *gracias, señora*. I never deviate much, my dear. I am thanking God," he added. "Magellan said a man should never go to sea without faith in his God." He looked up. "Here comes the Englishman, *señora*."

Catherine rose to her feet. "I pray you," she said urgently.

The mist was still thick. Fires burned on the beach. Their glow was eerie. David was walking past the fires, two Spanish officers were with him; they were talking rapidly, gesticulating, and Catherine saw David grin—a sooty, reckless grin. At the same moment, Flores rose; he went toward David with a steady stride; he met the three men near one of the fires.

"You cannot see her for the mist, sir, but she is safe. The fires are quenched."

It was one of his officers who had spoken. He continued, "I've left thirty men aboard to watch tonight."

"That watch will be changed at twelve, sir," Flores said. "And again at four, as usual."

"Sí, señor."

There was a moment's silence. On the beach, the Spaniards were sprawled, sitting or lying, after their grueling task. They watched and listened; sitting up now, edging closer. Flores was about to speak, when Lola came into the scene.

The Spanish officer stepped to one side, and Lola stood beside David. He put his arm around her, her face lifted to his.

"Your hands," she said, lifting his hand gently, and turning the palm up.

"Burned a little," David said.

Lola looked at Flores, seeing again the black eyes, the pale cheeks above the short white beard. But she waited for David to speak.

"Sir, I've come to surrender myself."

Flores measured David with his eyes. In Flores' nostrils was the smell of charred wet wood; the mist floated past him, bringing the stink of the wet wood off the sea. He looked at David; he noticed one of his men named Sebastian had come and was standing close behind David, his eyes fixed on his Captain.

"You are a brave man," Flores said aloud. "Your action has saved our ship."

Sebastian nodded vigorously.

David said, "Thank you, sir. When I left her now, she put me in mind of the Ark."

Flores stared at David.

"Like the Ark," David continued, "she will sail you to safety." He was conscious only of intense weariness; even the pain in his hands was second to the deep desire only for a place to sprawl out. With detached envy he glanced at the men lying on the beach, half asleep.

He was not conscious of fear. Flores would not hang him immediately, he was sure. Flores was too kind-hearted; he would allow his prisoner at least until tomorrow morning, at six. David tried to stifle a yawn. But Flores was still silent, his eyes filled with a kind of excitement. He held up his hand, and said slowly, "Sir, you have come to surrender yourself. But I do not accept it!"

David's arm tightened about Lola. "I thank you again, sir," he said.

"You are weary," Flores said. "This morning I learned why you mutinied against your brother. I cannot take your life. I am proud to welcome you among us. I shall give you all the aid I can. Even in Acapulco, for some day we shall land there. In our Ark."

"Gracias, señor," David repeated. He felt dizzy; he lifted his head and drew a deep breath. *"Buenas noches, señor,"* he said.

He walked the short distance to Lola's tent. She gave him wine, and he lay down on the pine bed. Lola pulled off the heavy boots. She gave him more wine; there was cold fish, and she fed it to him in her fingers, while her tears dropped steadily down her cheeks. He slept for a few minutes while she brought water.

She bathed his face and neck. She rubbed salve on the injured hands, and bound them up with strips of cloth torn from a petticoat. He dozed, and when he wakened at eleven, she fed him again, a thick broth of dried peas.

"It's good," he said, lying on his side, while she fed him with a spoon.

"Catherine lent me the spoon," Lola said. "Here, my love, you've not eaten it all."

"I shall," he said.

He finished the broth. He drank another cup of wine. Then he raised himself on his elbow and looked around the bare tent. Lola followed his eyes. His only shirt was soaking in a bucket of water.

"I shall mend your shirt," she said.

His mind was in the future. "It will be weeks before we can sail," he said. "We must fashion sails from this canvas."

Lola smoothed his hair. "It gives me great pleasure to do for you, David," she said. "Catherine has gold, though. From your brother, for you. I told her you would not take it." She stopped suddenly, and gazed at him. "Was that right, David?"

He regarded her long.

"Was that right, my lord?" she whispered. "You do not want his gold, do you?"

He said only, "Hand me that boot, Lola."

She obeyed.

"Now reach in and lift the lining."

Her fingers felt for the lining. It lifted easily. She withdrew her hand. Gold lay in her palm.

"Put it back," he said. "I have all we need. And some jewels. Put it back, now, and give me both boots. I'm going to place them alongside me, over here."

Lola put the boots alongside him, as he asked. "Can you sleep now?" she asked.

"Aye. Come to me."

She put out the lamp. He felt her lie down beside him. He turned over on his stomach, drawing her close to him, leaving his arm across her, laying his head on her breast.

"Good night," he said sleepily. "If I'm too heavy, push me off."

Chapter 24

ABOARD SHIP, Cosmos always rose at five. He rolled up the mat he slept on, dressed in the dark, and slipped out for water for his Captain.

He appeared in the galley just as the stoves were being fed their morning quota of wood. Cosmos filled a tin basin and set it atop the galleystove to heat. Then he disappeared in the direction of the head.

By the time he returned, the water was beginning to steam. It was still dark. The cook put a cup of wine and water in front of Cosmos.

"Thank you," said Cosmos gratefully. He did not always get an extra cup of wine. He watched the water.

"Here's the other basin," the cook said cheerfully. "How's the Captain?"

"Still asleep," Cosmos replied.

"We're under very short sail," the cook said. "They say he expects to sight land soon."

"So?" said Cosmos.

The cook grinned. "You never know anything, do you? Your water's hot."

"I take it," said Cosmos, flipping open a clean towel; he held the basin with the linen. "Thank you for the wine."

He made his way aft with care, for the water was very hot. Inside the cabin, he lighted the lamp, and began to shapen a razor. He filled a cup with cool water, and laid out the implements for his master's toilet.

Cavendish stirred in his sleep. Cosmos turned quickly to watch him, his almond eyes intent on his master. Cavendish muttered something; Cosmos listened. Then Cavendish said, quite clearly, "David!"

Cosmos turned away; if his Captain should wake, Cosmos did not want to be caught staring. He heard Cavendish sit up. There was a moment's silence, and then Cavendish said, "Good morning, Cosmos."

"Good morning, sir," Cosmos replied.

Cavendish stretched his arms over his head and yawned. Cosmos handed him his toothbrush and the water.

"The stars are still out, sir," he said.

Cavendish drank off the water. He stripped off his rumpled shirt, and Cosmos looked at his naked chest and shoulders with admiration.

"You want hurry?" he asked.

Cavendish didn't answer. Cosmos slipped a clean shirt over his head. Cosmos was used to his silence. The Captain never changed, Cosmos thought.

"We sight land this morning?" he asked, as he stood over Cavendish, razor in hand.

"Perhaps," Cavendish said.

"I hurry, then," said Cosmos.

He was very deft. "Some day you have mustache, sir?"

Cavendish smiled. "I used to wear one, in England," he said.

"Perhaps again, then?" Cosmos spoke hopefully.

Again there was no answer. Cosmos finished, dried the razor, and tied the lacing at the throat of Cavendish's shirt. Cavendish stood up.

"I'll return in thirty minutes," he said, as always. He closed the door behind him, and Cosmos went to work to clean up the cabin. It was always this way; it never changed. Cavendish was always on deck to see the sunrise. For thirty minutes each morning, he paced the poopdeck alone, while the world grew light. It had been this way for seven weeks. Even on the mornings on which they had still hoped to see the *Content,* it was the same. Now Cosmos knew there was no hope of ever seeing the *Content* again. The Captain had mustered the crew to speak to them about it, and he had said that he believed the *Content* had been lost that night in the mist; and he had bid them bow their heads and repeat a prayer with him. He said they must have faith.

Cosmos had been standing next to Tyler. He had tried to follow the words Tyler had repeated. Tyler had never taken his eyes off his Captain, and Cosmos whispered, after Cavendish was done speaking. "He is a wonderful man, is he not?"

"He is—" Tyler began, and then broke off. "He's a better shot than I am even, Cosmos."

This morning Cosmos hurried. It was getting light. Through the porthole he could see the sea heaving and gray, and Cosmos jumped to put out the lamp. He had forgotten to do it as soon as it was light in the cabin. And he had very strict orders never to allow the lamp to burn after it was not needed. Guiltily he gathered the wet towels and the basin, and struggled out with them.

At six o'clock the first calls came from the lookouts. Cosmos put the last mouthful of biscuit in his mouth, fished for the piece of salt pork with his fingers, and laid down the basin. He put his knife, with which he ate—there were no spoons—into his belt, and hastened up on deck.

"Land ho! Land ho!" the echoing steady call came from the lookout. On the poopdeck, Cavendish had lifted the glass to his eyes. Cosmos saw the smudge ahead of them, off the starboard bow. There it was. Land.

"It's Guana!" cried the man next to him. Cosmos watched him start up into the shrouds. He had no desire to follow; he stayed on deck, while most of the crew scrambled aloft to see for themselves. Cosmos saw de Ersola, smiling, mount to the poopdeck.

"You are almost as good a navigator as you are a chess player," he said. "You've accomplished the fastest Pacific crossing in history. Thus far," he added.

"Aye," said Cavendish thoughtfully. The crossing had cost one ship and the lives of twenty men. The price might seem high, but Cavendish knew it was not. It was a small sop to the vastest ocean in the world, uncharted, its many islands guarded by its blue swells. He had known, as he watched the sunrise this morning, that more lives would be lost before he should see England again; they were sure to be forfeit. He had begun his voyage with one hundred and twenty-three men; he had lost two ships, and sixty of his crew. He had lost his own brother. So much had it cost already to chart the courses that other men would follow some day.

The sea was gray, a mirror of morning. Off to the east, low clouds hung over the water, but above them the sky was palest blue, shot with gold, and suddenly the rising sun splashed a pool of fiery red against the gray ocean.

"With this gentle gale, we should fetch the island about one o'clock," he said.

"Are you going to land?" de Ersola asked.

"With only sixty crew, I do not dare," Cavendish answered. "I am going to spend about ten days in the Filipinas, sir, in Spanish waters."

"I see," said de Ersola.

Cavendish swung around to look at him. His blue eyes were level. "You remember your parole, sir?" He watched de Ersola carefully, steadily.

"Your words are a warning, of course," de Ersola said. "You deemed them necessary?"

Cavendish looked sardonic. "War," he said curtly.

"We fight for a rich prize, do we not, Captain?" de Ersola asked, almost dreamily. He glanced at Cavendish and smiled. "Would you care to see my map of China?"

Cavendish burst out laughing. "What a disarming fellow you are," he said. "Will you breakfast with me, sir?"

"Yes," de Ersola said. "You know, if you hadn't gambled your King's pawn last night, you would have won."

The sun shone. The half-naked sailors clustered on deck, waiting. The island was coming steadily nearer. Tyler squatted on deck, carefully guarding the five rude pieces of old iron; one he had tied to a fishing line, to be ready. Guana was two leagues to the west, yet, but the sea was already black with native canoes.

"There must be a hundred of them," Tyler said.

Master Fuller was standing before the mast. "Only about seventy, I'll warrant," he said. He raised his voice. "All hands aloft," he shouted, and Tyler reluctantly dropped his fishing line and started up the shrouds.

"Strike the tops!" Fuller shouted.

From the poopdeck came Cavendish's voice. "North northwest, Master Fuller."

The mainsail veered. The spritsail was furled. All around the *Desire* clustered the native war canoes with their triangular sails. The natives stared at the blue and gold paint, and the gunports, and the faces that looked over the rails at them.

"I want to stand into the harbor, Master Fuller," Cavendish said, as he came walking across the boat deck.

"Aye, aye, sir," said Fuller.

Cavendish walked over to Tyler.

"Do you see that, Tyler? Those canoes aren't above half a yard in breadth, and some seven or eight yards long. And those—those must be canes, thrust out on the starboard side. Toss the line down."

"Aye, sir," said Tyer, happily. He swung the fishing line, with the piece of iron, into the big canoe right below him.

The natives yelled and laughed. They tied a big fish to the line, and Tyler avowed that he had never caught so large a fish before. He tossed the line down again.

"Send a coconut!" he yelled.

A big naked savage, with his long hair twisted into two knots atop his head, grinned back. Tyler pulled up a coconut.

"The bastard looks like the carved devil on the head of their boats," Tyler remarked.

Cavendish laughed. He was trying to make out what the savages used for sails. "I believe they are made of sedge grass," he said, "and they sail as well against the wind as before."

Tyler had tied another piece of iron to his line. "What will you take for your wife?" he shouted down.

Cavendish smiled at him. "Are you married, Tyler?" he asked.

Tyler, said, shyly, "No, sir. I'm fickle. Like you, sir."

Cavendsh said nothing, but Tyler wiggled his bare toes a bit apprehensively. But Cavendish seemed to pay him little attention. He was looking down at the big canoes that clustered closer than flies around the *Desire*. Suddenly one canoe came too close. The *Desire* stemmed into it; the natives dived overboard and swam;

their heads appeared above water, and they swam like fish to the nearer canoes.

Cavendish straightened and looked around. The deck was piled with coconuts, potatoes, wriggling fish and fruits.

"Tyler, follow me," he said curtly.

Tyler dropped his line. "Aye, aye, sir," he said hastily, looking sideways at his Captain.

"And where did you hear such a rumor?" Cavendish asked.

"Everywhere, sir—on Fleet Street."

Cavendish strode ahead, saying nothing. Tyler climbed up to the poopdeck and stood waiting.

"You were confined before sailing, weren't you, Tyler?"

"Aye, sir."

"And have you been gambling lately?"

"No, sir. I swear to God I haven't."

Cavendish grinned. "Master Moon," he said, "have six muskets made ready and brought to me." He raised his voice. "Master Fuller, trim all sails, sir!"

The *Desire* quickened her way, but there were even more canoes around her.

"There are a hundred of them," Moon said. "Here are the muskets, sir."

Cavendish took one, and started to load it. "Give one to Tyler, Master Moon," he said. His own was ready to fire.

"Quick now, Tyler," he said. "We will discourage these natives with a little gunfire."

"Aye, aye, sir," said Tyler eagerly, as Havers came bounding back to the deck. He walked over beside Cavendish and raised the weapon.

Cavendish did the same. "The man in the head of the farthest boat dead astern," he said.

The gun fired.

"A hit!" Tyler cried, enthusiastically.

Cavendish was reloading the weapon.

Tyler did not hesitate. "The same boat, sir," he said, "the man in the stern."

Again the musket spoke.

"Another hit," Cavendish said.

From the five canoes near the one at which Tyler and Cavendish had shot all the natives plunged into the water fearfully.

"Hold your fire," Cavendish said. "I think they'll disperse now. Wait, Tyler. Try for the man in the head of the farthest boat abeam."

"Aye, sir," said Tyler, raising the weapon again. He fired.

"No," said Cavendish. He raised his own weapon.

"No, Captain," said Tyler, grinning. "You hit the canoe. Look at them dive for it!"

Cavendish laughed. He handed the musket back to Moon. "They'll leave us alone now, Moon," he said. "All right, Tyler, get back and help clear off that deck."

"Aye, aye, sir," said Tyler. He smiled at Cavendish. "Thank you, sir," he added. Then he said diffidently, "Wouldn't you like that big fish dinner, sir? It was so fresh, it was alive."

Cavendish said, "I would like it. And if there are any lemons, tell Cosmos I want half of one served with the fish."

"Aye, sir," said Tyler, happily. "I'll tell him, sir."

Guana dropped astern. The wind was still from the north, and the *Desire* ran before it, under full canvas. Cavendish alone was on his deck.

He had made landfall correctly. That much was done. So also was the warning of de Ersola accomplished. For ahead were the Filipinas, Spanish islands, and the *Desire* boasted only sixty crew. A small force. And only one ship to combat the many the Spanish could send out for him.

He began to pace restlessly. There was one more thing he should do, before the next day or so was up. It was three hundred and ten leagues to the Filipinas. Eight days of sailing—or more, if storms blew up. The weather since he had left California had been so mild that he now expected storms. He looked up at the sail over his head. The mizzen would have to have new sail, in the anchorage he wanted to find. Safe anchorage, pleasant, not too warm. Drake had used the Celebes, but it was foul with heat and fevers there. Anchorage in the Filipinas would be best, even if the Spanish were

near. Catherine had said the women were pretty
enough, and the natives friendly. Aboard he carried the
three Filipinos who had sailed on the *Santa Anna*. They
could translate for him, so he could talk with the natives. The men could rest and eat, and work, and enjoy
the native women. Eight days and he should be anchored in the Filipinas, unless they ran into foul weather.

They did. Six days out of Guana, the gray of morning
did not lighten as the invisible sun rose. There was no
wind; the *Desire* was almost becalmed on a molten sea.
The sails slatted disconsolately.

"The blow will be soon," Cavendish said. "Master
Fuller, strike all sails!"

The wind was upon them in so few minutes that men
were still aloft. Below, the helmsman disconnected the
whipstaff, and lashed the tiller. Cavendish went to his
cabin for a leather jacket, and came out on deck to ride
out the storm. It lasted for two days. On the fourteenth
day of January, at nightfall, the winds began to drop a
little. The *Desire* dared to show a little canvas, and
Cavendish spent his time between the poopdeck and the
compasses and charts in his cabin. At the beginning of
the middle watch, he went forward to speak to Fuller.
The two men talked in low voices. The night was black.

"We'll lie at hull all during this watch, sir," he said.
"I think we'll sight the Filipinas at daybreak."

"Aye, sir," said Fuller. The ship's bells struck the
hour.

"Time for the watch," Cavendish said. "I'm going to
get a little sleep between now and four, sir."

"Aye, aye, sir," said Fuller.

Cavendish disappeared; he made his way alone aft
with care, for the rain was slanting down into his face.
He stumbled against a kneeling figure.

"What do you do here?" asked Cavendish, his voice
harsh.

De Ersola shouted back, "I wanted something in my
sea chest, sir."

There had been no place below to store de Ersola's
chest; it had been lashed to this deck. De Ersola hung

onto the running ropes. "I wanted something in my chest, sir," he repeated.

"This is an odd time to want it," Cavendish said. Neither moved, and the *Desire* pitched suddenly, and both had to heed not being thrown overboard. The wind was howling around them, and they were soaking wet.

"I could not sleep," shouted de Ersola. "I have always had a weak stomach."

His voice sounded plaintive and Cavendish knew that the admission of a weak stomach might very well be true, and it amused him. "Good night," he said, and left de Ersola standing there, on deck, in the dark.

He made his way to his own cabin where Havers waited for him. He rose when Cavendish came in, but tired as he was, Cavendish did not sit down.

"What news?" he asked, his mind on de Ersola instead of his question to Havers.

Havers puffed on his clay pipe; the cabin was blue with smoke. He said, "John Gameford is sick again, sir."

Cavendish was not surprised. He didn't expect John Gameford ever to see England again. It was an old illness that troubled Gameford, who was a cooper and in charge of casks and barrels aboard the *Desire*.

"Is he keeping any food on his stomach at all?" Cavendish asked.

Havers took the pipe from his mouth and shook his head. "We tried the hot wine, as before."

"Then leave him alone and let him rest and sleep," Cavendish said "I'll see him in the morning. I've been watching the weight drop off him."

Havers put the pipe back in his mouth. "I have too," he said, and glanced at Cavendish, who looked drawn and weary. Was he losing weight, Havers wondered, or did he just imagine it?

"Gameford has excessive pain in the stomach," Havers said."But he doesn't complain. The storm tosses him a good bit."

"It will blow itself out in a few hours. We're lying ahull until daybreak, Havers. We ought to see the Filipinas when the dawn comes." He leaned over and pointed to his chart. "We should fall in with this cape,

Cabo del Espíritu Santo. It should be a matter of minutes."

"I know," said Havers. He watched Cavendish sit down and bend over the chart, resting his head in his hands; and he watched the preoccupied look come over his Captain's face. Then Cavendish lifted his head.

"Havers," he said suddenly. "I want to speak with you a few minutes."

Havers crossed his legs comfortably. "Certainly, Tom."

Cavendish hesitated. "I've made a new will," he said. "It's in the box with our commission and the reports. I wanted you to know it was there, in case I shouldn't live to return to England. In case of accident."

"I see, Tom."

"You know how I am. I thought it wisest to take account of the fact that I might not return. All my share of this voyage, sir, and all my estates, go to the Señora Catherine, unless David survives. Then Trimley is his, or his heirs'."

"I see," Havers repeated.

"You might be confused by the name of the *señora*." Cavendish paused, and Havers didn't know what he meant. "You see, Havers," he said, bluntly, "Catherine's my wife."

Havers, who rarely cursed, was startled into the first half of an oath. He took the pipe from his mouth.

Cavendish said, "It was complete madness, I know. It was eight weeks ago tonight, at just about this time, Havers."

"My felicitations, sir," Havers said. He started to rise and hold out his hand, but Cavendish was looking at the floor. Havers sank back into his chair.

"I lifted her out of the boat," Cavendish said. "I had wrapped a cloak of mine around her; her feet were bare. In the moonlight I could see her clearly."

He had been able to see the shadow of her lashes against her cheek; the wind had been soft, the moonlight shimmering over the water and the white beach. He had looked down at her, and holding her thus he had started up the beach.

Her eyes opened. "Where are you taking me?" she had whispered, finally.

"To find the priest," he said, almost roughly.

"But—" she said.

His even stride carried them toward the line of trees.

"I would wed you, Catherine," he said. "I want to wed you now!"

"Would it occur to you to ask me. Captain Cavendish?" she had asked.

Suddenly he had smiled. "It did not occur to me, wench." Happiness flooded him. "You have the most beautiful smile!"

Cavendish looked up at Havers. Then he said, "The priest consented to marry us, without witnesses. He lighted two candles, and we knelt; I took her hand, and we repeated the vows together. She was cold; she was shivering a little, the cloak fell off her shoulders, and I put it around her again. She was all mine, Havers, the way I wanted her to be. And now—I know it was madness to marry her!"

"It was," said Havers, concealing his anger.

Cavendish frowned.

"You are about the poorest man for a husband I can think of. The only consolation is that she wanted it this way. What a fever she put you in, Captain."

"Fever?"

"I don't know what else to call it," Havers said. "You were mad for her, Tom. Why not admit it?"

"I have admitted it!"

Havers smiled.

"I swallowed the hook. Deep, I told you," Cavendish ended.

"I know you did," said Havers. His gray eyes looked at Cavendish. "There's still the voyage, Tom, and that reminds me. The Portugal Roderigo wants to see you."

"Now?" Cavendish asked. "Tell him I'll see him when I'm ready. I'm not fond of him, Havers."

"He says it's important."

"Important? Tell him I'm the judge of what's important." Cavendish crossed his legs and leaned back. "I'll see him when I'm ready."

Chapter 25

THE DAWN had not yet come to California; the January day was not yet born. The stars were still bright, the night dark, but no light burned aboard the bulky *Santa Anna*, with her improvised masts and her dirty patched sails. Only in one tent did a light burn, and David sat on the bare ground beside it, hiding its light, so that a great shadow was thrown up on the tent walls by his seated figure. His hands were clasped over his legs.

"I could not tell you before," he said. "I did not want you to know."

I am glad you didn't," said Lola.

"We shouldn't burn this lamp!"

"But I cannot talk to you without seeing you, your eyes, for what you say to me is so often in your face, and not on your lips!"

"That isn't true," he said, shortly.

"Only in that—" she hesitated. " 'Tis true! I know *now* you want to take me; I didn't before! In the dark."

He rubbed at his bearded cheek. He frowned, his scowl deep. She didn't interrupt his thoughts. She knew he would speak them aloud in a minute. He did.

"Flores could not protect me, once we should land at Acapulco. Flores is part fool, Lola. He's too kind for command. He is likely to lose his head because of the wreck out there—" He gestured toward the water and the once proud *Santa Anna*. "From now on, Lola, I shall be a fugitive, and trust to myself. It will be safer."

"I would be so little trouble," she said.

For the first time in their talk together, he smiled.

"I am learning my English so well, now. Why should you teach me English and leave me?"

He threw his hands up helplessly, and began to laugh.

"I go with you," said Lola.

She did not smile. She looked extemely sober. Then she rose to her feet and began hastily to fill a canvas bag.

"Hurry," said David, glancing at the lamp beside him. "Don't let me forget this lamp. We need it."

"*Sí*," said Lola.

David watched her as she opened her one wooden chest and lifted out her sewing box. She put that into the bag, filled it with her clothes, and methodically began to fill the wooden bucket with the tin basins, the pan, the two spoons.

"Don't make a noise," David murmured, and then they both heard Sebastian's voice.

"*Señor*," *Sebastian whispered*.

David jumped to his feet and moved noiselessly to the tent flap. He opened it, and Sebastian slipped inside.

"We are ready, *señor*," he said.

"So are we," Lola returned, raising her eyes to Sebastian's face.

Sebastian looked at her, and then at David. David nodded. "I cook," Lola whispered. "I sew."

Sebastian pulled down the corners of his mouth. "I cook," he said. "I sew."

Without a word Lola handed him the bucket, with the few household utensils inside. There was little silence. Then Lola said. "I cook and sew better."

David grinned. "She comes," he said.

David put out the lamp. Lola carried the bag, and Sebastian the bucket. At the water's edge was a small crudely built boat; it had one seat. Lola crouched in the bow.

The little boat pulled away from shore soundlessly. The oars dipped. No one spoke, and when they reached the bark anchored so near shore, Lola stood up and grasped the ladder.

Sebastian held the boat steady. David climbed aboard, and pulled Lola up after him. Sebastian handed up the few belongings; the little boat bobbed, empty, alongside the bark as the three of them crossed the small deck and entered the only cabin.

Two men awaited them.

David set down the lamp. Sebastian put the bucket down and straightened up; between them stood Lola, carrying the canvas bag.

"She comes," David said.

A man named Juan nodded, smiling a little. The other man spoke.

"It is folly," he said.

David pulled out a leather pouch and tossed it to him. "Count it, Gomez," he said. "Fifty pieces of gold for your help tonight. What we agreed on."

Gomez felt the pouch with his fingers; he did not open it. His eyes fell from David's. "I count it later," he said. "But I am not sure. About—"

"What?" asked David. "What aren't you sure about?"

"We risk our lives to take you tonight. For this." He squeezed the bag in his hands.

"Whoreson coward," said Sebastian. "Your life is not worth a peso to anybody."

Gomez was the only man among the four of them who wore a sword. He put his hand on the sword hilt. "I go with you tonight," he said. "As we agreed."

"Good," said David. He motioned to Sebastian, and the two of them left the small cabin. Out on deck the stars still shone brightly.

"I'm going ashore," David whispered. "I'll be only thirty minutes. Watch Gomez."

Sebastian said, "A knife in his back, *señor*?"

David shook his head. He stepped down into the small boat. "No," he said. "Not yet."

It was only four minutes before he beached the boat. The whole camp was dark and still. He entered Catherine's tent.

Catherine was awake. She stood as he entered, but he took her arm and let her back to the hammock. She sat down in it and he knelt; their faces were level.

"It is time, then?" she whispered.

He put out his hands to take hers.

"Aye," he said. "Lola is going with me."

Catherine held back a little sigh. David squeezed her hands tighter.

"I leave you alone!"

"You can do nothing else," she said. "Nothing else. I have Kate and Tina."

"I know." He began to speak rapidly. "Gomez didn't want to be persuaded. He said he did not want to betray Flores' trust in him. But he took the gold, as we agreed. We are ready to sail. We'll watch him carefully. It is very easy, Catherine. There is no way of catching us. We shall cross the Gulf of California, and hug the coast; there are small islands too. I know them. Tom put in to a number of them. For his charts."

Catherine said, "Then where—"

"In Navidad," he said. "You will sail tomorrow, and I shall watch for you. The *Santa Anna* will be very slow."

She said, "But it won't be safe for you in Navidad!"

"No, but I shall see you there. Now, did you destroy the marriage papers?"

It was a while before she answered, and in the darkness he scanned her face anxiously.

"I hid them," she said. "They are safe."

"Safe? Catherine—I've warned you!"

"I shall destroy them, if it becomes dangerous."

"They are already dangerous," he said, more quietly. He rose to his feet; there was little time. "I shall see you in Navidad; it may be six weeks."

"The *Santa Anna* is very slow."

They stood together. David suddenly drew her into his arms. "I shall see you," he said, almost fiercely, "in Navidad!"

He turned and left her.

At his going she went back to the hammock slowly. The gray-white canvas made a spot in the darkness. She drew her feet up into the hammock and closed her eyes. The dawn would come soon. It would be the last dawn she would see here, in California. The days were gone, now; the colony was almost gone. On the beach the little row of women's tents was all that remained. The canvas of the tents for the seamen had been used for sails, and the men slept in the open, under the stars.

This morning would be the last morning that they would cook over the fires on the sandy beach. The men had gathered the last of the wood, the children the last of the pine cones. The flag had been hauled down over the wooden house; it flew now on the masthead of the *Santa Anna*. Her bulwarks were strong and new; she wallowed deep in the water; she had no upper decks at all, but canvas stretched across for protection from the sun and weather. She was ready to sail.

Sleep came to Catherine. She dreamed. Restlessly. She dreamed, and she saw Cavendish's face clearly. Only as she heard his voice and saw him smile, the dream changed, and instead, she saw his face on her canvas, and she was lifting her hand, with the brush in it, and instead of him himself it was the portrait in front of her. She had worked so hard on it these last days. She woke, quickly, remembering.

The first rays of dawn were in the tent. She rose. She was fully awake. Was the portrait as good as she remembered it? Yesterday she had finished it. Outside, it was barely light; she dragged the rough easel to the doorway of the tent and uncovered the portrait.

Her heart beat fast. She looked at it critically, her head to one side; the light was cold and gray on it. On the canvas the blue eyes smiled at her, the mobile mouth was curved in laughter, and the thick hair was short and rough. She brushed away the sudden tears. It was good. It was the best thing she had ever done, and the joy in creating and the pain of longing were close and sharp together inside her. She turned from the portrait.

The bay was smooth. The little bark was gone. David and Lola were gone, and—he—he was very far away. Across a wide ocean. He would have sailed by Guana by now; this morning he should watch the dawn from the Filipinas.

The beach was still quiet. There was no sound of voices. She covered the portrait, and left the tent. She walked along the beach, slowly. The sand was cool and its grains were wet against her bare feet. She walked faster, taking pleasure in movement, feeling the cool morning wind off the sea. She walked purposefully, in the direction of a single lonely tent. When she came near, she heard movement within.

"Padre," she said softly.

A deep voice answered her. The priest knotted his girdle around his waist; he lifted the tent flap.

"Good morning, *señora,"* he said.

His hair was gray and thin. His eyebrows were gray. From under them, he studied her.

"Padre—I—" She looked up.

"We'll walk this way," he said. "To see the dawn."

She fell into step beside him. The camp was rousing, and they walked along the shore, past the tents, toward the river.

"This will do my legs good," the priest said. "It will be the last time we shall walk here, *señora."*

"I know, *Padre,"* Catherine said.

"We sail on again," he said.

She said low, "You mean that for me."

"Yes," he said. "We go on."

"I want to go on," she said firmly. "I want to go! Why should it then—our going—make me feel that my last link with him is gone, too?"

She had stopped walking. The first colors of the rising sun were in the paling sky.

"Would you pray with me, *Padre?"* she asked. "If I knelt, would you say the words and I will say them after you?"

"Why?" he asked. "Why, Catherine? Can you not say the words yourself?"

"No," she said. "I want to, and then I think of all I have, and that I am strong and well, and that I can paint, and my child is good; that I have a man to love, and that the *Santa Anna* was saved. Then I feel grateful, Father. I have been given so much, Father! I feel it is wrong for me to ask for more, when I am so grateful for what I have!"

He said slowly, "Catherine, my child, the times when I feel nearest to my God is when thankfulness is in me."

Catherine said, "What shall I say to Him, then, Father?"

"What do you want from Him, Catherine?"

"I don't know!" she said.

"Think," he said.

"Enough courage and faith," she said.

___"Then kneel down and ask for it," he said. He looked out toward the sea and the beauty of the new day. He put his hand on her bright head. "I think it has already been granted you."

Chapter 26

IT WAS the fourteenth of January. The day had begun in California. But three thousand miles to the west, the night was still dark and angry. For four hours, all during the middle watch, the *Desire* had lain ahull, her helm lashed alee, while patiently she rode out the last of the Pacific storm.

De Ersola slept heavily. He shared a tiny cabin with Roderigo the Portugal. He slept on his back, his arms folded across his chest, his hands lying protectively against his body.

The Portugal slept less heavily. He was ready to wake. He had not drunk much wine last night, in the Captain's cabin, nor had he played chess with the Captain until two o'clock. Roderigo was not in need of more sleep, and at the first of the dawn's light, he roused.

The wind had abated. Roderigo could tell from the motion of the ship. He sat up in his hammock and looked to his sleeping companion. Jealousy filled him. Then he rose.

He walked the two steps to de Ersola. He leaned down and put his hand gently on de Ersola's chest, his fingers probing. It was still there—the paper. It had been there ever since the first night of foul weather. Roderigo stepped back and began to make more noise. He put on his shoes.

De Ersola didn't rouse until Roderigo had left the cabin. Then he turned over on his stomach and went back to sleep. He had plenty of time. He came up on deck much later, when the sight of the Filipinas was plain, for the *Desire* had fallen in with a mighty cape, with high land in the middle and low land trending far into the sea westward; she had fetched the Filipinas, in the sailing of the course from Guana, eleven days and a night.

He was almost alone on deck. He smelled food; it was the first cooked food they'd had aboard since the storm. Below, no doubt all hands were enjoying it. But de Ersola felt no hunger. He had drunk far too much wine last night, and lost the game because of it. But ale would taste good; he was thirsty. When Cavendish appeared, he would ask him to join him in a tankard.

The wind was gentle. The *Desire* had entered the Straits between Luzon and Camlaia; it was already hot, and the sun shone. He knew these waters so well. Just fifty leagues away was Manila. On the rail his brown hands lay listlessly, yet within he was conscious of uneasiness, and it wasn't due to wine. He stared ahead at the clustered islands, lying green in a blue sea. Thirty minutes later Cavendish appeared on the poopdeck.

He waved his hand to de Ersola, and lazily the Spaniard mounted the high deck.

Cavendish was looking through the glass. He nodded to de Ersola.

"Keep her on the larboard tack, Master Fuller."

"Aye, aye, sir!"

Cavendish lowered the glass. He handed it to de Ersola. "Capul," he said.

De Ersola raised the glass to look at the island. "Good harbor," he said. "Will you have some ale? Lord, I am thirsty!"

Cavendish grinned. "I'll join you later."

"Then I'll find Havers," de Ersola said, knowing it was no use trying to talk to Cavendish now. The Captain was intent on these waters; they were new to him. De Ersola watched Cavendish run down to the lower deck, glass in hand, and saw him start to talk to Fuller.

The island of Capul was palm-fringed and lovely to the eyes. The water was deep blue. Here was harbor. The harbor lay through a narrow passage between Capul and an unknown island. There was a ledge of rock lying off Capul, over which the tides rippled, and the great lines of breakers gleamed white in the sun. But the water between the reef and Capul was deep and running smooth.

"There'll be no danger," Cavendish said. "There's

water enough a fair breadth off, and within the point, a good harbor."

"Ten fathoms," called the leads man.

Cavendish noted it down.

"Eight fathoms," called the leads man.

Cavendish noted it down.

"Eight fathoms, eight fathoms, seven and a half, sir."

The *Desire* put about a little.

"Six fathoms, six fathoms. Five and a half, five, sir, five."

They were within a cable's length of shore. The beach, the palms, were very near. The anchor cables creaked, the *Desire* lay upon the untroubled water. She was anchored in four fathoms of water, hard aboard the shore.

No sooner was she come to anchor than a big canoe put out from shore. The *Desire's* crew hung over the rail and shouted. The canoe drew nearer; the English seamen stared at the occupants. They were tawny in color, their skin carved and cut with sundry devices. They were bringing food, for they had watched the *Desire* maneuver through the narrow channel between island and reef for an hour or more.

"One yard of linen for every four coconuts," Cavendish ordered, "and the same for each basket of potatoes."

Master Pretty gazed at the basket of potatoes.

Cavendish smiled a little at him. "Ah, sir, are they not excellent sweet, either roasted or boiled!"

The chief Casique climbed aboard and stood there, in his nakedness, looking around. Cavendish went down to talk to him.

The Casique thought they were Spanish.

"English," said Cavendish, "and we will pay you for food." He held up the linen. "This much for four coconuts." He demonstrated.

The Casique smiled, and nodded his head. He called instructions down to his companions in the canoe, and they began to row back to shore. In the meantime, Master Pretty took the basket of potatoes and disappeared in the direction of the galley.

"Camotas," the Casique said, pointing to the potatoes.

Cavendish said, "Potatoes. Bring more." He drew the man aside and started to talk with him further, memorizing quickly the Casique's names for the foodstuffs he had brought.

"Hogs," he said.

The Casique said, *"Balboye,"* and nodded, again smiling. "Hogs," he repeated after Cavendish.

The crew eavesdropped. They were going to get pig, fresh pig. Their mouths watered.

"Hens," said Cavendish. Havers brought up a bag of money, and Cavendish showed it to the native. "Eight *rials* for every hog, one *rial* for each hen or cock."

The native's eyes grew big.

"We are English," Cavendish said. "We trade, and pay you. We do not steal."

De Ersola had come up. He made a rude noise. "Are you the harbinger of a new era out here?"

Cavendish laughed.

"For a bloody pirate, you sound remarkably peaceful today," he continued, as Cavendish and he went up to the poopdeck.

Cavendish kept on chuckling.

"Trade," said de Ersola. "Trade mixed in with a little well-applied force, when it's needed. That's right, isn't it, Captain?"

"Look at the wench," Cavendish said, leaning over the rail to suit his words.

Right beneath them was a canoe with a small boy and a young woman. Both were using the long paddles. Cavendish reached in his pocket and pulled out a nail. He tossed it down to her, and she caught it deftly, and held it up.

"I guess this means a ration of nails issued to the men," Cavendish said. "Else they'll be digging them out of my ship."

De Ersola laughed. When he leaned on the rail, the paper under his shirt crackled; he stepped back quickly. "I'd like to plant a flag on this virgin territory," he said. "May we go ashore?"

He was well aware of the quick glance bestowed on him by Cavendish, even as Cavendish smiled at his words.

"Perhaps tomorrow," he said.

The smell of roasting hens was wafting though the warm air from the galley.

"Jesu, I'm hungry," said de Ersola. He hadn't eaten yet today.

"So am I," said Cavendish.

He was a magnificent animal, de Ersola thought. Hungry, and wary, too. He measured the distance to shore.

"There are sharks," Cavendish's voice said quietly. He did not give de Ersola a chance to answer him; he did not want an answer. The ship's bells sounded. "We can eat soon," he said.

Dinner took a long time. When de Ersola came out on deck later, the swift tropic night had fallen over the islands and the blue water and the shining white of the breakers on the reef. The stars were low and golden and there was nothing to hear but the sound of the surf.

The ship was silent. The boats had been hoisted back on deck; the ladders had been pulled up. Way below, the water shimmered. De Ersola made his way across the deck to his chest.

The lookout called down to him, his voice friendly. The officer of the watch was standing fore, talking low, and de Ersola opened his chest and drew out a clean shirt for the morrow. While he knelt alongside the chest in the darkness, he took the white paper from under his shirt, and put it in the chest, and with his shirt in his hand, he rose and locked the chest again. He went aft.

He walked slowly. The night was calm and peaceful. The wind was soft. Capul was in thirteen degrees; it was not so hot as usual. Sleep was what he needed, he knew, for his plans were made. Only sleep was what he needed.

The passageway was dark. He opened the door to his cabin. There was no light, but he didn't need one. He bent down to loosen his shoes, when he felt himself seized from behind.

He did not cry out; he did not fight the hands that

held him. One hand was clamped over his mouth; he was lifted and carried. And still he made no move to struggle or speak, because he knew that if he did he would be killed. Quickly. And he knew who it was who must have betrayed him.

The ship was silent. There was still no sound. On deck, the officer of the watch—it was Moon—did not move; he could see the chest dimly. In the passageway, aft, Tyler ran on bare feet, soundlessly. He knocked on a cabin door, opened it, and entered.

"Sir," he said.

Cavendish looked up from the chart which lay in front of him. "Well?" he asked. Tyler was trying to control his amazement and excitement. He tried to speak calmly.

"He went to the chest, sir, as you said he might. He took out a clean shirt. Then he went back to his cabin!"

"Go on," said Cavendish, laying down his pen.

"Then—by God, sir—then someone was waiting for him and they took him to the great cabin!" Tyler would have continued, but Cavendish's voice interrupted like a whiplash.

"How many?"

"Three of them, sir! He made no move to stop them, sir!"

Cavendish rose to his feet, and Tyler looked hastily away from his Captain's face. He was supremely thankful that he was not one of the culprits.

Cavendish flung open the door; he was running down the passageway to the great cabin. He did not pause. Tyler was right behind him when he opened the door and stood framed in it, his dark head bent a little, so he could enter.

The scene flashed before Tyler's eyes. Berkeley and Mills stood at each side of de Ersola. Tyler hadn't been able to recognize them in the dark. They had tied de Ersola's legs to the chair, and in front of him was Roderigo. Tyler even caught the last words of the sentence which he and Cavendish had interrupted. There was a knife in Roderigo's hand.

At the sound of the opening door, Roderigo whirled around. His face was pale with fear.

"He is a spy, Captain!" he cried, desperately, as Cavendish advanced toward him.

"He had a letter! I saw it!" Roderigo cried again. He dropped the knife from his hand and fell on his knees before Cavendish. "Captain," he said, imploringly.

"Be quiet," Cavendish's voice said over his head. Berkeley and Mills knew enough to keep silent; they waited until they were spoken to.

Cavendish said to de Ersola, "My apologies, sir."

He bent down himself and untied the knots of rope. There was no sight of blood on de Ersola. Roderigo hadn't yet had time to use the knife. He pulled one rope free.

"Thank you, Captain," de Ersola said, standing up. Then he was quiet, too, waiting.

"Now," said Cavendish, turning his gaze toward the two seamen. "What are your explanations? Mills?"

Mills said hopelessly, "None, sir." Then he pointed to Roderigo. "I believed him, sir," he said. "I thought you were being tricked."

Roderigo could not keep silent. "It is true He would have betrayed us!" He was still kneeling, crouched on the floor at Cavendish's feet, and without a word Cavendish raised his heavy boot. The heel caught Roderigo in the temple, and knocked the Portuguese sideways to the floor.

"You thought I was being tricked, Mills?" Cavendish asked directly.

"Aye, sir," Mills said.

"And you, Berkeley?"

Berkeley said, "The Portuguese said there was a letter, sir. We wanted to find it."

"You did?" Cavendish asked.

Tyler had thrust his hands into his pockets and was looking very superior and pitying. Berkeley glared at him.

"You will both be punished for this," Cavendish said. He looked up and saw Moon in the doorway. Moon's eyes were round and surprised.

"I left a guard on the chest, sir," he said at first. "I heard voices below. Señor de Ersola did go to his chest; he spent two minutes with the lid open."

"Tyler was watching Señor de Ersola," Cavendish said. "Tyler apprised me of this"—he waved his hand at the scene—"this attempt to make Señor de Ersola talk. Moon, will you summon Captain Havers, sir? And take these two men into custody. The Portugal will be confined to his quarters."

"Aye, sir," said Moon. Roderigo was sprawled on the floor, and he motioned to Mills and Berkeley to pick him up. They carried him from the cabin. Cavendish and de Ersola were alone, except for Tyler. Slowly Cavendish spoke.

"Your sword, please, sir," he said.

De Ersola pulled the weapon from its sheath.

"I had been watching you, sir," Cavendish said. "Tyler, light this overhead lamp."

"Your game, Captain," de Ersola said. He sighed.

"I didn't plan on Roderigo's interference," Cavendish said.

"I should have killed him before," de Ersola said. "But it might have made you more suspicious."

Cavendish sat down in his chair. He motioned de Ersola to the chair at the end. "Sit down," he said. "Havers will be here, in a minute. And the others. We are going to open your sea chest, sir, in full view of the gentlemen and officers who will be gathered here."

De Ersola reached in an inner pocket. He brought out a flat key. "I'll give this to Havers when he comes," he said.

"Thank you," Cavendish said.

De Ersola sat, unmoving. Havers came in, and spoke to him stiffly; the other officers appeared.

De Ersola only half heard the words that Cavendish spoke. He looked up at the silver lamp, lighted overhead. The cabin was hot; he was so used to this heat, here in the Filipinas. Manila was so close, and so familiar.

They had brought his chest in. Havers had taken the keys; he had opened the chest. For how long had that chest accompanied him? It held all his life. One by one they were laying his maps out on the floor. Havers was careful. Then, just as carefully, he laid out de Ersola's personal effects, his shirts, a red embroidered scarf, a Bible. Finally Havers had emptied the chest and de Ersola looked on calmly. Havers lifted the thin teakwood lining and straightened up. In his hand was a letter. He handed it to Cavendish.

The letter was heavily sealed with red wax. It was addressed to His Excellency the Governor of Manila. Cavendish broke the seal and began to read. The letter was short. De Ersola knew every word of it. Briefly, it described the *Desire*. It told of the capture of the *Santa Anna,* and of de Ersola's enforced position on the *Desire*. It gave the *Desire's* position at the island called Capul, being but one ship with small force, and said that His Excellency should use any means to surprise the English there at anchor, for the place the *Desire* rode was but fifty leagues from Manila. There was one last injunction.

"Let this Englishman escape," de Ersola had written, "and within a few years you must make account for your towns' and your ships' being besieged and attacked by an army of English."

Cavendish looked up from that last line. His eyes met de Ersola's. He handed the letter to Havers.

What de Ersola had written was the truth. Cavendish knew it, and he knew that had he been in the Spaniard's place, he would have done the same thing. Parole meant truce, and there could be no truce, because the war had not ended. Nor would it end for many years. But the penalty for breaking parole was death. De Ersola had gambled his life.

The officers had finished reading the letter, and Havers handed it back to Cavendish. Cavendish held it up. There were only a few brief words left to be spoken now.

"This is your letter, is it not, Señor de Ersola?"

"Yes, it is, sir," de Ersola said. "May I have it back now?"

"No," said Cavendish. "I wish to keep this evidence against you. For my report."

"I see," said de Ersola.

Cavendish said, "Then the matter is most manifest to us, now, having been made so by this trial and this proof."

"Yes, sir," said de Ersola calmly.

"Thus," said Cavendish, his voice well modulated, neither strong nor soft, "it is our judgment and will that you be double ironed and confined until six o'clock tomorrow morning, and at such time that you be hanged from the larboard fore yardarm, and may God have mercy on your soul."

De Ersola pushed back his chair and stood up. Moon jumped to his feet; de Ersola went to the door, with Moon following him. At the door he waited for Moon and Master Fuller to fall in step with him. Then he turned again. "*Adiós,* gentlemen," he said, bowing, and the door closed.

The letter still lay on the table in front of Cavendish. On the floor was de Ersola's sea chest, battered and scarred. Cavendish raised his eyes from the chest, and he was about to say that he hoped to God that he or any of them would have met defeat with as much courage, when he checked himself. De Ersola had no need for such a testimonial. He rose to his feet and left the cabin.

Below, de Ersola waited for him, knowing he would come. It was not very many minutes, either, that he waited; almost as soon as Moon had left him, he heard Cavendish's tread, and the door that Moon had closed and barred opened again. Light flared up.

De Ersola smiled at the sight of Cavendish. His arms were full. He was carrying tankards and ale, and under one arm was the chess set and board. He set the lamp down, throwing de Ersola's face in shadow, and de Ersola was glad because the shadows concealed the quick tears that had come to his eyes—unwarranted, he thought, angry with himself. But there were so many men who would not have had the courage to come and face him, and talk with him; this man who was his enemy was also one of the finest friends he had ever made.

Cavendish put down the chess board. Leaning down, he unlocked the irons around de Ersola's arms and legs. He moved the lamp over, and the two men, unarmed, faced each other within the small circle of light. They were both sitting.

De Ersola said, "I thought you would come."

"I wanted to spend the time with you," Cavendish said. "If you wanted me."

"I do," said de Ersola, and his brown eyes were warm.

Cavendish turned aside to pour ale into the two pewter tankards. He set one of them in front of de Ersola, raised his own to his lips. Both men drank, de Ersola quickly, as was his wont, Cavendish more slowly, as if he wanted fully to savor the taste of the dark ale. It was hot, too; Cavendish's shirt clung to his chest and back and shoulders. For a second, de Ersola played with the notion of flinging himself forward at Cavendish, who was still drinking slowly, but then he knew that would be folly beause even if he could possibly overpower his opponent, he still could not leave the ship. Else he would have left it before.

Cavendish set down his tankard. "D'ye want to play?" he asked. De Ersola nodded, wiping his mouth. "Black?"

De Ersola nodded again, and began to pick out the black pawns. He always arranged the pawns first.

"I like to use the blacks," he confessed easily. "I know my weaknesses," he added.

"One of them is that of not giving up," Cavendish said, placing the white ivory chessmen in their respective squares.

De Ersola smiled. He knew that was the only reference Cavendish would make to his breaking of his parole. He knew Cavendish understood why he had done it.

"Your move," he said.

Cavendish moved the King's pawn two squares. De Ersola followed suit; he stared down at the board, watching Cavendish's brown fingers pick up the King's Bishop.

De Ersola followed Cavendish's opening moves automatically. He said, "No matter where you go, Captain, you always leave something you love behind."

Cavendish picked up the tankard of ale. His blue eyes claimed agreement.

Again de Ersola stared at the board. The chessmen swam together; this was the last night he would live, and he had decided on this course himself. The fight had been unequal, and he had lost it. Again and again, Cavendish had warned him. He had even put the clumsy Tyler on guard, so de Ersola knew for certain that he was being watched. But tonight he had not thrown the letter overboard. He had still hoped there was some way he could get it to Manila. A native runner—so easy to bribe.

"Your move," Cavendish reminded him.

De Ersola concentrated on the board. He studied it for a moment, and he saw that his opponent had no intention of letting him win easily tonight. De Ersola smiled. Lord, he had put himself into a bad position, but—he squinted thoughtfully. He wondered if Cavendish knew that he perceived the trap that had been laid for him on the board. If he pretended ignorance, in nine moves he could checkmate. It was wonderfully neat, too. He started to rub his chin, and then remembered that would be a warning to Cavendish, for Cavendish knew he had that habit when he was pleased with himself. De Ersola moved right into the trap; he lost his Bishop in the third move after that, but he was still going to win. His brown eyes glinted as he moved his men precisely and without expression.

The dawn came. The sun was up and over the tops of the palm trees. The sky turned blue and gold. The wind was gentle, and strange birds sang. De Ersola came out on deck into the early sunlight. He came slowly forward until he and Cavendish stood together, and it crossed de Ersola's mind that Cavendish looked tired and worn, and then de Ersola thought that probably he did, too. They had been up all night.

He had dressed himself in his finest suit, with his red-embroidered scarf flung over one shoulder. He carried his Bible.

The crew were mustered on deck. The rope hung over the larboard fore yardarm, swinging lazily in the wind. The drum corps assembled before the mast. It was ten minutes before six.

De Ersola knelt down on the deck, clasping his hands over his Bible, and his eyes were closed, his head bent. He prayed silently, asking forgiveness for his sins, and even while he did that, he wondered what prayer he should use to his God, in these the last few minutes of his life.

Then he began, and the sonorous Latin, so softly spoken, was clearly heard by the men around him.

"Pater noster, qui es in caelis, santificetur nomen tuum—"

He raised his head and opened his eyes to see the light of the dawn.

Cavendish's blue eyes were on the dawn and the sky. Under his breath he repeated the prayer in English.

"And forgive us our trespasses," said de Ersola, "as we forgive those who trespass against us. And lead us not into temptation. . . ."

He rose to his slender height. He handed his Bible to Cavendish.

Cosmos offered wine to de Ersola, and the Spaniard took the silver cup with the arms engraved on it. He took a sip; it was the best wine the *Desire* had to offer, from Cavendish's own private stock, and de Ersola had tasted it before. He lifted the cup; once more, sharply, he felt intense sorrow, not only for himself but for Cavendish, and once more he wondered why they were here together and what forces had conspired to do this to both of them. The beauty of this beach-rimmed harbor, bordered by its reef, was a reproof to death, and yet the very manner of his living had brought death here, this morning, this January day. He lifted the cup. He wanted to drink to whatever it was that had brought them to this pass. Let him drink, then, to the vast continent they were both fighting for. Let him drink to the land, and not the sea.

"To America," he said, and let the wine pass down his throat. "A Spanish name, Captain."

He handed the cup back to Cosmos, who put it back on the silver salver.

The rope was ready. He reached up and tucked down

his collar, so that the noose would not slip on it. He did not want the hands of the hangman to touch him. He tucked the collar down carefully, turning under the edge with slim fingers, deft as a sailor's can be. He stepped forward, and then Cavendish did too. He held out his hand to the condemned man.

De Ersola took the strong hand, a small smile on his face. Then his face sobered, and his eyes grew intent. "Take care of my maps," he said.

"Aye, sir," said Cavendish. "I shall."

The noose slipped over de Ersola's head. The drums rolled, making echoing thunder in the little bay; they rolled for the space of two minutes; in ten minutes de Ersola's body was cut down into the clear blue water and into the outgoing tide. Cavendish turned from the deck and walked aft to the crowded poop. He put the chess set away. Havers didn't play chess. He stood alone in the small cabin.

After a minute, he sat down wearily. On his table was a chart he had been drawing of this harbor. De Ersola had helped with it; he had been eager about it; he had had so much eagerness which he had released so easily. It had been a joy to be with him.

He opened and unrolled the first map of the Filipinas that de Ersola had left with him. It was beautifully drawn, and de Ersola had decorated it. A big fat Neptune blew storms from a billow in the ocean. The Neptune looked pleased with himself.

As Havers came in the door, Cavendish pointed to the chart.

"Look, Havers," he said.

Havers said, "There was nothing else you could do, Tom. Everybody knew he had broken parole."

Cavendish said, "I'm abandoning the Portugal here. To Spanish mercy." He did not look up from the chart. "Manila is very near," he said. He rolled up the chart. He had no time now. There was too much to do.

Chapter 27

LOLA STIRRED UNEASILY. She felt cold. She turned over on the sand; it was cold to the touch too. She sat up. The fire was burning very low, and she knew why she had wakened. David was gone.

She looked past the remnants of the fire; she saw Sebastian's head, pillowed on his arms, and she recognized Juan's stocky figure, about twenty feet from her.

"Sebastian," she whispered. "Sebastian."

Sebastian was wide awake immediately. He sat, facing her across the smouldering logs.

"My lord is gone," she whispered.

Sebastian jumped to his feet, feeling for the weapon at his side. "Gomez," he said. He stood looking down at the water.

The little bark rode at anchor just as they had left her. She was very plain in the moonlight. Sebastian glanced at the moon. "It's about three o'clock," he said. Then Lola said, "Sebastian, there is the *Santa Anna!*"

He had seen it at the same time she had. He thought rapidly. "She has been visible about an hour," he said. He listened. There was no sound in the night.

Lola had run down to the water's edge. The little bay curved, and at the tide line she could see around that curve. She stood there, and then she said, "Oh, Sebastian, which way?"

"Toward the town, of course," he said, "but not you, *señorita*. It is better not. I shall go."

David made no noise. The sand slipped away under his booted feet. He ran easily, noiselessly, slipping from tree to tree, watching his quarry, who strode ahead of him on the narrow curving beach.

In the shadow of the trees David slowed his pace. He would need his breath. In a few minutes he and Gomez would meet, on that lonely moon-washed beach. David felt at his belt for the long dagger, then he dropped his hand, and came out of the shadow.

"Gomez," he said softly.

Gomez stood still; he was too surprised to draw the rapier at his side. David took that time to cross the beach to him.

"I've been following you for some time," David said. "You are going to Navidad."

Gomez snarled, "And if I am?" His surly face was angry, his eyes puckered by a scowl.

"You saw the *Santa Anna*," David went on, in the same low voice. "You thought it was time to betray me. In Navidad."

Gomez was unafraid. He had a sword; the Englishman had none. He said, "You'll be caught sometime, *señor*. Why not let me claim the gold?" But he found words none too easy at any time with his superiors. He reached for his rapier, to end the talking.

His right arm went over to his side; at the same instant David leaped forward. Gomez found hs right wrist pinioned just long enough for David's left hand to draw the murderous dagger.

"No!" he screamed, the sound shattering the stillness.

He was killed instantly. He lay on the sand under David's feet, and David knelt down beside him to unfasten his belt, and to claim the rapier which was still only partly unsheathed. Under his shirt, David found his papers and the money bag he was looking for; he wiped the smeared blood from them on Gomez' shirt. He stood up to see Sebastian running toward him.

"I have killed him," David said. "He would have betrayed me."

"*Sí, sí, señor*," Sebastian said. "That is good! You are sure he is dead?" He looked down at the sprawled figure.

"Perfectly sure," David said. "Here, help me carry him to the water. The tide's ebbing."

Sebastian bent down to take Gomez' ankles. David took his shoulders, and they waded out into two feet of water.

"This will do," David said. "I don't want to get too wet."

They dropped their burden. Sebastian leaned down to rinse off his hands. "We saw the *Santa Anna* too," he said.

They started back up the lonely beach. The clumsy shape of the *Santa Anna,* as she wallowed slowly in the offshore swells, was plain to see. Lola had put more logs on the fire, and it burned brightly in the distance.

"The *señorita* wakened me," Sebastian said.

"Did she?" asked David. "Look, Sebastian, I reckoned the *Santa Anna* will fetch Navidad tomorrow at afternoon, or thereabouts. We will put into the harbor after dark."

Sebastian frowned. "There'll be no moon till late."

"I want no moonlight," said David. "I accompanied my brother on just such a trip, after dark, in a small pinnace."

"*Sí, señor,*" Sebastian said, with relief. They were back at the fire.

Lola stood up to greet them. She had known it was David, from afar, and the trembling in her knees had gone, by now.

"You're safe," she whispered.

He pulled her down beside him, and Sebastian sat too, crosslegged. The flames illumined their faces, the two men's, bearded, and Lola's, still white under her tan. Juan was awake; he edged closer to hear.

"I have Gomez' papers, Lola," David said. "From now on, that is my name."

She did not ask what had happened to Gomez. David stretched out flat.

"We might as well get some sleep," he said. "There's nothing to do. We cannot sail until this afternoon."

"We got to Navidad then?" Lola asked, moving over, so he could put his head in her lap. She stroked his head with her slender fingers.

"Aye," he said. "I'm going to try to see Catherine. I'm afraid for her, Lola."

The harbor of Navidad was dark when the bark, on a larboard tack, stole close along her shore. At the tiller, David sat silent. It was not Tom who stood before the mast; it was Lola, the wind blowing her long hair. Suddenly she turned, and came toward him on her bare feet. She sat next to him, saying nothing, holding his arm tight, looking ahead. Finally he said, "I did not expect this."

"I know," she whispered. "You will not dare the town, David?"

In the darkness he smiled ruefully. "No, *señorita.*"

Sebastian's figure detached itself from the darkness fore. He knelt down at David's feet, to be closer to his ear. His whisper was fearful. "There are five of them, *señor,*" he said. "That is the flagship *Maria,* and four escort vessels."

David looked out over the harbor. Each vessel bore a light in her stern; aboard the flagship there were more lights burning in her cabins; the paint on her stern galleries gleamed red.

"That will be Captain da Gossa, *señor,*" Sebastian went on.

"A good seaman?" David asked.

"Very good, *señor,*" Sebastian murmured regretfully. "He will have sailed from Lima and he was probably searching for Captain Cavendish."

"We are near enough shore now," David said.

"*Sí, señor,*" Sebastian answered, rising to his feet.

They towed behind a small ship's boat. Sebastian pulled her alongside, and stepped in; David loosed the painter, and Sebastian dipped his oars.

"*Hasta la vista,*" he said softly.

The bark sailed on, slowly, then came about and drifted idly. "It will be four hours before the moon is up," David said. The ropes creaked as Juan furled the sail; the anchor splashed overboard.

"We shall wait," David said.

It was two hours before Sebastian returned. Silently he climbed aboard, and again he knelt at David's feet to speak with him, while Juan hauled up the anchor and the bark got under way slowly.

"I saw no man from the *Santa Anna, señor,*" Sebastian said first. "And no one there saw me."

"Good," said David, thankfully. He hardly wanted it

known that Sebastian had been in Navidad that night. "They will think us far from here, then."

"*Sí*," said Sebastian. "There is a warrant out for your arrest. There is bad news."

"What news?" asked David levelly.

"Captain Flores is in custody for dereliction of duty. For the loss of the *Santa Anna* and for your escape. They shall take him back to Acapulco for trial. And the Señora Catherine—Captain da Gossa has taken her aboard the flagship."

David said nothing. Over the water the lights of the flagship shone; aboard her was Catherine. David said slowly, "Her crew is ashore?"

"*Sí señor*. They have been six weeks at sea, searching for Captain Cavendish. They must stay here for a few days. They sail on to Acapulco, to land the *Santa Anna's* passengers. Then the fleet returns to Lima."

"It will be safer here than at Acapulco," David said. "This port is much smaller."

Sebastian did not understand.

David said, "I am going to try to get aboard her."

David judged the distance carefully. When the bark was roughly a hundred feet abeam of the flagship, he leaned down to take off his boots. He slipped over into the water.

"Stand off a little. Keep on her quarter. The tide's ebbing," he whispered to Sebastian. "I'll be back."

"God be with you," Lola said, trying to keep her voice even.

"I'll be safer swimming, Lola," he said, his head and his shoulders visible to her and the rest of them. "They don't expect boarding," he added, remembering. "Last time I boarded a Spanish ship, I was lucky too."

His head disappeared. Lola could see him for a minute before only the faint movement of the water showed her he was swimming easily and strongly toward the bulky *Maria*. The bark came about; Sebastian held her into the wind. No one spoke.

The water was warm and smooth. There was almost no current, and little wind. But David approached the ship with caution, not daring to splash; he used an even under-water stroke; he swam under the stern galleries.

A pool of light fell onto the water. David swam close by the ship's side; he pulled himself aboard at the stern ladder. Like a cat he made his way along the painted bulwark and swung himself over to the lower gallery. He pressed himself flat against the side of the ship. He looked sideways into a paneled cabin.

The cabin was large and spacious. A man sat at a polished table, in a high-backed chair as elegantly carved as his own high forehead and deep-set eyes. David was sure he must be da Gossa himself; this would be the Captain's cabin, and probably Catherine was near. Even as David watched, the door opened and he saw Catherine.

Da Gossa rose, he led Catherine to a chair by the table. David pressed back against the wood and listened.

Da Gossa had resumed his place at the table. He studied his visitor; she was much as he had expected, and yet there was a fibrous strength and dignity he had not expected. Still, he couldn't conceal the pleased look in his eyes that appeared as they watched her.

"You must be weary, *señora,*" he said, his measured tones coming clearly to David's ears. "You must be weary after such a voyage. We could not believe, when we saw you today, that the *Santa Anna* was once the proudest ship in the world. A little wine?"

"If you please, *señor,*" Catherine said. "We have endured with the *Santa Anna,* Captain, and to us she is still proud."

He poured the wine into two silver goblets and set one before her. "You are very white. The wine will do you good."

"Now that our uncertainty has ended, and we are safe here, we are all too relieved to be anything but tired," Catherine said quickly.

"There's no use pretending, *señora,*" he said, just as quickly. "You are still uncertain."

She had not touched the wine yet. Now she drank it. She set the goblet down and her fingers touched the small brassbound sea chest on the table. "That is mine," she said.

"From the Englishman Cavendish!"

"It belongs to me," Catherine came back.

He nodded, saying nothing. Then he sighed, dismissed the brief flurry of words that came to his lips, and went to another subject. "I cannot expect you to condone my action toward Captin Flores. Believe me, *señora,* I understand how you feel toward him. It is a misfortune that he allowed sentiment to come between him and duty." He had been going to continue, for he had wanted to evaluate this woman before he questioned her further. Instead he said, "You have been in the New World seven years?"

"*Sí,* Señor da Gossa," she replied.

"It breeds a certain toughness," he remarked. He smiled, and there was friendliness in his carefully hewn features. "I have been here seventeen years."

Catherine smiled back. "The dinner was wonderful tonight!"

He laughed. "White bread," he said. "Is there anything better, *señora,* after biscuit?" Then he said bluntly, "I know much of you. This is your chest, here on the table. These are your possessions, the jewels and the gold, are they not?"

"They are, *señor.*"

"And they were given you by the English Cavendish?"

"They were."

"Then I want you to see something, *señora.*" Across the table he handed her a heavy parchment. He put his finger against the sentence that began. "And if you should hear news of the ship or ships in which sails the English pirate Thomas Cavendish, you are to capture, kill or cripple him, at any cost whatsoever to yourself."

Catherine lifted her eyes from the orders signed by Philip of Spain. The parchment lay on the table beside the brassbound chest. Da Gossa's voice went on: "Let's not use veiled words. The English pirate was your lover. Since he is wanted for his many crimes against Spain, I must question you. Also, you have been the companion of his brother, David Cavendish, who is wanted by the Crown."

"Master David escaped in a small bark," Catherine said. "We on the *Santa Anna* have not seen him since San Lucas." She said it calmly, and while she said it, she wondered if it were possible that it had all been true. But San Lucas was real, and today the bay would be as blue as it had been the first time she had seen it. "Since San Lucas," she repeated.

"I know that, *señora*. What can you tell me of the bark's destination?"

"Nothing," Catherine looked straight at him, and she was sure he knew she was lying.

"Just so." he said dryly. "But that is of no great matter. We shall find him, eventually, certainly." He crossed his legs and regarded her. "What is of moment is what you can tell me of Captain Cavendish."

"Of Captain Cavendish?" she repeated. "What can I tell you?" she asked, low. "What do you wish to know?"

He picked up his pen. "First, a description. From you, it should be correct. Proceed, *señora*." He dipped his pen and his hand hovered over a blank sheet of paper.

Catherine began. "Eyes, blue," she said.

Da Gossa wrote. He listened to her voice. Her low tones were the only sound in the room, aside from his pen. He wrote, and once he raised his eyes quickly, to see her face, and he looked down at the paper again just as quickly, for it was as though he had intruded on something far too intimate. He felt a flicker of jealousy that this woman could love an Englishman so much, and he was sure that any attention he would get from her would be crumbs from another man's table. He said, "And now, *señora,* the Englishman's destination?"

She said, "Plymouth, England."

Da Gossa frowned.

"And before that, *señor,* Manila, Java, Sierra Leone and then England."

"He may be attempting to fool us, *señora*. Although it would be the height of folly to try to escape us in these waters much longer, with the forces we can bring to bear on him."

"Captain Cavendish wanted to round the world," Catherine said. She stood up. "Is this chest still mine, *señor?*"

He rose too. His lips twisted in a wry smile. "I believe so," he said. "It is late now. I shall talk with you

further tomorrow. You are in my custody; it may be that
they shall want to question you in Acapulco. I'll take
you there. We sail in a week."

He had started to the door with her. She turned and
held out her hand; she smiled at him, and he could not
help adding, "Do not worry, *señora!*"

Her hand was in his. "Thank you," she whispered, as
he kissed her hand.

"Your quarters suit you?"

"They are beautiful."

"Señora, I do not blame the Englishman!"

He watched the sudden sparkle come into her eyes.
"Good night," she said softly, and left him standing
there.

Alone, da Gossa removed his shoes, and went over
to the table to turn down the lamp. He was very sleepy,
but he saw the paper he had just written to Catherine's
dictation, and he sat down again and began to read it
over. It tallied exactly with other information he had
about Cavendish.

He rested his chin in his hands. He rubbed his short
mustache and loosened his shirt at the neck. It was hot.
It was January, and it was hot. He took off his shirt,
threw it over a chair, and turned the lamp out. In the
next cabin he heard Catherine moving about; he heard
her voice, and then, in the darkness, he stiffened. He
heard a man's voice.

He jumped to his feet, and for a second he stood un-
decided. Then he crossed the cabin, slowly in the blackness, and stepped out into the passageway. In his bare
feet he walked soundlessly. At Catherine's door he
paused and listened. He tried the latch.

It lifted, but the door was locked. He abandoned all
pretense of silence. He knocked, sharply.

"Open!" he ordered.

Almost immediately he heard Catherine answer him.
"Certainly!" came her voice, and then he knew she had
something to hide, for otherwise she would have asked
him why.

The bolt slipped, and he flung the door wide. There
was nothing to see, of course, and he said nothing, his
ears alert. Had he heard a splash? He started across the

cabin toward its gallery, and Catherine almost hurled herself in front of him. He stopped dead.

"What is it?" she cried, seizing his arm.

He shook her free, pushing her aside. His ears still listened for sounds outside the cabin. But he heard nothing now. He ran to the gallery, his voice raised; he called out orders. The ship came alive. "On the starboard quarter!" he shouted.

Then he heard a cry, and whirled around.

It was the maid Tina who had cried out. She was on her knees beside Catherine, who had slipped to the floor in a crumpled heap.

"Sangre de Dios," da Gossa growled, his ears still attuned to hear the sounds he wanted to hear—the boats he had ordered over the side to search.

"Help me," Tina said. "Help me!"

Da Gossa stared down at Catherine. Then he leaned down and picked her up in his arms. He stood with her, wondering whether the swoon was genuine, looking down at the closed eyes and white cheeks.

"Put the *señora* on the bed," Tina said, exasperation in her voice. *"Señor,* put her down!"

He obeyed. He laid Catherine on the bed; he was still watching her face. There had been a man with her, but he was gone now, and it might be too late to catch him. He was afraid it was too late.

"Raise her head, and I'll give her wine," Tina said, carrying the cup.

Da Gossa said bitterly, "She doesn't need it. The danger's past."

Tina's black eyes gleamed with anger and fear. "Fool!" she said. "Raise her head, and let her have this wine! She has been sick. She is with child!"

Chapter 28

CAVENDISH'S FACE was preoccupied as he bent over de Ersola's chart of the Filipinas. The charts were good, and complete, even to their warnings. Cavendish took the last draft of ale, and looked at the clock. It was seven; he had just finished his breakfast, and there was need for hurry.

The *Desire* was anchored between two narrow islands. Her course should be south, and directly on that course, on the chart, was marked neatly, "Danger." Cavendish scratched his head, took one last look at the chart, and got up. The *Desire* could sail no farther until he himself had gone ahead in the pinnace to take soundings, to find the channel. And in the meantime, these were Spanish waters. He had reached the cabin door when he heard the cry, "Sail ho!" and then it was repeated twice.

Cavendish grabbed for the glass and ran up on deck, and when he saw the small ship that had just rounded the point to the south, his first feeling was one of relief.

"Up anchor, Master Fuller!" he shouted, raising the glass to his eyes.

The Spanish ship was an oared frigate; she bore two sails, and she was sailing close along the shores of Panay.

Aboard the *Desire* the drums beat to quarters, the men swarmed aloft, the gun ports opened, and Master Fuller's voice was venting obscene epithets on the wind. The wind was so light. Slowly the *Desire* clawed around to windward; she began to bear down on her quarry slowly.

The guns roared. Moon was finding the range. The *Desire* came up on the frigate, and Moon himself touched off one of the sacres: the frigate was hit. Her foremast tumbled down on her decks. She struck her sails, and her long oars dipped into the water, rhythmically, flashingly, fast.

The wind dropped. There was no wind. The frigate was drawing out of range, and Cavendish handed the glass to Havers and ran down to the boat deck.

"Hoist out the pinnace!" he ordered.

Havers watched in dismay.

"Master Moon!" Cavendish shouted. The pinnace splashed into the water. "Bring muskets!"

Cavendish slid down into the boat. Men tumbled after him. Moon joined him in the stern sheets, and the pinnace pulled away from the *Desire,* with twelve men aboard. And by this time, the frigate had disappeared. There was no sign of her at all.

"There's no use hoisting the sail," Cavendish growled.

"Give way!" Moon commanded, having no idea why his Captain was so intent on risking his life to follow a Spanish frigate.

Cavendish said, "They must not carry word of us!" He paid no further attention to Moon; he was watching the shore.

The oars pulled fast. In fifteen minutes, Cavendish said, "By God, there's a river!"

The river disappeared into Panay like a crawling snake. Trees leaned over the shore; some lay in the water, lifeless, and there were long poles thrust upward along the shore. They saw a few native canoes, long and light.

Cavendish glanced back at the *Desire.* A hundred feet more would bring the pinnace too much to the leeward of the *Desire,* and he frowned, murderously. There was still no sign of the frigate.

"There's the wind again, sir," Moon said, heartily.

Cavendish swore. "A devil of a lot of good it does now," he muttered.

"Look, sir!" Moon said, for Cavendish had again glanced back at the *Desire,* to measure the distance between her and the pinnace.

A large canoe, or balsa, as it was called, had appeared as out of nowhere; she had her oars close to the water through holes, and she was attempting to escape. "Keep athwart her head," Cavendish ordered.

They were overtaking the canoe. There were seven Indians in it and one Spaniard. The natives were terrified; as the pinnace bore down on them, they dove overboard and swam under water until their heads reappeared quite far off, to the amazement of the English seamen. But the lone Spaniard was not such a swimmer.

Cavendish reached out to seize the prow of the long balsa; it was incredibly light and he could hold it by himself. He ordered the Spaniard to come aboard his own boat, and the Spaniard complied. Hands pulled him aboard, and he crouched at Cavendish's feet, crying that he was neither soldier nor sailor, but just a servant from a hospital in Manila.

"What are you doing here on Panay?" Cavendish asked.

The pinnace drifted toward shore.

"My master is one of the officers," the Spaniard said. "We came from Manila to man the new ship."

"What new ship?" Cavendish asked, and the men listened, trying to make out the Spaniard's answers, when two things happened at once. The frigate reappeared, and the pinnace ran aground.

Cavendish leaped overboard into the waist-deep water. Moon followed him, and two seamen. They pushed the longboat into deeper water, struggling through the muddy banks. Shots sounded from the beach. About fifty soldiers had appeared on the narrow beach, and musket fire rang out. Bullets whizzed around Cavendish's head.

The boat was freed. He and the men scrambled back aboard. "Hoist the sail!" he shouted, as he stood in the stern, raising the musket to his shoulder.

"The soldiers are from the big ship they've come out from Manila to man," the little Spaniard cried in dismay. He was still crouched at Cavendish's feet.

A bullet sang by Cavendish's head, and tore through the raised sail of the pinnace. The men pulled at the oars; the frigate was bearing down on them rapidly— her Captain had been lying in wait for the longboat; her guns opened fire.

The pinnace shuddered under the first hit. But no one was hurt, and the men bent low over the oars trying to keep out of danger.

"We'll be safe," Cavendish said calmly, reloading his musket. It was a narrow escape, but they had made it. The frigate was coming within range of the *Desire's* guns, and to make sure that the frigate's Captain perceived it, Havers, aboard the *Desire,* fired a booming salvo that splashed into the water twenty feet from her. The pinnace was safe. She slid up alongside the *Desire,* and her men climbed aboard.

Havers was waiting for Cavendish, smiling with relief.

Cavendish said angrily, "I don't dare take the *Desire* up that river. They acted quickly," Havers said. "Their commander did."

"Aye," said Cavendish grimly. "We can't storm that beach! We don't have any boats big enough!"

"Nor men enough," added Havers, calmly.

Cavendish turned. "Bring that Spaniard up here, Master Moon," he called.

The little Spaniard was trembling so that he could hardly mount the ladder. "I've just come here," he said, fearfully, before Cavendish could speak.

"Those soldiers—" Cavendish waved his hand toward the beach. "You said they'd come out here to man a new ship?"

"*Sí,* your honor!"

"How heavy is she?"

"Four hundred tons, *señor,*" was the answer.

Cavendish looked at Havers. And the Spanish probably had dozens of smaller craft to aid them. "We'd better set sail, Havers," he said, wryly, and Havers smiled.

"It might be best, Tom," he agreed. "Unless you'd like to hang from the yardarm of that new ship."

The *Desire* weighed anchor. The pinnance had been hit in the bow, but she was seaworthy, and once more Cavendish went ahead in her, for the *Desire* could not venture her stout keel in these waters. The hours passed. There was no sign of pursuit yet.

The two islands of Negros and Panay lay close together. Negros was flat and full of vegetation; Panay had marvelous trees. Master Fuller himself was calling out the fathoms, and astern came the *Desire,* on a lazy fanning wind.

Cavendish's pinnace increased the distance between the two craft. He was intent only on the soundings, and marking down the reefs and channels and the entrances to narrow rivers.

"What a maze this is," he said. "We've come sixteen leagues."

Ahead was a jutting piece of the island of Negros, lying flat out into the sea. The longboat's sails filled with the wind, and she came around the point.

"There's our opening," Cavendish cried. "A fair one, Master Fuller. Southwest by south."

The longboat put about, and the *Desire* hoisted more sail. The two came together once more, and Cavendish clambered back aboard. He called the Spaniard, who appeared, trembling.

"*Sí,* your honor," he said, before Cavendish had addressed him.

Cavendish smiled. "I want you to carry a message to your Captain."

The other bowed hastily. "*Sí, señor.*"

"I want you to tell your Captain to set aside a goodly store of gold, for I and my men mean to see you, perhaps at Manila, in a few years, and your Captain can have the gold ready for us." The members of the crew who could hear this laughed aloud, and Master Pretty, gazing at his Captain's tanned face, was remembering the words so he could write them down. "I did but want," Cavendish continued, "a bigger boat to have landed my men, or I would have seen your Captain this morning."

The Spaniard said seriously, "I shall tell my Captain, *señor.* To have the gold, for you'll be back."

"And do not forget to give our regrets that we had not a bigger boat for landing, else we'd have seen him today."

"I remember what you say. I remember."

He climbed eagerly into the pinnace that still bumped against the *Desire.* Fuller took him ashore and landed him on a lonely point of Panay. He started to walk rapidly up the beach.

The longboat was hoisted aboard. The *Desire* set sail again, her course southwest by south. For the third time she was going to cross the equatorial line. She was leaving Spanish waters. Ahead lay the uncharted South Pacific.

Chapter 29

THE SHIP *Eugenia* proceeded slowly. She was hugging the shore—a majestic and white-sailed searcher.

It was afternoon, late. She had passed Point Maldonado hours ago, and across her deck her Captain walked, back and forth, back and forth. The *Eugenia* was stately, but she was a good sailer, and her small victim should be near. The *Eugenia* had been searching for David Cavendish ever since the night he had escaped from the flagship in the darkness.

A point of land jutted out into the sea. The *Eugenia* was rounding the point, bearing in toward land. The Captain walked once more, back and forth. Soon, in a few minutes, the mouth of the river Verde would be revealed. When the *Eugenia* came around the point, the cries the Captain wanted to hear came from the lookout.

The light guns had already been served with powder and shot. Time was important. The capture of this little bark was tremendously important. With all sails squared, the *Eugenia* bore down rapidly on her victim.

The first gun was fired. It fell short. The little bark was putting into the small harbor, tacking toward the river.

The guns roared again.

"She presents such a small target, sir," one officer said. "But she hasn't quite time to escape us up the river."

"*Sí, señor*," the Captain murmured.

"But it must be Cavendish, the brother," the officer exclaimed.

"Quite true, *señor*," the Captain said, his words drowned in the sound of the guns.

The little bark was hit. The Captain smiled. The fight was unequal, and that was good, since he must win it, and bring back a prisoner so badly wanted by the Crown.

"I want him alive, though," he said, to his first officer.

"*Sí, señor*. If possible." The officer was staring ahead. The bark was near, she had been hit again and even while he watched, the bark heeled over, and righted again.

"We bear down on her," the Captain said. Satisfaction filled him. He glanced toward the shore.

The bark was within short range. The guns of the *Eugenia,* trained on her, thundered forth again, and again, until the Captain stopped them with a quick command.

"She will sink quickly," he said. "Hoist out a boat and aboard her, sir. I shall wait."

It had been done so easily. It was the discovery of the bark, not the taking of her, which was difficult. The Captain wished she had not been so near the river, then if she had not, he could have made sure to take her crew alive. Now he frowned as he resumed his pacing. He wished he hadn't had to use the guns.

The little bark was floating helplessly, almost at the edge of the river. The *Eugenia* stood off, under short sail; from her pulled a longboat, with twenty armed men.

"I pray the Englishman is alive," the Captain said aloud.

Aboard the longboat, the first officer watched the shape of the bark come close. She was almost gone; her decks were awash. Astern, her crude little boat, still hitched, bobbed on the waves, empty.

The Spanish longboat pulled up alongside.

The first officer stepped gingerly onto the deck. A man lay face down in the water. The first officer leaned down and turned him over.

He was small. This man was not David Cavendish, but it must be the renegade Juan who had escaped with the Englishman. The officer said, "Here is one of them. Dead."

One of the two men with him aboard the bark bent

over to release the dead man's foot from the rope in which it was entangled.

"He would have been washed overboard, except his foot's caught, sir."

The first officer narrowed his eyes, looking down at the rope. Had the man been hitched? Dead? By his foot?"

The two seamen with him had tranferred the body to the longboat. He waited for them to join him. He walked to the small cabin; its hinged door swayed brokenly. It was dark, but it was not too dark to see that the tiny cabin was empty except for the rising water. The first officer sighed.

"There is no one left alive aboard," he said. He thought to himself that had he been the Englishman, he would have much preferred to drown. That was the way the Englishman had taken, and he had taken his woman with him. The Spanish officer stepped into his longboat.

He reported to the Captain of the *Eugenia*. The Captain inspected his one prisoner, a dead man.

"But if I had not used the guns, she might have escaped us—" The Captain stared out at the dim shape of the sinking bark. He could barely make it out; it was drifting sluggishly toward shore.

"They did not attempt to use their boat, sir. It was hitched to the bark."

"*Señor,*" the Captain said, "we shall tow the bark back to Acapulco. 'Tis the best we can do."

"*Sí, señor,*" the first officer said.

He relayed the Captain's order. After half an hour, night had fallen, and the *Eugenia* was under full sail again, towing behind her the small bark, and its small boat, empty.

Chapter 30

HEAT. It shimmered down upon the *Desire*. The men wore nothing but their breeches, and walked the hot decks in bare feet. The officers and Cavendish envied them; every day Cosmos washed out the thinnest of Cavendish's lawn shirts and hung them in the bleaching sun to dry.

The *Desire* sailed on. At night the stars seemed to be lower in the sky and the ship's wake threw up great plumes of phosphorescent spray. Islands clustered close here; nameless islands, some of them sunk in the sea and nothing but sand any more. Gilolo was passed, its fingers of land thrust out green into the bluest of water, and at night the doubled lookouts aloft scanned the waters for the thin line of white that would herald the cry: "Breakers ahead!"

On the fourteenth of February, three degrees and ten minutes below the line, the *Desire* fell in with ten or twelve islands, rank and thick with vegetation. Low and flat, they lay drowning in heat. The *Desire* passed in the lee of them, close enough to hear the murmur of their jungle life. Havers was standing with Cavendish on the poopdeck. Suddenly he lifted his hand and struck at a fly that had settled on his neck. It left a bloodstain on his neck and hand.

"I like not the look of those islands," Cavendish said. "There is something rotten about them."

Havers knew what he meant. Fever and heat. Already twenty men were suffering with the fever.

"No man could exist long in those lagoons," Cavendish said. "We can get spice in Java. And we already carry a deal of it."

Java was to be the last port of call between the South Sea islands and the Cape of Good Hope, on the tip of Africa. Havers felt excitement when he thought of it. One more vast ocean to cross, and then their own Atlantic. What a joy it would be to see the gray Atlantic.

"I'm tired of tropic nights, beautiful as they are," Havers said.

That night was a wonderful night. They had sighted the chain of islands that would end with Java. The moon was full; on deck the musicians played, and the men sang softly. Cavendish let himself drift into a dream of Catherine; he let himself long for her, the touch of her hand, the sound of her voice. He brought her image into his mind; he let himself remember how great was his longing for her. He looked down at his hands and thought only of touching her with them. She would already be on her way to England. If Fortune smiled only a little on them—the bark had only to cross the gulf to Mazatlán, and hug the coast until she fetched Acapulco. And there was a smaller port, Navidad.

"Havers, he said suddenly, "how far was it—do you remember—from Navidad to Acapulco?"

Havers said, "I do not know, Tom." He got to his feet. "I'll find out for you; I want—" He reached for the rail to steady himself; he lurched. His hand grasped the ropes, and over him at the same time came a terrible nausea and weakness. He thought the *Desire* pitched, he tried to get his balance, and then he fell.

Cavendish leaped to his feet. He bent over Havers; he and Tyler picked him up. They carried him into Cavendish's own cabin.

Havers was unconscious. He began to retch, first chokingly and then violently. Cosmos ran for cool water and towels, while Cavendish took Havers' boots off, and stripped from him the soiled shirt. On Havers' back and chest the familiar sweat was beginning to stand out in great drops.

Cavendish was not afraid that night. He had seen many men fall into a faint with these tropical fevers. He covered Havers with blankets when the chills began. Later, Havers seemed to sleep, and Cavendish ordered a hammock for himself slung out on deck. His cabin was the largest and most comfortable, and he could look after Havers himself.

In the morning Havers was delirious. The vomiting continued all morning, and the chills that gripped him now thrust fear into Cavendish's heart. He watched him all that day, waiting for the fever to abate a little, waiting for Havers to become conscious of him.

The next day was the sixteenth of February. That day, John Gameford, the cooper, who had been ill a long time, died. Cavendish mustered the crew on deck and led the prayer. Gameford's body slid over the slide, and the *Desire* sailed on.

Heat. It dogged them. Among these teeming islands the *Desire* was lonely, a small ship against a heat-filled ocean. The men walked and talked in whispers. One man had died, even though it had not been from fever; the whole ship was afraid because Captain Havers was sick. He had lain unconscious for two days.

On the third day, at dawn, Havers recovered consciousness. Cosmos called Cavendish, who was on deck watching the sunrise. Immediately Cavendish went to Havers.

Havers was very flushed in the gray light. But his eyes were open and aware, and he tried to smile. "Tom," he murmured.

"Do not talk," Cavendish said. "Are you very hot, man?"

"Aye," was the answer. "My head."

Cavendish put his hand on Havers's forehead. To him it seemed less hot than it had been. "Cosmos and I will bathe you in cool water," he said.

He started to take off the blanket. When they had stripped Havers, they saw the rash. It covered his body, like a red network; then Cavendish knew Havers did not have ordinary tropical fever.

"Water," Havers whispered, with difficulty.

He drank thirstily, gulping. He lay back, exhausted with the effort. "Your cabin," he said, and closed his eyes.

"Aye, Havers," Cavendish said. "I thought you would rest better in here, alone."

They bathed him quickly, and wrapped him up again in the blankets. The chills came on again, the fever rose during the day and the sweating began, worse than before.

Havers was in terrible pain. Cavendish knew that by

the way he tossed and cried out. When he was conscious he did not speak at all, but drank water. Nothing else would stay down, and even the water caused vomiting. But most of the time he lay gripped with pain and fever.

On the seventh day he lay quietly. Occasionally he opened his eyes, and it was on this day that Cavendish knew there was little hope. He stayed by Havers' side, but Havers did not speak. On the eighth day after he had succumbed to the fever, he died. It was Ash Wednesday.

Cavendish could not believe it. Havers was dead. Cavendish sat beside him and could not encompass the fate which had struck at him. Here he sat, alive and well, and Havers was dead.

He dressed Havers himself. He used a linen sheet to wrap him in. He sewed it carefully. He left the shrouded body in the cabin.

Burial was before the mast, at sunrise. The *Desire* could not come to anchor. The *Desire* had to sail on, her white wake foaming, her sprit sail taut with wind. On her decks the company stood bareheaded and silent, their brown-bearded faces blank and still. There was no man aboard the Desire who had not loved Captain Havers.

The body was placed on a plank. Moon's gun crews manned the light cannon and all the small shot in the ship. Pretty held one end of the plank and made no secret of the tears in his eyes above the bearded cheeks.

Cavendish stood alongside Havers for the last time.

"Heavenly Father," he said, "this is our comrade. It is our duty to commit his body to the deep; in Thy hands we leave him, our beloved friend and countryman, who shall be buried here so far from his native soil."

Cavendish stopped.

"Let us pray," he said.

The men bowed their heads.

"Our Father which art in Heaven, hallowed be Thy name . . ."

They had dressed in their best for Havers. They were neat and clean, and in their strong voices they prayed to the Lord for Havers. They were using the same prayer de Ersola had used, only this time the language was English.

". . . For Thine is the Kingdom, and the Power, and the Glory, forever. Amen."

The last salute for Havers was fired. Master Pretty heaved on the plank, and the shrouded body went overboard into the waves. Cavendish dismissed the crew, the watch was set, and the *Desire* kept on her course. Cavendish went to his cabin alone. He sat down at his table and anguish gripped him.

"Oh, Catherine," he cried. "Catherine, he is gone."

An hour passed, and he still sat at his table. He felt intense weariness. His head was in his arms, and he knew he had slept a little, sitting there, sleep mixed with dreams, sleep mixed with remembering.

Suddenly he stood up. He picked up his brush and brushed his hair back, for the unruly lock had fallen across his forehead. He changed his shirt. It clung to him in the heat. He went out on deck.

Pretty was standing at the rail staring at the island of Bali. Cavendish approached him from behind. Pretty heard him and turned.

"It's you, Captain," he said, as if surprised to see him.

"Aye, Pretty," Cavendish said. He looked out across the gray water to the island of Bali.

"You knew him better than I, sir," Pretty said abruptly. He sighed deeply, a long sigh; he felt a little better with Cavendish there beside him. It came to him suddenly that he had written much about the man who was his Captain, and he was just beginning to understand him, a little. His Captain had heavy and terrible responsibilities, and there was no one to whom he could look for help.

"You have so much, sir," he blurted. Through his mind flashed the face of Catherine. "I mean so much to do that's hard, Captain. Sir, those charts you draw, the soundings we take, the ports we discover, the islands we name—do you think that men who come after us will know how much it cost? How *much* it cost?" He had turned and was regarding Cavendish with appealing directness.

Cavendish said, "Why, of course they will. Some. Never all, but always some. Will you accompany me now, sir?"

"Aye, aye, sir," said Pretty.

He followed Cavendish into the forecastle. Twenty-eight men lay there, sick with fever.

Cavendish paused before each hammock. Some men were sleeping like the dead; to the others he talked a little.

"How do you feel, Johnson?" he asked.

"Better, sir." Johnson smiled.

"What tastes best to you?"

"The lemon juice and water, sir."

Cavendish nodded. He put his hand on Johnson's forehead; the ship's surgeon came up.

"Moon told me you were here, sir," he said hastily.

"Johnson seems to have no fever," Cavendish said. "I'd suggest you move all men who have no fever out onto the fore galleries, where there's more air. I'll send men to move them. They shouldn't walk yet."

"Aye, aye, sir," said the surgeon.

"And there are plenty of lemons for the sick. The rest of us can do without."

Cavendish left, with Pretty trailing him. As he emerged onto the lower deck, a group of men sprang apart, their faces grim. Cavendish wanted to smile; he had evidently just interrupted what might have been a brawling quarrel. The tenseness aboard was apt to explode into flying fists and drawn pocket knives.

"Williams," he said, fastening whom he thought might be one of the main culprits with a stern eye, "report fore to the surgeon. All of you. Step lively, now. You can help your shipmates."

The men moved away. Oppressiveness had settled over the *Desire*. The volcanoes of Bali stood up like sentinels in the sky, rising over the lush green of its shores; and from the island came a rumbling like thunder in the distance. Fuller came up to Cavendish.

"The wind's holding," he said. "We should fetch Java by nightfall."

"I think so," Cavendish said. "Fuller, issue an extra

ration of wine to all men who are not on the binnacle list. It may help strengthen their blood.

"And there should be fish in these waters. Cast out the hames; we'll trail them. And man the harpoons in the head."

"Aye, aye, sir," said Fuller, happily, for at least it was something to do.

Tyler ran joyfully to the first harpoon. He readied it; he scanned the water; then he gave a shout and loosed the harpoon.

"A shark!" he yelled.

In a minute the water was red with blood, and gray and white with the swirling movements of the angry creature. Cavendish ran down, across the main deck, and mounted up into the beakhead.

"Any man overboard gets a week's confinement!" he roared, as one man perched himself precariously on the rail.

The man slipped down onto the deck, turning startled eyes on his Captain.

"D'ye want to lose a leg?" Cavendish asked him, grimly. He stared down at the writhing shark.

"Cut him loose," he ordered.

Tyler obeyed. Most of the well men were on deck, and with her tops reefed, the *Desire* entered the straits between Java and Bali.

The straits were narrow, and edged with foamy surf. The sun was setting over the mountains, and just before nightfall, as Fuller had predicted, the *Desire* heaved out her anchors in a large bay on the underside of the island of Java.

It was a strange scene, this bay at dusk. The *Desire* rode like a toy ship; the land looked mighty and savage. The bay was dotted with islands, and the shore was empty. The silence was deep, and through it Cavendish could hear drums beating. Suddenly there was a heavy rumble, and then from a crudely carved island to windward, a shower of sparks lighted the darkening skies.

"Volcano," Cavendish said to Pretty.

The drums beat plainly in the distance. There was no sign of human life.

"Double the watches tonight, Pretty," Cavendish said.

"Aye, sir," said Pretty. "This is a savage and barbaric land," he added. "So I've read, sir."

Cavendish stared at shore. He needed food and water. Ahead was the Indian Ocean. Two thousand leagues of ocean. He must have food and water, and he must get it here.

Pretty said, "Tyler asked me if you would like your hammock slung out on deck tonight."

"I would," said Cavendish. "I would very much."

"It's infernally hot, Captain," Tyler said from behind. Just then the volcano grumbled, grew strong and angry. The black night was illumined suddenly, as the hot lava was hurled upward.

"Jesu," said Tyler.

"It's called Krakatoa," Cavendish said.

"Jesu," Tyler repeated. "What would happen, sir, if—"

"It would blow you straight to hell, Tyler," Cavendish said. "Go sling that hammock."

"Aye, sir," said Tyler.

"Good night, sir," said Pretty. He walked slowly away. Below, in his cabin, he was alone, for Moon was on duty until the middle watch. Pretty sat down and took off his shoes. He got out his journal, and opened it to the first blank page. He started to write and he didn't know what to say. Finally he dipped his pen.

"On the twenty-first day of February," he wrote slowly, "Captain Havers died of a most fervent ague which had held him furiously for some eight days." Pretty dipped his pen again. The volcano rumbled. "To the no small grief of our Captain and all the rest of our company."

Pretty's eyes filled with tears. He put his head down in his hands. "God bless you, sir," he muttered, and he didn't know whether he was speaking of Havers or Cavendish. "God bless you."

Chapter 31

CATHERINE woke slowly. Her body was bathed in sweat, and as she raised her head, drops of perspiration ran down her throat and neck. The afternoon sun slanted through the portholes; there was no air at all.

High mountains protected the port of Acapulco, and shut out all the wind from the land. The port was only half a mile in breadth, so soon did the mountains rise from the bay they sheltered; the town clustered in five blocks along the waterfront.

Catherine sat up in bed. Her very being felt heavy, yet she must move, and must get dressed.

"I have the water ready," Tina said.

Alongside Catherine, Kate stirred in her sleep. Her long hair was tangled and mussed, her small hands were damp to the touch. Suddenly the weariness that enveloped Catherine mounted into activity; she turned over on her stomach and began to cry, with long sobbing cries that shook her whole body.

Tina said nothing. She moved about the cabin, laying out Catherine's dress; she emptied the water into a wooden tub.

Catherine buried her face in the soft pillows; after the first outburst she realized she did not want to waken Kate and have the child see her cry this way. Fear for the child had gripped her terribly in the last few weeks. Guilt nagged at Catherine, for if she had never left Manila, the child would be safe there now. She wiped her face with her hands, and sat up; she took Kate's wet hand in hers, and the child sighed in her sleep.

"I shall never leave her, *señora,*" Tina said.

Catherine blinked back more tears. She started to say something, but couldn't.

"I promise you, *señora,*" Tina said. "I swear it by the Virgin."

Catherine blinked and sniffed and wiped her nose.

"She sleeps still, do not waken her."

Catherine nodded and slipped off the bed, stripping off her thin shift. She stepped into the tub, and knelt down, splashing the water up gratefully on her face. She felt a little better.

"I love her with all my soul," Tina said. "I know you do, Tina," Catherine said, inadequately, feeling the tears rise again. "But you must take her to England, Tina. If anything happens to me, you must take her to England!"

"I shall, *señora*," Tina said, and Catherine looked up at her lean dark face and the wrinkled neck with the gold chain around it.

"Trimley St. Martin," Catherine said aloud, and Tina repeated it. "It is near Harwich," Catherine said, as if it were truly impossible to conceive of it. "The house is brick, and geese walk in the kitchen garden. And it is in Suffolk, Tina. Ah, it must be beautiful in England."

"We shall go there, *señora*," Tina said. "Your towel."

Catherine took it. The water felt good to her feet, and she dried herself while she was standing in the tub. On the chair lay her dress.

It was cloth of gold, made of the material Cavendish had given her. Its bodice was low; it had small panels over the hips, and a narrow skirt. Tina put it over Catherine's head, and stepped back to survey it.

Tina nodded, pleased. Catherine looked down at herself.

"I'll wear my hair loose with this," she said.

Tina brushed her hair back, and fastened it with two gold pins; she put a gold mesh net over the shining hair. "What jewels?" she asked.

Catherine said, "Why should I placate them? I'll wear the emeralds."

They were fabulous. They could be nothing but a pirate's loot, or an Aztec prince's. The ring was her wedding ring; the emerald on the narrow chain was the one she had tried to steal.

"You are beautiful," Tina said, matter of factly.

"It's the excitement," Catherine said. She went toward the door, just as there was a knock on the heavy dark wood.

"I'll rouse Kate, and get fresh water," Tina said, "and bathe the *señorita*. The sun is going down and I'll take her out on deck."

"Good-bye," Catherine said.

"*Adiós, señora.*"

Catherine had not far to go. The large cabin was only fifteen feet away. Da Gossa himself opened the door, and led her to a chair next to his. The other gentlemen rose when she entered, and silence fell.

Catherine saw the silver bowl of fruit on the polished table. There were nuts and sweetmeats and wine. It flashed through her mind that after they had finished with her, they would indulge in these refreshments and talk about what had occurred. Da Gossa was introducing her, and she curtsied to each in turn, repeating the names after da Gossa.

"The Alcalde of Acapulco, Señor del Cano."

"Your servant, *señor*," Catherine said. He was the last to be presented. Catherine studied his square face briefly, and he brushed his short pointed beard.

There was another brief silence. Da Gossa broke it. He lifted the sheet of paper in front of him.

"Señora de Montoro," he began, "I have here the questions I asked you and which you have already answered. I am going to read them aloud, and the gentlemen gathered here will then have an opportunity to hear them and your affirmations that the information is correct."

"Certainly, *señor*," Catherine replied.

"Then I shall begin," da Gossa said. "Gentlemen, the Englishman's description is as follows." He began to read. "Captain Cavendish; nationality, English; age, two and thirty years. Eyes, blue; hair, dark brown, tinged with gray, cut short. Face, clean-shaven—"

His voice went on. Catherine thought only of the man whom his words evoked. "Eyes, blue." She bit her lip.

Fifteen minutes went by. Da Gossa read on, and finally his voice stopped. He laid the paper down.

Another brief silence fell. Then the Alcalde folded his hands in his lap; he looked at Catherine. He said, "The *señora* has thus told us nothing that any other passenger or member of the company of the *Santa Anna* could not have told us."

"That is quite true," da Gossa said.

The Alcalde frowned. "We have the word of many crewmen that the English pirate was setting forth to Manila and the South Seas. I am wondering, sirs, whether that was a trick of the Englishman's. Let me tell you, gentlemen, that if he should return by the Straits of Magellan, all our heads would be in danger of falling!"

"But Captain Cavendish will not return that way, sirs," Catherine said.

The Alcalde frowned deeper. "How may we know you speak the truth, *señora?* You have been under no compulsion to tell the truth."

Da Gossa glanced at Catherine. He was about to speak, but the Alcalde interrupted him.

"Certainly, *señora,*" he said, "you know much more than you have told us."

"I do not, *señores,*" Catherine said levelly.

The Alcalde studied her openly. *"Señora,* Spain and England are at war. You are a Spanish subject, and in consorting with the English captain you are guilty of treason, I believe," he added, looking at da Gossa.

Da Gossa frowned.

"Thus," pursued the Alcalde, "it would better your position if you would reveal the secrets which you are withholding from us."

Catherine again kept her voice level. "I know nothing more," she said.

The Alcalde said to the others, "Of course, a man like that Englishman probably reveals little to his mistresses." There was a certain detached envy in the Alcalde's voice. "All of what he has told her may be lies, gentlemen."

Catherine said, lifting her hand to study the enormous emerald on the third finger, "Captain Cavendish does not lie, *señor.* To me, or to anyone." She raised her eyes from the emerald and looked at da Gossa. He smiled.

"A little wine, *señores?*" he asked. He began to pour some wine; he rose and brought a goblet to Catherine.

The Alcalde had accepted wine too.

"Possibly it might be best to send the *señora* to Lima," he suggested, over the rim of his goblet, "and wash our hands of the matter."

Catherine wanted to protest, but it was not time. They were talking among themselves, and she hardly heard them. The very word Lima was a threat. She looked up at the great map that stretched across an entire side of the paneled cabin. Her eyes found Lima. It was so far away—halfway down the Pacific coast. Acapulco was a red dot on the map; south of it the continent of America narrowed, and there was only a thin strip of land dividing the two great oceans. Across that thin strip of land was the Atlantic Ocean. Another red dot marked the port of Vera Cruz—and that was where she must go.

She didn't hear the voices around her. She heard David's voice, as it had been almost a month ago when she had come into her cabin and found him there. Da Gossa had almost caught him, but David had escaped. And David had had time to whisper, "Get to Vera Cruz! You must! I shall be there. From there we can take ship across the Atlantic!"

She stared at Vera Cruz on the map. It was near, compared to the distances of this land. And some leagues south of here, she saw on the map the thin line that drew in the Verde River. It was on this river that David intended to make his way inland, and to cross from the Pacific to the Atlantic. The Verde River. There it was on the map. Was David there now?

"In Lima," the Alcalde was pursuing his point, "the Viceroy will know what to do to please the Crown. And then we shall not be responsible for the *señora*, and it will no longer be our business."

Da Gossa said, "The Viceroy? But I am thinking it might be wisest to send the *señora* to Vera Cruz. If she is guilty of treason, it might be best to send her on to Spain."

Catherine fastened her eyes on his face. "Spain?" she said. "Vera Cruz?"

Da Gossa nodded. "That is what our orders are concerning the brother, David Cavendish. Although I imagine he is dead."

"Probably," said the Alcalde. "Drowned, or captured by the Indians. It would be easier on us if we could catch him. But, anyway, da Gossa, David Cavendish is the brother, and thus a prisoner of war." The Alcalde was loathe to give up his plan. "I think the Viceroy should decide."

Da Gossa sighed. He thought privately that Lima might be safer for Catherine de Montoro. "Perhaps you are right," he conceded. "I sail for Lima in two weeks." He had risen suddenly and was looking through the open port. "The *Eugenia* is putting in," he said. "She's towing a disabled bark!"

There was a brief silence. But Catherine had hardly heard da Gossa. She said, slowly, "Spain and England are at war?"

"I told you that before, *señora*," the Alcalde said sharply.

"Yes, but I did not realize," she said. She stood up and set down the wine glass.

"I told you, too," the Alcalde added, "that you were guilty of treason. Did you not understand me, *señora?*"

"No," said Catherine. She faced all of them. "I am not guilty of treason!"

The Alcalde said sharply, "You are! We shall send you to Lima! Do you know, *señora,* that Captain Flores was sentenced to death this morning?"

Catherine's eyes blazed. "You little fat coward," she said, contemptuously. "And you shall not send me to Lima, to stand trial for treason. Not I, sir! For I am not a Spanish subject!"

The Alcalde was red in the face, especially since da Gossa looked as though he fully agreed with Catherine. The Alcalde sputtered, and da Gossa interrupted casually.

"If you are not Spanish, what then are you, *señora?*" And as he said it, Catherine was sure he knew what her answer would be. He was leaning back in his chair, waiting.

"What am I?" she asked. She stood very straight. "I

am English, sir. You shall send me to Vera Cruz, and on to Spain by your orders. I am an English subject. I am not the mistress of the English Captain. I am his wife!"

Chapter 32

THE SUN ROSE BLOOD-RED. It splashed against the waters of the bay, and by eight o'clock it was burning down on the deck of the *Desire*.

All the company were on deck. They talked in low voices, and watched the shore. They could see it plainly now, in the white hot heat of the blazing sunny morning. And they saw no sighs of human life. It was there, but they could not see it.

Cavendish came out on the poopdeck, and the men turned to see their Captain. The three little Filipino boys, the de Dasis, whispered and nudged each other, and the big Negro whom Cavendish had taken from the *Santa Anna*—he stared toward shore too. He heard Cavendish call out his name; immediately he made answer, and everyone watched as he made his way to Cavendish's deck.

The Captain was dressed in a white shirt and canvas trousers. He waved one white-clad arm to shore.

"Can you speak their tongue?" he said.

The Negro nodded. "They will understand the Morisco tongue, sir," he said.

Again Cavendish pointed toward shore. "I see large canoes hitched to poles. They are fisher canoes. Yet this morning they are hitched up and unused."

"They are afraid," the Negro said.

"We'll go ashore and see," Cavendish said. "You shall come."

"Oh, no!" the Negro cried.

Cavendish said, "There will be no danger."

The Negro nodded excitedly. "They will die, if their King so orders it," he cried. "They are savage! Last night they beat the drums!"

"We'll go ashore," Cavendish repeated.

Cavendish's boat was put over the side. Pretty wanted to come, and then ten men joined them; the Negro crouched fearfully between the thwarts. The boat pulled ashore. When they were near, Cavendish told the Negro to call out in his own tongue.

The wall of green jungle did not answer.

"Call out again," Cavendish ordered, as the boat was beached. Cavendish jumped out onto the sand, and the men pulled the boat up on the beach.

The Negro stepped out too. He raised his voice; it echoed and trembled a bit, and suddenly, at the call, a figure appeared. A man stood, uncertain, at the edge of the trees, and slowly he made his way toward the white men.

"Ask him where we can find fresh water," Cavendish ordered.

The two Negroes talked rapidly. There were tentative smiles between them. The native pointed.

"He says, water there."

"Good," said Cavendish. "Now tell him to carry a message to his King. Tell him that we are English, white men, and that we come to trade for victuals and diamonds and pearls and any other jewels he may have, and that we will pay for all we get in either gold or merchandise."

The native smiled when he heard the translation. His face was bright with sweat and excitement. He made the men laugh. He volunteered to show them the fresh water; he went ahead, and they followed. But when they had reached the fresh pool and the little stream that fed it, he disappeared almost like magic.

The jungle was deep and airless and full of life. It had closed around them like a green net, and Pretty was conscious of unease. White men could be as easily trapped here as hapless flies in a spider web. But nothing happened. While the casks were being filled—just enough water for today—Cavendish and Pretty stood watch, their muskets loaded, both of them knowing that a few masket shots would be of no use at all before a concerted attack.

The walls of the jungle closed around them again as they made their way back to the white hot beach. The great volcano thrust itself upward; smoke curled from it. The sun beat down and the blue water sparkled in the heat; Cavendish had to squint to look out and see the *Desire,* riding so nattily at anchor and looking almost incredibly out of place in the blue bay of a savage and primitive island, so far away from home.

There were no fisher canoes on the surface of the bay, yet. There were only the *Desire's* boats, for some of the crew were fishing for tonight's meal. Cavendish knew that beyond the narrow strip of sand, before the jungle began, native eyes were watching. Soon perhaps they would dare to come forth and speak with the English. He stepped into his boat.

But the next day was the same. The land was silent. Fuller had set part of the men to cutting new canvas for the mainsheet; they worked during the early hours of the morning and evening, to escape the sun. The water casks had to be cleaned and filled. Cavendish went ashore with armed guards, while more of the crew cut wood. They lived on fish caught in the waters of the bay. And thus eight days passed.

"We must have food," Cavendish said.

Around the table in the big cabin, at midday dinner, the other officers listened gravely.

"I do not want to use force," Cavendish said. "I'm afraid to use it, because, should we approach their town through the jungle, they might make off with all their food, and leave the village bare." He threw his hands out, helplessly. "I don't want to try force," he repeated, "but, of course, we may have to. That is why, Fuller, I want to weigh anchor and stand in nearer the shore. We shall approach the town from the bay, then."

"Aye, sir," Fuller said, rising to his feet.

"We shall stand in nearer the town, and bring it within range of the guns. Then they will flee so quickly that they will not have time to take their livestock with them."

"Aye, sir," said Fuller again.

"We need the oxen I can hear lowing," said Cavendish, smiling, to ease the gravity with which he was being regarded. "And we shall wait one more day."

Pretty followed Cavendish. "You'll wait one more day, sir?" he asked, trailing behind his Captain.

"The danger," said Cavendish slowly, so that Pretty

knew from long observation that he was frowning, "is their preponderant numbers." He had emerged onto the deck ahead of Pretty, and he stopped so suddenly that Pretty bumped into him.

"Sorry, sir!" Pretty said, and stared at the bay.

"You see what I mean?" Cavendish asked. The anchor cables were already creaking, and the crew was tumbling out on deck. Pretty heard Moon's voice as the gun ports opened. Cavendish ran down to the boat deck. He did not raise his voice.

"Master Moon!"

"Aye, aye, sir!"

"Hold your fire until I give you word!"

"Aye, aye, sir!"

Slowly Cavendish walked to the rail. "Master Pretty," he said over his shoulder, "fetch the Negro from wherever he is hiding himself. We're going to talk first—if they'll let us."

Pretty gave one last look at the bay. He had never seen so many canoes in his life. The paddles flashed as they streamed toward the *Desire* in the midday sun. The wind was very scant, and the *Desire* moved lazily, her sails hanging, and Cavendish knew that if this was an attack, they had picked the day well, for the *Desire* was almost becalmed. He looked up at the sails. Then he turned and bellowed for Cosmos to bring the glass.

Cosmos came running with it. He handed it to Cavendish and watched as the Captain raised it to his eyes. Still squinting through it, Cavendish said, "You are not afraid, are you, Cosmos?"

"No, sir," Cosmos said.

"You needn't be," Cavendish said, and there was relief in his tone. He called out, "Moon! There are women in those canoes. You can save that fire!"

Moon came running up on the boat deck, his face wreathed in smiles. He took the glass from Cavendish's fingers.

"By God, sir, look at them!"

"I am looking," said Cavendish. "Where's the Negro?"

"Here, sir," said Pretty.

It was only twenty minutes before the first canoe slid

up alongside the *Desire*. There were ten men in it, and one of them was the native to whom they had talked eight days ago.

"Bid him good day," Cavendish ordered the Negro.

But the native had already begun to talk. He stood up in the canoe, waving his hands; he gesticulated and smiled, and Pretty was sure he was going to fall overboard in his excitement. Finally he was finished.

"What did he say?" asked Cavendish impatiently, cutting short the Negro who was answering the native in his own tongue, with more smiles and gesticulations.

The Negro stopped talking and turned to Cavendish. He could hardly get the words out. "He says you are welcome! He says the King says he is honored to welcome white man, English. He is most honored! He sends you gifts of food, and pearls, and wines, and bids his people make joy and dancing for you. He says you come nearer town, now!"

"Tell him we are honored too," Cavendish said, speaking slowly. "Tell him we shall stand in nearer the town, if the wind permits. Tell him we send our greetings from the Queen of England to his King."

The Negro translated Cavendish's words. When he heard them, the native waved his hands again.

"He has more message," the Negro said.

The native talked again.

"He says the King has sent his own Secretary, and his interpreter, and members of his court to welcome royal white Captain. And, sir, he says there are two white men coming to meet you!"

"Two white men?" Cavendish asked, frowning.

"Aye, sir, he says that, two white men."

"If they're Spanish, this is a trick," Cavendish said.

"What'll we do then?" Moon asked excitedly.

"Wait and see," Cavendish said.

The Negro interrupted. "They are Portuguese, Portuguese, sir!"

At almost the same moment the wind sprang up. The great mainsail filled, the *Desire* quickened her way, and spray flew up from her bows. Around the *Desire* the canoes were thick now; they followed her, streams of them.

The crew hung over the rails, waving. A canoe full of girls came up alongside, and Tyler almost fell into the water as he tossed down a rolled-up yard of linen. It was seized eagerly, and the girl who caught it put it over her shoulders carefully.

The native men were almost naked. The women wore a single garment, twisted under the armpits, and they were fair of complexion. Aboard the *Desire*, the men stared down at the laughing faces beneath them. Tyler was dissatisfied to hang over the rail; he showed his prowess by mounting high into the rigging and waving his arms to the girls as he perched up there. The wind held and the *Desire* stood in slowly toward the town; then she struck her sails and heaved out her anchors. She rode quietly about three cables length from shore.

The natives had brought food, precious food. Live hens, drakes and geese. Eggs, plantains, sugar in plates, coconuts, limes, oranges, lemons, salt and spices, and stores of wine.

And then the Portuguese came, with the officers of the King's court. They were dressed in European dress, with fine lawn shirts.

The two Portuguese tumbled onto the deck and came running to Cavendish. They seized his hands.

"We are so glad to see you!" they cried, simultaneously.

Cavendish said politely, "I am no less glad to see you, sirs."

"Our King," they were both crying. "Don Antonio of Portugal, is he dead?"

"No," said Cavendish. He started to explain Don Antonio's whereabouts, but the Portuguese were shouting loudly with joy and venting epithets on the Spanish who had told them their King was dead.

"Those thrice-damned Spanish," the one Portugal was repeating, over and over. Finally he asked, "Where is our King, then?"

Cavendish said, "In England. He took sanctuary in England, under Her Majesty Queen Elizabeth. Her Majesty has given him an honorable allowance."

"You fight with Spain?" the Portugal cried, pointing at Cavendish. "You have sunk their ships?"

"Twenty," said Cavendish, turning down the corners of his mouth so he would not smile.

They clutched his arm; one kissed him soundly on the cheek. Moon turned away to hide his face, and the crew giggled with merriment.

"We must have some wine," Cavendish said hastily, "and we can drink to your King, Don Antonio. And to the King of this land."

"They are preparing a feast for you," the Portuguese cried. He pointed to the town. "There is far more food for you, Captain, too! There are live oxen, and plenty of live hogs. Only, the wind was so scant and the canoes so deeply laden, they could not put out from shore."

Cavendish grinned with pleasure.

"We'll go below," he said, "and get out of this sun." He leaned down and picked up an orange from a big woven basket. He began to peel it, and between bites he told Moon how many men could go ashore now.

"I'm sending almost all of them," he said to the Portuguese. "God knows they need it. They're taking presents for the women."

He was leading the way to the great cabin. It was cooler there, and Cosmos brought wine and the fruit. The Portuguese and Cavendish began to talk.

When darkness fell, all the company were back aboard. Pretty had not gone ashore, either. He had stayed with Cavendish, and watched the men come back, laughing, singing, and most of them a little drunk. Tyler hurriedly helped a shipmate across the deck, and Cavendish pretended not to see. He looked the other way, and the Portuguese laughed.

"No incidents," said Cavendish feelingly.

The Portuguese said, for the twentieth time, "You come ashore now, Captain. We have prepared dinner, and wines. In the finest house."

Pretty grinned. There was open affection in his eyes. "Why don't you go, sir?" he asked softly.

"Come with me, then," Cavendish said, and he waved to Fuller and slid down into the Portuguese boat.

Ashore they took him to a house with carved wooden pillars, set under trees. Inside it was cool, and there were low couches with pillows. The Portugals could not keep from smiling.

"It is a joy to have you!" one kept repeating.

The food was wonderful. They had roasted chickens and pork, fruit, and rice, heaped high and served with a strange pungent sauce.

"It's marvelous," said Cavendish.

"How he eats!" said the Portugal to Pretty; and turning to Cavendish, "Taste this wine, Captain."

Cavendish raised the full cup to his lips. It was clear and colorless. "It's as strong as Scots whiskey," he said. "Or aqua vitae."

He was full of food. He had eaten a whole chicken besides tasting of all the other food.

"It's enough to make a man very drunk," the Portugal said, happily. "Like the islands from which it comes."

Cavendish drank it off. He leaned back against the pillows, putting his feet up. His whole body felt relaxed.

"We brought you something else," his host said. He spoke a few words in Javanese, and Cavendish turned his head lazily. The curtains of the doorway parted and a girl came into the room.

"She speaks a little Portuguese."

She moved like a cat. She wore a single garment wrapped around her; her bare shoulders were golden; she went over to Cavendish and sank down on the earthen floor beside him.

"She is virgin, Captain," said the Portuguese.

Cavendish looked at her. The Portugal grinned. "A nice present, is she not?" He stood up and filled Cavendish's cup. "You have a long voyage ahead," he said.

"I wanted to hear more about China and India," Cavendish said, letting his eyes rest on the girl beside him.

"I tell you," the Portugal said eagerly.

The lamps flickered. Outside, the jungle insects sang softly. Cavendish listened to the Portugals talk; strange names rolled off their tongues; Cavendish tried to remember them. Suddenly he sat up and unbuckled his belt. Without a word, the girl took it from him and laid it on the floor beside her.

He lay back again, stretching luxuriously. He reached one hand over to touch the bare shoulder so near him. The Portugal kept right on talking about Soychin, and Canton, and Paquin; the girl moved a little. Her skin was smooth under his fingers. He held out his empty cup to her.

She stood up like a fluid column and refilled his cup. The wine was stronger than whiskey and it rolled down his throat, burning like fire.

"Are you writing all this down, Pretty?" he asked, his eyes half closed.

"Aye, sir," said Pretty.

Cavendish turned over on his side. He was a little drunk. The girl's dark eyes were fastened on him; he held out the cup to her again.

She brought it back to him. He took it from her and sat up drinking off the white liquor in one draught. A lock of short hair fell over his forehead as he leaned back again, and the girl smoothed it back with her hand.

He said low, "Do that more."

She smiled, her white teeth gleaming. He felt her fingers as she stroked his head. The Portugal was still talking, and Cavendish did not hear a word he said. Then the Portugal rose to his feet.

"We leave you, Captain," he said.

Pretty said, "Good night, sir." He started for the doorway, but he gave one last look at his Captain, who had not waited until he left the room. He had already pulled the girl down beside him, in a close and passionate embrace.

Chapter 33

THE MULE TRAIN was very slow. The heat was intense. The spring sun burned down on the sand, as the mules struggled onward across this strip of continent that separated two great oceans.

The mules walked slowly enough to allow the native bearers to keep up with them. There was little talk among the men; the journey was coming to an end, soon. The Indians who walked alongside the burdened mules slapped lazily at the animals with whip or broad-leaved branch which they used also as a fan. Only a few natty horsemen rode ahead of the train, and in the middle came a few litters, borne on the shoulders of four dark-skinned Indians.

Catherine wore a broad-brimmed hat to protect her face and throat from the sun. The same kind of hat was worn by Kate, who rode at her side on an ambling mule, with Tina walking beside her.

It was midday. In the swaying litter, Catherine dozed in the heat. It should be time to stop; all morning they had been crossing this belt of sand that meant that Vera Cruz was near.

Suddenly there came the sound of voices, the natives began to chatter, and ahead the first horseman pointed with his whip.

Kate cried excitedly, "I see the blue of the ocean!"

Catherine raised herself up. Across the shimmering waves of heat and sand was the faint blue of the sea, and the outline of the old town clustered at the side of the harbor. She looked forward eagerly.

The sea. It was homecoming. Across its pathway some day they would meet again, and she felt happiness rise in her, for during this long journey she had been bound by land and hemmed in by rough mountains, and now, once more, the sea would pound on the beaches near and she would be nearer to him because of it.

It was two o'clock before they entered the town. Even the arrival of the mule train failed to rouse it from its afternoon siesta. The sun beat down on the harbor, gleamed on the brilliant blue of the water. The harbor was narrow, bordered with long reefs, dotted with islands, and the surf near those barriers was so glitteringly white that it was hard to look at it.

The wind was offshore. The bay was quiet as a lake, except for its surf, and the adobe houses lay baking in heat that had already turned them the soft colors of palest pink and faded green.

The mule train came to a stop before a long low building. On its rude porch a number of seamen lounged, idly talking, looking now at the few Spanish women. Not far away, a few hundred feet from shore, rode a large ship, dwarfing the other smaller craft, and the native fishing boats.

The horseman rode up to Catherine, spurs jingling, swarthy face beaded with sweat.

"I shall take you directly to the Alcalde," he said, smiling. "I expect you'll be glad to get there."

Catherine said, "I shall, and, tell me, *señor,* is it always so hot here?"

He grinned. "Always, *señora.* But there's the *Concepción.*" He pointed to the ship. "She sails tomorrow with the tide."

He wheeled his horse again, and barked a few words to the native bearers, who increased their pace reluctantly. Catherine lay back again, for the litter was swinging back and forth.

They passed the long low building, and Catherine scanned the faces of the men there. None of them was David. None of them could be. He was dead.

"This is Vera Cruz at last, Tina."

They stopped again quickly, before a house, low and square, with the semblance of a garden; the grilled door opened, and the horsemen leaped down, just as the bearers set the litter down gratefully. The horseman helped Catherine step out, and lifted Kate down from the brown mule. The two Indians with the mules which bore Catherine's boxes, two strapped on each side, waited patiently in the sun.

Inside it was cooler. The lattices were shut, and no sun was allowed to show itself inside. The house was quiet, and Catherine heard the sound of water playing in the inner courtyard. It reminded her of Spain. Then a woman entered the room.

Catherine was surprised. She had expected to see the Alcalde himself. Instead she saw a rather voluptuous woman coming toward her, hands outstretched in greeting.

"My poor child," said the woman. "What a trip you have had!"

Catherine took her hands in her own sweaty ones, and returned the firm friendly grip. Then Catherine took off her hat, brushing the hair back from her forehead, and Tina removed Kate's hat.

"It was a bad trip, *señora*," Catherine said. "We are glad to be here." She was a little cautious.

The woman smiled, as if she understood Catherine's caution. "My husband—the Alcalde—is asleep," she said. "I wanted to welcome you myself."

She had dressed herself especially, in her finest black gown of satin and lace. It had been a pleasure to get dressed even though the Alcalde had snored heartily and had not been on hand to admire her. She studied Catherine while the booted Spaniard presented the two women.

"And my daughter, Señorita de Montoro," Catherine said.

"You pet," Señora Araceno said, "you little pet. Now, sir, if you'll have the *señora's* boxes brought in, I can show her to her chambers."

The Spaniard bowed and disappeared.

"I'm going to take you right back to your chamber," Señora Araceno continued. "It is a corner room, having a window on the courtyard, too."

"Gracias," Catherine said, with such undisguised pleasure in her voice that the word of thanks was sufficient against the other woman's volubility.

She hurried Catherine along. If she was going to do what she had planned, as soon as she had learned that Catherine was coming to her, she would have to do it quickly and act quickly.

"There is a small chamber next, for your woman and the little one."

"That is marvelously kind of you. Truly," Catherine said. "Even if we are here for such a short time. The *Concepción* sails soon, I think."

Señora Araceno sat down on a stool. "Sit on the bed," she said.

Her eyes met Catherine's and she watched Catherine settle herself gratefully on the soft bed. "Pull the pillows in back of you," she continued, for Catherine's figure was aready full. Catherine sighed a little, and leaned her head back, her long lashes fell against her cheeks, and Señora Araceno looked at her with a certain proprietary air, for she knew that Catherine was a woman defenseless now through her love for a man. She also knew instinctively that Catherine would not mind demands for money, and she would be prepared to meet them as frankly as she, Señora Araceno, intended to ask for them.

She said, "I wanted to talk with you before my husband wakened."

Catherine's eyes flew open; a quick excitement and hope gleamed in them. "I have brought you a gift," she said. "A string of matched pearls. They were a happy choice for your coloring."

Señora Araceno smiled. "Your name is Catherine. I wish you would call me Antonia."

Catherine swung her legs over the side of the bed. She had kicked her shoes off. Her boxes had been brought in, and she opened the small one, and drew out what she wanted. She held up the pearls.

"For you, Antonia," she said. She got back onto the bed.

Antonia fingered the pearls with delight. "I was going to help you anyway," she said. "As soon as I heard of you, and that you were coming here."

Catherine said simply, "Why?"

Antonia said, "I've been in trouble, too. Perhaps that is why." She laughed; she was very handsome, and her zest showed readily when she laughed. "I have been thinking that if you stayed here with me until your child is born, then you could sail to Spain and you would be better able to—make your way. Captain Cavendish is your second husband?"

Catherine nodded, curling her legs up on the bed.

"I've had three," Antonia said companionably. "When do you expect your child?"

"In the first weeks of August," Catherine said.

"I shall tell the Alcalde, my husband, that you cannot be moved till then. He will listen."

Catherine said, "*Señora*—Antonia, I am not very well." She drew her brows together, and then, with no warning, as had happened so often lately, she felt the dizziness descending. Antonia leaped to her feet and called for Tina.

Vera Cruz slept. Out in the harbor the little islands lay blanketed in the sun. Under a rude shelter, on the farthest island from the town, a woman lay asleep. She was dreaming.

She dreamed that she could not breathe. Across her chest a band of steel prevented her from drawing breath. In the dream the water was not cold, as it had been that day some months ago. But everything else was the same.

Around her waist, David's arm was gripping hard. Her fingers clung to the side of the bark, but she was drowning, and David would not let her put her head out of the water for air. He had said he would drown her first—that was the last thing he had said.

She hadn't struggled against him. She could hear nothing. She had watched the Spanish longboat approach the bark, and when it drew near, David had drawn her over the side, and he and Sebastian had got a good grip on the hanging rope. Then they had waited.

When the Spanish officer stepped onto the deck, David had pulled her under. She held her breath until the agony forced her to suck in water. He did not let her go. She could not plead. He lifted her up. She drew in air. Then he pulled her down again, the cold water closing over her head; her hair floated around her face and the agony set in again, only this time it did not last long. It pounded through her chest, and then she lost consciousness.

She remembered little. The Spanish had gone for a few minutes. It had been time enough for Sebastian and David to swim to shore, supporting her between them. On the river bank, where they had laid her for a minute, Sebastian had said, "She'll not die."

"It might be just as well," David said. Then they had carried her to the trees and watched while the Spaniards came back and towed the bark away.

That night David had stolen an Indian canoe, and they had started their voyage up the Verde River, to Vera Cruz. Now the Spaniards thought David was dead. They thought she was dead, and Sebastian too. Now David was pleased with the whole adventure, and he was waiting for Catherine to come to Vera Cruz.

But the dream persisted. Lola stirred in her sleep; she wakened, gratefully. David's arm lay across her breast; it was heavy, and she moved it. He was back, then. He must have come while she lay sound asleep. He slept himself, soundly, and she was conscious of nothing but joy that he had returned again.

He was restless here, on this tiny island. Two days ago he had left her here, with Sebastian, and he had gone to Vera Cruz to learn what news there was. But now he slept alongside her, and she put her hand in the tousled hair. Had he been with another woman in Vera Cruz? His lashes were thick and short; they lay against his cheek; he smelled of wine. Suddenly his eyes opened.

Lola lay still.

"What are you thinking?" he said.

The sound of his voice made her sigh. He would know she had been regarding him while he slept.

"I was only thinking I love you," she said. "You drink, David? In Vera Cruz?"

He chuckled lazily. "Not much, wench." He drew her into his arms. "I have good news. Catherine has come to Vera Cruz!"

Lola lay on her back and looked up at his face. She said slowly, "Do you love her, David?"

He plainly showed his amazement. "Love her?" he repeated.

"*Sí*," whispered Lola.

"No!" said David.

"Oh," said Lola. "You see Catherine tonight?"

He nodded. "I must be careful; she thinks me dead. And I am far from dead. Not so, wench?" He paused, regarding her. "You thought I was in love with Catherine?"

Lola said timidly, "You see, *señor,* I thought perhaps you *thought* you were."

"Nonsense," he said. "Catherine is Tom's wife. What other nonsense have you been thinking in your little head?"

Lola said, "No nonsense. Were you with a woman in Vera Cruz?"

He grinned. "Very many," he said. "But I still want a kiss."

"I am tanned like an Indian," Lola said. "I have brown hands." She held them up. "How can I suit you?"

He laughed. "Show me where you are still white."

"David," she said.

"Soon I will take you to England," he said. "Soon we shall be able to sail, now that Catherine is here." His hands were on her unfastening her blouse. Her red mouth was ready for his kisses. Her dark eyes were open; he knew that soon she would close them in surrender to his passion. He slipped off her blouse, and it was true, what she had said. She was tanned, an even golden brown; only her breasts were white and the flat stomach and rounded hips. He whispered, "Lola. Lola, you know it's you I love."

At sundown, David had his usual swim. Afterward he put on the loose canvas trousers he had bought in Vera Cruz. He pulled on his boots, and walked back from the sea through the brush to the little camp.

The fire was going. Fish stew simmered atop the flames; there were meal cakes to eat with it. David took his clean shirt off a branch where Lola had hung it to dry. Lola stirred the stew with a large wooden spoon. Sebastian waited for his dinner. David sat down.

"The Señora Catherine is here, Sebastian," David said.

Sebastian nodded. "I know, *señor!*"

"Sebastian, it is known that she is Madam Cavendish. She is being sent to Spain."

Sebastian wriggled his bare feet. He wanted to say something comforting, but the Señor David was thinking, and he was afraid for the Señora Catherine, and Sebastian prayed that the Señor David would be able to think of a way to help the *señora* since he wished it so much.

"I am sorry," Sebastian said, finally.

David picked up a handful of sand and watched it trickle through his fingers to the ground. "Thank you, Sebastian," he said.

The sun was going down. Lola ladled out the stew; the men ate it, picking the pieces of fish out with their fingers, drinking the liquid from the tin basins. When he had finished, David washed his hands. Lola gathered up the basins and started down the beach to scrub them with sand and wash them in the sea. She came back and dropped down beside the two men. It was cooler now.

Sebastian scattered the pieces of wood that were still smoldering. The three of them sat in silence, and just at sundown David stood up.

"I'll go now," he said.

Sebastian rose. "I go, also?"

"No. You guard my *señorita*."

He went down to the beach again. He put his boots in the canoe, and carried it into the water. In five minutes he had beached it on the mainland, and hidden it in the brush. He began to walk toward the town.

It took thirty minutes of fast walking. By the time he reached the outskirts, the night was dark and only the stars illumined the night. He passed an ale-house. He came to the house of the Alcalde of Vera Cruz.

Two lights burned inside. David was glad to see the house was low and square. At one of the windows should be the woman he wanted to see. He might have to wait, but eventually she would come to one of these rooms, and he had only to step into the window.

But he waited only another thirty minutes before a lamp shone out of a corner room. He heard Catherine's voice, and he crept along the wall until he looked into the slatted window. He knew he should wait longer, but he could not help himself.

"Catherine," he said, insistently, softly.

He saw her turn toward the window. For a moment she stood motionless. Then she ran toward it; she said. "Wait!"

He watched her go to the lamp and set it on the floor, and only a faint glow came from it. Then she came back and raised the blinds; he threw his foot over the sill; the blind dropped again.

"David!" she said. She was trembling with excitement; her eyes filled with tears. "You are alive! I thought—I thought—they told me you were dead!"

He had taken her hands, holding them tight, while she looked up at his face, seeing the quick smile and the eager exuberance. Catherine said, "You are more alive than ever!"

He smiled. "And you are here!"

She could not believe he stood before her, tall and strong. She said, "While I was in Acapulco, the *Eugenia* returned, with the little bark."

"I could not let you know the truth," he said. "But it is best now, Catherine, for I can move about freely enough. I will be able to sign on as a seaman aboard the *Concepción*."

"The *Concepción?*" There was so much to tell him. "I shall be allowed to stay here, until my child is born."

His eyes took in her figure. "You are bearing Tom's child?"

She said, "Whose else?"

He laughed. "I'm not doubting your virtue." Then he added quickly, "Why are you allowed to stay here?"

"Señora Araceno. She will help. She has helped."

He did not have much time. It was imperative that his presence should not be discovered; it was imperative that he stay safely dead.

"Do not trust this woman until you are sure, until time has passed," he said, frowning. "But I am here now. I shall come again. I will not leave you again, Catherine." He was thinking that later in the summer, Catherine could use Lola. They could all sail after the baby was born; Lola and Catherine and Tina, together. He told her that, quickly, summing up the plans. Then he said: "I cannot stay longer; I must go."

He went to the window.

"Sleep well," he said. "I am here, now."

"Oh, David," she said.

He took her bright head in his hands; he kissed her lightly.

"I'll bring you to Tom. The bastard. He has complicated matters."

She was smiling at him. He knew she felt happy. And much safer. He told himself there was no reason for the disquietude he felt as he looked at her.

"You can trust this woman?" he asked. "Señora Araceno?"

"I'm sure, David," she said. "I can tell."

He nodded. "Then sleep well. Dream of Tom." He was out the window. The blind closed behind him. He walked on, deep in thought.

Chapter 34

"THE REST OF MARCH, and all the month of April," wrote Master Pretty in the leather-bound journal, "we spent in traversing that mighty and vast sea between the island of Java and the main of Africa, observing the heavens, the Southern Cross, the other stars, the fowls, which are marks to seamen of fair weather, foul weather, and approaching of islands; the winds; the tempests; with the alternating of tides and currents."

Pretty looked up as Moon came into the cabin. He nodded but Moon was preoccupied with putting on another pair of boots, and was not disposed to conversation. Pretty wrote on:

"The tenth of May we had a storm at the west, and it blew so hard, it was as much as the ship could stir close by under the wind, and the storm continued all that day and all that night.

"The sixteenth day of May, about four o'clock in the afternoon, the wind came up from the east a very stiff gale, which held until Saturday with as much wind as the ship could go before, at which time by six o'clock in the morning we espied the promontory or headland called the Cape of Good Hope."

Moon stood up. "What are you saying?" he said, looking over Pretty's shoulder into the open book.

Pretty said embarrassedly, "Nothing much, Moon."

Moon said, "Aren't you going to put in that the Captain corrected the Portuguese sea charts by one hundred and fifty leagues, in the crossing of the ocean?"

"Certainly," said Pretty, laboriously writing it down under Moon's eyes. He tried to pretend Moon was not watching the words as he wrote them down. He continued doggedly, with Moon repeating the words aloud to himself as Pretty's pen scratched on.

" 'The eighth of June,' " read Moon. "You're bringing this up to date, I see. 'We fell in sight of the island of St. Helena. The next day having a pretty easy gale of wind, we stood in with the shore, the Captain having his boat sent away before to make harbor, and about one o'clock in the afternoon we came to anchor in twelve fathoms of water two or three cables' length from shore, in a very smooth and fair bay under the northwest side of the island."

"Aye," said Moon, buckling his belt, "and you'd better hurry, or you'll hear that Captain asking Fuller where the devil you are. We're going ashore."

Pretty grinned. "I'm coming," he said. He closed the book. "I want to observe this island, Moon. I like to write about the lands we see."

"Well, don't forget it's hot, fair as it seems." And he added, "And for your information, Pretty, the island lies in 15 degrees, 48 minutes, to the southward of the equinoctial line."

"I know it," said Pretty stiffly.

Moon mounted the narrow ladder, using cheerful and obscene language about the absence of women on this island. He was talking as he reached the deck. Cavendish heard him and began to laugh.

"There are flocks of goats, Moon," he said, sliding down into his boat. He watched the shoreline as they pulled to the curving beach.

Pretty was staring ahead too. There was a valley spread out before them; from the trees and the sloping hills behind the valley rose a church spire. They tumbled out onto the beach and there was a path, well defined, leading into the little valley. It was like a big fruitful garden, cradled in hills.

Cavendish walked ahead, his musket held loosely under his arm. He walked along under the fig trees; there were pomegranates and date trees. The air was sweet, and through the valley a stream tumbled, coming swiftly from the hills that had given it birth.

Walks led to the few white houses with porches. The church was tiled, and it boasted a porch, too. He set the musket against the stoop, and entered the small church. He closed the door behind himself.

It was cool and half dark inside. At the upper end was a large table, and on it a picture of the Saviour on the Cross and the image of the Virgin. The sides of the little church were hung with tapestries.

He knelt down and bent his head. The church reminded him of Havers; kneeling there reminded him of Catherine, and the night they had taken their vows.

It was June. June already. By now she should be in Spain, or perhaps even in England. She had only one ocean to cross, and the great Spanish galleons plied that ocean regularly and often. That made him remember that he himself might sight Spanish ships soon. He rose to his feet, dug in his pocket for a coin which he put in the box on the table. Then he went out, closing the door again and picking up the fowling piece he had laid against the stoop.

Moon was waiting.

"There's nobody here, in these houses, save six Negro slaves who keep the gardens. Smell the spices, sir!"

Cavendish sniffed. There were radishes and mustard plants growing here in the orchards, parsley and fragrant basil and fennel.

"The Portuguese use these islands as a stopping place only. The Negroes said we missed the East Indian fleet by twenty days. And the place is crawling with pheasants, sir!"

Cavendish smiled. "Call all hands," he said. "We'll have a shoot."

But there was more to be done than to shoot partridge, important as that was. The next day Cavendish set about to clean up the ship, and ready her for the voyage home.

The *Desire* had taken very heavy seas for the last weeks. Her decks were crusted. The men took white sand from the beaches to scrub her with.

Her sails were torn. She had only the one suit of sails left; these were patched, with leather patches, sewed on carefully. The men cut new spars; the ship's carpenters worked all during the days, and all the water casks were cleaned and filled once more.

During these two weeks the men grew fatter again. There were flocks of wild goats on the island—flocks so big they seemed at least a mile long as they traveled together, their shaggy beards hanging down almost to their feet, climbing the steep mountains with incredible surefootedness. But swift as they were, the *Desire's* crew caught them. They caught wild fat vicious hogs, which they slaughtered and salted. There were guinea hens, black and white, with red heads, and these laid eggs. The eggs tasted marvelous, boiled or made into omelettes. Cavendish had an omelette every day for breakfast, and he too gained weight, after the weeks at sea.

It was the twentieth of June before the *Desire* was ready for the sea again, her patched sails brave, her new spars gleaming with oil and tar. Once again she was well provisioned; once again she had fresh water and fresh-cut wood aboard. That night, at eight o'clock, she set sail. The wind was at the southeast, and the *Desire* haled away from the island northwest by west. On the fourth day of July she crossed the equinoctial line for the fourth time. The *Desire* set her course for the Azores.

Now foul weather set in; the *Desire* reefed her weakened topsails and sailed on, close under the gales. It was summer now, and the weather was warm, but the summer storms were swift and unpredictable, and they lashed themselves at the sea-weary *Desire;* deeply laden, she struggled with the winds and currents of her own ocean.

It seemed to Cavendish that every sunrise showed him patchy clouds and a gray and white ocean. The storms blew down from the northeast; August passed, and the weather grew worse; all August it was bad, and now every morning, as he paced the deck, he looked upward at the straining sails.

On the twenty-fourth they sighted the Azores. He did not put into the islands. They were too near England. The ocean was calm, the wind from the southwest, a gentle wind, and the *Desire* was carrying full canvas. Even so, he watched the sails again that day.

"We should be done with foul weather," Moon said.

"Aye, we should," Cavendish replied, but there was no assurance in his tones.

Moon looked surprised. "The weather seems fair enough," he offered.

But the wind had dropped even as they talked. The

sea looked molten and heavily and satinly gray. Over their heads the gulls screamed, and then the seabirds wheeled, in a flock, and soon they were lost to sight in the gray skies. The birds knew well when storms were coming.

Moon fidgeted. "We're so near home," he said.

"You can drown here as anywhere else," Cavendish said. "Send men aloft to brace the rigging and run preventer rigs up the yardarms. Batten all hatches except the main hatch. Double lash all boats." He was staring ahead, frowning. "That's all Moon. This blow is going to be soon."

He went below. He was working on his charts of the Straits. It had not been accident that he had taken twenty-two days to go through the Straits. His charts would be vastly important to the men to follow him. His charts would be accurate and complete, and when he worked on them he could forget that Havers did not smoke his pipe and lounge in his hammock, talking; he could not forget it perhaps, but it was better to work.

The first sign of storm came when the *Desire* began to roll a little. He was out of his cabin in a second, and up the narrow stairs to the poop. Wind greeted him.

The ocean had already responded. Now, before his eyes, the heaving quiet gray was gone. Like a harp whose strings had been violated by a restless hand, the sea was answering the call of the wind.

Spray was flying. The *Desire* was beating now to windward, taking the seas across her bows; her decks were awash as the water foamed over them.

Cavendish raised his voice. "Master Fuller, strike all sails!"

The wind blew the words away. Men were in the shrouds, in the rigging. It was almost dusk. Cavendish had allowed no fires tonight in the galley stoves, but he had ordered an extra ration of wine. And they might need more in the night to come of that strong powerful white liquor from the East Indies.

The wind had a high whining sound to it. It was blowing directly from the northeast. The rigging braces creaked; and the great ocean was moving itself and bestirring itself as it prepared for an Atlantic summer storm that was going to leave its mark on history. Leagues to the north, a Spanish and English fleet were locked in battle for the control of the seas, and the building of a vast empire was in its beginning.

The *Desire* shuddered as she took the next roller. Her timbers protested; she had fought many battles against the seas. She plunged heavily down the next crested wave, and before she could lift herself, an angry twenty-foot comber of water came crashing down on her decks. Even on the high poop, the water flew up in Cavendish's face. He knew before the end of this storm she would be taking water across the stern.

It was almost dark. Dead ahead, he saw the curtain of slanting rain coming, steely and strong and cold. He reached quickly for the clasp of his leather jacket and fastened it tightly around his neck. Automatically his eyes squinted, his head bent a little, and then the rain began to beat down on the *Desire*. Moon came struggling up the poopdeck.

"Jesu," he said, "you were right about the weather." Cavendish looked out to sea. The night had come; with the storm the night had descended, as though to make the tasks of men and ships more stern. Out of the blackness, the terrible crested rollers arose dead ahead, almost upon the weary ship before they could be seen.

"It's foul weather!" Moon yelled. His hat blew off in another gust of wind, and he snatched vainly at it, stumbling to regain his balance as the *Desire* pitched sharply. "But we have gold as ballast!"

Cavendish did not smile. "This is what the Indians call *huracán*," he said.

Now they both had to hold onto the ropes to keep from being swept overboard. Moon felt fear for the first time. The *Desire* shook as she took the next wave, and again water poured over her decks, and poured from her scuppers as she lifted herself, and came up to the head of a huge trough that suddenly appeared in the water beneath her.

This time she took water worse than before. It came crashing down on her and at the same time there was a splintering sound, and a tearing sound, and Cavendish knew instantly what it was. He ran down to the main deck.

The lanyards on the great mainsail had broken loose; the yardarm swung outward, and Tyler, on the deck, threw himself flat on his face and slid across to the rail, the water splashing over him, carrying him down the deck like a toy. He seized a hatch top and clung to it frantically.

The *Desire* lay on her side. Then she righted. Cavendish jerked Tyler to his feet. Both men struggled forward to the broken lanyards and as they did, a piece of sail came free, tearing free; the wind caught it.

Cavendish started up the shrouds. Braced in the top, he drew his knife and began to cut.

There was no need to shout orders. They could not have been heard anyway. The men knew what to do. The yard hung lopsidedly. The sail was whirled out by the wind and the mast must be freed from the torn sail; it was too weak to take the strain.

He clung with one hand, bracing himself while he slashed through ropes and braces with his knife, great tearing slashes. The howling of the wind and the crashing of water were in his ears; faintly he heard shouts, as a great wave caught the *Desire* amidships. She rolled over; Cavendish threw both arms around the mast. He was over the water, angry beneath him. A terrible ripping sound told him the sail had gone; the mast was freed; they had saved it, perhaps. But there was no sail left.

Fuller, at the helm, felt the ship right herself. Cavendish slid down onto the deck. The waves were waves no longer; they were mighty rollers, as though from the bottom of the sea, and they were crested and thirty feet high as they surged up on the ship.

The *Desire* shuddered from bow to stern. Cavendish clung against the shroud. He could not move. A wall of water crashed over his head; the force of it almost sent him hurtling across the deck, his fingers stiff on the ratlines. But he held on, and when the water surged past him, he saw that the foresail had gone too. Pretty must be fore. He knew grimly that even if they could save the ship, only the mizzen's lateen sail would be left.

He struggled forward, foot by foot, to reach the safety of the poop. It was no longer possible to stay on deck.

Below decks, it took three men to hold the helm. Men were manning the pumps; all through the night the sound of the pumps would be in his ears. If the ship survived.

"North northeast," Cavendish said. The water dripped from him.

"Aye, sir," Tyler said.

The whole ship trembled. Above their heads the weight of tons of water buried the *Desire* and sounded like thunder. She keeled over, then she righted. The sweat was pouring down Tyler's face. Cavendish shouldered him aside. He took the helm himself. If they didn't hold the *Desire* into the wind, she would go. The sound of the pumps was insistent.

At two o'clock Fuller relieved Cavendish at the helm. At the end of the middle watch, Cavendish went out on deck. The boats were gone, all save one. The *Desire* was still taking water over the stern.

When the gray dawn came, the *Desire* pitched on an angry and lonely ocean. The wind had shifted to the northwest; the waves still washed over the decks as the *Desire* slowly and laboriously mastered the troughs and the crests, and her great mainmast still towered over her, bare and empty of sail.

Chapter 35

ON THE MORNING of the twenty-fourth of August, Catherine woke in pain. She stirred, stretched her legs, raised herself on her elbow. In the faint gray of morning light she saw Lola.

Lola was sound asleep. She had placed her mat on the floor, near the window, and Catherine didn't want to wake her, so she settled back, pushed the sheet down with her feet.

Gradually the room became lighter. On the table was her sewing basket, with the almost-made linen blouse for Lola spilling over it. In the corner was her easel. The seascape on it was not done; indeed it was scarcely begun, for though she walked every day at sundown on the beaches of Vera Cruz, she had no will to paint. It was quite enough to walk the beaches, lazily, at the very edge of the water, where the sand was damp, gray and hard from the outgoing tides. Then the sand was cool under her bare feet, and the murmur of the sea was in her ears, the smell of it in her nostrils, and the sketch of the narrow harbor she had begun was unfinished.

The pain was not bad. Twenty minutes passed before it came again, warningly, and she thrust the thought of it away after it had passed. Lola's clothes were almost done. Lola had needed clothes so badly; she had almost nothing when she had come to live here with Catherine. For soon would come the time when they would set sail for Spain.

August had passed slowly. Catherine and Lola and the Señora Antonia sewed in the mornings. In the afternoons they slept away the heat of the midday, and at night, when the Alcalde was away, they gathered in Catherine's room, shut away from prying eyes, and drank the heady wine and talked about the clothes they were making, for themselves and the new baby, about the men they loved or had loved.

Time stood still in August. They waited for it to pass, hour after hour, night after night. The summr was very hot. Night brought scant relief, unless the wind from the sea blew gently and coolly across the gulf.

David never came. There was no need to take chances. Even aboard ship he and Lola would never speak. He and Sebastian had stayed on the island until the *Concepción* had put into port again. Then they had circled the town at night, and come into Vera Cruz from the south two days later to sign on as crew. The master of the *Concepción* had been glad to get two seamen.

It was hard to wait. Restlessness gripped the three women, and at night, the wine or ale offered the only surcease. This morning Catherine's mouth was dry. She started to get up to get water, when the pain came again.

This time it had come more quickly, and she said, softly, "Lola."

Lola wakened instantly. She sat up, pushing back her long black hair; in the gray dawn her face looked very white.

"Please call Tina," Catherine said.

"It has come?" Lola whispered. She picked up a shawl to wrap around her nakedness. In a few seconds she was back in the room; she began to dress with hasty fingers.

"There is plenty of time," Catherine said. "I am so thirsty, Lola."

Lola fastened her skirt. "I'll fetch water," she said.

She ran out of the room and into the long narrow kitchen with the stove at one end. She put some light wood on the fire, and set a pot of broth over it to heat. She poured cool water into a jug and carried it back to Catherine's room.

Catherine drank gratefully. Lola arranged the pillows, and Tina came into the room.

"I'll fetch Señora Antonia," Lola said.

Antonia was already awake. "I heard you in the kitchen," she said. She was combing her hair; she didn't bother with her busk, but slipped a dress over her shift.

"It is hot already," she said. "A plague on this weather, Lola; it will make it hard on her."

"I know," Lola said.

The broth would be hot by now. She went again into the kitchen and poured a cup of the liquid.

Tina was bathing Catherine. She had braided her hair and fastened it on top of her head like a heavy crown. Catherine got out of bed.

Lola gasped, to see her stand. "You should not!"

"I want to," said Catherine.

"You should drink this," Lola said. "You need the strength."

"I'll take it," Catherine said.

Tina stripped the sheets off the bed. Deftly she tucked the clean ones in. Catherine finished the broth and sat down on the bed again. Lola picked up the cup. The sun was coming up. From the kitchen came the smell of cooking.

Antonia was making an omelette for Catherine, but when she brought it in, Catherine could not eat it. An hour passed.

The room was bright with light. Little Kate was dressed and having her breakfast with the Indian cook, and the three women sat quietly with Catherine, watching her as she moved restlessly in the big bed. They had tidied the room, and everything was ready. There was nothing more to do. Antonia went over and shut the blinds. The room was dim.

Tina mopped the sweat off Catherine's forehead. Suddenly Catherine opened her eyes. She saw Antonia sit down, and she said, "I want the sunlight! And please leave me! Please go away!"

Tina wrung out the wet cloth and put it on Catherine's brow. Antonia and Lola looked at her for advice. Tina said, "The *señora* wants to try and sleep, I think."

She motioned to the door, and they obeyed her unwillingly. Lola left the door open a little. Tina went back to the bed.

"I didn't want them watching me," Catherine whispered. Now that they were gone she made no effort to conceal her pain. Her face twisted, she rolled her head from side to side, drawing her legs up, turning on the bed.

"Ah, *Dios,*" she said. "I had forgotten. I had forgotten how bad it was!"

The sun moved higher across the burning blue of the sky above the sand of Vera Cruz. The sun was coming to the windows, and Tina lowered the blinds against it. This time Catherine did not protest. She pushed the pillows onto the floor.

"Can you drink something, can you, *señora?*" Tina asked.

"No wine," she whispered. "It made me sick this morning. Don't you remember?"

Tina replied, "I'll get fresh water."

Outside the room Lola and Antonia waited, sitting on the floor. Tina shook her head when she saw them. "Not yet," she said. "I am afraid, Lola."

Lola searched her face. Tina moved down the little square hall, and Lola went after her. "Does she call for me?"

"No, *señorita,*" Tina said. "She calls for no one, not even him. She is bleeding badly."

Tina's eyes were hooded by the heavy lids. She turned. "Do not weep yet," she said.

"If only he were here!" Lola cried.

Tina's wrinkled face was set. "He cannot be here; she knows that. She knows she is alone. She will not call for him. For you, maybe, later. I go back to her now."

She found Catherine out of bed. She took her back. Catherine whispered. "I wanted to see my portrait of him," she said. "I thought of it, and I wanted it."

Lola, who had followed Tina with Antonia, brought the portrait to Catherine.

"Hold it thus," Catherine said impatiently. The canvas started to roll up, and Antonia caught it. She and Lola held the picture.

"It's the best thing I've ever done," Catherine said, her breath coming swift, pride in her voice. "He will be on the Atlantic now, Lola, across the ocean." She raised herself to look at it. "I feel so dizzy," she said. "And, Tina, I'm bleeding so much." She lay back and closed her eyes.

Lola grabbed up her shawl. In the doorway she paused a moment. "I'm going to get David!"

Antonia moved to her side. She seized Lola's wrist. "Are you mad?" she cried, in a whisper.

"No!" Lola came back. "She needs him."

"Madre de Dios!" Antonia muttered. "You'd bring death to him and you! Are you mad!" She held Lola's wrist hard, pulling her.

Lola wrenched away from her. Tina's voice stopped her. "Fetch the priest, *señorita*," she said. "Go fetch the priest!"

Antonia dropped her hand, as she was about to seize Lola again. Lola stood still, just for a second. Then, with a quick stifled cry, she threw her shawl over her head, pulled it around her shoulders. Her light, running footsteps grew fainter and fainter.

Three hours later Catherine's baby was born. Antonia took the child, and bathed it, and dressed it in the clothes Catherine had made. She came back into the room with the baby in her arms, and Tina did not even look up. Tina was not concerned with the baby; she knew Catherine was going to die.

The priest knelt by the side of the bed. Lola knelt beside him, her fingers clutched over her beads.

"She is bleeding to death," Tina whispered to Antonia. "I cannot stanch the flow of blood." She reached under the sheet to feel the soaked linen she had wrapped around Catherine in a vain attempt to stop the bleeding.

Suddenly Catherine opened her eyes.

"It is all over," she said.

"Sí," said the priest. "You have had a little girl." Catherine smiled. "Bless her, *Padre.*" Then she whispered, "And christen her Elizabeth. Then he can call her Bess."

Lola had wiped her face on her skirt. Her huge eyes were dark and full of desperate appeal. Antonia said, "Would you like to see your daughter?"

Catherine did not answer.

Antonia held the baby up, and Catherine moved her hand to show Antonia she wanted the baby. Gently, biting her lip, Antonia laid the baby down beside its mother, tucking the sheet in around both the child and the mother.

Catherine saw Tina's face hovering above her. She remembered telling Tina she had forgotten how bad the pain was. Now she said, "I had forgot how wonderful it was to have a baby, too."

Her eyes closed. The priest took her hand. The baby slept.

Tina brought little Kate into the room. Kate's green eyes looked at her mother.

"She sleeps, Tina?" Kate asked, very softly.

"*Sí*, my own," Tina said.

"And the baby sleeps, too," Kate said. "I thought the baby would be bigger."

"No. Babies are very small."

"I will take care of her," Kate said. "I am big."

The priest drew her into the circle of his arm. Kate watched her mother.

Lola lifted her head. She reached forward to touch Catherine's hand as it lay against the sheet. "Oh, Tina," she whispered, "does she know she is going to die?"

"No," said Tina.

After a little while Catherine's eyes opened again. She looked at the baby. The baby's head was dark.

"She has his hair," Catherine said, suddenly. Then she saw Kate.

Kate said, "You were asleep when I came in."

"Darling," Catherine whispered. "Do you like the baby?" She paused; she wanted to ask a question. "Are her eyes blue?"

"*Sí*, Catherine," said Lola.

The faintest frown crossed Catherine's face. "But all babies' eyes are blue." She would have to wait a few months before she would really know whether her child would have its father's blue eyes. "I shall have to wait, again," she said.

Lola hardly heard her. She held Catherine's hand. The priest took Kate from the room and returned alone.

He and Lola and Antonia stayed with Catherine, even after her light breath stopped.

The women prayed, with the priest; the baby slept. Finally the priest lifted the child from its place beside Catherine, and laid it in Lola's arms.

"Your duty is to the child," he said. He covered Catherine with a clean sheet Tina had brought. "You are needed," he said. "And the *señora's* other child."

He blessed the baby, while Lola held it. When the baby's eyes opened, and Lola saw the clear blue eyes, her slight shoulders shook with sobs. When the priest was finished, she could wait no longer to ask the question.

"Why, *Padre?*" she cried desperately. "Tell me why!"

"I do not know," he said.

"You should!" Lola said. "If you do not know, who can tell me?"

"Only yourself," he said gently. "I am going now to the child. Ask yourself, daughter, whether she does not need me more than you."

Antonia said, "You'll not leave us, Father?"

He said, "Not yet, and I shall come back this evening, my daughter. To stay with you. And I want to help with the arrangements to have these two children returned to Spain with Lola and the Filipino woman. I shall see the Captain of the *Concepción.*"

"Oh, *gracias, Padre,*" Antonia gasped out.

He put his hand on her shoulder. "I shall be back," he said. His bony feet stuck out from under his swinging robes, his head was bent a little as he walked away. Lola took the baby into the room where the cradle was. But she didn't put the child down; she held the baby close.

In Catherine's room, Antonia moved about silently, with Tina. They carried the stained linen from the room, and Antonia lighted four candles to burn at each corner of the white-shrouded bed.

"I am going to brush and comb her hair, *señora,*" Tina said. "Would you want to leave me?"

"No," said Antonia. "I am not afraid of Catherine."

Her foot struck a soft impediment, and she reached down, her eyes so full of tears that she could hardly see. Her fingers felt the roll of canvas. She picked up the picture, and she unrolled it a little to see the top of a dark head, touched with silver, and a pair of blue eyes. Antonia rolled the picture up again and put it away.

PART

4

Chapter 36

THE *Desire* tossed helplessly on a still-troubled sea. The wind had shifted to the northwest, but the great mass of water that had endured the wind tumbled from the northeast; the wind took the crests of the waves and flung them high in the air for the pale sun to shine through. Master Fuller kept the *Desire's* bow into the wind, and the waves slapped her sides; her decks were wet and slippery.

But the hatches were already thrown open to the sun and air, and curls of smoke came from the galley stoves. The ship was very still.

Some of the men were sleeping, Tyler among them. Cavendish was shaving and getting dry clothes on, and Master Pretty was readying himself for the first watch. His face was grim and hopeless. Before he left his cabin, he sat down for a moment and wrote in the log he kept.

"We suffered a terrible tempest," he wrote, baldly, "which carried away the most part of our sails." He closed the book and went up on deck. The Captain was waiting for him.

"Call all hands, Master Pretty," Cavendish said.

"Aye, aye, sir," said Master Pretty, his voice lagging. He went off slowly, throwing a look upward at the bare mainmast. Tatters of sail clung to the yards, the wind blew them raggedly; the *Desire* was carrying her lateen mizzen, but Pretty could see that it would not last in any kind of stiff wind.

Cavendish paced the poopdeck as he waited. He was wearing a clean shirt, and a leather sea jacket; the spray flew up even to this high deck. The sun felt good on his face and he paced on restlessly, for he was so weary that he must keep walking to stay awake.

The crew who assembled before him were weary too, after the night of tempest. Their faces were drawn and tired, yet they came quickly enough, they knew that what he had to say was important.

They had no sails. They were leagues from any land, and they had only a bit of rotten mizzen that the wind tore at. Cavendish spoke.

"We have a deal of work to do this morning, but first you'll get a good hot meal." He smiled, and the men smiled back at him, tentatively.

"I have examined the mainmast," he went on, "and it was weakened last night. Also, you know well enough we have no sails." He paused, and they looked up at his face, intently.

"We shall have to cut new," he said.

Pretty's eyes were startled. They had no canvas to cut. There wasn't any, and yet—Pretty felt the tense hope rise in him as it was rising in the men whose faces were upturned to his as he stood on the quarterdeck with Cavendish. He heard Cavendish's voice go on, and each single word came like a promise.

"In the hold," the Captain said, "we stowed chests of very heavy silk damask."

Pretty wanted to shout aloud and he had difficulty remembering to restrain the words that tumbled to his lips, for Cavendish was still speaking.

"After your meal, we shall set to work to cut new sails from the silk, and we will wrap the mainmast in the cloth of gold, like a heavy bandage." He frowned a little, wondering just how he was going to do it, and then he realized that the men were staring up at him with a sort of reverential awe. Master Pretty was remembering the day in San Lucas when Cavendish had warned him not to let the damask get wet, and he had a wonderful smile on his face because he had not been able to think of the damask himself. But Cavendish had.

Cavendish said, "Master Pretty knows where the damask was stored."

"Aye, aye, sir!" said Pretty.

There was a moment's silence; the crew looked very different after his few words. They looked at him with unspoken love, and Cavendish felt the blood beat in his temples as his emotions rose. They were his crew, and they had been with him through every kind of disaster, every kind of stormy sea; they had mourned with him when he had buried Havers. The kinship between them was at this moment so strongly evident that he found himself completely speechless, and a little shy. "All hands will help cut the new sail," he said, inadequately.

Master Pretty dismissed the crew from mess.

By evening the new sails were up. The mainmast was bandaged in cloth of gold, and the sunset gleamed on the wind-filled silk. The wind was large for England.

Four days later they spied a sail off the starboard bow. The *Desire* overtook her, proving to Cavendish that the *Desire* was still swift and alive. She was beautiful in her new dress. As they bore down on her, Cavendish said to Pretty, "By God, she's a good sailer!"

Pretty said, "She's not Spanish!"

"No," said Cavendish, "she's within hailing distance, sir." He lifted the trumpet.

He hailed her, his voice ringing out over the choppy water, the words evenly spaced. "Ahoy there! What ship are you?"

She was Flemish, she called back. "What ship are you?"

"The *Desire!*" Cavendish shouted back. "Out of Plymouth two years!" He could not help adding this.

"Two years!"

"Aye!" shouted Cavendish. "What news?"

The Flemish ship's master could not believe his ears. But he had news for the Englishman. "You sank the Spanish Armada," he yelled. "The great fleet was sunk. And a tempest finished it!"

The *Desire's* crew let out a long hard yell; cheers echoed over her decks; it was incredible, but it must be true.

"You English sank the Spanish fleet!" the Flemish repeated. "Where are you from now?"

"The Cape of Good Hope," Cavendish shouted back, "by the Indian Ocean, the Pacific, and the Straits of Magellan!"

The crew of the Flemish vessel waved their caps and cheered. "Good luck! Good luck!" they chorused.

The *Desire* dipped her flags in salute. Cavendish ordered extra wine for the crew to celebrate the defeat of the Spanish Armada. The sea turned gray and choppy.

The wind held good. It was just wind enough for the *Desire* to carry all her canvas, and the next morning, England was sighted off the larboard bow.

It was so lovely a sight that the men stood transfixed on deck, and Moon had to shout orders twice. Tyler was at the helm. Moon threatened to confine him, and Tyler nodded and smiled.

"Aye, sir," he said, happily.

All sails were trimmed. The *Desire* was seaborn and beautiful; her silken sails gleamed, and news of her coming went ahead of her into Plymouth. When she came proudly into the roadway, the third ship ever to circumnavigate the globe, the city bells were already ringing. The men were aloft, straining their eyes to see an English town. The bells rang steadily. The *Desire's* flags flew bravely, and the gun ports opened, the guns were run out.

The heaviest cannons were fired in a salute to Plymouth. The crew cheered wildly. Master Fuller roared orders.

"In the to'gallan's'ls!"

The men gave the old yells as they heaved on the ropes. The tops furled.

The lateen mizzen held the *Desire* into the wind as the great mainsail was reefed and made fast. The anchors splashed overboard.

Pretty was beside himself with excitement. "I cannot credit it!" he exclaimed to Cavendish.

Cavendish laughed. "I cannot myself," he said. Pretty glanced at him. Cavendish was smiling, the brilliant smile that let the boyish eagerness and tenderness free. "I cannot credit that that"—he waved his hand—"is Plymouth!"

"It is, though, sir," Pretty said. "It is!"

The ships's bells struck five times. "Two-thirty," Cavendish said, just as the lookout in the fo'c'sle head repeated the helmsman's strokes.

The *Desire* rode at anchor in Plymouth harbor. The bells of the city kept on ringing. An Englishman had come home again, from the far corners of the earth. A man called Captain Cavendish had sailed a ship around the world and sailed her home again.

"We're in port, Master Pretty," Cavendish said, with finality. "We're in port."

"Aye, sir," said Pretty. "What are you going to do, sir?"

"Do?" asked Cavendish. He didn't speak further, he looked toward shore, not half seeing the sun shining on the city's roofs, her docks, her shipping. The day was colder than the day when he had left, for this was September ninth, and the last time he had seen Plymouth had been a July day. Incredibly, the task begun that summer day was done. Off his shoulders now came the responsibilities that had been carried for two long years and three months. Incredibly, there was nothing much to do. And yet he said, almost defensively, "Do, sir? I've a deal to do. I'm going below."

He went to his cabin. He got out pen and paper. He dipped the pen in the ink. Now, in a few short words, he must write what could never be written to make it understandable to one who had never been a part of a ship at sea. He must write to Lord Hunsdon, the Lord Chamberlain—a letter for Her Majesty. He dipped the pen in the ink again, and stared at the wet point.

The paper lay before him. "Right Honorable," he wrote, and then he paused. Just to one side on his table lay a part of his notes; he had been studying them last night. His eyes read, "A note on the varying of our winds." He pushed at the paper, lifted it. Underneath it was another. "A note on the winds which we found between the coast of New Spain and the Islands of the Filipinas." His writing, heavy and deliberate, went on. He knew the night he had written of. He could remember clearly that night of mist. When he had left Catherine and David at San Lucas.

"The 19th day of November," he had written, "in the year of our Lord 1587, we departed from the cape of California, and we found the winds to be between the east and the east northeast, until the 29th day of January, being then in the latitude of 9 degrees."

He shoved the notes away, his mind changed, gathered them neatly, and stowed them in the right place. They were valuable, these notes on the prevailing winds. He dipped the pen again and began to write.

"I desire Your Honor to make known to Her Majesty the desire I have had to do Her Majesty's service in the performance of this voyage." That was commonplace enough. He was satified with that opening sentence. He dipped his pen.

"It has pleased God to suffer me to encompass the entire globe, in which voyage I have either discovered, or brought intelligence of, rich places of the world. I navigated along the coast of Chile, Peru and New Spain, where I made great spoils. I burnt or sank nineteen great ships." He frowned, Should he try to include all the lesser craft? His lock of hair fell over his forehead, and he pushed it back. There was a knock on the door.

He looked up and told Tyler to come in. Tyler did so; his face openly excited. "You wished to see me, sir?" he asked.

Cavendish said, "I did, Tyler. Would you like to carry this letter to London for me, tonight?"

Tyler's face broke into smiles. "I would, sir," he said.

Cavendish grinned. "Tyler," he asked, without preamble, "would you wish to stay on with me, ashore?"

Tyler was taken aback. He fumbled with his hands. "I would, sir," he said, low. "Thank you, sir." He paused, looking at his Captain. "Thank you, sir," he said, his eyes shining.

Cavendish reached into his table and brought out a heavy bag of gold. He tossed it onto the table. "Take this with you, then. In London, after you've delivered this letter to Lord Hunsdon, go to the Cock and Pheasant, on Ludgate Hill, and get rooms for me. I'll bring Cosmos, and Anthony de Dasi and his brothers."

"Aye, aye, sir," said Tyler, happily.

Cavendish picked up his pen, and Tyler went to the door.

"Be ready to go in thirty minutes," Cavendish added.

"Aye, sir," said Tyler. He closed the door, and Cavendish read over what he had written. He could hear plainly the noise of voices and laughter from the *Desire,* and from the boats that already hovered about her. Sentences fell into his cabin.

"Did you bring gold? How does England look? We sank the Armada!" He shut out the clamor of welcoming voices and began to write again.

"The matter of most profit to me was a great ship of the King's that I took at California, which ship came from the Filipinas, being one of the richest in merchandise that ever passed those seas. Which goods and ship, I was forced to set afire, for my ship was not able to contain the least part of them."

His pen was dry. Two sentences covered the taking of the *Santa Anna*. Two sentences, and nothing of a woman was in them.

He started a new paragraph.

"The stateliness and the riches of the countries among which I navigated, I fear to make report of, lest I should not be credited, for if I had not known sufficiently the incomparable wealth of these islands, I should have been as incredulous as others will be—those who have not my experience. Our countrymen can trade freely at these ports, if they but will."

He smiled a bit as he wrote that, one eyebrow arching up. There was little more to say. He added a brief itinerary of his voyage and the course he had charted through the Southern Pacific. "I leave Your Lordship to the tuition of the Almighty," he ended. "From Plymouth this ninth day of September, 1588."

He sealed the letter and stamped it with the heavy ring that bore his crest. That much was done, and he could feel the restlessness, the old restlessness creeping in on him. He gave the letter to Tyler, and went out on deck.

Most of the crew had been given shore leave for tonight. Shore leave, and ten pieces of gold. No more. He watched them almost tenderly as they mustered on deck for Master Fuller's inspection. They wore, proudly, the wide trousers which marked them as the seafaring men they were. They wore heavy belts, with shining daggers, and jackets of all kinds and descriptions—most of them obviously Spanish.

"Jesu," Cavendish said to Pretty, as he watched them

disembark for shore. "There will be fifty happy wenches in Plymouth tonight."

Pretty grinned. "Going ashore, sir?" he asked.

Cavendish hesitated. He stared at Plymouth. It had been ten months since he had left Catherine. If she were coming to him, she would be waiting for him now—in Plymouth. His hands clenched on the rail.

"No," he said, "I'll wait."

Chapter 37

ON FRIDAY, Cavendish paid off his crew and dismissed them.

One by one they filed past him.

"If you have a return of that fever, let me know, Johnson," Cavendish said, as he paid the man.

"Aye, aye, sir," Johnson said, smiling. He picked up his heavy bag of gold.

"And don't lose all this tonight," Cavendish said to the next man.

The seaman grinned. "I'll not, sir. You'll be in London, Captain?"

"I shall."

"Good-bye, sir." He went. The line went on. It was over, the voyage. The hatches were wide, and out of them were hoisted now the heavy chests. Damask, gold, spices. Wealth and money. Now he had them. And fame, too, although he was hardly aware of it, now.

Another crew was going to take the *Desire* into drydock. The first of Cavendish's money went into the pockets of the men who were going to fit her for the sea again. He left the *Desire* before the alien crew took her. In his own cabin, with Cosmos beside him, he stood for the last time. There was nothing in it now but a roll of canvas. Moon came in, with Pretty at his heels.

"Master Fuller says that the shipbuilder is here, sir," Moon said. Moon looked a little lost.

"I'm coming," Cavendish said.

"What's that, sir?" asked Moon.

"A portrait," Cavendish said. She had given it to him. She had painted it herself.

"Of the Señora Catherine?" Moon asked, guilelessly. "Lord, she was fair. I wonder where she is now? Probably she's been in Spain for months. Probably she's married, don't you believe sir? Lord, she was marvelously fair."

Marvelously fair . . . That she was—and suddenly the thought of her pierced him sharply; the longing he had so carefully tried to cover, was there, naked, within him.

Moon coughed and went on talking. "The carriage is here from London, sir. And Tyler has brought your horse. I wish I could ride part way with you, sir, but I'm going home."

"I'll see you in London, Moon. I'm going to take a house there."

"I'll come, sir, thank you," Moon said.

"You, too, Pretty," Cavendish said. "Where are you off for? Suffolk?"

"Aye, sir. Will you be at Trimley?"

Cavendish said slowly, "I don't know." He didn't know. How could he, with this sharp uncertainty lodged in him?

Pretty was suddenly silent. He looked down at his boots. Then he said, "I'm sorry, sir. I forgot about Master David."

Cavendish held out his hand. "I shall let you know when I'm in Suffolk," he said.

Pretty gripped his Captain's hand, hard. "Good-bye, sir," he said, and he turned away hastily, carrying his leather-bound journal.

Moon and Fuller came over to Cavendish. Another crew was boarding the *Desire*. Moon said, "I hate to see these other men swarm over her, sir!"

Cavendish laid his hand on the rail. He picked at it with his finger, and the blue paint chipped off in flakes. "She needs them, Moon," he said. "For her, she's a slow sailer, now. They'll take care of her."

Moon scrambled down the ladder. The gun ports were closed. "Good-bye, sir," he said.

Fuller said quietly, "The shipbuilder is in the fo'c'sle, sir. Wait. Here he comes."

A heavy-set man came walking toward them. To Cavendish he gave a bow. "I have the specifications, and the drawings, sir," he said. "I brought them to you."

Cavendish took the papers he held out. "I'll let you know. Soon. I'll be back in Plymouth in a month or so."

He and Fuller went over the side, one after the other. Ashore they parted, and Cavendish handed Cosmos the portrait and the papers the shipbuilder had given him. Cosmos was in the coach; he decided to ride up front so that he could see better. He opened the door for Cavendish.

Cavendish shook his head. "I'm going to ride," he said, and he swung up into the saddle.

The carts had gone ahead. The carts with all his personal belongings, and his share of the spices and the cloth; only the heavy sea chests with the fortune in jewelry and gold, and his commissions, traveled with the coach. And there were the three Filipinos, and Cosmos. The Mayor of Plymouth had proudly provided an armed escort.

Cavendish set the pace. He rode ahead. The riders and the coach left Plymouth behind. . . .

They reached London forty-eight hours later. Cosmos was still riding up front. Cavendish galloped ahead, and London was ready to greet him. Cosmos had never seen anything like this before in his life.

For hours he had been watching the city come closer. He was shaken with riding, and the pounding of hoofs sang in his ears. And then, suddenly the city had swallowed them up; its inhabitants almost stopped the coach, and stopped the Captain. They clung to his saddle and the stirrups; they swarmed over the coach, and pushed the mailed riders aside with high good humor. They yelled and shouted, and leaned out of the high windows, and they threw flowers.

The women were as many as the men. They said all manner of things to Cavendish which Cosmos did not understand. Their voices were high with excitement as London welcomed her returning hero.

The coach barely moved. All the way up Ludgate Hill, the coachmen struggled against a sea of humans, and Cosmos was breathless with excitement too, his almond eyes darting this way and that, to be sure not to miss anything of the buildings, of the houses, the gardens, the bridges. Wonderful bridges, and a great silver river where ships were anchored and river craft plied.

Tyler was riding at the head of the coach. His face was covered with smiles. The three Filipinos hung out of the coach windows, a little terrified, but not too terrified to look, round-eyed, at this English city which had certainly gone mad. And, ahead, Cavendish rode, trying to answer the questions hurled at him, trying to keep from riding down the men and women who flung themselves at his horse.

His scarlet seacap was perched on the side of his head. He wore Spanish mail, pure gold, and polished Cordovan boots with gold spurs, and heavy fringed gauntlets. One woman seized the bridle of his horse. When he tried to release her fingers, she snatched for the glove. He let her pull it off, and she waved her prize proudly.

The Cock and Pheasant was just ahead. The coach stopped. Tyler pushed his way to Cavendish's side, and took his Captain's horse. Cavendish grinned at him.

"We're home, Tyler," he said. "We're home."

Chapter 38

THE COCK AND PHEASANT was crowded. It swarmed with court gallants, waiting to see their Cavendish. The landlord was very proud and a bit apprehensive. They sat on tables; they were gambling with dice and cards; they were drinking. When Cavendish appeared, they milled about him, excitedly, and they all talked at once.

Cavendish pushed them aside and sat down at one table. Sir George Carey was at his side. Sir John Harington had arrived; he was allowed a place at the table. Gradually the room settled down again, and again the dice rolled. The landlord served dinner, and the wines flowed.

Cavendish was drinking ale.

"Where in God's name have you been, Tom?" Carey asked. "I was going to ride down to Plymouth if you hadn't come today."

Cavendish said, "The Admiralty Court was dividing the spoils, George."

"What did you do in Plymouth?"

"Nothing," said Cavendish. "I stayed aboard most of the time."

"You stayed aboard?" Carey grinned. "I heard that, but I didn't credit it."

Cavendish said sharply, "It was true."

"I know a wench who would be charmed to know you."

"I believe he means that biblically," Harington put in.

Cavendish laughed. "I'll choose my own wench," he said. Suddenly he added, "I have picked her."

"This wench is—" Carey made a gesture.

"No, thank you," Cavendish said, applying himself to his food. No wenches—while he still cherished a vision. There was yet time. He thought of Carey's certain admiration when he saw her. "I've picked out a lady," he repeated.

Carey nudged Harington. Harington winked. The conversation went on. Then the landlord came up.

"Captain," he said, timidly.

Cavendish looked up, frowning.

"Captain, there is a lady to see you."

Cavendish jumped to his feet. He was conscious of the pounding of his heart. "Where did you put her?" he asked, intently glancing around the crowded room. "In my rooms?"

"Aye, sir," the landlord said, wondering if he had done right or whether a tempest would be loosed on his head.

"Thank God," Cavendish said. He didn't bother to excuse himself. He pushed out of the room, and ran up the narrow stairs. He ran down the crooked corridor. He flung open the door of his own room. He stopped short.

His hands clenched. He stood tall in the doorway.

"Who are you?" he asked. He stared at the curved figure, veiled heavily. Anger filled him. He came to the center of his room; he had left the door open.

"Leave," he said.

"Then I shan't win my wager," she replied. The voice was low and tentative.

He was unappeased. "D'ye want me to use force?" he asked.

"Would you?" she said. But she was a little afraid of him.

"I would," he answered. "And I shall."

She moved toward him slowly. He smelled faint perfume.

"You're costing me twenty pounds," she said.

"Twenty pounds?"

Her voice had a hint of laughter in it now. She was daring enough, to come here.

"You have so much gold, Captain," she said, "you could at least pay my gambling debts."

She was passing in front of him, toward the door. Her veil, artfully arranged, did not conceal the generous curve of her breasts above the low-cut black dress.

"A moment," he said, reaching out his hand. He tried to see through the veil. He couldn't.

"Remove your veil," he said.

"Ah, no," she said.

"I'm used to 'Aye, aye, sir.' "

"I might disappoint you. You expected another. Did you not, Captain?"

"No!" he said. He shut the door. It banged sharply.

"You lie," she said. "You expected someone. I am sorry."

"Take the veil off. I cannot buy a pig in a poke."

She was very lovely, so she removed the veil. He had never seen her before. He took the cloak from her shoulders and surveyed her. His experience marked her as submissive and lustful and generous.

"Carey brought you," he said.

"True, Captain. We had a wager. Whom were you expecting?"

"No one," he said. He moved toward her. "I've been a foolish man, mistress."

"I came as a jest only, Captain," she said, and she laughed, her teeth sparkling white. "Call Carey."

"The devil I will," Cavendish said.

"Oh," she said, "but you must."

"Must? Who are you?"

"Martha Howard."

He knew her, then. She was one of the sprawling Howard family; her sister had been one of his mistresses; they were long on love and short on virtue. He drew her into his arms, slid one hand down her body. She did not resist. She was made for love; he picked her up in his arms and carried her to the big bed.

Five hours later he sent her home in his coach with Tyler—the richer by fifty pieces of gold. He felt only a trifle guilty. He dismissed her from his mind and went downstairs to join Carey and Harington.

Carey laughed when he saw him. Cavendish sat down and slid his long legs under the table.

"How much did you give her, Tom?" he asked lazily.

"Fifty pieces of gold," Cavendish said. He banged on the table for the landlord.

"Jesu," Carey said, "you'll spoil all the whores in

London. But I doubt if Mistress Howard has been paid in gold before; she's not a bad wench."

"She remonstrated a little," Cavendish said, remembering. "I told her to take the gold."

"You drip with wealth," Harington said.

They questioned him about the voyage. As usual, he answered their questions briefly. He ate and drank; later he settled down to gamble, and he won enough to pay for his night's pleasures. At five in the morning he sleepily let Cosmos help him undress, and he rolled into bed pleasantly drunk. Yet an uneasiness held him awake long after he should have been asleep.

The next day he bought a house. The town house of the Earl of Shrewsbury. It was near the Globe Theatre and near the Bear Gardens. Its grounds sloped down to the river. Then he took Catherine's picture to be framed.

Two busy weeks passed. He rented a warehouse on Fleet Street to store the spices and merchandise he had for sale to the merchants of London and Europe. A crew of workmen swarmed over his new house, redecorating the long second-floor gallery that would be used for entertainment; on the study walls they put up the painted leather panels that David had shown Catherine. The house had been unused; the chimneys were swept, the larders stocked, and a new wine cellar relined with shelves.

The stables were newly painted; a new carriage was ordered, and he spent three days in the purchasing of fine horseflesh. He spent one long afternoon closeted with the Queen. But in these two weeks, no word, no letter, no courier came from Catherine.

Her portrait hung over the mantel of the fireplace in his bedroom. The painted green eyes looked down at him; from the wall, her warm red mouth smiled at him tantalizingly, and the shining hair gleamed. But she did not come. He had given her enough gold and jewels to keep her wealthy for the rest of her life; she didn't need to come. And besides that, he thought bitterly, there were only too many men who would be glad to heap more wealth on her.

The first day of October dawned. That day, when he walked into the room, he didn't look up at the picture. Cosmos was in his room, and Cosmos was pale with excitement. He was staring at himself in the mirror; his livery was made of velvet, his buttons real gold. He was going to Court.

He turned hastily as Cavendish came into the room.

"Admiring yourself?" Cavendish asked.

"Aye, sir," said Cosmos, truthfully.

Cavendish laughed.

Cosmos studied his master's appearance. He was fully satisfied. "I am a good barber," he said.

"Jesu, you are becoming vain," Cavendish said.

"Thank you, sir," said Cosmos, happily.

Cavendish put into his hands a carved ivory box. Cosmos held it in sweaty hands. He followed Cavendish again, out of the house, into the carriage.

The city was familiar to Cosmos by now, but he still liked to sit up front and absorb the stares of Londoners who had never seen a Japanese before. Cosmos was proud of being a celebrity in this alien land.

The coach drew to a stop. Cosmos hopped down, and opened the door. Cavendish stepped out, and Cosmos fell into step behind him. After him came the three Filipinos, dressed alike in white satin.

As they approached the throne room, Cosmos heard the subdued murmur of voices. He came to a stop outside some huge double doors which were flung open. Cosmos stared at the halberdiers, who looked down at him from under their helmets with interest. They didn't speak, and Cosmos saw his master go ahead of him.

Cavendish stood in the big doors for only a second. He paused between the two guards at the door. Fifty feet away from him sat the Queen.

There were a great many people in the room. Cavendish saw the French ambassador, with his wife and daughters. There was Don Antonio, exiled King of Portugal. Cavendish's mind went back to Java and the two Portuguese who had been so glad to know their King was safe in England. Cavendish saw other faces, some familiar, some not familiar, and ahead of him was the

Queen. Her ladies were grouped around her, and he started forward, down the narrow carpet that covered the path to the throne.

He walked swiftly through the hushed room, and knelt at her feet.

"Your Majesty," he said.

Behind her, tall candles burned in wrought iron holders. She rose to her feet. She was still tall, only a little bent, and she drew herself to her fullest height. This was her kingdom, and she its Queen and mother. It was her power, her gift, to draw men to her like the one before her now. To him she was more than woman, perhaps a goddess, at the least a Queen. This England that she ruled sent her without stint its bravest men; for her they labored, and she turned their services into great returns for the nation that bred them. Here were romance and practicality thrust together, to raise England high, to wrest the power of the seas from Spain, to place it on a green island whose ships already circled the globe.

The power of Spain was partly broken. More battles there would be, but now, at this moment, she was sure that she had won, and that it was England that would go forward, and Spain that would wane, slowly, like a dying candle, sputtering annoyingly and flaring up briefly—but dying at the last.

Lord Hunsdon, to the left of the throne, stepped forward slightly. Elizabeth noticed him, and she knew he was going to speak. With a gesture of her hand she cut him short.

She had spoken to Cavendish before, in private. She had seen the charts, the map of China; she had heard the tales of incredible wealth, of rich islands; she had listened long as Cavendish had recounted to her his adventures and the sights he saw. She had seen his notes, and she had heard him end by saying, with a downward twist of the mobile mouth, "With a little force, you may take spoil of them all."

"But you believe in trade?" she had asked, reminding him.

"Aye, but with a little force—"

She had talked with him thus in private. Today, this

was display. She liked it. So did he; so did the crowded Court; so did the people who would hear of it and tell it over among themselves. Today she was not a harassed woman, finding the conscience, the will, the time to do what she must do; today she was the Queen, dramatic, lovely, and buttressed by this pageantry.

She was looking down at Cavendish's dark and gray head. Softness filled her face, restoring youth to it, giving it a quickened loveliness that had been hers once, and like a miracle returned to her when emotion moved her.

"Your sword," she said. She held out her hand.

Surprised as he was, he acted instantly. He drew the narrow blade, fashioned in Toledo. Elizabeth knew, as she took it in her hand, it had been stolen from the Spanish. Her quick humor was pleased.

The candlelight winked along the length of steel, as she touched his shoulder with it. She leaned over, she was very near him, and regardless of stares, she laid her hand on the dark head for just a moment. Then she reversed the blade and handed it back to him.

Cavendish heard her bid him rise. He stood, now he looked down at her, and he sheathed the weapon.

"Your arm, please," she said.

She placed her hand on his arm, and she seated herself. One of her ladies nearest her moved aside a little, so that Cavendish could stand beside her. At this moment Cosmos appeared in the big doors, a small figure.

"Your Majesty," Cavendish said. "Cosmos is Japanese, taken from King Philip's treasure ship. He would wish to present you with a token of our esteem. And the three behind him are Filipinos."

Elizabeth smiled. There was a hum in the crowded Court. Cosmos came forward again. He thought his master looked magnificent standing thus beside his Queen, with the lovely ladies grouped around them. He knelt, as Cavendish had taught him.

"We are proud to bring Your Majesty a small gift," he said.

Elizabeth smiled at his accent.

"Open the box, Cosmos," Cavendish said.

Cosmos snapped open the ivory lid. On a satin bed, a

huge ruby ring gleamed. Elizabeth picked it up and slipped it on her finger.

"We thank you," she said to Cosmos.

Cosmos rose to his feet, and stepped to one side, allowing the three satin-clad Filipinos to kneel in front of Elizabeth.

Each of them presented her with a box.

"From Java," Cavendish said, as Elizabeth looked down at a creamy circlet of pearls, at a jade pendant studded around with diamonds, at a great black stone from the East.

She smiled delightedly at her treasures. Before, she had received the Crown's share of the voyage; but these were as beautiful as the brilliance of her own Court, in fullest flower and plumage today.

The Musicians began to play, softly. The sound of voices arose. Cosmos smelled food. He stuck close to his master, eagerly listening to snatches of conversation.

"Sir Thomas, would you permit me to send you the poem I have written commemorating your voyage?"

"Tom, Tom! Jesu, man, I'm glad to see you! I arrived in London only today!"

"Sir, sometime would it be too great a favor if I might see you and if you might tell me if I could sail with you, next time?"

"Sir Thomas, could I beg a favor of you too, and ask you to receive my father, Lord Bedford?"

"Sir, I wonder if I might speak with you on a matter of business—about spices—"

Cosmos was amazed at the informality of the court. At dinner the Queen ate sparingly, summoning her favorites, talking with them. Her eyes roved over the room and once they fastened on a young man she did not know; she stared at him and his color came and went until finally, with a wave of her hand, he came to her side. She told him to present himself. Then, after a little while, she beckoned to Cosmos.

He talked to her for fifteen minutes while she questioned him about his native land. In another part of the long room, Cavendish and Essex and Carey and two other men were gambling. Once the Queen heard an explosive oath and she turned her head to look; her ladies clicked their tongues, plied their fans, and glanced over at the men. At nine, the Queen rose.

But her going did not put a stop to the festivities. The musicians played, and Cosmos stood behind Cavendish's chair and watched the card game. They were playing primero and the stakes were high. They interspersed their gaming with talk about the women. Three young men stood and watched Cavendish play. They listened too. Cosmos heard Cavendish say, as he pushed a pile of gold coins forward, "Who's that dark-haired wench?"

Carey looked, and then consulted his cards and matched the gold, and turned again to look at the dark-haired woman. She was sitting decorously, her hands folded over her fan. Carey flipped his cards over. "Fifty-five," he said. "She's Southerly's wife."

"That fish?" Cavendish asked. "A flush, gentlemen." He spread his hand and scraped in the money. "Southerly is poor, too."

Carey picked up the cards and began to deal.

Essex said, picking up his cards, "He has a name, though. She didn't."

"Oh," said Cavendish.

"She's been pursued by many," said Essex, discarding two cards and waiting for the draw. "Give yourself a month of assiduous attention."

"A month?" asked Cavendish. "All I have is two hours."

Carey looked up and grinned. Cavendish's blue eyes were full of laughter, and Harington said, "Well, Tom, what are you going to do about it?"

Cavendish laughed. "I'm studying the lay of the land. Tell me more about the fort and her commandant."

Carey said, "At least call her a fortress, Tom."

Cavendish got to his feet. He said, "I'm going to reconnoiter."

Carey watched him go over to Nora Southerly.

"What'll he do?" Essex asked, and Carey said, "You don't know him very well, but he has some mad plan ready." He started to laugh. He watched, and across the room he saw Cavendish beginning to talk to Nora Southerly. In an hour, Cavendish came back to the table; the men were still playing cards, and there was evidence that a great deal of wine had been consumed. Nora Southerly was walking away with her husband.

Cavendish slid back his chair, which one of the men had vacated for him instantly.

"You failed," Essex said.

"I've time for one hand," Cavendish said.

Carey rocked back in his chair. "Out with it," he demanded. "What are you going to do?"

"I'm planning a military action," Cavendish said. "If no one is going to deal, we might as well go now."

"What are you going to do?" Carey repeated.

Cosmos appeared with Cavendish's cloak.

"Come along," Cavendish said.

He picked out three of the younger men who had been waiting. "You cannot come, Essex," he said. "Bess might not like this."

The October night was brilliant with stars, and cold. In the courtyard, the torches of the linkmen lighted the faces of a group of men who stood around Cavendish. He was tying a handkerchief across the lower part of his face; he swung up into the saddle, and riding abreast with Tyler, he and his group of riders pounded out of the palace gates and into the city streets.

Their quarry was ahead, but their horses' flying hoofs ate up the distance. In ten minutes, the outlines of a coach could be seen in the darkened street. Cavendish and Tyler spurred forward, galloping past the coach, and reached out to stop the horses. The coachman shouted for help, and waved his long whip. Tyler seized it and wrenched it from his grasp.

The coach stopped jerkily; it was surrounded by masked riders. Harington pulled his sword and flourished it.

The footmen fled, jumping down and taking to their heels. Cavendish slid from the saddle, and flung open the door of the stranded coach. The horses danced, and along the street, windows flew open so the people in the houses could see what was happening.

The torches flared high. "To me!" shouted Southerly to his grooms, even as he stared at Cavendish's masked face.

Cavendish pushed him backward against the seat. "I want the wench," he said, holding Southerly back with one arm as he leaned over him to take Nora's arm. His big hand fastened over her wrists, and he pulled her out of the coach.

Southerly was stammering with rage, but he did not move. "I know you," he was saying. "I know you, Cavendish!"

"Send your seconds in the morning," said Cavendish, his voice clear in the street. "And tell Bess. Good night, sir."

He swung Nora up into his arms, set her on his horse, and mounted. The big roan wheeled; Carey and Harington put spurs to their own animals.

"We'd best leave," Carey said.

The man next to him said breathlessly, "Jesu! He'd known her only an hour!"

Carey was pounding down the street. "He's always been like this."

"Southerly's like to kill him," the younger man ejaculated.

Carey shook his head. "Not the Captain," he said. "Not Tom."

Chapter 39

CAVENDISH killed Southerly the next day at dawn. He and Essex and Carey had forgotten one thing—that Southerly was the deadliest shot in England.

Southerly had sent his seconds that same night. Tyler took the news to Carey, and Carey arrived with Harington at four in the morning. Over a tankard of ale, Carey said, "For God's sake, Tom, it's your place to choose the weapon. He's challenging you."

"He has asked to use pistols, and I'm not disappointing him," Cavendish said.

"In that case," Carey said quietly, "shoot straight."

Upstairs, Nora Southerly watched the men ride away in the early dawn. On Marylebone Heath the two men met. Two shots were fired, but Southerly was angry and Cavendish was not. Southerly fell with a bullet in his heart. Cavendish lost only the tip of his ear; when it healed, it would hardly show.

That night he took Nora Southerly to Court. She was dressed in black, Elizabeth summoned Cavendish with fire in her eyes. But all she said was, "Take her home and never dare to bring her here again!"

Cavendish complied. He sent Nora Southerly to Paris, and the incident was ended. He went to Plymouth for a week.

When he returned, his eyes lighted on one of Elizabeth's ladies-in-waiting. She was tall and fragile and high-born and virtuous. He abandoned the wenches of Fleet Street for a week and was seen at Court every night. At the end of that time, the lady-in-waiting was accompanied everywhere by a Filipino page, the ten-year-old de Dasi, and Cavendish was in possession of a key. This palace intrigue amused him for a while, for his mistress was madly in love with him, and his hurt vanity was soothed somewhat. No other man had been successful with her, and Cavendish relaxed under her obvious devotion. October passed.

During November, he began again to visit Fleet Street, and the taverns, and the theatres. His mistress shut herself in her room after his adventures had been recounted to her. He had taken a masked woman to the theatre with him and set her beside him on the stage. A riot had stopped the play, and it was said that the seamen in the audience had won the battle. The theatre was closed for four days for repairs.

When Cavendish came to see her the following night, he laughed when she reproached him. But she was sweet, and for two weeks he behaved himself. At the end of November, leading twenty other men, he and his followers raided London's most exclusive bawdy house. Tyler fetched him home in the morning, still drunk.

He slept all the next day. When he rose it was evening. He walked down into his study. His eyes roved around the room, and his secretary, a little apprehensive, said placatingly, "Another poem about your voyage was printed and sent to you, leather-bound, sir. And there is a new globe, a present!"

Cavendish picked up the book and glanced at it, riffling the pages. He laid it down on the table.

The globe stood near. He twirled it idly; a red line marked his voyage, and it was substantially correct. He stared down at the tip of California—stared at it, and suddenly the lack of her seized his heart again with relentless fingers. He gave the globe another twirl.

"A marvelous gift, sir," Cosmos said. "I brought your ale, sir."

"A marvelous gift, sir," the secretary repeated. "And there is something else for you. From Mynheer Hoogstraaten. He asks if you would receive him Thursday."

"He wants me to sell him some spices. He's a Dutch merchant."

"He sent a chess set. Look!" The secretary opened an inlaid box. "Ivory and gold, sir! A pity you don't play chess."

"I play chess," Cavendish said in such a tone that the secretary hastily shut the box and retreated.

Cavendish turned on his heel abruptly. "I'm going out, Cosmos," he said. "Come help me to dress."

It was the next day, in the afternoon, that Master Pretty came. He waited in the library, alone for a few minutes, and he walked about, looking. Then the door opened and Cosmos came in. Cosmos was apologetic.

"I'm sorry, sir, to intrude."

Pretty smiled. "I'm glad you did, Cosmos," he said. "I was thinking of you; this room makes me think of our voyage." He waved his hand. "It's all here. Even to Captain Havers' pipes." Pretty thrust his hands into his belt, and stood in front of the fire. "How have you been, Cosmos? How do you like England?"

"Very much, sir," said Cosmos politely.

"Where is the Captain?" Pretty asked.

Cosmos leaped into speech eagerly. "I don't know, sir." He spread his hands helplessly.

Pretty frowned. "You don't know?"

"No, sir! I never know." He had started forcefully, but his voice trailed off.

"Where's Tyler? Doesn't he know?"

"The Captain always takes Tyler with him," Cosmos said. "The Captain came home, then he changed his clothes. He is wearing regular seamen's clothes, with his leather coat. He's gone again, sir."

Pretty rubbed his chin. "I'll wait for a while," he said. "I've been hoping he would come to Suffolk. But he never has. If I tried to find him, where would I look?"

"Along the waterfront, in the taverns," Cosmos said. "At the theatre, in the upper balconies."

Pretty said, "A hopeless task. But is he always out and away?"

Cosmos shook his head. "Oh, no, sir." He pointed to the table, and Pretty went over to look at the chart affixed to it. He looked admiringly.

"The Straits," he said to himself. "He knows them like the back of his hand." He tapped his finger against the wood. "I'll wait for an hour, Cosmos," he said.

At that precise minute, Sir George Carey was looking for Cavendish. He came out of a tavern, and started along the street, under the shadow of the Tower. It was cold, with a wind off the river. Ahead of him he saw a familiar figure; he hurried his steps.

He did not call out. When he came close to Cavendish, he suddenly slackened his pace. Cavendish had stopped too. His arm was around the woman who walked by his side, and while Carey watched from behind, Cavendish turned her to him and kissed her, there in the street. Carey heard Cavendish's voice, and then both he and the girl entered the tavern where they had stopped before.

By the time Carey entered the tavern, Cavendish was seated at a table talking to some men. In the dim light, he looked unshaven; his elbows were resting on the table and he was drinking ale. The wench lounged at his side, leaning against him. Carey walked forward.

"Sir Thomas," he said, pursing his lips.

Cavendish looked up. "Sit down, George," he said. "I present Delight." He pulled at a loose curl, and Delight caught at his hand and pulled it so that his arm was around her again.

"Delight?" asked Carey, smiling.

"Captain calls me that," she said, turning her head to look at Cavendish.

"Were you looking for me, sir?" Cavendish asked, while the rest of the men at the table were quiet and listened.

"Have you forgot, Tom," Carey said, "that you're giving a party tonight?"

Cavendish laughed. "Jesu, so I did. Let me finish the ale." He raised the ale to his lips. He set down the tankard gingerly.

"Does it hurt, my honey sweet?" Delight asked.

"No," Cavendish said, grimacing a little and flexing his arm. "Let's go, Carey."

Delight grasped his arm, and none of them saw a man pause in the doorway, a tall man, who looked in at the scene, saw Cavendish get up and pat Delight on the backside. The man smiled a little, and turned away with his companion.

"Did you expect him to change?" he asked.

The woman with him answered in a flurry of Spanish. They turned the corner.

Cavendish reached his own house just as Pretty was deciding to leave. Pretty had picked up his cloak and was starting for the door when he heard his Captain's voice in the hallway, he heard Cosmos' voice answering, and then Cavendish's quick stride to the library. The door was flung open.

"Pretty!" Cavendish said, his smile eager. He held out his hand.

Pretty took it. "How are you, sir?" he asked. "How are you?" He was holding his cloak in one hand and he was smiling broadly. "How has everything been with you?"

"Splendid, Pretty. Put that cloak down. You can't go now." Cavendish was taking off his leather jacket; he pulled it off his left shoulder carefully, and Pretty jumped forward to help him.

"You're hurt, sir," he said, worry in his tone.

"A thrown dagger," Cavendish said, looking at his blood-stained shirt. "I was in a brawl last night."

Pretty opened the shirt to look at the crude bandages on the upper left arm.

"Cosmos will change the linen," Cavendish said, sinking down in a chair. "Tell me, Pretty, how are things with you? Sit down, man. Cosmos will bring you some wine. Javanese wine, do you remember?"

Pretty kept his smile. "Aye, aye, sir!"

Cavendish settled back comfortably. "Well, Pretty?"

"I'm splendid, sir. I was hoping to see you come to Trimley. Before I reached London. And I'm married, sir!"

"Married? Jesu, man, my congratulations! The wench is lucky to have you."

"Thank you, sir," Pretty said. "She waited for me. For more than two years."

"Some women will," Cavendish said. "Here's Cosmos."

Cosmos came in, carrying a tray with powerful white wine and glasses.

Cosmos poured the wine.

"Drink hearty," Cavendish said. "You'll stay for dinner?"

Pretty lifted the strong wine to his lips. "I wish I

could, sir," he said, "but Lucinda, my bride, is waiting for me. We're staying with her uncle, on Villiers Street."

"How do you like the room?" Cavendish asked.

"It's beautiful," Pretty said. "I remember when we cut down those leather paintings. I remember that kris over the fireplace."

"Java," said Cavendish.

Under the leather painting, at each side of the fireplace, ran bookshelves, and on one of them stood a rack of pipes. Pretty said, "I see Captain Havers' pipes, too, sir."

Cavendish said, "I kept them, Pretty."

Pretty looked straight into the blue eyes of his Captain. "You think Master David dead, sir?" he asked, steadily.

"There is no news," Cavendish said. "None. I was hoping for news."

Pretty said, "Oh, sir, I—"

Cavendish filled his glass. "Have you seen Moon?" he asked.

"Aye," said Pretty. "He's wed too, sir."

There were voices in the hallway, and Pretty got to his feet.

"I have to leave, sir," he said, reluctantly. He picked up the book he had been reading. It was bound in leather and had "To Captain Cavendish" printed in gold letters. "May I have this to read tonight, sir?"

"Certainly," said Cavendish.

"Have you read it, sir? It is good. Good poetry. I wish I could write as well. My account is factual. It's being printed, though, sir," he ended proudly. "Richard Hakluyt is printing it."

Cavendish looked pleased and surprised. He regarded Pretty with affection. He walked to the door. "I'll read yours. I remember the first day you came aboard; you were carrying a leather journal."

"Just like now," said Pretty, lifting the book in his hand; "only, this time, the words have been written and the voyage is over."

"Aye," said Cavendish. "The voyage is over." He opened the door. "Good-bye," he said.

He went upstairs to dress and bathe and shave. Cosmos put a plaster on the knife wound in his upper arm and fixed a black velvet sling to match his master's doublet. By ten that night Cavendish was royally drunk.

He had served all kinds of wonderful food and wines. There had been musicians hired and dancers and entertainers. His guests were masked and the long gallery was full of men and women. Fires blazed at either end of the room in marble fireplaces.

At exactly ten, a man and a woman, unmasked, entered the big room. Cosmos saw the gentleman and he let out a startled gasp. The woman brushed by Cosmos and stood looking at the room and the scene it presented. Her eyes searched the room quickly; she found the man she wanted and she started toward him, walking fast.

She approached him from behind. Cavendish was leaning against the table watching his feminine companion throw the dice for him. She made a good throw; he scraped up the coins and dropped them down the front of her dress. He looked up to meet black eyes that rested on him with smoldering anger.

"You drunken beast!" said their owner, coming to stand right before him.

His startled expression turned to one of amusement.

The woman raised her fan and struck at Cavendish's companion. "Leave us!" she commanded.

"Wait a moment, mistress!" Cavendish said.

"Make these whores leave!" She was breathless with anger.

Her dark hair was arranged on top of her head. She wore a white gown, and from her ears swung long pearl earrings. Just as the memory of her face came to his mind, one of the men near by put a familiar hand on her shoulder, seizing her roughly. Startled, she cried out. And then Cavendish did remember. Lola again faced him, as she had done that day in the pine forests of San Lucas. And Cavendish said, "Take your hands off her!"

"I'll do it this time, Tom," said a voice behind him. David reached out leisurely and took Lola's admirer by the front of his jacket. He shook him slowly and ended the brief encounter by sending him backwards onto the floor, into the dancers and the men and women who were watching.

"The next time you lay a hand on Madam Cavendish, I'll kill you," David said pleasantly. He held out his hand to Cavendish.

Cavendish gripped it hard. "David," he said, low. "David." He could say nothing else.

"Aye, Tom. Hadn't you expected me, sometime?"

"I hoped," Cavendish said. They must be waiting for him to do something. Gently he put Lola's hand in his arm across the sling. "My congratulations, Madam Cavendish," he said. "Come." Again he looked incredulously at both of them. "We cannot keep her here, David."

Lola's hand, still brown, rested on the black velvet uncompromisingly.

"I am glad that you at least realize this company is not fit," she said, lapsing into quick Spanish that reminded him of Catherine.

David smiled unperturbably. "Oh, I don't know, Lola. A man must play."

Lola drew a deep breath; they were going downstairs. In the study, Cavendish shut the door. David looked about the room appreciatively.

"Beautiful, Tom," he said.

Cavendish blurted. "You knew all the time you were alive, but I didn't, David!" He suddenly smiled, the brilliant wonderful smile, and Lola's expression softened.

"Now you look like your portrait!" she said.

Cavendish didn't hear her. Lola walked over by the fire. She thought England was frighteningly cold. She heard David's and Cavendish's voices, and quick tears filled her eyes. She thought of Kate and the baby. She and David had come late tonight because the baby had cried. She sank down into the chair by the fire and listened.

"We saved the *Santa Anna*," David was saying.

"You saved her?" came Cavendish's incredulous tones.

"The fire freed the starboard stern anchor, Tom. I cut

the larboard cable. We payed out the fore cables and beached her. The wind changed. I had started the men at the bilge pumps to protect the hull." He looked at his brother's face. He smiled. "Do not worry, Tom. They'll never use her again.They dismantled her in Acapulco."

"Then, " said Cavendish, "then, what happened?"

"I used the little bark you built. She was sunk by enemy action." David grinned. "At the mouth of the Verde River. One of the men with me was killed, and I tied him aboard so they would find one body, and we went underwater until the Spaniards left. Lola almost drowned. After that, it was easier. They thought us dead. I brought a man named Sebastian home with me. We came home from America as seamen, together. It was another easy matter to leave Spain for France, and then England."

"Very easy," said Cavendish.

Lola said, "David is a wonderful man."

"She's mad about me," David said.

Questions trembled on Cavendish's tongue. But he couldn't voice them. David was saying, "I am told Brule must have foundered."

Cavendish nodded. "We lost the *Content* the night we sailed from San Lucas." But he could hold back the question no Longer.

"I warrant the Señora Catherine sailed on the *Santa Anna,* then?"

"Aye," said David.

Cavendish eyed Lola. "Did you see aught of the Señora de Montoro, madam?"

Lola's voice came from over her shoulder as she watched the flames.

"*Sí, señor,*" she said.

"I understood the *señora* was Madam Cavendish," David said.

Cavendish said, "She is. But I'll warrant it's not much hindrance to her." He felt the black anger beating through his body. In a minute he would ask whether she was in Spain or whether she had stayed in America. In either place, he had a quick vision of capturing her; he saw himself raiding a town in America, and facing her again.

"Is the *señora* in Spain?" he asked, his voice dangerously low.

Lola started to answer, but David cut her short. "So your vanity is suffering, is it, Tom?" he asked. "I wish she were in Spain. I wish she were sitting now, as you vision her, telling the richest man in Spain that unfortunately you had forced her to marry you. I wish it were true, Tom. But it isn't."

Cavendish said roughly. "Then where is she, David? In America?"

"Aye," said David. "Your vanity doesn't need to suffer any longer. She loved you. Catherine would be here if she could be. Catherine is dead, Tom. She died in childbirth. You have a daughter. Catherine named her Bess."

For a moment he stared at them—white, unbelievingly. Then he turned abruptly, flung open the door, and went out. After a few paces, the sound of his footsteps ceased echoing, and there was only silence again—a dead silence broken finally by shouts and laughter in the distant gallery.

Chapter 40

SNOW WAS FALLING GENTLY. The flakes were big, and they floated quietly to the ground and melted quickly on the dark bare earth. Only to the brown branches of the trees did they cling, and to the slate roof of the sprawling brick house.

Smoke came from its eight huge chimneys. The yews were laden with the wet snow.

"I've never seen it before!" Kate said, excitedly, letting go of the reins with one small hand and holding out her palms to catch the snow. It melted on her glove instantly.

Cavendish said, leaning over to grasp the reins, "No more galloping in this."

"We're almost home," Kate said. "There is a carriage, too."

"We have visitors," Cavendish said, looking ahead. He reined in, and jumped to the ground, lifting Kate from her little mare, and settling her on her feet just as the big door opened.

"It's the Countess of Earlsham," Cavendish said to Kate. "Come, you must be presented." He looked at her critically, his Kate. She was dressed in velvet riding clothes and her hood and gloves were edged with fur.

"Madam," he said, bowing. "We are so glad we did not miss you. May I present my daughter, Catherine."

Catherine swept a curtesy. Just then little Antnony de Dasi came running up. Kate's green eyes sparkled.

"May I go to the stables, sir, with Tony?" she asked, as Tony took the reins of her mare. "I'll not stay long."

"Certainly," said Cavendish, looking at her proudly, and she started away.

The Countess arched her brows. Did she disapprove? Cavendish frowned, and said, "She will be the finest horsewoman in Suffolk, madam."

"She rides astride?"

"I've forbidden sidesaddle," Cavendish announced. "It is a silly fad."

"Is the little dark boy her page?" the Countess asked, drawing her cloak close around her.

"He is," said Cavendish. "He's a Filipino."

"How old is your daughter?" asked the Countess, knowing perfectly well.

"She is seven, madam," Cavendish answered, seeing Tyler out of the corner of his eye. "Well, Tyler," he said, sharply, "it took you some time. Get him dry." He turned back to the Countess who was waiting. "Excuse me, madam."

"The little one is your stepdaughter, then?"

"Kate is Madam Cavendish's first child," Cavendish said.

The Countess moved toward her coach. "She is very lovely," she conceded.

"She is as fair as her mother," Cavendish said, helping her into the coach. "I am happy for you to have met her and seen for yourself."

He stood out in front of the house, bareheaded, while the coach disappeared down the drive. Tyler came around the corner of the house.

"Her daughters look like horses," Cavendish said to him. He turned, and strode into the hall, brushing his wet hair back. The hall was empty, the fire blazed on the hearth, and he started up the wide stairway. Cosmos met him at the top.

"The bailiff is with Master David in the study, sir," he said.

Cavendish strode along to his own room. Cosmos divested him of his heavy boots, replacing them with comfortable leather house shoes lined with fur.

"I'll go see the bailiff," Cavendish said.

He went out into the hall; he stopped at the entrance to a long low room with bright new painted furniture. He saw Lola.

She had the baby in her arms; she was sitting before the fire in a low chair, and when she saw Cavendish, she rose, and brought the baby over to him.

"Listen to her talk, Tom," said Lola, making little noises that the baby answered eagerly.

Cavendish felt again an enormous thankfulness for Lola's obvious love for the baby. "The Lord must have sent you," he said.

Lola smiled. She put the baby in Cavendish's arms. He said, "She is finally accustomed to my voice."

The baby's blue eyes were on him. She looked a little uncertain at the sound of his deep tones; then she made a small grimace.

"Is she smiling?" Cavendish asked.

"I don't think so," said Lola, laughing at him.

"Her hair is turning lighter," Cavendish said. "I wanted it to."

Lola said seriously, "I think her hair will be auburn, dark red, a combination of yours and Catherine's."

The baby began to breathe fast.

"I'm beginning to know when she's going to cry," Cavendish said. "Faith, Lola, look how angry she is."

"She's sleepy," Lola said, taking the baby. She laid her down in the blue-painted cradle. "She'll not cry long," she assured him.

He was not sure. "I'll wait here till Tina comes," he said, sitting down by the cradle. Lola left him there.

The baby stopped crying. He sat quietly, staring into the flames. There really was no need for him to see the bailiff. The bailiff was competent; never had Trimley and its farmlands and tenant houses looked so well. And David was competent, too. Trimley would run itself, and David would run it, and he and Lola would live here and raise their own children, here in this peaceful English county. David was writing, too. Every afternoon, after the morning duties were done, he sat alone at his table. David would stay at Trimley, so near to Ipswich, where the sea pounded. In the direction Cavendish was facing this moment, through the brick wall, a few miles away the sea would be gray and winter cold now, heaving, immense.

He looked down at the baby. She slept, her arms folded, her hands tightened into little balls. The more he looked at her, day after day, the more beautiful she became to him. Already she seemed to know Lola, and Tina. But she didn't know him—not yet.

He reached over and touched her little hand with his finger. She slept on. In the silent house, he suddenly heard Kate's voice, chattering eagerly in her broken English with Tony. He heard her excited laughter.

"No, no, no!" she cried, and then he heard her running steps going away from him. "Lola! Lola!" she called. A door banged, and then there was silence again.

They were forever taken care of, these children. He had given them everything—his name, these wide estates, the fortune which was his. Even though David's son would inherit, Trimley's was theirs to live in, always.

Lola and David were very happy. They were so happy together that sometimes their happiness thrust a stinging pain through him. Yesterday he had to go out; he had ridden to the sea. Yesterday, the water had been deep blue, the deepest blue that colored the water when the northern sky was cloudy except for small patches of blue sky. When the water changed from gray to blue, because the sun had pierced through, then it became that wonderful shining deepest blue.

The baby slept. The house was still quiet. David would be with the bailiff, and Kate was with Lola.

He had not heard Tina's soft steps. "I waited for you," he said.

His voice wakened the baby. She opened her eyes, and Tina reached out for her.

"Your dinner is ready, sir—in five minutes."

He bent down himself and lifted the baby in his arms. "You're going to feed her?" he asked. The baby looked into his face with the puzzled faraway expression she still had, and he put his lips to the side of her face. Then he laid her in Tina's arms and went from the room.

At dinner, the polished table shone. The candles were set in silver sconces about the walls, and the paneled room was ruddy with firelight. The food was excellent. He sat at the head of the table, with Lola at the other end, and David between them. One of the plum puddings that had hung from the rafters in the room atop the long kitchen was served hot for dessert.

"The house couldn't have a better mistress," Cavendish observed, and Lola smiled, pleased.

She was working at her handwriting. After dinner she sat frowning over a list of household orders that Cavendish had written out for her; she had insisted on copying them herself, because that was right. She concentrated on her task.

"Every guest room," she wrote laboriously, being careful to space the words evenly as Cavendish had done, "should be cleaned, aired, and supplied with fresh sheets and linens, in no less than four hours after the departing guest has left."

She finished that, and looked at the next instruction. She read it, and then she asked, "Tom, what does this mean?"

Cavendish looked up from his place by the fire. He was lounging idly; David was reading.

Lola read, "Any man who uses the courtyard to make water will be fined two shillings."

Cavendish grinned. He started to explain, just as Lola realized what the words meant.

David smiled and put aside his book. Cavendish seldom read; and David felt a trifle guilty because he and Lola were both occupied and Cavendish was not. He started to speak, but Cavendish interrupted him.

"I'm going to Plymouth tomorrow, David."

David was not surprised, he glanced at Lola as if to remind her that he had been right, and had anticipated this. "Tomorrow, Tom?" he asked.

"It's been a month since I was there," Cavendish said. "I haven't told you before, David, but I am building a new ship. I started to build her last September."

David was surprised, now. "You are? A new ship?"

Cavendish nodded.

"It's time for me to go, soon."

"Oh, no!" Lola said. She had forgotten her writing; she was leaning across the table, her eyes on him. "Oh, no, Tom!"

Cavendish shook his head.

He got up and stood with his back to the fire. "I

want to go to sea again," he said simply. "I want to go."

"No!" Lola cried.

David caught Lola's eye. She was silent, and David said, "How soon, then, Tom?"

"Not till spring," Cavendish said. "My new ship will be christened *Galeon*."

David thought a moment. "Stillness of the sea, calm," he translated. "I'm surprised you remembered your Greek. You always surprise me, Tom."

Cavendish smiled, affectionately. "Captain John Davis will command the *Desire*; the *Desire* is ready to sail now."

"You couldn't have a better man," David said.

"Except Havers," Cavendish said. "Or de Ersola."

Lola interrupted. She rose and went around the table to stand before Cavendish.

"Tom!" she said.

But he wouldn't let her speak. There was no use. "There's a moon tonight, Lola," he said. "I think I'll ride out for a while." He went to the door, he closed it, and his voice was raised in a call for Tyler. Lola stood in the center of the room, looking at the door Cavendish had gone through. Slowly David came over to her. He turned her to face him.

"What he says is true," he said. "He wants to go."

"No!" she said desperately.

He tipped her face up to his; his smile was tender. "Lola," he said, "there are some men born with a gallantry that leaves them no rest until they have pitted themselves against insuperable odds."

"I don't know what you mean," she cried.

David said, "What Tom said was true. He must go."

"I know he loved Catherine!" she said. "But—"

"That is not the point," David interrupted. "Tom is not running away from sorrow. He told us he started to build his new ship before he knew Catherine was not coming to him. He would have left her. Lola, he lives with a dream. He knows it. His dream is the conquering of the seas, the expanding of the world, the building of America, the making of an empire. He would die for it."

"Die for it?" she said. "Oh, David, do not say that!"

PART
5

Chapter 41

"THE TOWN of Santos lies here." Cavendish's finger jabbed at the map of the coast of South America.

"Aye, sir," said John Davis, and Captain Cocke nodded solemnly. Pretty rubbed his hand over his face to conceal the stifling of a yawn. He was very sleepy and he knew he would have nothing to do with the action Cavendish was outlining for the other two captains. John Davis commanded the *Desire,* and Cocke the bark named the *Blake.* Pretty yawned openly.

Cavendish said, "We will provision here at Santos. It will be a very simple matter to take the town. Very simple." Again his fingers jabbed at the map, pointing to the long sand bar that lay across the harbor.

"Anchor outside this bar," he said, looking up from the map at the two Captains. "Anchor Saturday night after dark. Use two longboats and the pinnace. Sunday morning the people will be in church. At nine, church time, surround the church and keep the people within its walls as hostages. We want food, and only food."

John Davis said, "As you say, sir, it is very simple."

Pretty yawned again, throwing a glance at Cocke, who looked a little surprised at the strategy. Pretty knew it was good strategy, good Cavendish strategy.

In the meantime, Cavendish was saying to Davis, "It may be simple, but it is vastly important." He frowned a little. In his restless haste to reach the Pacific, he had put off reprovisioning until now; rations were dwindling. "I want you to take the town at church time on Sunday morning. I hope to be there myself, but the *Galeon* is not so good a sailer as the *Desire*, and time is important. Sunday morning we catch them unawares. We must have food."

"Aye, sir," said Captain Davis.

Cavendish smiled at him. He trusted Davis absolutely. In his hands the expedition should be well executed.

"Good night, then," he said, for there was no time to lose.

"Good night, sir," said Davis, and he and Cocke went up on deck with Cavendish, Master Pretty trailing behind the three captains. In the darkness, the lights from the *Desire* and the bark *Blake* flickered faintly across the water. Cocke commanded the *Blake*, Davis the *Desire*, and Cavendish waited on the deck of the *Galeon* to watch their boats pull away toward each of their ships. It was the fourteenth of December; they were anchored at the Isle of San Sebastian. The next night should see the two smaller, swifter ships anchored outside the bar of the town of Santos, ready for the action of Sunday morning. It was then Friday night.

As Cavendish had expected, the scant wind and the bulk of the *Galeon*, his new ship, allowed the *Desire* and the *Blake* to go ahead. At dawn, he did not see them on the sea. Sunday night he anchored outside the bar at Santos, almost a full day later than the *Desire*, which rode nattily at anchor in the dusky evening light. Cavendish wondered whether it would ever not be a joy to see her once more.

The *Galeon* had no sooner thrown over her anchors than a longboat was hoisted over the side of the *Desire*, and Cavendish saw Davis clamber into it. Captain Cocke was with him. Cavendish did not think it odd. He waited in his own cabin for them, a smile on his face. But the smile disappeared as soon as he saw Davis's face.

Davis was in a diffcult position. He did not know how to begin his tale. Cavendish asked sharply, "You took the town?"

"Aye, sir. This morning, as you said."

Cavendish heaved a sigh of relief. "Good," he said.

"The people were in church, as you said. We surrounded it—I did—with but twenty-four men, who had come ashore with me in my longboat. We guarded the church."

"Good," said Cavendish, more heartily. "You lost no men?"

"None, sir."

"Then you immediately began to provision?"

Davis said slowly, "No, sir, I did not."

Cavendish's tanned face hardened. He brought his fist down on the table. "Why?" he asked.

Davis could not help throwing a swift glance at Captain Cocke, and Cavendish saw it. He turned to Cocke. "Suppose you tell me," he said, "why you did not immediately secure the food?"

Cocke cried, "The Indians carried off the food! They escaped and ran off into the hills! They took everything!"

There was quiet in the *Galeon's* great richly paneled cabin. Moon looked incredulous and contemptuous; Pretty paid scant attention to Cocke and his confession of failure; he was wondering what Cavendish was going to do.

Cavendish said, "While Captain Davis took and held the town, you allowed the Indians to make away with the food we needed?"

Cocke said despairingly, "Aye, sir. It happened like lightening! They were there, and then they were gone! And the town as clean as a whistle!" Cocke had jumped to his feet, as he explained, for Cavendish himself had risen. Cocke was standing between him and the cabin door.

Cavendish reached out one hand and took Cocke by the front of the shirt. "You incompetent fool," he said quietly, and pushed him aside.

He walked to the door and threw it open. He would have to go to the town of Santos himself and see if he could repair the damage that was already done. There was a faint hope that it was not irreparable.

He took Davis with him. Men from the *Desire* still patrolled the town, and its inhabitants had been relieved of all weapons. Davis had done his part, but Davis did not think so. He blamed himself, and he said so, briefly, shyly.

Cavendish said, "You are not to blame, sir."

The boat pulled swiftly toward the town, and Cavendish watched the black water and the white breakers on the beach. He jumped out onto the sand.

Ashore, he conferred with the mayor of the town, seeking now to get by treaty what he had failed to get by force. In addition to that, he posted a guard at each house. In the morning they searched Santos again. They obtained cassavi meal, and that was all.

"With your permission, sir, we could roast a few Indians," Moon said.

Pretty laughed. He had an idea that the intrepid Moon would eat Indians, too. He glanced sideways at Moon, wonderingly.

"And as far as pursuing those Indians up into the mountains, why, they might as well be as far away as the Pacific, sir," Moon went on. "As if you didn't know it, Captain," he added.

Cavendish looked up from the list he had been making.

"We'll make many a meal from meal," Moon said, with a grin. "By God, we'll have a meal cake for Christmas."

"If you'd stop talking, Moon," Cavendish said, "I might be able to."

Moon sat down in one of the chairs. "Fire away, sir," he said.

"Captain Cocke," said Cavendish, speaking the name indifferently, "carries the most part of our remaining victuals. He'll be relieved of those today, Moon. Here's the list. In the event of his foundering, or losing the fleet between here and Port Desire, we shan't have lost the most part of our food. And since we don't have much time, we'll set sail tomorrow for Port Desire."

"Aye, sir," said Moon. He stood up. He left the cabin. He wasn't worried. He depended on Cavendish. And the *Galeon* was new and sturdy; her great masts rose over his head, towering upward. Even though the worst part of the voyage lay ahead, even though the rations would be short from now on, Moon wasn't worried. He looked down at the list in his hand. The first thing to do was to get the food from the *Blake* aboard the *Galeon*. For Moon did know that Captain Cocke had shown incompetence, and after that, he might show cowardice. He might desert. Moon settled his cap firmly and made ready to relieve Captain Cocke of his list of foodstuffs and wine and ale. It would be a pleasure, he told himself. . . .

On Christmas Day the first bad storm blew down on the *Galeon* and the *Desire*. The storm lasted three days, and when its might was spent, the *Galeon* was alone on the seas as they surged heavily across her bows. The *Galeon* was alone; she had been blown way off her course. She had lost her fleet and she would not see the *Desire* again for almost three months.

They were long months. Close hauled under the gales, the *Galeon* fought the fury of the South Atlantic, and her seamen endured with her. They were as tough as her hewn timbers. They buttoned their jackets close, and wore woolen caps pulled down over their heads. Master Fuller got sick, but in four days he was up and around again, bellowing orders in the teeth of a fresh storm. Moon's round face was thinned, but his obscene expletives came as sharply as before, and Pretty was growing a beard; Moon avowed it would keep him warmer, and Tyler had decided to grow one too, even though the Captain shaved himself each morning, as usual.

"I'm getting used to this," Moon said to Pretty, in their own cabin, as he changed his wet clothes for some that were at least not wringing wet. "I'm always wet, Pretty," he said. "You see, I'm working up to bedding a mermaid."

"You'll be in fine shape," Pretty said.

"It'll be worse, soon," Moon said cheerfully. "We are in forty degrees now. The roaring forties. More gales, sir."

Pretty said, "I've been here before."

"You're as mad as I am. There must be something rotten in our heads." He finished lacing his boots. The *Galeon* pitched and Moon stumbled. "Oh, land, where art thou?" he asked. "Good-bye, Pretty. Get some sleep, if you can."

On this he left the cabin. Cavendish was on deck, talking to Fuller. The men were building a long boat. In the last storm the *Galeon* had lost all her boats. The gray Atlantic heaved itself; a mountainous roller bore down on the *Galeon;* the ship lifted; the roller washed across the decks and through the scuppers. The sea settled itself again, lazily, after the effort.

"I think the sun's coming out," Cavendish said. He was looking to the west. Sun broke through the clouds. Cavendish spoke to Tyler, who was on his knees, hammer in hand.

"Fetch my glass, will you, Tyler?" he asked. "And bring out those wet clothes of mine; string them up on the poop."

"Aye, sir," said Tyler spitting three nails out of his mouth. He rose.

"I'll take the nails," said Cavendish, holding out his hand. He knelt down in Tyler's place and began to hammer with quick, even strokes. Fuller thought he took pleasure in it; he was watching Cavendish when Tyler came back.

Cavendish got to his feet and took the glass. Already, the other men had hung out the wet clothes.

"The ship looks like a wash house," Fuller commented, coming to Cavendish's side. He waited eagerly.

Cavendish was looking again to the west.

"We were blown back toward land," Fuller said. "Thank God."

"We've been blown all over hell," Cavendish said. But he was smiling. He lowered the glass. He handed it to Fuller. "Land," he said.

After all these weeks, they had sighted land. It was almost March. In a few weeks, incredibly, it would be spring in England. Down here, it would be fall.

Fuller was staring through the glass, his face deep with creases. "Land," he breathed. "By God, sir, land!"

It was bare and desolate. The *Galeon* was in forty degrees. Day by day she haled southward; she showed as much canvas as she dared, and day by day it grew colder. On the eighteenth of March the weary *Galeon* put into Port Desire. And in the harbor, riding quietly, was the *Desire* at anchor.

It was bitter cold, already. Cavendish buttoned his leather jacket tight against the wind, as he stood on deck with Pretty. They could hear Moon's voice shouting orders above the wind, and the crew, aloft or on deck, raised their voices to cheer the *Desire,* as she dipped her flags and fired a welcoming broadside, to greet the flagship sailing slowly into port.

The anchors splashed overboard into the black water. A flock of birds wheeled upward from a lonely rock, and great breakers crashed unceasingly across the northern shoals that bordered the harbor.

"She found port, sir," Pretty said lovingly, looking across the narrow strip of water that separated them from the *Desire*. "Here comes Captain Davis."

They saw Davis' figure standing in the stern of his longboat. He waved his cap, they heard him shout to them, and Cavendish shouted back. The crew cheered, wildly, because death had sailed with them many weeks, and they knew that it would follow them relentlessly, through the seas ahead. For a few days, now, they were in safe harbor, forbidding harbor, but safe. And this port was their port. Their Captain had discovered it, named it after the ship that rode close to them. He knew these waters. They looked up to the deck on which he stood, and watched him come running down to greet Davis. Davis brought penguins, plucked, for stewing. He brought a few smelts.

"We've been catching them with hooks made out of pins," he said.

Cavendish looked into the basket at the meager pile of small fish. Standing there, on the deck of the *Galeon*, here in the gaunt port he himself had discovered, he smiled somberly.

"Come below," he said. "We'll eat and talk."

Davis and he said little during the meal. Cavendish ate the smelts, bones and all, crushing them between his teeth. The officers talked, cheerfully. Moon told how bad the storms had been; how much rigging and sail had been lost, and all their boats.

Cavendish had finished eating; there was no more to eat. He said, as an end to Moon's tale. "We have no more sail than masts. No victuals, no ground tackling, no more cordage than is over your head, Davis."

The cabin was cold. The lamp swung overhead. Ice bumped against the sides of the ship.

Davis said, "We are so near the Pacific."

No one spoke. This meeting, after months of lonely sailing, was now a time for reckoning.

"There are no more sails than masts," Cavendish repeated quietly.

He rested his hands on the table; his eyes swept the circle of officers, noting them carefully, noting their thin faces, the circled eyes. Pretty very badly wanted to say something, but he shut his lips tight. Moon tried a cheerful grin; he spoke.

"I'm ready to go on, Captain," he said. He rattled the pair of dice he had in his hands.

"Don't bother to roll them, Moon," Cavendish said. "It's not going to be based on a throw of the dice. The *Galeon* cannot go on. She must turn back."

Pretty's eyes looked startled.

"I," said Cavendish slowly, "am going to return to my old cabin aboard the *Desire*. I'm going to sail her to the Pacific again."

Through Pretty's mind flashed a picture. A picture of a warm sunny beach where the south wind blew gently. "California," he said, aloud.

Cavendish met his eyes. Cavendish smiled a little. "I shall not return to England," he went on evenly, "but with me, aboard the *Desire,* I'll take only those who want to go."

Pretty said, "I'd like to go, sir," and even as he said it he knew what the answer would be. A hopelessness fell on Pretty; he bit his lip. His hands were trembling, and he told himself it was hunger that did this to him. "Captain Cavendish!" he said.

Cavendish said, "You are needed, Pretty. You and Moon and Fuller are needed. The *Galeon* must return. You will be responsible for the lives of a hundred and fifty men. I take only forty with me."

Pretty heard his voice go on. He heard him say that they must catch penguins and dry them. He heard the rations issued for the men who were to sail on the *Desire:* six ounces of meal a day. Pretty looked at Cavendish's broad shoulders; he couldn't live on that, not a man who weighed as much as his Captain.

Then Davis said, "I shall sail with you, Captain Cavendish." His face was tired and drawn. It was not late, but sleep was one compensation for hunger. Cavendish went out on deck with Davis, to bid him good night, him and his officers. He watched their boat pull away to the *Desire*.

"I'll be aboard her tomorrow myself," he said.

Pretty said nothing. The wind blew. The sky overhead was dark, moonless, starless. A single light shone from the *Desire*.

"We'll sail as soon as possible," Cavendish went on.

Pretty leaned wearily against the rail. He could not think of anything except the man beside him.

"In England, you'll have an heir by now, Pretty. It's time you saw your child."

"I'd rather go on," Pretty said.

"I'm sorry," Cavendish said.

"I can't forgive you for it," Pretty said evenly. "Moon feels as I do."

Cavendish did not answer. A lonely gull mewed sharply over their heads. The tides of Port Desire, the great surging tides, slapped against the ship like waves. Across the black water the single light aboard the *Desire* shone out. Pretty knew that after a few days he might never see her again.

Chapter 42

THE ENTRANCE of the Straits of Magellan is bounded on the north by Cape Virgins. It is a great broad opening in the land, standing in fifty-two and a half degrees. It is the end of the continent of America, the entrance to the Pacific, one hundred and ten leagues in length. On the sixth of April the *Desire* sighted Cape Virgins.

The weather was fair. The wind was moderate. The *Desire* entered the Straits.

The rolling tides here dropped forty feet at their ebb. Along the shore, rock thrust upward, and even as the *Desire* sailed by, the water ebbed out and a sandy beach lazily threw itself outward into the blue water. Leaning on the rail, John Davis watched the shore line.

Cavendish was beside him. The two men had just come out on deck. "Look your fill," Cavendish said, "for the land will drop away for a few hours."

They had just come from the charts. Davis spent much time studying Cavendish's charts. They talked of nothing else, in these last weeks; they talked of nothing but seas and shores and currents. And food. Davis stared down at the swift water.

"The channel is wide here," Davis observed, "but Jesu, man, what currents!"

"They run as much as eight knots," Cavendish said. His voice was tired. He had told Davis that before, he knew, but it was hard to remember.

"We need speed," Davis said, not expecting an answer. They had food for two weeks, a little food—enough, perhaps, to last. Only one man had died since they had left Port Desire. Again he glanced at the man beside him. He had expected to know him better in these last weeks. He had expected the man Cavendish to emerge. He hadn't. The wide shoulders were very thin, even under the heavy leather jacket. John Davis said, almost timidly, "Sir, there is a little wine."

"We might need it, Davis," was the answer. It was said gently, but the gentleness did not conceal the determination not to let any guard down yet; not to give one bit of the battle yet to this enemy, this cold mighty southern sea and the mountains that guarded it. Davis knew that the man who was his Captain was hungry. He knew that the magnificent six feet of bone and flesh and blood and muscle must cry for food.

"I'm smaller than you, Captain," he said.

But he saw Cavendish had hardly heard him. The *Desire* was sailing through the outer narrows, close hauled against the wind.

"You're thinking of those charts," Davis accused.

The word charts made an impression. Only the words, the sentences, the thoughts that had to do with this fight to enter the Pacific, were the words that mattered to Cavendish. All his will was straining toward one object, and only that object had his attention.

"The wind is stronger," he said.

The sprit sail strained under full canvas. All other sails were sheeted. The ropes and braces creaked. The wind blew steadily. The inner narrows were upon them.

"In with the main sheet!" Cavendish called out.

Ice crackled as the crew furled the mainsail. The sun came out and glistened on the ice-coated ship. The water turned blue, and the sun winked evilly on the floating icecakes. Ahead was Cape Froward.

"It is unearthly. Beautiful," Davis said, under his breath.

Seven thousand feet up into the sky, Mount Sarmiento towered whitely. Cape Froward, black rock that it was, was sprinkled with snows.

"Famine Reach," Cavendish said, indicating the narrowing channel toward which the *Desire* tacked on the starboard tack.

"You named it," said Davis. Again they spoke of nothing but charts and channels, seas and currents. Only the sea mattered. Davis thought Cavendish's eyes as blue as the sea water itself.

A great chunk of ice slipped off the nearest glacier and splashed into the water, settling itself lazily to float. Long trails of seaweed drifted past the ship.

"At least the cold keeps her bottom clean," Cavendish said. "And there's no water in the well."

"She's dry. We just sounded the well," said Davis.

"We shall double the Cape before noon," Cavendish went on.

They did. At eleven they doubled Cape Froward. They were in the narrowest stretch of the straits. Then the day turned hell dark, and fury came out of the skies.

The *Desire* heeled over; the wind screamed over the sound of the tortured wood and canvas. Davis and Cavendish clung in the shrouds as they furled the mizzen. The *Desire* clawed to windward; the shore of Famine Reach came closer. Cavendish's voice pierced through the wind:

"Helm to starboard!"

The *Desire* steadied her course.

"Sheet anchor to seaward!"

Cavendish slid down onto the deck, with Davis after him. There was no need for further orders. Cavendish was already unlashing the heaviest boat. Davis was beside him. Tyler was there.

The boat swung over the side. Cavendish scrambled down into her, seizing an oar. A great breaker took the boat, stood her on her stern, and crashed it down again. They pulled frantically.

The shore was close. Cavendish jumped out into the icy water, carrying rope. His hands fumbled with the knots. They moored the *Desire* to the heaviest trees, for there was no real anchorage there. Then they pulled for the *Desire*.

No man was lost. Cavendish ordered a fire lighted to dry the men. They were anchored in the Straits, and until the weather lifted, they would have to stay.

"Famine Reach," he whispered. "You named it yourself."

The fourth day they buried the first man to die of starvation. The *Desire* was moored on a narrow shelf of rock, very near shore. Beyond, the water was unfathomable; the current itself so swift that it ran free always although ice floated in it, dotting its blackened surface, running along merrily, bobbing with the water.

The sound of the wind was high and strident. It blew from the north northeast, prisoning the *Desire*. The great ropes, the heaviest the *Desire* had, moored the ship to shore; the cables were soon crusted with ice, and when the snows began to fall, ridges of snow lay along the ropes and over the forms of the trees so near.

Seaweed floated near the ship, long and trailing. They ate it. The leather on the yards was frozen solid. They could not strip it off and boil and powder it for food. They ate mussels, raw, for Cavendish thought there was more nourishment in them raw.

On the eighth day two men died. After the prayer had been said, and the bodies, sewed into the hammocks, had slid into the black sea, Cavendish took the men ashore to cut more wood, and to find the precious mussels. A blizzard blew down on them that day, and continued in intensity for five more days.

Incredibly, it was almost May. In England the blossoms would be burgeoning; in California the skies would be drenched with south winds and lazy mists that the sun pierced at morning. But in the Straits of Magellan it was winter. The world turned white; only the black water swirled along past the ship, and there was no sound in this world but the sound of the wind.

Twenty men died. Twenty men were buried in the frozen seas, and the gale winds blew steadily. The wind made its long familiar sounds, the waves slapped at the sides of the ship; the wind wakened Cavendish early on the morning of the tenth of May. More than a month had passed since he had entered the Straits.

Hunger and the wind wakened him. It was not yet dawn. He sat up wearily; he was fully dressed. He wriggled his toes; they felt frozen, as always. Yet they could not be, because he could move them a little.

He tried again to sleep. He must sleep. But he was conscious of only one desire, and that was food. For days now he had been aware only of hunger— everything else was gone and only hunger was left, and he knew it was the same for every man aboard the *Desire*. He got up and stumbled in the darkness. He found the lamp and lighted it.

Last night he had put away the chart that had lain on

the table for days, and which Davis had been studying. Wearily Cavendish extracted paper and ink. He began to write to David.

He wrote long. In his own cabin, here aboard the *Desire,* the only sound was the scratching of his pen. Sometimes long after he needed ink he would keep on with the words, and then he would have to retrace the lines where they were too faint. He had told David about the first part of the voyage; now he went on:

"Such was the fury of the west-southwest wind and southwest winds that we were driven from shore four hundred leagues, and constrained to beat from fifty degrees to the southward into forty to the northward, before we could recover near the shore. In which time we had a new shift of sails clean blown away.

"Thus we had been almost four months between the coast of Brazil and the Straits, being in distance not more above six hundred leagues, which is commonly run in twenty or thirty days."

He dipped his pen.

"Now, being anchored here in the Straits, some days the snows fall so thick we cannot see but for two and a half hours, in the middle of the day."

He looked back over what he had written.

"Bear with this scribbling," he ended, "for my fingers are cold to hold a pen in my hand."

He frowned, looking down at the words. He looked at his thin brown hands; he clenched them slowly, watching the fingers, the short clipped nails.

He laid down the pen, and blew out the lamp; it was getting light, and he really shouldn't have used the lamp. Everything aboard should be conserved, for the hours and days ahead. It must never be lost sight of— his objective. It was all that was left, except hunger.

There was a knock on the door. It was John Davis. He came into the cabin; he carried a silver cup of wine.

"Good morning, Captain," he said. "I brought you a little wine this morning. They—the men—wanted you to have it."

Cavendish's blue eyes concealed themselves from Davis. Davis was deeply touched. Emotions were near the surface today, and yesterday, and the day before.

"They wanted you to have it," Davis repeated, setting the cup down gently, slowly releasing his fingers from the precious liquid, to make sure his unsteady hands didn't tip it. He knew Cavendish was waiting for whatever other news he had brought.

"There'll be no burials this morning, sir," he said.

Cavendish sighed with relief. A gust of wind shook the *Desire,* and Cavendish stood up. He picked up the wine. He started to drink it. He sipped it slowly, and handed it, half-empty, to Davis.

"You take the rest," he said. "Issue the same amount to each man. We're going to sail this morning, wind or no."

At eight they went ashore to loose the *Desire* from the trees and ropes that moored her to the land. Thirty minutes later, the anchors laid to seaward were weighed. The sheeted cross jack held her close into the wind; the sprit unfurled, and close hauled, on a larboard tack, she edged out into the currents of Famine Reach.

The wind, like a miracle, dropped a little. The heavy seas washed over her decks and the bowsprit turned to ice, chunkily. The sun shone through a patchy sky; the water turned deep blue. On deck, Cavendish watched; he paced the high deck to keep warm, and he stopped walking when it was physically impossible for him to walk longer. Then he leaned against the rail. The sun was setting when the *Desire* entered the Pacific.

The Pacific was rolling blue and mighty. Cape Deseado crouched against the shore line, a monstrous sentinel of the world's vastest ocean. Across it, the sun was sending its last light of the May day; long purple streamers flung upward against the white-gray sky; westward on the horizon a pale golden haze was over the ocean. Cavendish straightened up and his voice rang out. The objective had been reached, and he spoke only four words to tell of triumph.

"North northwest, Captain Davis!"

The course was set for the Juan Fernández islands.

He slept that night from eight to twelve, the beginning of the middle watch. The *Desire* had only nineteen officers and men. Cavendish was taking the middle

watch himself. It was during that watch that the wind
sprang up again. The wind blew from the north northeast.

All sails were furled. The helm was lashed alee. For
six hours the *Desire* lay ahull, and for six hours she was
driven south. When dawn came she was three leagues to
the leeward of Cape Deseado.

There was only one way to save the ship. She was
being blown southward, as Drake had been, into the uncharted Antarctic. She must put back into the Straits; it
was the only way.

The *Desire* was not half so big as the icebergs that
floated in the seas here—great hunks of glacier whose
white sides came down into the seas and broke off as the
endlessly churning waters tumbled at them. Those seas
broke over the *Desire,* broke over the poop, and clung
to her ropes and rigging and turned them to ice.

On deck Cavendish said, "We must double the Cape
before noon, or die." He said it bluntly, leaning back
against the ropes and steadying himself. A great wave
broke over the poop and washed past his feet. "Get sail
up," he said to David, "and we'll put it to God's
mercy."

The Cape on the southern shores of the Straits was
two leagues distant. On the north shore was nothing but
a company of dangerous rocks and isles and shoals. The
seas were churning now as the *Desire* unfurled her sails
and began her battle once more.

In half an hour the foot rope of the foresail broke.
Nothing was holding the sail but the eyelet holes. The
Desire was falling more and more to the leeward of
Cape Deseado. It did not seem possible that she could
double the Cape and enter the Straits; instead, she was
going to be dashed onto its rocks.

Only a half mile of leeway separated the *Desire* from
the Cape. She was so near shore that the counter surf
rebounded against her sides. In desperation Cavendish
ran down to the lower deck; he started up the shrouds;
Tyler was with him.

Between the two of them, they veered the mainsheet.
The *Desire* leaned perilously; she quickened like a live
thing, the spray flew up as she dipped and steadied her

course. High in the shrouds Cavendish clung; the *Desire* hesitated; the wind blew, and the sound of the heavy surf was crashing over the ship. Then the *Desire* shot past the Cape, close.

Tyler and Cavendish took the mainsail. The foresail was furled. Below, it took three men to guide the helm, and the *Desire* spooned before the seas without an inch of canvas. In six hours she was within the Straits by twenty-five leagues. Cavendish stayed on deck. He knew these waters.

At seven o'clock the three ounces of meal were doled out; the precise wine parceled to each man. Cavendish went below for the first time in twenty-four hours.

"Call me in half an hour," he said to Tyler. Davis was asleep. "Just let me have half an hour, Tyler," Cavendish repeated. He stumbled. He was wet through, and there was a knifing pain through his back between the shoulder blades. He bent over suddenly with a cough.

"Captain?" said Tyler.

"Call me in half an hour."

He stood in the center of the cabin. "We'll try again tomorrow, Tyler," he said. "Call me in half an hour."

He sat down in his hammock; he stretched out on his side curling his legs up and wrapping his arms around his chest for warmth. He was back in the Straits, and the sun-drenched tip of California seemed as though it must be farther away than heaven. Surely, this was hell.

He opened his eyes. He felt a little warmed, and the pain that had tormented him all day seemed less. He moved his head a little, to ease the throbbing, and he felt bitter cold, but there was warmth in his body; he could feel the warmth with his hands. He could rest a full thirty minutes, and he knew these seas well. The immediate danger had passed. They hadn't foundered on the rocks of Cape Deseado. They were back in the Straits.

His eyes were closed, and he wasn't asleep; yet he knew he must be dreaming. He saw Catherine plainly; she was coming nearer to him, running, and she spoke to him in Spanish, forgetting her English. He must be dreaming; and he opened his eyes and he was in his cabin, alone. Yet she was near. All during these months she had been near. It was here that he had told her he loved her; it was here that he and de Ersola had played their endless games of chess; the paneling in the cabin must be impregnated with the smoke of Havers' pipes.

He was here, in his cabin aboard the ship *Desire*. He felt quite warm, and his eyes closed again; there were twenty-five minutes left to rest. He had used but five of the thirty.

The hammock swayed. At Trimley, in the spring a year ago, he had slung a hammock for Kate, under the trees. She was probably there now, and Bess would be old enough to sit in the hammock and be swung to and fro. He sighed, and the intake of breath was painful. He breathed lightly, and his eyes closed again. He had twenty-three minutes left to sleep. And he would sleep, he knew. Before the deep sleep came he would dream of Catherine. The memories were so close today, and the image of her so vivid. He moved his hands up under his head, his arms against his chest. His legs were still drawn up for warmth. For the last time he opened his blue eyes, to make sure which was the dream and which the reality. The cabin was just the same, neat and tidy, and cold and dark in the light of the stormy day. The wind was still blowing outside, but he was warm, and Tyler would not call him so soon. There were all of twenty minutes left—so long does it take time to move when it is mixed with eager dreaming. He went to sleep.

Chapter 43

TYLER LOOKED DOWN at his worn boots. There had been silence when his voice had stopped for a moment.

The fire crackled. He could feel its warmth. It was hard to believe that he was safe here at Trimley, and the fire Lola had insisted on lighting while they waited for David was a real fire, and that it burned so close to him.

He lifted his eyes from the boots that had carried him across England from Cornwall, and alone down the curving lane to Trimley, lying there secure under its slate roofs and its beechwood trees. He knew Cosmos was standing behind his chair, and Cosmos moved around and put a footstool in front of Tyler. Gratefully, Tyler lifted his feet onto it.

"Thank you, Cosmos," he said. Cosmos stayed at his side. Across from him, David sat forward in his chair; beside David sat his wife.

"Go on, Tyler," David said.

Tyler continued where he had left off. It was not hard to remember.

"The Captain and I veered the mains'l," he said. "We shot past the Cape, and within six hours we were twenty-five leagues in the Straits. We spooned before the seas, without an inch of sail; it was hell dark, sir, but the Captain—he knew those waters like the back of his hand. He went below, then, and told me to call him in thirty minutes." He stopped. "I asked him—I didn't truly ask—I said, 'Captain?' And he said, 'Tyler, call me in thirty minutes.' So I left him, Master David. I left him, and when I went back—I couldn't rouse him. He was asleep, I thought—and then I knew, when he didn't answer me right away. You know how he was aboard ship, awake in a second. I knew, then."

Tyler took a deep, unsteady breath. He looked at Lola; her dark eyes were luminous and full of compassion as they rested on David, and then on Tyler. He remembered her first words to him, "You shall stay with us always, Tyler. You will get well!"

Then Tyler remembered Cosmos, standing alongside him. He looked up at Cosmos' face, and he spoke directly to him.

"Captain missed you," he said. "He said he'd bring you a wife back with him, too."

Cosmos said unsteadily, "I get you more wine."

"I can't drink much yet," Tyler said.

Cosmos picked up the wine decanter anyway. It was the ship's decanter that Cavendish had used on his first voyage. Cosmos held it up. "You buried him?" he asked. "Where, Tyler? On the land?"

Tyler shook his head. "We buried him in the South Atlantic," he said, and through his mind went the scene of that day, with the great ocean swelling beneath the bows, and the gauntness of the land near, warning men of the might of the seas and nature. Tyler remembered the scene well; the bareheaded men, woollen caps in hand, the figure of John Davis, lean, with lined face, his voice rising above the sound of wind and water and creaking ropes and spars and canvas.

"We used the Lord's Prayer because it was what Captain always used. And," Tyler said, his eyes looking past the fire into the past of a year ago, "Davis made a prayer. He said, 'Oh, God, with whose power the mightiest things around men are matters of no moment, I most humbly beseech Thee that this intolerable burden may through the blood of Jesus Christ be taken from us and end our days with speed, or' "—Tyler held out his hands and his tone rose strong—" 'or show us some merciful sign of Thy love and preservation.' "

Tyler said simply, "The prayer was answered, Master David. The next day we sighted some unknown islands.* The Captain would have liked that. They saved us. Weeks later we put into Port Desire.

"After a month," he went on, more quickly now, "we

---

* The *Desire* was the first ship ever to touch at or put into the Falkland Islands.

had a goodly store of penguins; we'd eaten their eggs and the smelts we caught. We had plenty of fresh water and dried penguin. But—although it was all right for a while—the penguins weren't dried enough, I guess. They got worms in them. Those worms—you've never seen the like of, Master David. They grew and grew and ate everything; they bored into the wood; they were an inch long and they ate our clothes, our boots, hats, shirts; there was nothing they didn't devour except iron, and they crawled over us at night and they bit, badly. They—"

Again Tyler stopped. Lola's face was white with horror, and Tyler hesitated.

"We had thrown the penguins overboard, but the worms kept growing mightily." Tyler moistened his lips and continued, again quickly. "We had sixteen men left. Only five could move. We put into a few ports, to get food and water, but we were so weak, we didn't dare much with the Spanish and the Indians. So we set sail again. Later, even I could not heave out or take in a sail; nobody could. So our tops and sprit were all torn to pieces by the wind, and Captain Davis and I took turns at the helm. Captain Davis said we were lost wanderers on the sea, and it was only by the Grace of God we fetched Bearhaven in Ireland on the eleventh of this month."

David said, low, "Go on, Tyler."

"We ran the ship on shore. The Irish helped us take in the sails, and moor the *Desire* and float her again. It cost Captain Davis ten pounds. Then, in five days, when we could walk, we took passage to England in a fisher boat, to Padstowe in Cornwall. Then I came here, to Trimley."

Davis stood up. "You need rest, Tyler. You need long days of rest, and good food. I've sent word to Pretty; he'll want to see you. And Moon. We'll fetch the *Desire*—" He broke off. "Excuse me, Tyler," he said, and he went to the door. He held in his hand the letter Tyler had brought. "I want to read this," he said. He opened the door and left them.

Tyler pushed aside the footstool. Cosmos moved it

out of his way. Slowly Tyler rose; he walked over to the window, and he looked out at the green country.

"It's June," he said.

Cosmos moved over to the window, too. His long eyes were on the figure of Kate in green riding dress. "They haven't told her yet," he said. "I will tell her, and you, too."

Tyler said, "Not now, Cosmos. Let her go now." He watched the two, Tony de Dasi, the Filipino, and Kate, as they rode down the curving lane he had walked up just an hour ago. "Let them go now," he said, and added, "Tony has grown."

Cosmos nodded, his eyes still on the receding figure of Kate. Then he heard something. He said, "Come here with me, Tyler. Come here a minute."

He went to the door. In the hall he paused, and looked toward the stairway. Tyler looked too.

"Ahoy, Tina," he said.

Tina came down the last steps. Tight in her hand was the small hand of a three-year-old girl. The child saw Cosmos, and without a word she let go Tina's hand and took hold of Cosmos' outstretched fingers. Her level gaze was on the stranger.

"I don't know you," she said.

Tyler dropped down to one knee. The clear blue eyes studied him.

"I knew you when you were a baby," Tyler said. "You're Bess."

"Bess Cavendish," she corrected.

Along the stair wall were two portraits. She pointed to them. "That is my mother. And that is my father, Captain Cavendish."

"I know," Tyler said. He stood up, a bit unsteadily.

Again the blue eyes studied him. Then they looked at Cosmos, and back to Tyler again. She held out her hand. "Would you like to walk with Cosmos and me?"

Tyler nodded. Her hand was very small in his. "I would, Mistress Bess," he said, and the three of them went slowly to the door and down the shallow steps, into the garden.

ABOUT THE AUTHOR

JAN WESTCOTT was born in Philadelphia, Pennsylvania and grew up in Laurel Springs, New Jersey. "All around were spreading farms and pasture land. We woke to my father playing Mozart and Chopin, Rachmaninoff or Beethoven." In 1943 she began to write and has since authored *The Border Lord, The Tower and The Dream, Captain For Elizabeth, The Hepburn, Captain Barney, The Queen's Grace, Walsingham Woman, The White Rose* and *Condottiere,* among others. Jan Westcott lives with her husband, Robert P. Barden, a radiologist, writer, physician and Doctor of Science.

RELAX!
SIT DOWN
and Catch Up On Your Reading!